FULL Domain

Kindle Alexander

A *NICE GUYS* NOVEL

Full Domain

Edited by Jae Ashley
Cover art by Reese Dante
http://www.reesedante.com

ISBN Print: 978-1-941450-09-3
ISBN ebook: 978-1-941450-08-6

Full Domain is a work of fiction. Names, characters, places and incidents are either the product of the author's imagination or are used fictitiously, and any resemblance to any actual persons, living or dead, events, or locales is entirely coincidental.

Licensed material is being used for illustrative purposes only and any person depicted in the licensed material is a model.

FULL Domain
Kindle Alexander

A *NICE GUYS* NOVEL

Honor, integrity, and loyalty are how Deputy US Marshal Kreed Sinacola lives his life. A former SEAL now employed by the Special Operations Group of the US Marshal Service, Kreed spent most of his life working covert operations and avoiding relationships. Never one to mix business with pleasure, his boundaries blur and his convictions are put to the test when he finally comes face-to-face with the hot computer geek he's been partnered with. Hell-bent on closing the ongoing case for his longtime friend, he pushes past his own limits and uncovers more than he expects.

Aaron Stuart strives for one thing: justice. Young and full of idealism, his highly sought after computer skills land him a position with the National Security Agency. Aaron's biggest hazard at his job is cramped fingers, but all that changes when he is drawn into the middle of a dangerous federal investigation. Aaron gets more than he bargained for when the FBI partners him with a handsome and tempting deputy US marshal. His attraction to the inked up, dark-haired man provides another kind of threat altogether. Aaron tries desperately to place a firewall around his heart and fight his developing feelings, knowing one misstep on his part could ultimately destroy him.

The solution isn't as easy as solving the case, which is treacherous enough as it is. But the growing sexual attraction between them threatens to derail more than just Kreed's personal convictions as he quickly learns temptation and matters of the heart rarely fit easily into the rules he's lived by. Will Kreed be able to convince Aaron to open his heart and face the fact that sometimes the answers aren't always hidden in code?

Dedication

Kindle, you are forever in our hearts.

Perry, you're missed every day.

Reese, Jae and Ena, for all you do. We hope to never have a release without you.

Trademark Acknowledgements

The author acknowledges the trademarked status and trademark owners of the following trademarks mentioned in this work of fiction:

Advil: Wyeth, LLC
Apple: Apple, Inc.
ASUS: Asustek Computer Incorporation Corporation
Atlanta International Airport: City of Atlanta
Back to the Future: Universal/U-Drive Joint Venture
Barbie: Mattel, Inc.
Bose: Bose Corporation
Bud Light: Anheuser-Busch, Incorporated
Call of Duty: Activision Publishing, Inc.
Coors: MillerCoors LLC
CTFxC: Charles Trippy
CVS: CVS Pharmacy, Inc.
Dulles International: Metropolitan Washington Airports Authority
ESPN: ESPN, Inc.
Ethan Hunt (Mission Impossible character): Paramount Pictures Corporation
FBI: Federal Bureau of Investigation
FedEx: Federal Express Corporation
Flo Rida: Dillard, Tramar
Glock: Glock, Inc.
Google: Google, Inc.
Hallmark Channel: Hallmark Licensing LLC
Hawaii Five-O: CBS Studios Inc.
Heineken: Heineken Brouwerijen B.V.
Holiday Inn: Six Continents Hotels, Inc.
Home Depot: Homer TLC, Inc.
iPad: Apple, Inc.
iPhone: Apple, Inc.
Jack in the Box: Jack in the Box Corporation
Justin Timberlake (SexyBack): Tennman Brands, LLC
Levi's: Levi Strauss & Co. Corporation
Lush: Cosmetic Warriors Ltd.
Marine Corps: US Marine Corps, a component of the US Department of the Navy
MIT: Massachusetts Institute of Technology Corporation

Monsters, Inc.: Disney Enterprises, Inc.
Mountain Dew: Pepsico, Inc.
Nine Inch Nails (Closer): Michael Trent Reznor
Oreo: Intercontinental Great Brands LLC
Pay Day: Tournament One Corp
Samsonite: Samsonite IP Holdings S.A.R.L.
Shinedown (Call Me): Smith, Brent
Sonic: America's Drive-In Corp.
Speedo: Speedo International
SpongeBob SquarePants: Viacom International Inc.
State of Decay: Microsoft Corporation
Subway: Doctor's Associates Inc.
Superman: DC Comics General Partnership
The Creatures: The Creatures LLC
The Matrix: Warner Bros. Entertainment Inc.
The Men's Warehouse: The Men's Warehouse, Inc.
Tahoe: General Motors LLC
Tim Tams: Campbell Soup Company
Underoos: Fruit of the Loom, Inc.
US Navy: The Department of the Navy
Walmart: Wal-Mart Stores, Inc.
Whataburger: Whataburger Partnership
X-Files: Twentieth Century Fox Film Corporation

Note from the Author

This is not the hacker's bible – please don't use it as such. Technology changes by the second. Creative license was taken with this story. It is a work of fiction.

Chapter 1

"Man, this is turning into one *suck-ass* day," Aaron mumbled quietly to no one in particular as he edged his way through the overcrowded and lengthy terminals of the Atlanta International Airport. He swore his backpack weighed at least fifty pounds and the small carry-on he tugged behind him easily added another twenty-five. He'd tried to stick to the bare necessities for this trip, but with all his gear, electronic equipment, and his most important ASUS ROG notebook, which he never left home without, he still managed to over-pack.

The gates and corridors were congested with rude, indignant travelers, more than he'd ever seen gathered in one place before. From the conversations he'd caught snippets of along the way, the irritable attitudes were due to unexpected flight delays across the eastern half of the United States.

A winter storm had blown through, dumping a shit-load of ice in its wake. Apparently the magnitude of the storm had caught the southern half of the US by surprise. The meteorologists had completely missed this monster of a storm before it bore down on its intended target. At least that was the continued excuse he kept hearing from the airport personnel as to why they weren't better prepared for this crippling event during one of the busiest traveling days of the year. Words like *happy* and *holiday* were used with increasingly angry bursts of *fucking* and *asshole* added to the mix.

Not even the Christmas carols playing overhead helped lighten the mood surrounding him. So much for peace on earth.

Keeping his eyes focused on the large information screens, Aaron scanned the arrival and departure listings, watching as hundreds of delayed flights were canceled all across the East Coast—not that any of that actually mattered to him. His flight from Miami had arrived so late he'd have missed his connecting flight regardless of the inclement weather.

No way in hell would he spend the night in some corner of this overly congested airport, waiting for the flight schedules to open again. The Federal Bureau of Investigation would just have to work their magic and get him on a different flight tomorrow or when things let up outside. Until then, he'd find a vacant room in a five-star hotel—preferably the Drake—his favorite place to stay when he stopped in Atlanta.

Aaron sighed as he followed the discontented masses toward what he hoped was an exit. If the weather was as bad as everyone kept hinting, he might not get a chance to eat at Poor Calvin's, Aaron's favorite little Asian-fusion eatery on Piedmont Street. The lobster fried rice was to die for and thoughts of the dish had actually been the only thing keeping him sane as they'd flown high above the city; it felt like they'd been circling for an hour and a half, waiting for their chance to land. His stomach picked that second to protest, the loud rumble reminding him he hadn't eaten anything since the protein shake he'd choked down for breakfast.

Aaron looked around and spotted a food kiosk about fifty feet away. That should take care of his urgent food needs until he could get to the hotel. Taking a deep breath, he carefully dodged his way through the crowd, attempting to move toward the kiosk, which proved a trickier process than he'd anticipated. He apparently hadn't truly experienced the vexed people in this airport until he tried to work his way between them.

"Hey, move it!" the guy behind him bellowed as Aaron slowed to merge farther to the left.

"I'm sorry. Excuse me," Aaron apologized when he accidently stepped in front of another person in his rush to get out of the middle of traffic and away from the jerk behind him. The woman in his path huffed, and although he'd never touched her, her hands flailed dramatically like he had tripped her in some way.

"Dude, watch it," the man beside her quipped, making a show of keeping the woman on her feet as she reached out for his arm. Aaron moved quickly to the opposite side, tugging his luggage out of the way and inadvertently stepped into the flow of traffic going the opposite direction.

"Shit!" he exclaimed loudly when a large trunk-style suitcase rolled right over his sandaled foot.

The scowl he'd been holding back slid firmly in place as he watched the person who'd so rudely rolled over his foot, glance back over his shoulder to give him a very clear *fuck you* glower as he kept going without any hesitation.

Seriously, this place was worse than Black Friday on *motherfucking steroids*. Aaron took a deep breath and tried to move farther out of the way. He made it to the far wall and stopped outside the flow of manic pedestrians to catch his breath and regroup. The only reason he was in this godforsaken mass of pissed off travelers during the airlines' busiest and most miserable travel week of the year was a job, and no job on the planet was worth this kind of bullshit.

Time to reassess his life. No more Mr. Nice Guy. He was done with that. Look what being nice had cost him. He was standing in the middle of hell. If the FBI insisted he be onsite, then he shouldn't have any problem becoming the biggest pain-in-the-ass on the planet.

Except that just wasn't his personality. He'd tried everything to make the bureau see that he wasn't needed in Washington, DC, for this assignment. He could carry on as he was, monitoring everything from home with the equipment he needed to do his job properly. Look how far he'd gotten on his own, from the privacy and comfort of his living room.

Yet the stuffed-shirt egomaniacs in DC said it would be in everyone's best interest if they were able to look him in the eye when they spoke. In other words, no matter what he had done to prove himself, they didn't trust him as far as they could throw him.

But not even the FBI could control Mother Nature—even though the majority of them had huge God complexes—and he wouldn't arrive there today as he'd been ordered. That thought eased a little of his tension. Honestly, their demands meant nothing to him, and the only reason he'd eventually given in and flown to DC had to do with his friend Mitch Knox.

Since Mitch had first asked for his help, something about this entire case needled at him. Aaron couldn't tolerate injustice, bigotry, or hatred in any form, and the fact that this case had hit so close to home for Mitch had an effect on Aaron as well. Those few minutes after Cody had been shot were some of the most frantic of Aaron's life. He'd shown his true ability, hacking into everything as he'd desperately tried to find answers for Mitch.

At the time, Aaron's belief in the justness of a situation had overpowered any reasonable thought. He wanted the best for the world, especially for those who couldn't fight for themselves. Cody shot in the chest... Mitch trying to get to him... No one getting Mitch the answers he needed... Yeah, there was nothing fair in any of that at all.

More than anything, Aaron hated bureaucratic bullying. The arrogance of that act just pissed him the hell off. Life should have buffers in place to protect people from Big Brother beating them down and stalling the process for their own gain. They could have gotten Mitch his answers, but hadn't, and that wasn't right. Life should be nothing more than moment after moment of peace, love, and rock and roll—or some shit along those lines.

Aaron finally manned up, found a break in the traffic, and began moving again. He made his way to the long line waiting at the food kiosk, and took his place at the end with the rest of the hungry patrons. He looked over the menu board and groaned in frustration when he found absolutely nothing good to eat. He could choose from an extensive list of foot-long hot dogs or, for an exorbitant price, he could upgrade to sausage. His arteries hardened at the thought.

"I heard it's turning to snow outside."

He looked over his shoulder to see who had spoken the first kind words he'd heard since arriving in Atlanta and found an older couple behind him.

"Snow? Really?" he asked, just to be nice. At this point, he didn't give a shit. He needed food and to get to the hotel and unpack. He'd planned for colder weather in DC, but left Miami in his standard attire of walking shorts, T-shirt, and a CTFxC hoodie.

"Yes, they're calling for snow, maybe up to an inch. They're saying the highways are backing up already." Those words actually caused Aaron a slight panic. He needed to get moving.

"Thanks," he said absently before he broke from the line, braving the pedestrians bustling toward the exit. He absolutely wasn't getting stuck in this airport overnight; he could go hungry until he arrived at the hotel. He'd live. He shoved his way through the corridor until he spotted the closest exit. He pushed through the doors and the biting wind took his breath. Nothing but more chaos awaited him on the other side. People were packed three deep from the curb, waiting for any way possible to get out. The airport shuttles were filling to capacity and the taxis couldn't stop fast enough to pick up passengers.

Aaron pushed his way to the curb and called out to a guy lifting a trunk lid to load his luggage inside a Checker cab. "Where are you going?"

"Downtown," the stranger yelled back, never really looking up from his task as he scrambled to load his baggage. An upturned suit jacket collar and keeping his head bent in were the man's only defenses against the biting wind and heavy snow.

"I'll pay the fare if you let me ride," Aaron offered. The slush hit his uncovered legs and feet, causing him to shiver as the freezing temperatures registered with his body.

The guy finally looked up at him, eyeing him closely before he replied, "Sure."

Aaron tossed his backpack with his laptop in the backseat and went for the trunk. The driver stayed inside the taxi with the heater blowing, offering zero help. Aaron pulled the hood of the hoodie over his head, slid the zipper as high as it would go, and reached for his suitcase. At that exact moment, another taxi came barreling past. The taxi splashed the length of the left side of his body with slushy ice water. The shock of the cold attacking his body caused him to lose his grasp on his suitcase, which then tipped over but, luckily, landed intact on the wet pavement.

There were only seconds of relief as another car ran over it. The Samsonite held together until the third car. After that, it didn't stand a chance. He watched in horror as four cars hit his suitcase before an attendant could get involved and direct traffic away from all his belongings being spread across the parkway. With no other choice,

Aaron trudged through the ice and falling snow in his sandals and gathered all his now-ruined clothes as everyone watched from the safety of the covered sidewalk.

As he worked, the taxi started honking. The guy he was riding with took pity and jumped out, tossing Aaron's drenched, dirty clothes into the trunk. By the time they finished, Aaron felt like his clothes looked: frayed, inundated, and completely wrecked. He was soaked and shivering as he finally got inside the taxi. The driver pulled out before he was able to get the door fully closed.

"Here," the guy said, shrugging out of his coat.

"It's okay." Aaron was surprised he got the words out, his teeth were chattering so loudly. The older man didn't pay him any attention, draping the warm, dry coat over him.

"You should take off those wet sandals," the guy suggested. Aaron did, rubbing his feet together when he noticed they were completely numb.

"Where are we going?" the cab driver called out as he merged into traffic. At least the driver had positioned all the vents to point in his direction, pushing the warm air back on him.

"The Drake," Aaron called out first, fighting against the cold chill gripping his body. "Do you have a place to stay?"

"I was going to the Holiday Inn."

"Take us both to the Drake." Aaron involuntarily shivered as he pulled his iPhone out of his pocket and dialed his father's assistant.

"Hey, Aaron," she answered. He couldn't remember her name but did remember she was younger than him by almost six years. His father liked them young.

"Hey, listen. I'm stuck in Atlanta overnight. I need you to get me a couple of rooms at the Drake."

"Okay, no problem," she said. He could hear her typing on the other end of the line.

"They're filling up fast. Let me make a call," she said professionally. At least this one seemed to have some communication and secretarial skills. That was more than most who'd filled this position over the years.

"I can't afford the Drake," the guy next to him said.

"It's on me." Aaron left off the part about it being a family-owned property. That kind of thing usually made people look at him differently and ended up costing him more money in the long run. The guy started to argue, but Aaron held up his hand to silence the protest when his father's assistant returned to the line to give him the details.

"You've got two rooms. They're suites. Non-connecting and on two different floors. It's the best I could do. I hear the weather there's a beast."

"You have no idea. Thank you."

"You're welcome. I'll tell your dad you said hello." Aaron let that one go without a response. He'd never tell his dad hello. Much like his father, they both liked to pretend the other didn't exist.

"The Drake," he instructed the taxi driver as he shoved the phone back in his pocket. When he realized he wasn't being tossed around the backseat like a normal taxi ride, he glanced out the windows to see they were inching along in bumper-to-bumper traffic, not even to the highway yet. Aaron shivered again and rubbed his feet on the floor mat to build friction. His feet were fucking freezing.

"I can't let you pay for my room."

"It's the least I can do. You restored my faith in humanity," he said, sticking out his hand. "I'm Aaron. I get a corporate discount. It's not a problem."

"I'm Ted. Thank you," the guy replied.

"Now, let's see if we can make it that far," he said, looking back out the window. The heater was blowing harder now. He handed the coat back to Ted and tugged the hood off his head to run his hands through his thick bleached-blond hair. He'd changed the color about a month ago and added purple and black to the tips. He'd planned to add turquoise just to mess with the boys at the FBI, but he'd run out of time.

The cold wetness of his shorts riding across his skin sent a shiver up his spine as his phone vibrated in his pocket. The only reason he checked it was to see if the hotel reservations had changed. A text from Kreed. Aaron swiped his finger across the screen to open the message.

"Let me know if you were able to ice skate your way through Atlanta so I don't make a wasted trip to the airport."

Interesting how even Kreed's texts read in that cocky way he normally spoke. For some reason it grated on Aaron's nerves more than usual. With a small smile, he shoved his phone back in his pocket, deciding to ignore the text. Let Kreed make the trip to Dulles to pick him up. Kreed deserved at least that much trouble for his part in insisting Aaron fly to DC in the first place.

~~~

SpongeBob SquarePants reruns played on the television set in the hotel room the FBI had assigned to Kreed Sinacola. He'd arrived late last night under a mandatory directive from the powers that be. Sadly, he'd had to leave his parents on the command of Director Carpenter who apparently hadn't seen the need to end his own holiday vacation like he'd demanded of Kreed, Aaron Stuart, Special Agent Connors, and Special Agent Brown.

If Kreed chose to care, that would probably piss him off. But with twenty years of being a government employee under his belt, he knew how the top brass generally operated—all posturing, little performance.

Boredom more than anything had Kreed sprawled across the king-size bed, a couple of pillows tucked under his head as he absently tossed a blade in the air, artfully executing a perfect spin before catching the handle solidly in one hand each and every time. He didn't pay much attention to the act itself, it was second nature to him. Where his longtime partner and buddy Deputy US Marshal Mitch Knox had his video games to keep him occupied during the long hours of downtime in their jobs, Kreed had his knives. The scars along his hands and arms proved the time he'd put in to becoming an expert bladesman.

A couple of minutes, maybe more, had passed since he'd texted Aaron Stuart, the little computer hottie he was assigned to pick up from the airport. The guy hadn't responded. Since he'd seen the weather alerts crossing the bottom of the screen, he figured Aaron was stranded, pissed off, in some terminal somewhere. Hell, pissed off was probably mild because the guy had already been pretty damn upset he'd had to make this trip in the first place.

Kreed gave a little chuckle at the memory of the fit Stuart had thrown when he'd found out about the mandatory directive. Just wait until the sexy IT guy heard he was now being officially reassigned from the NSA to the FBI to help solve the case. Aaron had proven himself invaluable, negating all the years of government skepticism or maybe the better word was *"fear"* regarding his expert hacking ability. Kreed laughed out loud at that one. Yeah, they were scared shitless of Stuart's skill set.

There was absolutely no doubt in the kid's talent. Anyone who spent more than a few hours with the guy had to walk away impressed. Years ago, when Aaron was still a teenager, he had bested both the FBI and Department of Homeland Security when he'd broken into a system thought to be impenetrable—all as a fraternity prank or some shit like that. Of course, at the time he'd been "dealt with." And like most of those types of things turned out, the kid ended up working for the NSA, doing what he did best, finding weaknesses in computer systems and networks. It was just like the government to turn a blind eye when they needed something from someone.

Aaron probably didn't understand how badly they were using him. He was a genius in his field, but young enough that he still had that youthful idealism about him. No doubt he'd believed he could make the world a better place and proved that fact when he'd gone over a closed case file, found a problem, and made calls on Christmas Eve to everyone involved.

His brother Derek had that same way about him, too. Man, he missed his brother.

Instant grief blanketed Kreed, gnawing at the raw void in his heart. He'd spent Christmas at home with his parents for the first time in years to help ease the burden of this being the first holiday without his little brother. Yeah, that sucked on every level. His pop had already been in his late thirties when Kreed had been born thirty-eight years ago. His brother was twelve years younger than him. Derek had come as a surprise and no matter how old he'd gotten, everyone always considered him the baby of the family. God, that kid was so loved.

The loss had taken a major toll on his family. Kreed could see the decline in his parents since the Marines had informed them of Derek's death. Damn if grief wasn't a bitch to deal with.

For Kreed, his true problem lay in all the unanswered questions and the refusal to release information about the cause of Derek's death. He knew that secretive side of military too well, probably better than anyone. Their refusal to provide any real information had him questioning everything and suspecting the worst.

Honestly, the whole thing just sucked balls. He fought the anger forming. There was more to the story than what his parents were told. He stopped the monotonous flip of the knife, grabbing the hilt of the blade a little aggressively as he moved his free hand to rub a palm across his aching heart.

The possibilities of what caused his brother's death… "Stop, Sinacola," he growled and mentally forced himself to quit thinking about all the inaccuracies, anything to keep from going to that dark place deep inside his soul. Nothing would be gained from him losing his shit right now.

Lifting his head, he looked for something to focus on, anything to help keep him on a level playing field so he could tie this case up for Knox. A weather alert beeped loudly on the TV and the information began to run across the top of the screen. The weather… Okay, he'd think about the weather.

Thank God he wasn't sitting in an airport somewhere waiting out the storm. Somehow, on his trip from San Antonio, he'd just managed to bypass the storm blanketing the Southeast. Connors and his family were in one of the Carolinas visiting family for the holiday. Aaron was traveling from Miami. Both men were en route and most likely stuck in that icy mess.

From what he'd heard—and the best he could tell—the storm was fast-moving. Good thing, because the Southern states weren't equipped to deal with the extreme cold weather. Hopefully, the temperatures would rise quickly tomorrow, but for now, it was enough to be a major pain in the ass for travelers.

Once it had become apparent they weren't working on the case today, Special Agent Brown had done the standup thing and invited Kreed over for dinner. That had been a nice team-oriented gesture. Kreed appreciated the thought, but it was the holidays, and Brown had a house full of small kids… Kreed again crinkled his nose at the thought. Yeah, that just seemed torturous as hell, so he had respectively declined with a straight up *hell-fucking-no* and ended that with a loud bark of laughter. Good thing Brown had a sense of humor—that being the key difference between Brown and his partner, Special Agent Connors, who would have taken great offense to his invitation being so rudely declined.

All in all, seeing Connors get upset would have been kind of fun to watch, too. Connors's straight-laced, by-the-book, goodie-two-shoes persona just drew guys like him and Mitch to the task of rattling his chain any chance they got.

Kreed's cellphone started playing Justin Timberlake's "SexyBack," alerting him to a call from Mitch Knox. Mitch had assigned the song to himself when he was going through his Timberlake-slash–Flo Rida phase.

Looking down at the phone, Kreed paused. He'd been waiting for this call. All agents were under strict orders not to tell Mitch about the latest development in the case. The guy had been placed on mandatory leave for the time being, and Kreed had received a very private message from their director stating he'd be reassigned to a new partner as soon as this detail was complete. He figured that meant they were just waiting to tell Mitch he was on desk duty from this point forward. That caused another little ache to trickle across his heart.

Mitch had to see this coming, but his buddy had a way about him. He could change minds when he chose to, but Kreed didn't think that would work this time. Mitch had been directly targeted by the people they were investigating, and his lover, Cody Turner, had been shot at point blank range as a message to Mitch. Only a freak occurrence had Cody surviving the vicious attack. At this point, Mitch was a liability to anyone he worked with in the field, but Kreed hadn't wanted to be the one to tell his best friend he'd be becoming a suit if he wanted to continue being a deputy marshal.

Yeah, like having Mitch Knox in an office all day was ever going to work out for anyone involved. Kreed huffed a laugh and pushed that thought from his overactive head too. He didn't want to think about all that right now either. Instead, he let the phone ring four times before he answered. Mitch Knox hated waiting for anything, and Kreed loved pushing his buttons. Kreed grinned as he swiped his finger over the screen to accept the call.

"A man takes a vacation, gets engaged, but calls his partner? Aww…you missing me already? Trouble in paradise, princess?" Kreed couldn't resist teasing his long-time friend.

"Fuck you. Fuck the making me wait thing you always do when I call, and fuck the FBI. You should have fucking told me," Mitch responded.

"You know I have to strut around, be the sexiest thing in the room, every time I hear your ringtone, Knox. And what exactly should I have told you?" Kreed asked. There was a laundry list of things Mitch didn't know.

"Fuck you, Sinacola. You should have told me Aaron found something critical. And you need to tell me everything you know. These little surprise attacks aren't cool." Mitch sounded annoyed and angry, and Kreed knew when to back off. Now wasn't the time to joke around. This case they were working had been Mitch's baby. Mitch had painstakingly pieced together case after case of brutal attacks all on his own dime when their superiors had refused to allocate any money to the investigation. Kreed whole-heartedly agreed that Mitch shouldn't be left out now.

"You're too high profile, Knox. You're considered a liability," Kreed repeated what the higher-ups had said to him.

"Fuck that. I can be there on the inside. I know this case like the back of my hand," Mitch barked out the exact same argument Kreed had used in his partner's defense.

"You know I agree. I fought for you, man. I'll still fight for you. But they're firm. I'm gonna need the whole team to fight against their decision. And what are you gonna do with Cody while you're here in DC? You need to consider that before I throw a massive fucking fit to get you here."

Silence ensued. Yeah, Kreed figured Mitch hadn't gotten that far in his thought process. He was just pissed off he'd been excluded.

"He's still off work. He can come with me. Move the rehab to DC," Mitch argued, clearly thinking and talking at the same time.

"How'd you find out?" Kreed asked, contemplating Mitch's plan.

"The case file opened back up. I got an alert. I called your parents and they told me you were back in DC."

"You called my parents?" Everything stopped right then. If Mitch were in this room, he'd have thrown a blade at his partner. Mitch shouldn't have used his parents to gain information. That was one hell of a low blow.

"Fuck yeah, I did. You didn't fucking tell me what's going on," Mitch accused.

"That's low, even for you, Knox."

"No lower than you. I'm heading down there. Cody's coming with me. He's smarter than the both of us combined anyway—"

"Man, don't do it this way." Kreed cut Mitch's rant off. "The whole team's really worried about you and Cody. It's personal to them. I wouldn't be surprised if they don't have eyes on you two at all times. They're serious. Hang tight. I'll keep you updated, I swear. I was going to anyway. Everybody's just stuck in the shitty weather."

"Who's everybody?" Mitch asked.

"Brown's here. They're bringing Connors back in from vacation, and your gaming buddy Stuart's being brought to work inside."

"No shit? What'd he say about that?" All the anger had dissipated from his voice, and Mitch sounded astonished.

"It wasn't pleasant." Kreed condensed Aaron's bitch session about the decision into those three little words.

"Yeah, I bet." Mitch barked out a laugh. Just like normal, he rarely stayed angry, and Kreed appreciated that about him.

"Seriously, man, stay put. Enjoy your family and your man. Let me get a feel for what they're thinking. It won't be but a day or two longer and we can decide what to do from there," Kreed advised, praying that pacified Mitch.

"Keep me in the loop or I'm bullying my way in." Yes, Kreed had no doubt Mitch meant those words.

"Does Cody agree with this plan?"

"He will when I tell him." Mitch sounded defensive.

"Already keeping secrets. Tsk, tsk, princess," Kreed chided, tossing out his favorite nickname for Mitch.

"Fuck you. I'm not playing. Keep me posted or I'm showing up on my own. I'm not being left out of this. I want this finished. Cody's not safe until they're stopped."

"You're not either," Kreed countered.

"Neither are you. I've had your fucking back for almost ten years. Watch yourself until I can. Nobody kicks your ass but me," Mitch added a little more quietly, but still firm.

"Fuck you, Knox, and I will. I swear, as soon as we move, you'll know."

"All right. And record Aaron's first experience in that building. That shit's gonna be funny," Mitch said, laughing.

"I will. Stay put, Knox. We're gonna be smarter where we're all concerned. No one's getting hurt this time, and based on Stuart's intel, the threat still looks very real."

"You already said that. You did your job today and kept me out of it—I'm not balls to the wall anymore. I'm hanging up now."

Mitch disconnected the call, and Kreed chuckled, slower to drop the phone back on the bed. That had been the right thing to do—keeping Mitch safe in New York—but Mitch had a point about having his back. Sure, they would take their aggression out on each other at times, but that was all it was, just blowing off steam. No matter how many scuffles they got into with each other—and there had been plenty over the years—no one had his back like Mitch Knox. For whatever it was worth, when the tables were turned, he would always be there for Mitch. The stakes were higher in this particular case. Kreed needed to be at his best to keep any one of them from being hurt again.

Kreed picked up the blade and continued tossing it in the air. They were back to playing tactical games once again. His mind drifted to thoughts of his brother and his resolve firmed. He was done losing the people he loved.

Chapter 2

Twenty hours after landing in Atlanta, Aaron stepped off the overly-packed plane at Dulles International Airport, thankful he'd finally landed. Honestly, it wouldn't have mattered where they landed as long as he was able to get off that hell ride he'd been trapped in.

The airlines had rescheduled him to a coach seat in order to get him out on the first available flight. Not one of his best decisions. He ended up smack in the middle of a family. The mother with her crying baby sat in the row in front of him. The father and another smaller child took the seats beside him. Then their two tweens sat a row behind him.

It had seemed like such a reasonable suggestion when he'd offered the mother his seat so she'd be more comfortable next to her husband instead of dealing with all the back and forth and corralling the kids. The father had been useless in controlling anything, but the mom never seemed to get the clue or take the hint. She just kept rocking the crying baby and snapping those damn fingers at the other children.

His sound-resistant Bose headphones never stood a chance against that family of six. Thankfully that flight was over and they'd disembarked.

Since overcrowded airports seemed to be the new norm, Aaron tried to block out everything as he kept an eye on the overhead signs in search of baggage claim.

Honest to God, he tried to hurry because he knew Kreed was parked in front of the baggage claim exit, waiting for him there. Aaron shrugged on the new coat he'd bought when his other one was ruined, relieved he didn't have to wait with the masses of people in line for their rental car. And since the clothing he'd been able to salvage from his taxi-suitcase disaster now fit inside the backpack on his shoulder, he could also bypass waiting for luggage, making it way easier to get the hell out of there.

Aaron followed the signs directing him out of the terminal. He went down the double set of escalators then through the baggage claim interior doors. When he entered the large, open room, he scanned the back wall, looking for an exit. But he put that undertaking quickly on the back burner when his gaze landed on a tall, dark-haired guy wearing a leather jacket, standing by a wall. Jesus Christ, he had to be at least six-five with every inch solid muscle, and hot as holy fuck. Big, muscular guys in leather had always been a weakness for him, and this one was certainly his walking wet dream personified.

He smiled as he took in the sight. All of a sudden, Dulles International Airport didn't seem such a bad place to be.

The guy was turned away from him, and since Aaron wasn't one to miss an opportunity, he lowered his gaze, taking in a nice, firm ass that made his mouth water. Aaron could only imagine what sinful temptations were hidden under all that leather. The guy was probably waiting for his wife...or not. Who knew? Pity he didn't have time to find out. Duty called. Well, that and his need to escape the post-holiday travelers sucking his will to live. Thanks to Mr. Tall, Dark, and Menacing, Aaron had all the material needed for his spank bank later when he was alone in his hotel room.

Redirecting his focus to the task at hand, he finally located the sign he needed across the room, but as he headed for those doors, he couldn't help the quick glance in the leather-clad man's direction. It hadn't taken more than a thought for Aaron to convince himself he needed a face or, at the very least, a glimpse of the guy's lips to put with the body, then he'd be a fucking happy boy for the rest of his trip. Well, maybe that was pushing it, but whatever… Aaron wanted one last look.

He glanced over and this time, their gazes connected. One heartbeat, maybe two, later and Aaron stumbled over his own feet.

Fuck!

Holy fucking hell, he recognized those eyes.

Shit.

Kreed Sinacola.

In real life, those eyes and that body were about a million times better looking than on a computer monitor. Aaron groaned at the memory of shooting the guy down the first time he'd seen him on a Skype call with Mitch, while they were in Kentucky. Aaron mentally shook his head at his own stupidity, but in his defense, he'd been so busy cyber-chasing shit for Mitch he obviously hadn't judged the situation clearly.

What the hell had he been thinking? He made his living paying attention to the finer details. Shit. Clearly he was lacking in that department in this case.

"Excuse me." A hard bump from behind caused Aaron's heavy backpack to slip off his shoulder. In that brief moment, he'd somehow forgotten the crowds swarming about, trying to leave the building. Thankfully, the contact gave him the second he needed to collect himself as he looked away, mumbled an apology, readjusted the strap, and tried to gather his wits.

Feeling on steadier ground, he took a couple of steps forward, looking everywhere but Kreed's eyes. He nervously ran his wet palms down the sides of his brand new jeans as he adjusted his path and headed toward the guy. Kreed hadn't moved. He was still propped against the back wall, brawny arms crossed over his expansive chest. When Aaron finally worked up enough nerve to meet Kreed's stare, he swore there was a smirk on that very handsome face.

Shit! The man oozed swagger, and the air of confidence, combined with all that *fuck me* leather, was just so damn hot.

"Hey. You're Kreed, right?" Aaron asked once within earshot, trying for casual and unaffected, the exact opposite of everything raging inside him.

"The one and only, at your service," Kreed replied, using that same cocky attitude Aaron remembered from the Skype calls. But that unapologetic boldness went with the whole 3D package. His damn dick certainly agreed. "Got any luggage?"

"Nah, just this." He pointed to the backpack. "I had a slight mishap at the airport in Atlanta, so I'm gonna have to get some new clothes." He dared to glance back up at Kreed. There was definitely a smirk on his face, and it intensified, turning into a full-fledged smile as Kreed studied him. The grin surprised Aaron. He honestly hadn't thought Kreed could be any better-looking; clearly he'd been wrong. For the second time in less than three minutes, he needed to compose himself. This guy seriously threw him off balance, and that fact alone frustrated him to no end.

They stood in silence for what felt like several long minutes before Kreed finally moved, shoving his hand into the well-worn leather jacket he wore.

"I almost didn't recognize you. Your hair's different than I remember and you have this." Kreed indicated Aaron's stubble.

"I like change," Aaron said and looked away, his heart racing in his chest. What the hell was going on with him? The fact Kreed remembered such small details caught him off guard and sent a tickle up his spine. Aaron was always finding new ways to reinvent himself. Changing his hair color and style was something he'd started playing with in junior high during his defiant phase. At first, he'd colored his hair for pure shock value—a fuck you, more or less, to his father and the private school's administration. But then he found he really liked the change and kept it up.

From Kreed, though, those words felt like a personal caress and affirmation that he'd chosen well in changing the color of his hair. Kreed was a trained deputy marshal in the special teams division. Of course he would remember the little things; it was what he was paid to do. With another mental headshake, Aaron scolded himself. If he didn't get his responses under control, this trip would be a total disaster. Besides, Aaron didn't go for cocky guys and that was exactly what Kreed Sinacola came across as.

"I'm parked outside," Kreed finally said, nodding in the direction of the exit doors. Aaron didn't move right away. Now that he stood closer, he could confirm his earlier estimate; Kreed was around six-five, a few inches taller than his own six-two frame, and thicker, much thicker, beating him hands down in sheer broadness. Aaron caught a glimpse of the ink peeking over the top of Kreed's T-shirt. He couldn't see all of the design because it was mostly hidden beneath a dark material as well as the leather jacket. The temptation to immediately tug that shirt right off the man and admire all the rest of that inked canvas rode him hard.

Kreed Sinacola reeked of intimidation. He could see where the bad guys didn't stand much of a chance when Kreed went for the arrest, yet Aaron just found himself intrigued. Another thing he hadn't planned on.

When Kreed nodded toward the exit and took a step in front of him, Aaron's eyes immediately dropped to the man's ass. *Oh fuck me!* It was even better up close. The man radiated *perfect* in every sense of the word. Kreed's body-hugging black jeans showed off a tight bubble butt that led into thick, meaty thighs. Aaron followed Kreed, his gaze still glued to the guy's ass.

Out of the corner of his eye, a reflective flash caught his attention. He glanced up, catching their images in the glass of the sliding doors. Surprise and embarrassment swamped him when he realized Kreed was watching him in the same reflection.

Double fuck. He could feel his cheeks warm and he quickly looked away.

Shit! Aaron rolled his eyes at himself and his reaction. What the hell was he doing? He had shot Kreed down in flames, and now, he was drooling over him. Typical of his life. Clearly, he'd spent too much time alone and wasn't fit to be in public.

"This way," Kreed said, slowing his stride to walk beside Aaron. Kreed clicked the key fob and pointed out the black Tahoe two or three spaces down. He tried everything to ignore the guy, thankful when Kreed finally moved around the vehicle to the other side. Aaron carefully placed his backpack and coat in the backseat.

Taking a deep breath of the fresh, cold air seemed to clear his mind and help his perspective. Aaron stopped before opening the passenger door. All his thoughts needed to be centered on getting to the FBI headquarters, figuring out how to get his job done then getting the hell out of there. Once he got home, he had some serious soul-searching to do. In this moment he had absolutely learned his lesson about helping people out. Him standing in the middle of a DC airport, ogling Kreed—a freaking deputy US marshal, for God's sake—when he had more work than he could ever possibly accomplish, all sitting on his desk back home…Yeah. He needed to seriously rethink his entire life.

Aaron had a carefully planned life for a reason. He couldn't allow distractions—not FBI "requests" or lusting after men like Kreed Sinacola. He swore if he made it through the next few days, he could bet his ass that this would never, ever, ever happen again.

~~~

Kreed jumped inside the SUV and started the vehicle. He quickly flipped the heater knob to full blast, pushing the vents toward the passenger seat then just waited. Hooking an arm around the back of the passenger seat, Kreed used the rearview mirror to watch Aaron carefully place his things in the backseat. Man, Aaron had turned out to be an unexpected surprise. Last time he'd gotten a glimpse of Aaron Stuart, the guy had dark hair, that messy, just fucked style that grabbed Kreed's attention, but today his hair was blond with black and purple spiked tips.

While he'd waited inside baggage claim, of course he'd noticed the hot, edgy guy as soon as he'd hit the top of the escalator, but he was searching for the dark-headed gamer. He'd been attracted to Aaron with brown hair, but now… Damn, his attraction ascended to a whole new level. Kreed kept his eyes trained on that mirror, staring at Aaron. Yeah, this guy was something else.

Quickly, he ticked back over the information Mitch had given him. His buddy's words had been something like, "*you're barking up the wrong tree, Sinacola,*" leading Kreed to believe Aaron was straight.

Kreed smiled to himself. Nah, Mitch must have gotten it wrong. Kreed had definitely seen interest as Stuart eye-fucked him in front of the entire lobby of the Dulles baggage claim area.

How had Mitch missed that monumental bit of information? Knox was usually smarter about those kinds of things. Of course, he could have misread the guy. They only dealt with each other online. But whether Aaron was gay, bi, or straight, Kreed was sure of one thing—he hadn't ever had anyone appraise him quite so completely, and he most definitely wanted more.

Besides the different hair and his five o'clock shadow, he wore glasses that fit the shape of his face perfectly. Stuart was as hot, if not hotter, than Kreed remembered. On the screen, he'd have guessed Aaron to be shorter, but in reality, he stood only a few inches below him—the perfect height in Kreed's estimation. He liked his men about Aaron's size.

His men... Like he had men*? Where the hell had* that *come from?*

Chastising himself, Kreed tried to put the brakes on his wayward thoughts. They were there to do a job, not for him to fuck the hot computer geek. Kreed cocked his head and played devil's advocate to that thought. But hey, if the opportunity arose, he was gonna grab it by the balls. Kreed almost chuckled out loud at that thought.

With another look over his shoulder, he watched Aaron shut the back door then just stand on the curb. Kreed shifted his position, trying for a better view. Why was the kid standing outside in the freezing weather like that? Surely he knew hypothermia wasn't a sufficient excuse to get out of working this case. Kreed watched Aaron for a second more before turning back to the front. He would give Stuart a minute or two before braving the elements and pushing his ass inside the car.

Drumming the fingers of his left hand on the steering wheel, he patiently waited, while moving his free hand down to adjust his hard cock. Man, he'd thought he'd been attracted to Aaron on the computer screen, but that didn't begin to compare to the attraction coursing through him at the moment. Aaron Stuart in person was truly a mouthwatering sight. Something about the new hair had his fingers itching to feel those spikey blond strands. The black-rimmed glasses Aaron wore drew his attention to gray-blue eyes, framed perfectly by thick, dark lashes. He could have sworn Aaron had brown eyes last time he'd seen him, but what the fuck ever, this guy, with any color eyes—or hair, for that matter—was hot.

The guy's mouth alone made Kreed's dick sit up and beg for a little attention. Fuck! Aaron's full, pouty lips, perfect for kissing and so many other things, had immediately drawn his attention. Kreed had almost reached out to run his palm along that square, firm jawline, but quickly caught himself, stopping before he made the whole situation any more awkward. That very close-cropped beard would feel amazing against his skin.

If they had met in a bar, you could bet Kreed would be taking this guy home and directly to his bed. Aaron appeared muscular, but not thick, with long legs. Kreed couldn't tell for sure because they'd been hidden by a coat and jeans, but he would guess they were muscled in all the right places, perfect for wrapping those long limbs around Kreed's waist.

Kreed shook his head, trying to push that last thought down. Sex with Aaron would only complicate things, at least that was what his conscience kept screaming. Kreed didn't make it a habit of fucking the guys he worked with, never had. The fall-out could get too messy.

Kreed could feel the wicked smile pulling at the corners of his mouth. *Technically* they weren't on the job yet. So a little fooling around might be the best thing to help ease the building tension. Just to get the temptation out of the way, of course.

A shivering Aaron finally opened the passenger door and slid into the front seat. He now wore nothing to protect him from the cold weather outside. Kreed sat there with one hand on the wheel, the other still resting across the back of the seat, and stared at the guy. Aaron rubbed his hands together, putting them in front of the heater, then blew on them before rubbing them together again. Kreed continued to sit there, gawking.

"What?" Aaron finally asked, not looking over at Kreed.

"I think you got it wrong," Kreed replied.

"More than you know, but what are you talking about?" Only then did Aaron finally glance his way.

"You're absolutely my type," Kreed declared and resisted the urge to reach over and fix the thick, silky strands of Aaron's wind-blown hair. He held back a groan; this kid was tempting as fuck, seriously affecting him to the point of utter distraction. Aaron looked away as soon as he spoke the words.

"I believe you have your words mixed up. It was said the other way around," Aaron shot back. A hint of red crept up his cheeks.

"Well, you definitely got that wrong. You liked what you saw, and I've been wondering about you for a while now. We need to find a way to release all this sexual tension, clear our minds. That way we can give our all to this case without any distractions. So, if we're gonna fuck, we need to hit it now before we get to the bureau and we're officially on the clock," Kreed stated.

"What? Are you kidding me?" Aaron asked, clearly shocked, though maybe Kreed heard a little stunned curiosity in his voice as well. "Not saying I would, but what does being on the clock have to do with anything?"

"I don't get my honey where I get my money. And that's too bad 'cause you're fucking adorable." Kreed watched as Aaron's body visibly tensed.

"Huh?" It took Aaron a second to digest his words. "No, I'm not fucking you. I don't even understand what you're saying. Honey? Money? Adorable? All that thinking you're trying to do over there must be using up all the oxygen in your brain."

Aaron's aggravation came through loud and clear. All right, maybe he'd pushed a little too hard; Kreed had a way of doing that. But Aaron hadn't looked completely appalled by the idea either. At least that was something, right?

"You sure?" Kreed asked, never really any good at accepting no as an answer. "We got a few hours we could kill waiting on Connors's flight to arrive." This time Kreed gave a suggestive waggle of his brows.

"I'm not sleeping with you. I don't even know you." Aaron turned away and stared out the front windshield of the rental.

"I can't think of a better way for you to get to know me, can you?" Kreed asked then waited for something other than the incredulous look now being shot back at him. Kreed shrugged before finally speaking again. "Your loss. It's a onetime offer."

When Aaron said nothing more, Kreed dropped the gearshift into drive and pulled out from the parking spot. He didn't have enough time to wine and dine the kid, but Aaron's continued silence disappointed him. Clearly, the direct approach might not have been the best way to accomplish his most immediate goal.

Whatever. Can't fault a guy for trying. Kreed turned his attention to the traffic, reading the exit signs, following them out of the parking garage before taking the south airport exit.

"So like honey…meaning sex, and money…meaning the office? You don't have sex with the people you work with?" Aaron finally broke the tense silence about ten minutes later.

Kreed kept driving, eyes focused on the road as his grin grew. Aaron was thinking about his offer—maybe even reconsidering his decision, making it not quite the solid no he'd originally thought. "That's surprising. I assumed you and Mitch hooked up."

Kreed gave a deep chuckle at that one. Most people went there. Everybody assumed he and Mitch hooked up on a regular basis. It was just another part of the stereotype that gay field partners got. Instead of telling Aaron he shouldn't assume shit, he decided to be honest.

"We did a time or two, a long time ago, before we worked together as partners. It didn't work out. Now we just give each other shit. He's like my family," Kreed offered and gave Aaron a side glance. "It's still not too late to accept."

"What and be another notch on your bedpost? Nah, I think I'll pass. There's no reason to complicate things, especially when I don't even want to be here. I'm gonna do what they want then get the hell out," Aaron said, turning his head toward the passenger side window.

"Hmmm. Why's that?" Kreed asked. "I mean the getting the hell out part." Kreed left the notch on the bedpost remark alone, accepting it for what it was—an attempted slam to help create distance between them.

"All I was trying to do was give you guys the information I found. It wasn't that big a deal. I could do this from home. I don't need to be here and up in the middle of all this bullshit," Aaron said, somewhat disgruntled.

"Hmm." Kreed couldn't help but notice all the aggression in Aaron's words and wonder why. "You've been instrumental in this case. I'd pretty much say that if it wasn't for you, we'd still be chasing our tails."

"Whatever. Anything I did was from my house. I don't need to be under their thumb. I have a life and things to take care of. I should be there now…where it's sunny."

Kreed barked out a laugh. "I thought all you computer geeks stayed locked up in the house, away from the sun and people"

"I have a balcony," Aaron tossed out.

Kreed laughed again. Aaron had to get out of the house more than just onto his balcony to get that nice of a tan. Coming to a stop at a red light, Kreed gave a sideways glance toward the kid. A little prickle of intuition spiked, making Aaron more than just sexy. There was more to this guy than he'd originally picked up on and he didn't usually miss things. He could typically get a feel for someone within the first few minutes of meeting them.

Looking back, from the beginning, he couldn't get a read on Aaron. It bugged the shit out of him. The guy was an enigma, and Kreed realized that figuring Aaron out would be a challenge, but he always welcomed a good challenge. He'd investigate quietly, but completely. If nothing else, it would help fill the holes of boredom that Mitch had always been good at filling.

"Okay, beach bunny, again your loss on the offer. Guess you'll never know why they call me Sin." Kreed lowered his voice and turned toward Stuart. "I can tell you this much, though. It has nothing to do with my last name." Kreed gave Aaron a wink and focused his attention back to the road. The huff he heard coming from Aaron had a huge grin expanding across his face. Oh yeah, this was getting better by the second.

"How about some lunch? We can sit and talk. I have a feeling you'll be assigned as my temporary partner in this deal. We need to get on the same page. There're a few things we need to go over. Just for the record, I'm not any fonder of working with the suits than you are. I'm good with gettin' in there, gettin' the job done, and gettin' the hell out as soon as humanly possible."

"Sure, whatever." Aaron dismissed him and continued staring out the passenger side window. Kreed could feel the frustration rolling off Aaron in waves. Whether it was the FBI assignment or the sexual tension sitting between them, he couldn't tell yet. Secretly he hoped for the latter, especially since he'd been so solidly turned down.

Kreed pulled into the first restaurant he saw. Aaron Stuart was on his radar and Kreed wasn't about to let this kid out of his sight.

Chapter 3

Aaron stepped out of the SUV and immediately adjusted himself. His ever growing hard-on pressing against the tight new Levi's hurt and annoyed the shit out of him. Unfortunately, the slight adjustment hadn't been enough, but he couldn't very well stick his hands down his pants and rectify the situation in front of the very man who caused all this discomfort.

Kreed Sinacola hadn't minced words.

Damn, if it wasn't such a turn-on to be hit on. He couldn't remember the last time anyone had made their intentions so undeniably clear. The heat in Kreed's eyes had cemented the suggestion they go back to the hotel and fuck like bunnies. And his traitorous dick jumped right on board that train wreck of an idea.

As he contemplated the advantages and the complications of the notion, his brow furrowed. Aaron couldn't really remember the last time he'd had sex. Well…other than with his palm. Yeah, he did what he needed to do to get his rocks off, but he really didn't consider jacking off anywhere in the vicinity of having sex. It was quick, perfunctory, and got the job done. A means to an end.

The whole going out to get laid lifestyle grew old about the same time life had become so serious. Between work and the changing culture of today's gay community, it seemed every guy he met wanted a committed relationship. It was their right. But commitments took work, and that was something he didn't have time for. Sex for the sake of sex wasn't that easy to find anymore. Somehow strings were always attached, no matter what was agreed on before the deed.

Yet, his dumb ass had just been offered that very thing by the handsome guy standing in front of this rental car and he'd turned him down flat. Aaron glanced Kreed's way. Any doubt that he'd gotten it wrong and Kreed wasn't as hot as he'd originally thought vanished. Honestly, Kreed might be the sexiest man he'd ever seen.

Aaron had a gut feeling that sex with Kreed Sinacola would fall somewhere in that gray area between black and white. If Aaron couldn't untangle himself from this case, Kreed would be there pushing his way in, which would make the deputy marshal one of the biggest complications of all. Aaron absolutely didn't need anyone looking over his shoulder right now.

Dammit to hell! He hadn't expected all these contradictions and desires warring inside him. Aaron reached out to slam the passenger door shut before opening the back door of the SUV to retrieve his coat. Out of nowhere, the image of Kreed taking him from behind on the SUV's soft leather seat flashed in his head. His ass clenched and his knees buckled. *Fuck!* Aaron shook his head to push the thought away. He had to finish this case ASAP and get the hell out of Dodge. Aaron shivered involuntarily as the cold wind blew against his now-heated skin. He quickly regained his composure and grabbed his coat. He shrugged the thing on, zipping everything completely up to ward off the wind.

All bundled up, Aaron ran his fingers through his already-disheveled hair. He released the pent up breath he'd been holding. Kreed was dangerous—too sexy, too hot, too direct, and too smart. He'd known before he ever got on that plane that he needed to watch this guy. Aaron had thought he had it under control. He hadn't felt any sort of attraction for the deputy marshal until he'd actually set eyes on the hot-ass guy propped against the wall in the baggage claim area...then everything changed. This wasn't the time in his life to be playing around with a senior deputy US marshal. The man had a classified military past that was so tightly secured Aaron had had a tough time breaking into that file. Deputy Marshal Sinacola was one intelligence badass—no question there.

"Get a hold of yourself, Aaron. Kreed's one of them and an arrogant ass to boot," he mumbled quietly to himself. That was all he needed to remember to have the pressure in his overeager cock begin to ease.

Feeling a little more on solid ground, Aaron moved and shut the door behind him. He looked over at Kreed as he rounded the bumper of the Tahoe and their eyes locked again. Aaron knew the guy was trying hard to get a read on him as their gazes held. After all, that was what Deputy Marshal Kreed Sinacola was known for. That bit of information had shown up in Kreed's files over and over again—from the very start of his military career. Kreed had a well-documented innate ability to read a situation and come up with the correct assessment. He was sought out by many agencies and had been for years because of his reputation for closing the cases he worked.

Kreed was a force and Aaron didn't want him looking too closely at him for any reason during their time together. That was the true reason he hadn't shed his clothing and taken the guy up on his offer right there in the front seat of the SUV.

He absolutely couldn't allow himself to get caught up in the aspirations of his hard dick.

Aaron's entire strategic plan had been to stay aloof and completely disagreeable to keep both the bureau and Kreed's intuition at arm's length. He needed to always remember himself around Kreed, especially now. He had too much at risk.

"Did you lock the door?" Aaron asked, his voice may have been an octave or two deeper, but he doubted Kreed would notice. He still cleared his throat to keep himself even. Aaron couldn't let on how much the guy actually affected him. Kreed lifted his hand, held the key fob in front of his face while looking him straight in the eyes, and pressed the button, that damn smirk making another appearance. *Fucker!*

Aaron took a deep breath to calm himself as he heard the door locks click into place and the horn beep once, reassuring him the car was secure. Lord, Kreed could hold a stare without flinching. Aaron tried to return the gaze, fought not to look away, but damn, it was hard. Kreed's intensity disconcerted him and intrigued him in equal measure. In the end, Aaron forced his eyes away, cutting them toward the mom-and-pop restaurant across the parking lot.

"Are we eating?" Aaron asked, sounding a little overly disgruntled, even to himself.

"Beauty before age," Kreed said on a chuckle and stuck his hand out to direct him. Aaron eyed him again as he passed by and headed for the front door, ready to get out of the fucking cold-ass weather.

"Clothes new? Didn't have any cold weather clothing?" Kreed questioned, trailing behind.

"I had plenty until they were scattered all over the ice at Atlanta International." Aaron looked back over his shoulder. He caught Kreed's gaze lingering on his ass while he walked. Aaron rolled his eyes. Out of all the scenarios that had played out in his head about this man and this trip, none of them had included Kreed having the sexual maturity of a horny teenage boy. "Dude, seriously. It's not gonna happen, so stop."

"I've got a couple of hours before you become my colleague. I can look all I want right now. Just so you know, from where I'm standing, the view's magnificent. Bet it's even better without all your new, shiny threads in the way."

Aaron spun around in the middle of the parking lot, the icy wind stinging his cheeks as he faced off with Kreed. He had to get a hold of this situation. Aaron dropped his fingers to where he thought Kreed's gaze was and held them much like an inverted peace sign then lifted his wrist, directing Kreed's stare up to meet his. He used those two fingers to gesture between their eyes, keeping an intense look of irritation on his face as he spoke the words.

"My eyes are up here. Now, listen to me. Whatever fantasy you have bouncing around in that oversized head of yours… Not. Gonna. Happen. I'm here until I can convince them to send me home. That's it. End of story!" The amused look Kreed gave made him wonder if the man had heard anything he'd said. Aaron threw his hands in the air and growled in frustration, such a better emotion to hang on to.

Aaron tossed out the next words just to get a dig in. "So, you better get over it, old man."

Kreed barked out a laugh and started moving forward again, passing Aaron. "Say what you want, but I know what I saw in your eyes when you walked up to me at the airport. You can fight it all you want, kid. But I know you want a piece of this."

Aaron sighed, letting his head drop back between his shoulders, and just stared up at the dark, cloud-covered sky in total disbelief. Dammit to hell, he was in so much trouble here. Yeah, Kreed was absolutely right about wanting him, but it didn't matter, because he wasn't going there. The horn that blasted behind him startled the fuck out of him and had him jerking around to find he'd come to a stop right in the middle of the parking lot, blocking traffic.

Kreed seriously got under his skin.

The annoyingly loud bark of laughter coming from the front door of the restaurant brought him back to reality. Aaron lifted his hand, sending a quick wave of apology to the people in the car. After pulling himself back together, he took a deep breath then jogged toward the door where Kreed was now doubled over in amusement—all that jovial attitude directed straight at him. Aaron definitely wasn't laughing. The deputy marshal had him so wound up. He was almost certain that with just one click of Kreed's fingers his resolve would snap and his whole world would spin completely out of control. Aaron felt the scowl settle into place as he walked past his handsome tormentor, feigning disinterest as he went inside to get a table.

~~~

Kreed's brow furrowed as he listened to Aaron rattle off his extensive food order to the waitress—two large appetizers, an entrée with extra sides, and a dessert. Was this kid serious? The server finally looked over at him for his order. Before he got a chance to speak, Aaron called her attention back to him. He had her repeat the order back to him, stopping her every other word to change or add something. She wrote quickly on her pad before she turned her somewhat dazed expression toward him.

"Cheeseburger. Medium." He stared at Aaron as he spoke the words. He only broke eye contact to hand the waitress his menu. To be nothing more than a good-natured smartass, he grinned at Aaron before he spoke. "Can you repeat that for me?"

She started to turn away and stopped abruptly, turning back, a little startled. "Umm, yeah. You wanted a cheeseburger cooked medium."

Kreed nodded slowly, pretending to contemplate her words. "Yes… A cheeseburger…" He stared at Stuart when he said those words and laughed out loud at his own joke. Aaron didn't seem to find the humor in his action. He waved a hand toward the waitress and gave her a wink. "I'm messing with him. Ignore me."

She looked almost relieved before quickly turning away and leaving them alone again.

"You seriously gonna eat all that?"

"Every bite. I have a very fast metabolism and I haven't eaten today," Aaron replied, linking his fingers together on the table.

"Not the first time you've been asked that question?"

"Nope, it's not." Aaron stared back at him, holding eye contact. This time Kreed was less affected by all that hot, sexy, edgy hipster thing Aaron had going on, which was a good thing. Kreed had started them off all wrong. He shouldn't have gone there so quickly, but there was something about that adorable nerdy thing that did it for him. Kreed knew he could come across a little strong when he wanted something—clearly not the right approach to take with Aaron. If he could make Aaron comfortable, then he'd open up more, and that would greatly help in connecting some of the missing dots in the questions circulating through Kreed's overactive brain. Based on all the attitude in the stare he was getting right now, Aaron had resurrected the walls Kreed had managed to dislodge with his earlier innuendos.

"You gonna share any of those appetizers?" he asked, trying for friendly.

"Umm…I guess, but you should've ordered something more for yourself."

Kreed couldn't help but bark out a laugh at the pained look he received. Mental note made: Aaron didn't share or play with his food. Got it.

"I'm good. I can't eat all that crap anymore. I'm too old. It's gettin' harder to work it off." Kreed reached down and patted his belly. Aaron's gaze followed his hand before skittishly darting back up to meet his eyes.

"You aren't ready for social security. You can't be that old," Aaron finally replied.

"You know my age," Kreed said. There was no way Aaron hadn't come prepared, with intel on everything and everyone involved. The kid was too smart for that.

A slow smile parted Aaron's lips. "It makes people uncomfortable when I rattle off personal details. For the record, I wasn't just searching you, so don't get a big head. I can tell you Connors's and Brown's ages too."

"A foursome. I could be into that..." Kreed murmured, leaning back against the booth seat. The stern expression on Aaron's handsome face fractured, and to his delight, the kid even laughed a little at the joke. Interestingly enough, Aaron had a funny way of easing his heart. The banter between them left him feeling lighter than he had in months. For the first time since the awful news, his brother's death wasn't the most pressing thought on his mind.

"Is it brains or some sort of photographic memory?" Kreed asked. Aaron studied him for a full minute before the corners of his mouth curled, turning the smile into a challenging you-tell-me grin. Kreed watched Aaron's face lighten, smoothing out his features, making him look even younger and more handsome. Kreed was slightly mesmerized for a brief moment.

"You know my IQ," Aaron challenged.

"I know what the bureau profile says. I'm guessing it's probably higher," Kreed reasoned.

"Why would I lie?"

"Not sure. You would have to answer that." The smile faded and Kreed hated he'd caused its loss. He was supposed to be drawing the guy out, not closing him up tighter. "I didn't think you were truly twenty-nine. I've been twenty-nine for nine years, but you look young. Are you?"

Kreed leaned back as a heaping mound of nachos and a plate of potato skins were placed in front of Aaron. The waitress sat a small empty plate next to the cute computer guy. The question he'd just asked was forgotten as the look of delight on Aaron's face morphed into confusion when Kreed had an identical plate placed in front of him.

"Don't worry. I'm not mooching in on your grub." Kreed lifted two hands high, making sure Aaron knew he wasn't going to hone in on his food. Aaron eyed him closely before digging in, filling his plate to capacity. When done, he took one nacho and placed it on Kreed's plate with a little you're-welcome smirk. They both laughed at the move. "So I'm guessing you're the youngest in your family?"

"Why do you say that?" Aaron asked after swallowing his first bite.

"Experience. The youngest in the family's least likely to share. And that's magnified by the number of siblings. I'm thinking you're probably the youngest of a big group of kids—like four or five."

Aaron nodded, swallowing another bite before taking a big drink of the ice water. "Very observant, Deputy Marshal. I make number five."

Before he spoke, Aaron lifted the napkin from his lap and wiped his mouth. He used utensils to eat his nachos and potato skins, chewed with his mouth closed, and frequently wiped with a napkin. No matter the rebel-meets-hipster style Aaron donned, he had an ingrained sense of manners that usually came from wealth, which just intensified the questions already forming in Kreed's brain.

Kreed understood that in order to solve a puzzle, you had to start by placing the first piece, then the second, and over time the whole picture would slowly be revealed, making the game more time-consuming than complicated. Good thing Kreed had time.

"We should be going over the facts…" Aaron suggested, leaning back to make room as some pasta dish was placed in front of him. "That's the reason I'm here."

Kreed moved the plate in front of him to let the waitress place his there. He unwrapped the napkin, listening to Aaron ask for more butter, salsa, and ranch dressing. For Kreed, he was good with a Jumbo Jack from Jack in the Box for dinner. Somehow he didn't see Aaron as a fast-food junkie. He'd probably reject that idea in such a way that it would be fun to taunt him with the stops. He made that mental note to remember to do that and gave a simple, "I'm good," to the waitress when she asked if he needed anything more.

"So you and me, plus Connors and Brown, are the new team?" Aaron questioned. Kreed built his burger, adding mustard to the bun.

"I don't think anyone else got called in from vacation."

"What about the assistant who helped Mitch?"

"Anne? I don't know. We'll have to see. We have a two o'clock report time." Kreed lifted his burger to his mouth and took a big bite.

He'd found this little hole-in-the-wall place last time he was in town. His memory of the food didn't disappoint.

"So I'm probably not getting out of this?" Aaron asked. The honesty of the question intrigued Kreed, since he'd assumed the surly disposition had been an act. Aaron had always been ready to help, day or night.

"Probably not," Kreed stated, giving Aaron a truthful answer.

"Dammit," Aaron mumbled between bites. Kreed cocked his brow, watching the kid.

"Ahh, I'm all warm and fuzzy with sentiment. I'm looking forward to working with you, too." Kreed took another big bite of his food. He held back his smile as he watched the never-ending flow of food from Aaron's plate to his mouth. The guy was thin, yet he was consuming more food than Kreed had eaten in the last forty-eight hours. With his mouth still full, Kreed added, "But on the bright side, we'll team up against Connors and bully our way through. The more we get done unsupervised, the faster we can wrap this up."

"All right. Good backup plan. I'd rather find a way out of being here, but if I can't, I'll concede to that. Get done and go home. Connors and Brown up for that?" Even though the food intake never stopped, Aaron never spoke with food in his mouth—impressive and a bit of its own art form, truth be told.

"Brown is. Connors surprised me with that interrogation of Agent Langley—the way he pushed that through—so the jury's still out on him." Kreed took another bite, letting Aaron process that bit of information. Aaron had to know he couldn't talk his way out of being a part of this task force, especially with Mitch sidelined, and Aaron had been there from almost day one, helping Knox find all the dots that connected the cases. He was the most logical choice to fill the Mitch-shaped hole in their investigative team.

"So if we were gonna close this file for good, where would you start?" Kreed asked after a moment of silence. The biggest concern Kreed had about the case right now was who could be trusted. With the discovery that Special Agent Langley had been on the inside— and that he hadn't acted alone—there were most likely other dirty agents, either in the FBI or other government agencies. Aaron was technically the only one he really trusted right now and that said a lot. Aaron had single-handedly broken the case wide open when he'd identified Peter Langley's attorney being at Kreed's brother's funeral when no one else had—or maybe they had, and never shared.

If he and Aaron were on the same page going into the meeting today, they could bust out of DC by tomorrow. And if they weren't under someone's thumb, and he and the kid worked closely together, it might not be much of a stretch to close this case by week's end. Because with Kreed's gut and his willingness to allow Stuart to do whatever it took—both inside and outside the law—to find this information, he figured they could wrap this case up tight.

Aaron stayed silent for so long that Kreed figured the guy had caught on to his ploy to entice Aaron to close this investigation quickly rather than encouraging the man's desire to leave the case behind. The kid surprised him when he finally answered. "It's hate related. It's not rocket science that hate masks itself in religion all the time. Religion means a church is involved. Before I left, I narrowed it down to three satellite churches. All had members involved in the rally. "

"So you're thinking like I'm thinking—there's a religious organization behind this whole deal, probably starting back before even the Colt Michaels accident?" Kreed laid his burger on the plate, pushed the food aside, and took a deep breath. Being on the same mental page gave him the validation he needed to continue with his plans.

"Pretty much," Aaron said, before taking another bite of pasta.

"Have you looked into any of them closely?" Kreed asked, and Aaron went silent, eating the rest of his plate without making eye contact.

"If we're gonna be partners and get this solved so you can get out of here, you need to come clean with me, Aaron," Kreed said quietly. He leaned in a little and whispered the next words. "I want this done. Mitch and Cody aren't safe until we figure this out. You can trust me. I swear."

"We aren't partners yet, and the less you know about my processes, the better," Aaron quipped and Kreed leaned back a little disappointed.

"Well, that's fucking cryptic for a government employee who wants the hell out of here," Kreed snorted. He needed to remember Stuart wasn't someone to push. Aaron needed a gentle hand to help guide him where Kreed wanted him to go. "So if you were looking at the churches, when will you know something?"

Aaron wiped his mouth and gave an exaggerated eye roll.

"I've narrowed it down, but won't know for certain until I can get a secure connection," Aaron replied, before finishing off his pasta dish. Kreed nodded in agreement. That was all he'd needed to know. Kreed lifted his hand for the check. All of a sudden, getting Aaron to the office was the only thing Kreed was interested in.

"I ordered dessert," Aaron said defiantly when he realized Kreed's intent to leave.

Kreed shoved from the booth, heading toward the back where he saw the waitress go. He quickly asked her to bag Aaron's dessert and handed her his credit card for the meal. There would be little more than a skeleton crew at FBI headquarters, and they could work reasonably undetected. Maybe he could access Mitch's old office and stick Aaron in there, see if he could gather any more valuable information before they all met this afternoon.

Chapter 4

Dammit! Aaron knew better than to think he could worm his way out of this mandatory onsite request. To make it worse, he had no one to blame but himself. Society's shady-ass behavior always intrigued him to the point of trying to figure out motives and the potential next moves they planned to make. Add that to his innate do-gooder attitude and he always went after the bad guy when any sort of injustice made its presence known.

Good versus evil and all that superhero shit made him feel better at the end of the day if he had to break a few rules to expose the bad guy. His online buddies called him the modern-day Robin Hood, hacking information and releasing it to the disenfranchised. Knowledge was power, and the power should be with the people, not corporate overlords. Typically, that was a source of pride, but right now, riding in this car, he had the major heebie-jeebies—times about a million—at the prospect of walking into the front doors of FBI headquarters. This shit just got way too real and wasn't funny at all.

Aaron looked down at his palms. They were sweaty from his overactive nerves, and he quickly ran them down the front of his jeans before tucking his hands under his thighs. Up until Mitch's case that somehow inadvertently got dumped on his shoulders, Aaron had been able to do his Robin Hood thing from behind his computer screen in the safety of his own home. Now, as they pulled into the parking lot with the massive *Federal Bureau of Investigation* stamped on the entrance, a fear Aaron hadn't known, became his number one focus.

While working adventures with his merry band of brothers, Aaron might be branded the king of manipulating and exploiting limitations in the proxy servers of large organizations—more specifically, the largest corporations in the world, who tended to regularly exploit the little guy. And there might have been a time, or perhaps a few dozen times, where he may have orchestrated a complete flood on their system by simply issuing a calculated DDoS—Distributed Denial of Service—attack. And since Aaron's particular talents included systematically evading any reverse proxy servers in their way, allowing the unsuspecting flood to penetrate, some legal eagles might consider that a planned global cyber-attack. Aaron dubbed it more a wakeup call to the senior administration when they'd gotten a little too big for their britches.

Honestly, it had all been in good fun. Hell, they'd had a blast. He loved hacking for the sake of hacking. When corporate blowhards declared things like their systems being secure and unbreakable, hack resistant… *Hmm, okay, challenge accepted.*

Those hacks were the best times ever! And at the end of the day, he loved leaving his calling card of a fire breathing dragon avatar for the IT department to eventually find.

Aaron had his ways of leading anyone who might see him into a very wild goose chase. Okay, amend the previous thought. Spoofing his source address, redirecting his activity, and leading the authorities to an old abandoned house in Nebraska while they tried in vain to track him down… Yeah, that was the best time of all.

The problem with all that hacking was that he'd learned too much about the true evil side of excessive greed and ego. As much as Aaron liked and believed in Mitch, he didn't trust the federal, state, or local government as far as he could throw them. He'd hacked into too much, seen disgusting classified information that only the top of the top could access. Very few knew that his true reason for being a government employee was to keep his friends close and his enemies closer. The FBI represented that enemy tenfold.

After Kreed parked, Aaron paused for several seconds before he opened the car door and got out. Where the hell were Neo and Trinity from the *Matrix* when he needed them? Grabbing his gear, Aaron silently followed Kreed inside. A small, unreasonable fear trickled up his spine for about the hundredth time. What if this was a setup? Had he finally given them enough evidence to piece together his extracurricular activities? Kreed held the door open. Aaron entered, but let Kreed lead the way to the front desk as he tried to mask his face and calm his ass down.

"Tension's rolling off you in waves," Kreed said casually, flashing his ID at security. Aaron watched everything and everyone behind the desk. Even in holiday skeleton mode, they were way overstaffed at the entrance. Kreed went through the motions of logging his weapon while having security issue the proper identification to enter the building.

"It's weird being on this side of things." Since he hadn't been arrested the minute he'd walked inside, he redirected his pent-up anxiety and pushed forward his disgust. He wasn't necessarily sneering at the security guards but more the entire building, as he pulled out his government employee credentials and handed them over the counter, following Kreed's lead. The smartass officer took the documents to a desk behind a bulletproof barrier.

"Connors is gonna love you being on this case," Kreed teased, giving Aaron a wink and smile. Aaron appreciated his attempt to lighten the mood. It didn't work, but the thought was there.

"Maybe he could throw a fit and send me home?" Aaron replied eagerly.

"Whatever gives you hope," Kreed tossed out, tucking his badge back in his pocket. He turned to fully face Aaron and leaned against the counter. He'd been cleared for entrance, but he waited on Aaron, whose gaze danced between Kreed and the guys talking behind the bulletproof window.

Since Aaron's arrest record always popped up, he mentally began to count, three…two…one… Yep, perfect timing. One of the security agents behind the desk picked up the phone while the other came forward, flanked by two additional well-armed agents.

"If you could come this way," one of the men-in-black said to him while reaching for the backpack still slung over Aaron's shoulder. Aaron turned his shoulder away as Kreed's subdued attitude faded. Kreed stretched to his full height, sticking out a hand to stop the guard from taking the bag. Yeah, Kreed's move didn't go over well. All that security muscle tensed as waves of testosterone hit from every angle.

"I've been instructed to bring this man, NSA employee, Aaron Stuart, into this office to work an open case with me. He's authorized and under my supervision," Kreed explained, his voice deep, actually frighteningly threatening, and Aaron lifted a brow in surprise at the huge fucking turn-on that was, even during such a clearly intense time.

"It's not their fault. Keep my computer for me. I'll go with them. It'll take about fifteen minutes to go through the chain of command to prove I have access," Aaron said, trying to neutralize this situation. He quickly looked around. Eight against one… Aaron shook his head. Kreed was a badass—no doubt there—but he sure didn't see the guy coming out of this unscathed against all this bulk raining down on them.

"This shit's not right. I just told them I'll take responsibility for you," Kreed argued, clearly not used to having his word dismissed. Kreed wedged his body where his arm had been and got right in the agent's face.

"Deputy Marshal Sinacola, I don't have a problem with you."

Aaron took a small step to the side and looked around Kreed's massive body. Now, he wasn't a body language kind of guy, but from the sight of the ever-growing anger blooming on the men's faces, Aaron decided the agent's words were probably untrue.

"Apparently, you do. I just gave you my word as a deputy marshal of this justice system and that's not good enough for you?" The sentence might have been phrased in the form of a question, but it carried all the attitude of someone ready to kick ass.

Fuck. He needed to calm this situation. Aaron moved between the two of them, shoving his computer into Kreed's chest. "Keep an eye on this. Don't let it out of your sight." Aaron quickly turned to the guard, giving Kreed his back. "Take me wherever."

"Director Skinner has a personal note in his file. He's to be admitted," the agent behind the desk called out, his eyes still trained at his monitor. It still took a few seconds to defuse the cock-measuring contest currently underway. Kreed held his stance as the security guy eased his. Even relaxed, the agent confronting Kreed held his stare as he stepped aside, handing Aaron his identification. Kreed didn't ease; his formidable scowl and narrowed gaze stayed trained on the agent as Aaron took his laptop case back and moved to the desk to get his temporary badge. Another officer patted Aaron down to make sure he wasn't carrying a weapon. All the while Kreed monitored everything going on around him. Aaron had never felt safer in his entire adult life. Without question, if Aaron got himself in a bad situation, Kreed was the guy he wanted on his side.

Based on what he'd just witnessed, Aaron conceded that Mitch wasn't the most dangerous part of the dynamic duo of K & M. And he realized right then, the urban legend he'd read about Kreed could quite possibly be true. Aaron glanced back to see every single eye in the area still trained on Kreed, with every agent's palm resting on the butt of their weapon. Anger wafted all around him.

He'd been fooled by Kreed's laid-back demeanor. That casual, overly easygoing guy of the last hour had evaporated in less than a second, leaving no doubt Kreed could have taken out many of those agents by himself.

Aaron remembered reading Kreed's military file. It was filled with intense moments of heroism along with large black holes of missing documentation. That stayed consistent until he went to work for the marshal service. Since Aaron had that knowledge and had still underestimated Kreed, he wondered if anyone—even Mitch—could fill in those blanks in Kreed's military career.

"You'll be admitted under the supervision of Deputy Sinacola…" the guard behind the desk asserted carefully.

"Like I fuckin' said," Kreed growled at all the agents standing around the area. After getting to his feet, the agent came around the desk, his hands up in the air, trying for calm.

"Until we can get your identification properly loaded, stay with him at all times so we can keep this from happening again. It's precaution, nothing more. You know how different security is in today's world. We've gotta be overcautious…" It was a valiant effort to ease the agitation. One that didn't work at all if the tension level was any indication, but still a solid try.

"We're speeding that process along."

Aaron looked over to see Agent Brown jogging quickly in from the side, a big giant grin made the corners of his eyes crinkle. His hand came forward as he reached the group of them, and he shook

Kreed's hand. "The place's going nuts about a big, crazy Southern redneck causing problems. I knew immediately it was you, Sinacola."

Brown patted Kreed on the shoulder. Aaron grabbed his identification from the sneering guard and hung the temporary lanyard around his neck, never looking back. While Kreed and Brown did their thing, Aaron glanced around the room and watched the guards continue to eye Kreed with an occasional glance in his direction as they spoke in hushed voices near the desk. They were no doubt grandstanding simply because they knew exactly who Kreed Sinacola was and wanted to make a show of going toe-to-toe with the big guy, maybe to earn a few pats on the back and bragging rights later in the locker room.

Agent Brown stuck his hand out toward Aaron. "Good of you to come."

"It wasn't a choice." He only lowered his eyes for a second to clasp the hand before cutting his gaze back across the room to take in the animosity still brewing.

Brown followed his glance and waved a hand dismissively. "Yeah, that's standard around here. Why don't we get you settled in?" Brown had Kreed by the shoulder, pushing him toward the elevator; Aaron followed, staying close to Sinacola. "That's Roger Covington, Anne's husband. He and Knox got into it when Mitch first arrived too. It was kind of comical. Wish I could have seen it firsthand."

"He's a douche," Kreed said loud enough for everyone in the lobby area to hear. He looked back over his shoulder and pinned all the agents still watching with a warning stare.

"Yeah, I think Mitch had a few choice words of his own. Covington's just doing his job. He's clearly good at it," Brown stated matter-of-factly, waving his badge in front of the elevator security pad. The doors opened and Brown ushered him and Kreed inside. The tension slowly began to fade once the doors had closed.

"I don't know how you do it, man," Kreed muttered. Aaron watched as Kreed took a few deep breaths and visibly forced himself to calm down. Kreed's mood control was an impressive sight. He wasn't sure he'd ever seen anyone have that much self-discipline over their aggression before.

"It happens every time I have to show my credentials in a government office. That shit's never gonna come off my record, but it's also why they hired me," Aaron said as the doors opened. Brown was off first, but Kreed made Aaron exit the elevator before he followed.

"That doesn't happen to me. I served this country with a spotless record for the last twenty years. When I say something, it needs to be at least noted," Kreed tossed out. Aaron didn't respond as he pinpointed all the cameras lining the walkways of this floor. That uncanny big-brother-watching factor was high, and he wondered how many cameras were monitoring them right now. His stomach churned under the stress of the moment.

As he continued his forward motion, following Brown, Aaron did a complete circle. There wasn't a space that a camera wasn't trained on them. His eyes collided with Kreed's and stayed there longer than they should have. Kreed was right. Failing in his first goal of being sent back home, they needed to team up and get out into the field as quickly as possible. Nothing would be solved under all this oppressive monitoring. How the hell had Mitch gotten as far as he had with the investigation? Aaron turned back around toward Brown and readjusted his attitude. He'd find the information Kreed asked about so they could get the hell out of there.

~~~

The overhead fluorescent lights flickered as Kreed shrugged out of his jacket, absently tossing the worn leather aside on a side chair in the conference room he'd called home for several weeks last fall. Clearly, not nearly enough investigating had gone on in this room since he'd left. All the victims of this case had their pictures exactly where Connors and Knox had placed them on the wall. The handwritten notes were still scribbled on the rolling dry-erase boards. The monitor they'd brought in to conference in Aaron during meetings still sat in its place at the table. His counterparts in the marshals' division would be mighty pissed off to know the FBI had all this space while they doubled up in just about every field office they had.

Not paying any attention to anyone, he went for the break room. He needed a Mountain Dew and a minute alone to regroup. He rolled his head on his shoulders and shook the aggression out of his arms as he tried hard to re-center himself. The sexual buzz then the confrontation downstairs over Aaron had escalated into straight up pissed off on a level he hadn't experienced in a very long time.

All these erratic mood swings reeked of the PTSD diagnosis he'd been given upon discharge from the military, probably resurfacing after his brother's death. Honestly, he'd been spoiling for a fight for the last few months. Kreed knew the signs. He was a ticking time bomb, and he needed to get his fucked-up shit under control.

"Hey. Where's everybody?" Connors came from out of nowhere, stood directly in front of him, and effectively diminished his bad mood. Kreed couldn't hide his smile. Connors was dressed in khaki walking shorts, flip-flops, and a frayed sweatshirt. Putting aside the fact it was freezing outside, he'd never seen the guy in anything other than his standard issue FBI crisp blue suit, stark white dress shirt, and matching silk tie.

"I'm not even sure I know who you are." Kreed's smile grew. He reached in his pocket for some change then dropped the money into the slot and pushed the button.

"I'm not here because I chose to be." Connors shoved past Kreed.

"They're in the conference room," Kreed called out then thought better of it all. He quickly grabbed his drink then spun around. He jogged the few steps back to the conference room, bypassing Connors as he went, because he wanted a front row seat to Connors meeting Aaron for the first time. After all the hate the man had spewed to Knox about Aaron's presence in the case—not trusting him as far as he could throw him—there was absolutely no way Kreed would miss this moment. Besides, Mitch would want a play-by-play. He owed it to his buddy to capture every minute. He made it inside the door, crashed into a front row seat, sending the chair rolling backward, bumping into the table as he kicked back to watch the show. Guaranteed entertainment. Too bad he didn't have a bucket of popcorn; it would go really well with his Mountain Dew.

"Aaron Stuart, meet Special Agent Connors. Yep, it's him—pale legs and all," Kreed called out as Connors entered the room. He couldn't see what Aaron did because his sole focus remained on Connors, who didn't disappoint. He didn't miss the wince, that little brief narrowing of Connors's eyes at the introduction. Aaron's hand came into his peripheral vision and Kreed laughed out loud as Connors hesitated to extend his hand. The guy was too much.

"Good to meet you," Aaron said with definitely more manners than meaning. Connors didn't seem to possess that same attribute though.

"We should get started," Connors said. Kreed tracked the guy when he bypassed Aaron altogether as he rounded the table to shake Agent Brown's hand. They were actually assigned partners. *Huh.* Kreed couldn't see how Brown managed day to day with that stiff and formal agent. Kreed would never greet Mitch so formally. Actually, he and Mitch were more into greetings by way of insult.

Aaron's gaze slid his direction. "You need to Google 'mouse and Mountain Dew experiment' sometime, just for the hell of it." Aaron's nose scrunched up as he nodded to the green can in Kreed's hand before walking away.

"What? Why?" Kreed looked at the soft drink then shrugged before bringing the can to his lips and finishing the last of the sugary drink in one big gulp. He tossed the can in the nearest wastebasket and headed back to the table before the briefing got underway.

Aaron drew Kreed's attention over to him. His laptop was out and he typed quicker than any man Kreed had ever seen before. Kreed watched Aaron's long slender fingers fly across the keys as he gathered information. He couldn't help but wonder how well Aaron used those deft digits for other things.

The wall-mounted monitor lit up, drawing Kreed's attention back to the FBI meeting room and what he was supposed to be concentrating on. *Shit! Get your head in the game, Sinacola.* Numbers and letters in no particular order scrolled across the screen as Kreed's focus centered back on the task at hand.

Kreed turned his attention toward Colt's picture—the New York Panther's freshly out-of-the-closet quarterback whose automobile accident spurred this entire investigation. He'd never met the guy or his partner, Jace, yet he felt a bond with both of them.

"Do we need a refresher synopsis?" Connors asked from his seat at the head of the table. Since Mitch was out, Connors would, of course, be the sole lead. Kreed wrinkled his nose, remembering how many times he'd wanted to kick the guy's ass during the brief time they'd worked together on this case.

"I think we're good," Kreed started but Brown cut him off.

"I'll do it. I'll hit the high points," Brown said, taking his seat and opening a file. *Thank God.* Kreed breathed a sigh of relief. Connors could get windy. "Secret Service Agent Peter Langley was arrested in the attempted murder of State Trooper Cody Turner. Charges were also filed on the attempted murder and abduction of Elliot Greyson, Senator Greyson's college-aged son."

Aaron typed quickly and the agent's mugshot appeared on the screen. Brown was silent a second, turning pages in the file before he spoke again.

"He pled guilty to a number of crimes but was found dead in his cell of an apparent suicide before any additional information was obtained. It was widely believed—albeit not with most of the parties present in this room—that Langley worked alone in master-minding and carrying out a long list of hate-related crimes against nine men, ranging from murder to kidnapping. Then, Stuart here spotted Langley's attorney in the picket line at Derek Sinacola's funeral…" Brown stopped and looked up at Kreed a moment, worry clear on the guy's face.

"Are you sure you can handle this?" Connors chimed in with the words that were so plainly expressed on Brown's face.

Kreed already knew that Connors didn't do compassion. The tone he used was clear; Connors thought Kreed might be a liability and he got it, but this was the one damn thing he *could* do. There were victims and families out there who deserved answers and he was going to make damn sure they got them. He knew how much this meant to Mitch, and he wouldn't rest until the sons-of-bitches that did this got exactly what they deserved. He looked at Connors and just cocked a brow.

"You aren't pushing me off this case, hot shot. I owe it to Knox."

"How are they?" Brown asked, drawing Kreed's attention off Connors.

"As good as can be expected." Kreed assumed Brown meant Mitch and Cody. Then he smiled as he said, "Mitch knows, if that's what you're really asking. He's pissed he wasn't included, but he's worried about Cody, so he'll behave. If Stuart's lead turns out to be valid, Cody isn't safe. Hell, no one's safe. We need to get 'em while they're still regrouping."

Brown nodded, shutting the file and pushing it out of his way.

"And we all agree Agent Langley more than likely didn't act alone, correct?" The entire table nodded their agreement. Aaron made eye contact with Kreed for the first time since his fingers hit the keyboard.

"We should act fast before word can leak," Aaron suggested.

Connors stayed uncharacteristically quiet while he looked over at Aaron.

"Right now's our best chance. We need a plan before this holiday break ends and agents we haven't vetted for possible involvement return to their posts. Stuart and I talked before we got here. I think what he has to say's pretty solid."

"Let's hear it," Connors said. Kreed would watch this play out. If he had to step in to create the outcome he wanted, he would.

Aaron gave a long pause before he bent to work at his keyboard again. "Agent Langley's attorney was spotted across the street from the church."

Kreed watched the screen fill with images of the religious haters picketing his brother's funeral and his stomach turned. Stuart only showed shots of the crowd, and Kreed was grateful to avoid seeing the church or the funeral procession, not that those images weren't burned into his brain anyway. The picketers hadn't only disrespected his brother but Kreed's entire family with their 'God hates fags' and 'Pray for more dead soldiers' antics.

Three or four pictures passed with shots of the attorney, wearing a baseball cap, pulled down low, and a high-collared jacket, but the facial shots were clear. There was no mistaking his identity, even behind the cap.

"I've narrowed it down to three churches involved in that rally. I haven't had a lot of time with a secured line, but in the few minutes I had before this meeting started, I received the information I needed." Aaron continued his keystrokes and three church names appeared on the screen. East Hill Fellowship, Jonesboro Baptist, Four Square Temple.

Kreed's jaw clenched and his gut churned. How any of those organizations hadn't been added to the national list of organized hate groups was beyond him.

"I don't think any of this is a surprise," Connors started, but Kreed lifted a hand. They were progressing, and if Connors took the floor, they'd be there hours listening to him think out loud.

"Hang on. We came up with an idea. Let Aaron tell us what he thinks. We need to get it out before we rehash everything. Keep going, Stuart."

"Well, those three churches are satellite branches of the bigger, angrier Redemption Apostle Tabernacle," Stuart said, looking back at him. Kreed nodded, a little distracted when their gazes made contact. He couldn't seem to tear his gaze away from the kid but got the break he needed when Aaron finally looked down in order to bring up several images of the founder of the church.

"This is Pastor Gerald Albert Helps. These other three are the church's top deacons. What's important here is this one." The screen changed again as one picture expanded to take center stage. "Deacon Silas Burns has a military past. It took me months to stumble on the information. He's come up on a couple of lists, but his file was hidden away tightly for some reason. He was special teams for the army."

Okay, that got all of Kreed's attention, and he sat forward, leaning his arms on the table. The cut brake lines, all the different bombs... Burns would have easily gained that knowledge in the military.

"Anything else?" Connors asked.

"The deacon's taken a mission trip to Mexico, per his credit card usage. Not saying he's really there, but my gut says they're trying to create an alibi."

"Damn, you're good," Brown said. "How did Knox find you?"

"We played *State of Decay*," Aaron answered absently, causing Kreed to laugh. A technology genius wasting his time on online video games. What a riot.

"All right then, here's my plan. We go undercover inside the hub. We need to do it immediately, get the wheels turning this week while everyone's gone. I'll get Skinner to approve it," Kreed said, dropping his plan in the middle of the table.

"That's a shot in the dark. Besides, what do any of us have to offer to get inside the door of the church?" Connors asked, but Kreed talked over him.

"You haven't heard me out. To me, they're homegrown terrorists. So they're extreme and need to be handled as such. We'll pair up. Go undercover. Connors, you stay here and work your magic by buying us time. Brown, you monitor all the surveillance we feed you, and Stuart and I will go into the field." Kreed pointed to Aaron.

"Wait... What? I thought I was wrapping things up to go home," Aaron said, his gaze darting over to Kreed's.

"We need you. You're the only one who can get inside the church," Kreed explained.

"What? When did *that* become the plan?" Aaron shouted those words. He could tell Aaron was aggravated as hell, so he hid his smile at the outburst.

"He's talented enough to create a completely new identity for himself. No one outside the four of us needs to know who he's become. We'll clean him up and get him a job in the inner workings of the church. Every company I know needs a knowledgeable IT guy. Am I wrong?" Kreed asked.

"Yes, you're wrong. I can infiltrate them from my home office," Aaron shot back.

"Not good enough," Connors said, staring at Kreed as he thought through the potential plan. "It's what you'll hear on the inside that's important. IT guys sit quietly and absorb everything. Every employee knows to go to them to get the gossip. Sinacola, your plan has merit."

"No, it doesn't," Aaron countered defensively.

"Sure, it does," Kreed argued, but never looked Aaron's way. "I'll wire him up, set up shop somewhere close by, and be there to handle anything that goes down. The threat's real, but I've got your back." Kreed spoke the last line to Aaron and meant it. Nothing would touch the kid.

"So no one outside of this room knows what we're doing?" Brown asked.

"Skinner knows some," Kreed offered. "But he's given us the complete green light and came back from vacay to be our direct senior advisor."

"It's critical to the success. Their congregation's too massive and far-reaching. That's been proven with Langley," Connors said as he contemplated the idea.

"Yeah, exactly. It's already reared its ugly head inside the Justice Department. No telling who else in here shares their beliefs and the same hatred," Kreed reasoned aloud, validating Connors. "I'll have to tell Skinner parts, but I trust him with my life."

"No local law enforcement?" Brown asked, and Kreed shook his head.

"I'll track Stuart closely. And I've read that anything electronic can become surveillance." Kreed stopped and looked over at Aaron for confirmation. When Aaron did nothing more than give him the death stare, he took that as a thumbs up. "We can all keep an eye on him and gather intelligence," Kreed told Brown and Connors.

"I want access to every bit of data in real time," Connors stated.

"Of course. That's critical to the success," Kreed affirmed. Connors bit at his nail, his gaze locked on Kreed's before he turned toward the wall of pictures. Half those men had lost their lives and this was the closest lead they had.

"We have to get it right," Connors commented, still staring at the pictures.

"Do I have a say in this at all?" Aaron finally asked. For the first time ever, Kreed and Connors had easily agreed on a plan of action, but Aaron kept throwing little wrenches in their system.

"No," all three said in unison. After several moments of silence, Kreed finally addressed Aaron's concern. "If we can wrap this up, you won't ever have to hear from us again."

"Well, that's an incentive," he added dryly.

"Pull up the information you have on Redemption Apostle Tabernacle. Let's get started. Looks like we'll have a long night ahead of us, guys," Connors informed them, rising and going for a dry-erase board. As if on cue, their collective groans filled the room. Normally Kreed would have stopped him, especially since he'd already moved this in the direction he wanted them to go. But out of respect, he held his tongue. He could sit there quietly and let Connors beat them in the ground, trying to decipher the exact implementation of this part of the investigation.

Chapter 5

What seemed like hours passed with Connors rehashing everything concerning this case about a million times, droning on and on and on. Aaron could have sworn the agent was just talking to hear himself. Every once in a while, Brown or Kreed would inject a thought, but Aaron stayed silent through the whole lecture, still pissed off and not even a little bit resigned to his new undercover fate. No matter how hard he pounded the keyboard or how many grunts he gave, no one paid any attention to him.

To top everything off, the rumbling in his stomach had turned to pain a while ago. One pepperoni pizza split between the four of them wasn't nearly enough food, and damn it, if he hadn't left his dessert in the car. He glanced down at the clock on his computer screen and tried to ignore the noises rumbling through his stomach again. Agitation got the best of him. What the fuck was wrong with these men? Why was Kreed just sitting there, letting this happen? It was already past eight at night. At this rate, all he could see was Connors keeping them there all night long, rambling on and on about nothing, while they had a lot of ground work to cover before he could ever officially apply for any position inside that church—not that he had agreed to do any such thing. His irritation levels were sky rocketing with every second that ticked by.

Out of desperation, Aaron finally said loudly, interrupting Connors's flow, "I think you should find someone else. I'm not trained for this sort of thing, and you guys are beatin' the crap out of me right now."

All eyes turned toward him.

"No, you're the one for the undercover work, but the kid's got a point, Connors. I can't take much more of your discussing the same fucking thing over and over, man. I tried…" Kreed stood and stretched, reaching for the pizza box in the middle of the table. There was one piece left and Aaron had eyed that thing for the last hour. Kreed lifted the thin crust pepperoni and pineapple slice and took a big bite, before dropping it on a paper plate in front of Aaron. He wished he'd grabbed the piece first, half the damn thing was gone in that one bite Kreed took. But at least Kreed shared.

"So what're we gonna do with Knox? I know him too well. He'll bother us all to death until he just forces his way back in." Kreed stated.

"He can't," Connors said, sounding a little disgruntled, but surely to God that wasn't the first time he'd been told he talked too much. "He's got to stay put and let us wrap this up."

"Not gonna happen," Kreed replied, moving toward the water cart placed by the door. He grabbed two iced bottles of water. "We have to give him a job."

"It's too risky. His face is too well known," Brown said, stretching his arms over his head. Evidently he hadn't been the only one bored out of his mind with Connors. From the look on Brown's face, he'd had enough too. Kreed placed one of the water bottles in front of Aaron, still never really looking his way. Since they'd arrived at the FBI building, with the exception of the little show downstairs, Kreed had basically ignored Aaron, so the food and water gesture took him by surprise. Maybe the guy wasn't half bad after all. Aaron picked up the pizza and took a bite then opened the water bottle as Kreed kept talking.

"Besides, he's got security attached to him. So if we're busy keeping an eye on Stuart and Mitch is secretly watching us and his security's over there watching him watch us… Something's gonna fuck up."

When no one responded, Kreed hooked a thumb toward Aaron as he took a big gulp of water. "We need to decide what we're gonna do and wrap up this meeting. I need to feed him before he starts eating his arm."

"We just ate pizza," Connors protested loudly.

"That's just a snack for him. You should see him eat."

"Where do you put it?" Brown looked over at him incredulously.

"Focus," Aaron said, his mouth full of pizza. He didn't normally like to talk with food in his mouth, but extreme times called for extreme measures.

"Send Mitch to Dallas to guard Colt and Jace. It'll keep him busy. Plus, if something goes wrong, he's in close proximity to Redemption Apostle Tabernacle. Midlothian's about thirty minutes from Dallas," Kreed said, reaching for his jacket.

"That would keep him busy. What story are you telling him?" Brown questioned.

"I'll keep it vague, but he's persistent," Kreed responded.

"Yeah, but he usually uses me to gather his information," Aaron explained. Eagerness to leave had Aaron quickly displaying the job listings posted on the church's website on the mounted monitor. Kreed had been right; it was one of those massive, mega complexes that sprawled out over several acres. The church was enormous and just happened to have a permanent job opening in the IT department.

Typing quickly, Aaron split the screen. He'd had more than enough time during the hours of Connors's ramblings to build a proper undercover background specific to the job's requirements. He'd also done a quick mockup of a fake Texas driver's license. His new name was Josiah Smith of Krum, Texas. He had a master's degree in computer science from New Found Faith University. Linking himself to a strict fundamentalist college had been cause for giving himself a mental high five.

"If you agree with all this, I can load this information, get it in the required databases, and apply for the job tonight," Aaron offered, pulling the cords from the electrical outlets. He really wanted to get the hell out of Dodge.

"It's great. Looks good," Brown praised, reading the screen.

"You can't look like you…or at least not like you do right now," Connors said, staring up at the screen before turning back to eye Aaron. "Those church boys are clean-cut. I don't think they have multi-colored hair. You would stand out like a sore thumb."

"Yeah, you need to look like Connors," Kreed added, giving a chuckle.

"No offense, I'm not doing that." Aaron removed everything off the screen, frustrated with the turn of this conversation. He should have just uploaded the information on his own. It was far easier to ask forgiveness than permission—technically, the anthem of his entire life. Besides, he'd combed through his picture files to find a photo from his brother's wedding where his hair was styled reasonably well.

"Yeah, you are. I'll get him cleaned up tomorrow morning. I'm sure the hotel has a salon. Can you add a new picture in the morning before you send all this out?" Kreed asked.

"It doesn't matter. I'm not cutting my hair or looking like him." Aaron didn't look up as he began packing his shit up.

"Yeah, kid, you will."

Great. The most annoying side of Kreed Sinacola's personality was coming out to play—the one where he had all the answers and would just wait for everyone else to catch up. The air around him changed, and he glanced over to see Kreed's booted feet extremely close by. Aaron slowly lifted his gaze to meet Kreed's, where the man now stood, towering over him. The deputy marshal's dark stare bore intensely through him and the smirk on those full lips was about as close to a freaking *you'll-do-whatever-I-ask* grin as you could get.

Goose bumps prickled along his skin and his body tightened in response. Desperation made Aaron want to kiss that smirk right off Kreed's face, feel the plumpness of his beautiful lips. For a second, Aaron completely lost himself and would have agreed to do anything Kreed wanted him to do in order to stay lost in that intense and sultry gaze. Brown coughed on the other side of the room and broke the spell Kreed held over him. Aaron quickly looked away, hoping no one else in the room heard the pounding of his heart.

Aaron shook his head to clear his thoughts as he continued packing his equipment away. *Damn it to hell!* Aaron couldn't believe he'd let Kreed get to him. It wouldn't happen again. He took a deep breath and straightened before turning, this time scowling at that handsome face that mocked him, letting Kreed know he wouldn't win this argument or any other, for that matter. Aaron slammed his laptop shut. Not too hard, but enough to get everyone's attention.

"Why are you mad? It's hair. It'll grow back," Connors stated, confused.

"I'm starving and your scraps just piss me off. I'm out." Aaron shoved his laptop into the bag, slung the strap over his shoulder then spun on his heels and started moving toward the door, not waiting for Kreed. The guy could go jump in an ice-covered river for all he cared. He should have never been in this position in the first place. Today had gone from bad to worse. Now, he was the asshole going undercover. How had he even let that happen?

"I guess we're done for tonight," Kreed joked, gathering his things. The guy tossed his plate in the trash as Aaron hit the conference room door.

"No, you guys continue. Stay all fuckin' night talking about the same thing and over." Aaron added his own hint of mockery to his tone. Aaron walked out the door, leaving it open, and never looked back as he headed toward the elevators. Fuck Kreed Sinacola!

"He's got his period," Kreed drawled from behind him. Aaron quickened his pace. Maybe he could get on the elevator and downstairs before Kreed caught up to him. Did taxis wait out front of the FBI building? Only one way to find out.

"Fuck you. I'm taking a cab to the fuckin' airport." Aaron readjusted his laptop bag strap on his shoulder as he reached for the elevator call button. He absolutely wasn't cutting his hair or wearing the standard Men's Warehouse rack suit—not that they had even mentioned that yet, but he knew it was coming. No fucking way. He drew the line right there.

Lord knew he'd dedicated his life to helping the underdog, but this was asking too damn much. He reached out and punched the down button again when the doors didn't open. The small arrow lit up then went dark. Angry, he pressed it again, achieving the exact same results. Why didn't the elevators work? Immediately he scanned the small entryway, looking for the stairwell.

"Come on, smart boy. It's not so bad," Kreed taunted from behind. "You need to wave your badge in front of the reader like this if you want to get anywhere." Kreed pressed the button and when it turned green, he lifted his wallet over a small section above the button. The doors opened.

Smartass!

Aaron stayed rooted in his spot. He didn't want to get in the elevator car with Kreed. He'd take the next one down. In Kreed's typical annoying way, the guy stepped toward him, hooked an arm around his neck and hauled him against his side, forcing them both inside the small box. Kreed's scent filled the air around him, engulfing him in exotic spices. His brain cells momentarily went on hiatus again as his dick plumped and, damn it, that pissed him off even more.

Aaron was mad as hell, nowhere close to being attracted to the cocky guy, no matter how his body betrayed him. Aaron couldn't afford to get involved with anyone right now, and he damn sure wasn't going to get tangled up with the irritatingly bossy Deputy US Marshal Kreed Sinacola. It had to be that damn cologne Kreed wore—cinnamon, clove, and a hint of citrus. Aaron liked that scent way too much for his own good.

"I promise to get you all fixed up tomorrow—just a little styling. You won't have to look like Connors. Believe me, nobody but Connors can pull that tight-laced, chronically constipated look off with such ease."

A laugh came from behind them and Aaron jerked his head up. He hadn't noticed Brown or Connors stepping on the elevator with them. Brown gave a few quiet chuckles before a hearty side-splitting laugh erupted.

"Fuck you all," Connors said, pressing the first floor button. "Short hair's easier to deal with."

"I'll feed you and make everything better. You'll see." Kreed stared right at him, and he finally lifted his gaze to look back. Great. Another teasing jab, but Aaron took a deep breath and chose to let the remark go. The mention of food seemed to work in elevating his mood. Aaron didn't say anything more. His earlier annoyance hadn't dissipated by much, but he also hadn't moved out from under Kreed's arm. The weight of the guy's arm over his shoulders somehow calmed him, plus Kreed smelled too damn good and his attitude was contagious. He'd stay right there in that quasi-embrace and think about what he wanted for dinner.

Chapter 6

Kreed stirred, listening to what sounded very close to a mechanical typewriter clicking away in the distance. He cracked an eyelid and looked toward the curtain. There wasn't any light peeking through the bottom yet so that meant it was still dark outside. When the sound didn't lessen over time, he looked at the alarm clock by the bed. *4:30 am*. Weirdly enough, this had been the first night in longer than he could remember that he'd actually slept. He wasn't in a mindset to give that up. Kreed turned over, pulled a pillow over his head, and snuggled back underneath the warmth of the blanket, hoping to fall back asleep. Several minutes passed and all he could do was concentrate on whether he could hear that irritating noise.

Yep, there it was. *What the hell?* Tossing the pillow aside, he fisted the blanket and threw it toward the end of the bed.

Kreed kicked his legs over the edge and stood, before quietly padding across the hotel suite toward the partially opened door separating his room from Aaron's. He'd insisted on leaving the door open before bed. He knew that made no sense to Aaron, and it honestly hadn't made much sense to him either, but it was something he and Mitch had done while in the field. Being on the marshals' special teams task force meant they hauled in the worst of the worst criminals. On rare occasions, the bad guys found the deputies first and Kreed never wanted a locked door to be an obstacle that slowed him in getting to his partner's side. Now, apparently that same protective instinct applied to Aaron as well.

The sounds grew stronger as Kreed ducked in the closet to grab his gym shorts before pushing the door to their adjoining rooms wide open. Aaron sat at the desk in the dimly lit room, two monitors, a keyboard, and a tower in front of him. Where the hell had all that equipment come from?

"Have you slept?" Kreed asked, stifling a yawn as he pushed his fingers through his hair. Aaron looked up from his computer, a startled expression crossed his face as their gazes met. That was when Kreed noticed the earphones. Aaron reached up, pulling one of the earbuds from his ear, letting it dangle from the wire around his neck. He looked younger than his twenty-nine years, especially in the light reflecting off the monitors. Aaron was shirtless, wearing only a pair of shorts as he sat kicked back in the desk chair. He'd stretched his long muscular legs across another chair, the one originally placed in front of the suite's window. He must have moved it across the room. All the screens went dark as Aaron angled his head to look at him over his shoulder. Kreed had no idea how he accomplished the feat of turning off the monitors when his hands were no longer on the keyboard.

"What?" Aaron asked.

"Have you slept yet?" Kreed sucked in a breath when Aaron dropped his legs to the floor and spun completely around in his desk chair to face him, exposing a well-defined chest, inked with an impressive tatt that ran across his shoulder and down his chest. A flash of silver on the kid's nipples caught Kreed's attention and held it. Nipple rings?

Oh fuck me, yes!

Kreed couldn't believe all that had been hidden under Aaron's clothing. The kid was just full of surprises. He was staring, but he couldn't help it. Damn it, if he was going to hell, he might as well enjoy the view. Kreed's eyes dropped lower to follow the treasure trail of dark hair disappearing into the waistband of the nylon shorts sitting low on the kid's hips. Shit, the guy was mouthwatering. Kreed's cock hardened instantly. What the fuck? He'd never reacted like this to the men he worked with. He'd offered sex before they started the assignment, but once they made it to the FBI building, that was off the table. Yet, his behavior bordered on inappropriate and he absolutely hated he couldn't get a hold of his attraction for this guy. *Damn it.*

"Yeah, I just don't sleep a lot. Did I wake you?" Aaron scrubbed his fingers through his hair.

Kreed really wanted to be the one to do that, but instead he casually reached inside his shorts and straightened his dick. He tried for a normal guy move, something that didn't reek of creepy pervert. He really hoped it was convincing.

This kid was going to be a problem.

Kreed took a seat on the edge of the bed, praying he didn't tent as he chastised himself. Why the fuck had he even come in here? Kreed's sexual arousal kept him on edge, and outside of Aaron's momentary visual appraisal at the airport—*had that even really happened?*—Kreed wasn't certain Aaron was actually gay. At dinner earlier, Kreed had observed Aaron closely. The guy seemed to have a wandering eye, especially for the ladies, which raised more questions than it answered.

"Where did all this come from?" His brain hadn't registered Aaron's question, so he asked the first thing that came to mind.

"I had it shipped. The box was waiting for me when I got here."

"Huh. Were you working?"

"Nah, gaming. I usually game this time of day. Mitch's on. He still plays when Cody's sleeping. Cody isn't into video games."

There was a small creak in the desk chair as Aaron leaned back. Kreed's eyes were drawn to Aaron's lap. The keyboard covered his dick, but it sure didn't look like the kid was having his same problems.

"You don't game, do you?"

"Nah, but Knox sure plays the shit out of 'em. It sounded like someone was typing on an old timey typewriter."

"It's the mechanical keyboard I have." Aaron lifted a hand and randomly typed some keys to show the clicking. "It's kind of the thing right now in this world. Sorry I woke you."

"It's good. Where are your glasses?' Kreed asked, looking at Aaron's face a little closer.

"They aren't prescription. They're just vanity glasses. I wear 'em like I change my hair, whenever I want something different,"

Aaron replied, and Kreed just nodded. This kid seemed to always keep him guessing.

"I'm probably gonna go get a workout in," Kreed said on a yawn as he put his hands on his knees and pushed up from the bed. Between the options of a cold shower or working out, he chose the latter. He needed some serious meditation time too. Something was off over how attracted he was to Aaron right now. He shouldn't be so caught up in this kid he barely knew. He needed to stop this crazy infatuation from developing further.

"I did that already," Aaron said, swiveling in his chair to keep an eye on Kreed as he got to his feet and headed toward their shared door.

"You left without telling me?" Kreed asked, looking back at him.

"You were asleep."

"We're partners now, with a crazy man on the loose. My job's to keep you safe while you gather intel. You gotta tell me where you're going and when." Kreed shook his head as he left. When he made it back to his room, he called out, "I can already tell you're gonna be a pain in the ass about that."

"We're not in Texas yet. And I'll probably be the best pain in the ass you'll ever have," Aaron replied sarcastically.

Kreed stuck his head around the corner and watched Aaron lifting the earbud back to his ear. He swiped across one screen, turning the monitor back on. He picked up the keyboard and placed it on the desk. Kreed remembered that was Mitch's preferred gaming stance, too. Aaron had called him back in the room with a sexual innuendo then just completely dismissed him. Why in the world was that so hot? Nobody on the planet dismissed him like that except, on occasion, Mitch. But he could make Mitch crazy, and Aaron seemed completely unaffected by most things, unless he was hungry. Maybe if he rubbed whipped cream and hot fudge all over his body, he could get the guy's attention.

No, asshole. You don't want his attention now. He's your partner, dumbfuck.

Now he was mentally arguing with himself. Huh. Okay. Kreed turned and left the doorway, adjusting himself again, and made his way to the closet. He grabbed a T-shirt and his tennis shoes before heading out. So much for his good night's sleep.

~~~

Aaron listened to the door of Kreed's room bang shut, and he let out a pent-up breath he hadn't realized he had been holding. That whole "leave the door between their rooms cracked" thing Kreed insisted on had thrown Aaron for a loop. He'd been as silent as possible, but he'd known this damn noisy keyboard would be a problem. He needed to stop sometime today and buy something a little quieter. He tended to use this one while on the road to help mask his activities. People in the know would write him off as a gamer simply because he used the mechanical keyboard.

Aaron rose quickly and shut the door between the rooms, sealing himself in. He had about an hour to get his shit done and over with for the day. This on-assignment job was really cramping his style. It wouldn't be too much longer that he even needed to stay employed with the federal government. He relished that day. What kind of idiocy would ever pull someone like him from their desk job and out in the field to work an open, active criminal case?

It was past dumb, but so were most of the entire workings of the federal government. Why in the hell would they hire someone like him to break into their systems? All they did was teach him exactly how they operated and the methods they used to keep him out. Yet, this was where he excelled—in this world of manipulating code and forced entry into systems.

Screw the need to hold up a bank. Anyone could rob the average citizen blind on the pretense of opening a company in the true capitalistic society of American business. Case in point, this company he was currently working his way inside—if the senior executives would quit pocketing every extra dime they made, then maybe they would have been better equipped in their defenses to keep him out of their shit. They'd realize that soon enough.

Aaron worked steadily for another thirty minutes before he made it through the barriers and was given carte blanche to do whatever his little heart desired. And there it was. All the financial data for all their customers. Another very stupid way to conduct business. Aaron quickly went to chat, clicking on his screen name before issuing instructions.

"You're in. Get it started," Aaron said out loud in the quiet room.

"That was fast even for you," came a distorted reply, seemingly out of nowhere.

"Stop wasting time. Get it started." Aaron quickly did what he needed to on his end and shut his systems down. Thank God Kreed wasn't into the technology. If he were, he'd know he didn't need all this equipment to play *State of Decay* with Mitch, yet Kreed had bought it hook, line, and sinker. What a relief. The only problem with Kreed Sinacola was that gut feeling he kept hearing about. It was why he'd planned all his extracurricular activities in the middle of the night. He had to stay off Kreed's radar at all costs.

With that worry sitting on his shoulders, Aaron went ahead and dismantled his equipment, deciding to pack it all up again. If the schedules held, they should be heading to Texas at some point today. By putting everything away, he hoped to accomplish the theory of "out of sight, out of mind." He could ship the boxes wherever he needed before they headed out. Working fast, he managed to get everything all boxed up and tucked inside his closet before Kreed returned from his workout.

Chapter 7

Anchored with his arm propped on the counter, Kreed bent forward, listening intently to the list of services each spa package included. As the young woman spoke, Kreed looked back at Aaron and surveyed him closely. The kid was hot as fucking hell like he was, but he had a feeling cleaning Aaron up was going to make him a thing of beauty. Probably not the best idea with Kreed's current attraction problem, but he needed to bite the bullet and do it anyway. Church boys needed to look wholesome.

"For him, we need hair and face. He needs to shave…"

"I'm not shaving my beard," Aaron called out, and Kreed looked back at the woman behind the desk. Kreed gave her a smile, drawing her attention back to him.

"I wouldn't call that a beard—more of a dusting—but it's gotta go." Kreed used his finger to instruct her to write that treatment down. "Let's get him the facial and he needs at least a manicure. It looks like he bites his nails."

"How do you even know that?" Aaron asked a little defensively. Kreed looked back to see Aaron balling up his fingers into two fists. He laughed again, loving how Aaron eased him. He wasn't sure why, because certainly Aaron always carried an air of pissed-off whenever he was around, but he liked poking at the kid. Regardless of what Aaron kept projecting, Aaron was a do-gooder. He'd proved that over and over again, so Kreed suspected the irritated attitude was more of an act than Aaron's true nature. Gamers hated leaving their homes. He faced the girl across the counter.

"The kid's surly. Probably need to give him to someone who isn't easily put off." Kreed forced himself not to look back for Aaron's reaction to his words. For some reason, it helped him put Aaron in his place by referring to him as a child. "We need a full shave, no matter what he says. It's a work deal. He's gotta get cleaned up. He's just being ornery. And I want to decide on his hairstyle. I know what he needs to look the part."

Based on past experience, Kreed decided Aaron would probably be in there for a couple of hours, which would give him the opportunity to get some work done. Kreed glanced up at the menu board again and began ticking off the services he wanted. A shave, facial, nails, feet, and if there was time, he wanted a partial wax. He ignored Aaron's snicker from behind. Mitch gave him enough shit about his spa days and Lush products to last a lifetime. Besides, he hadn't been laid in a while. Clearly with all the lusting he'd done after the kid, he needed to fix that. He needed a quick hook-up from someone he wouldn't ever see again.

"Add a massage in there too," he added.

"All right, I have everything down. Give me a minute to get you two lined up and I'll come get you soon," the receptionist said before disappearing behind a wall. Kreed bypassed Aaron, going for a row of seating against the front wall. When Aaron didn't turn, he decided he liked this position. Kreed got to stare at the kid's backside. Aaron had a nice-shaped ass. He'd seen for himself this morning that Aaron was very well put together. The tattoos were a nice surprise. Kreed cocked his head, studying the guy in front of him closely but never seeing any telltale markings under Aaron's clothes. Kreed had never been that smart with his ink. There was no missing the love he had for body art.

"Has anyone ever told you that you're a bully?" Aaron asked out of the blue, still not turning around. Kreed smiled at the back of his disgruntled partner's blond head.

"Not a bully so much, just resigned to my fate. We have a job to do. The quicker we get done, the sooner you're free of me. Looking the part's critical in that goal," Kreed reasoned quietly. Okay, technically he did bully his way through things all the time, but it would be better to have Aaron on his side, rather than fighting him every step they took. "Today your eyes are a gunmetal gray. They were more ice blue yesterday. Brown when we worked together a couple months ago. Are those colored contacts vanity or prescription?"

"Why would you even remember the color of my eyes?" Aaron shot back defensively.

"I think my job title probably makes that an easy question to answer without assistance. So is it the same deal with the hair and glasses, you always changing it up?" Kreed asked.

"Yeah. Pretty much," Aaron finally answered, not engaging at all.

Just on the tip of his tongue to question that further, Kreed's right leg started tingling with numbness. The modern-style, unforgiving chair made his ass hurt and might possibly be cutting off the circulation in his legs. He moved to reposition himself. Damn it, these small seats weren't the most comfortable things he'd ever sat in. They looked cool as shit, with their contemporary design, until he sat on the hard square. He adjusted himself again, repositioning his numb ass. Kreed continued to squirm, not able to find a comfortable position, clearly not designed for the sheer mass of his body. He stood briefly to tug his arms out of his coat and drape it across the back of a chair, disappointed that didn't help him fit any more comfortably.

"Did Knox ask about the meeting yesterday?"

Another long pause happened before Aaron answered, "No, not that I remember."

Kreed's brow drew in. That didn't make any sense. He'd dodged two calls already this morning by claiming he needed a private area to talk. Mitch was a dog with a bone and this case had a T-rex size artifact that Mitch wanted to gnaw on.

"Aaron, we're ready for you," the woman said as she stepped back into the room.

Aaron kept his back to Kreed as he followed the woman behind the screen. Kreed grabbed his coat before following, not letting him get too far out of his sight to make sure his temporary partner got the full makeover.

~~~

Who knew Kreed Sinacola liked facials and mani-pedis? The alpha dude that always got his way seemed to know his way around a spa like the back of his hand. Not so much the layout, but he was familiar with every aspect of the services offered. He knew the differences in scents and treatments. Whether to use milk or lavender… Whatever the hell that meant.

Since they started with the hands and feet, he and Kreed stayed paired up, sitting side by side. Apparently Kreed liked his spa sessions quiet. He never really spoke until he had them include Aaron in a pedicure.

When Aaron genuinely objected, drawing the line there, refusing the service due to an unspoken, yet very traumatic childhood injury involving a swing set and an ill-placed foot, Kreed scoffed at him, like he did with everything else. The technician removed his shoes and gently, but thoroughly worked over his feet. It took a full hour to remove all the dried, dead skin, but honestly, once he got over the initial internal anxiety, he realized he'd really been missing out. And a bonus for everyone around? No one got a foot in the face like normal when someone ventured out to touch his toes.

Next, they were both shaved clean before the facials began. Aaron sat for quite a while with a warm towel wrapped around his face. Being pampered like that was something he could definitely get used to. He actually nodded off, startling when he opened his eyes to see Kreed leaning down over him, right in his personal space, surveying the work done. The guy took Aaron's chin and moved him one way, then the other, before a huge grin curled the corners of his mouth.

"You look even younger with a clean face. Ready for the hair?"

"I know I look younger. It's the reason I keep the beard. If you give me one of those church boy haircuts, I'll look even younger. They won't believe I'm old enough to do that job." Not surprisingly, Kreed ignored him completely.

"I wanna talk to his hairstylist—" Kreed was interrupted by a short, sexy looking Italian man wearing all black.

"I'm Sergio. Which one of you is Aaron?" He clapped his hands, before rubbing his palms together excitedly. To give the guy credit, he did look between the both of them as he spoke, but his eyes came back to stay on Kreed and his olive skin turned a little flushed. Whatever. Kreed had that same effect on him. He supposed it just came with the territory of being the super-hot Kreed Sinacola.

"He is," Kreed said, hooking a thumb over his shoulder. "But I'm deciding his cut and color." Sergio became visibly disappointed at that news. Probably sized Kreed up as single and then the deputy marshal's words made him think they were a couple. Aaron didn't set the record straight. Instead, he rose from the lounger he sat in and moved forward, passing Kreed.

"He gets to decide within reason," Aaron countered, but the wink Sergio gave Kreed said it all.

"Come on, smart boy. Don't look so down. It's gonna be okay. I promise," Kreed said, following Sergio toward his workstation. When Kreed passed him, he patted Aaron's ass and winked, staying a step or two behind Sergio. At the small counter separating the stations, Kreed and Sergio spoke quietly to one another. Aaron didn't intervene, thinking he could change the plan once Kreed left the room then realizing his mistake when he looked into a wall of mirrors and watched Sergio's face light up before looking back at him with an assessing eye.

"It's a perfect cut for your young man, and the color will bring out those gorgeous eyes," Sergio said, his accent thicker this time, causing Aaron to furrow his brow, wondering if Sergio was even truly Italian. "Take a seat here. Let's get a look at what we're working with. Would you like to sit close by?"

Okay, the accent turned British, and for some reason, that annoyed Aaron that much more. "No, surprise me. I'm gonna see if I can get a quick wax while you're working on him," Kreed said, before reaching down to pat Aaron's thigh.

Aaron caught his hand, whispering as the stylist turned away. "You're a douche."

Kreed's smile grew brighter and he winked again. "It's gonna be hard to keep the guys off you when we're done," he said loudly, puckering his lips, blowing him an air kiss before walking away. Sergio was back with a comb in hand, a big giant grin in place as his eyes tracked Kreed's ass in the mirror.

"Oh, he's something," Sergio cooed, his accent changing again. Aaron said nothing as his own eyes followed that strut out of the room. He was in so much trouble.

~~~

"It's about damn time you picked up your damn phone, dickwad," Mitch barked by way of greeting. The inpatient tone of his friend's voice made Kreed grin. He'd missed their interactions. They were fluid, very comfortable with each other. Man, he was so going to hate losing that more than he was willing to admit.

"You kiss little Cody Turner with that mouth?" Kreed mocked. Cody was a big guy, bigger than Mitch, actually, and it always made him smile to tease Mitch about his boyfriend's age. Cody was seven or eight years younger than Mitch, which made joking about robbing the cradle fair game.

"Don't talk about Cody, just fill me in. Nobody's answering the fuckin' phone. I hate that shit."

"That's because I was supposed to call and fill you in. I just got somewhere reasonably safe to talk." Kreed could just tell Mitch and put him out of his misery, but where was the fun in that?

"It sounds like you're standing on the highway."

"Well, I'm close to one actually. I had to walk out in the freezing weather to the middle of the parking lot of a salon where Aaron's getting a makeover," Kreed explained.

"Okay, that's weird. I knew you liked all that girly shit, but he does too? That changes my opinion of him a little bit," Mitch said, snickering.

"Do you wanna know?" Kreed stopped his pacing, looking up as the cloudy sky began to part, the sun peeking through the drab gray of a DC winter day.

"Keep going."

"Officially, your gaming partner and I are going undercover, and we need you to go to Dallas to keep an eye on your buddy Colt Michaels and his guy. Make sure they aren't at risk until we can get this thing wrapped up." Kreed summarized the info and waited for Mitch's inevitable questions.

After a couple of heartbeats, Mitch responded. "Why? They haven't had any trouble."

"For the bureau, it gets Colt covered and you out of their hair. Here's the unofficial part. I'm almost certain the bad guys are local to DFW and watchin' everything right now. It puts you with two of their intended victims. Actually, it puts all of you together in the same place. The way I see it, they have to hate you even more now. So if they're keeping an eye on things like I think they are, you being in Dallas with Michaels would set up a pretty good target close to home. They'll come out of hiding just to cut you down, especially after everything you did to get in their way."

"Okay…" Mitch was silent. Kreed could almost hear the wheels turning in Mitch's head. "And you'll catch sight of their plan by being on the inside. Is it a done deal, getting you two on the inside?"

"Close to. As done as anything can be. It's a solid plan or I wouldn't be asking you to put yourself or them out there like that," Kreed added. Mitch had always been balls to the wall, but now that he had Cody to consider, his partner was a little more cautious. It was kind of weird.

"I fucking know you wouldn't. I've gotta tell Cody," Mitch barked back.

"Of course, it'll be hard to be everywhere by yourself. He needs to be prepared. And there's another side benefit. You'll be close if I need you or vice versa," Kreed added, laying it all out there.

"Huh, so you're working this deal like you normally do. I bet they even fucking think this was their idea." Mitch knew him too well; No need for Kreed to reply to that statement. "And this part's just between me and you?"

"Yeah, I haven't said a word to anyone else. I think Skinner suspects it, but it was never spoken."

"Okay, so you'll be close to me?" Mitch asked.

"Reasonably, but you'll have to be on your A-game. There's five—now six—people that know Stuart and I are goin' in undercover. Who knows who we can trust out of any of 'em? And honestly, it doesn't matter. Same philosophy applies. I think even if someone on the inside is part of the problem, you, Cody, and Michaels being in the same location will be too much temptation. They'll have to be drawn out. If I don't get 'em, you will." Kreed dropped his head and closed his eyes, praying the outcome would turn out as simple as that sounded. He had to trust Mitch as well as himself that they could keep everyone safe from harm. It was a lot to ask.

"We'll head out right now," Mitch finally said.

"Keep me posted, but keep it secure, Knox, and watch yourself." Kreed was serious about that. "We're heading that way in a couple of hours."

"Yeah, you got yourself out of the ass kickin' I planned for you the next time I saw you." Mitch chuckled.

"I told you to trust my ass. I had to get everybody working together under the guise of it being their idea," Kreed responded. He knew Mitch must have gone through hell being forced to sit back and wait.

"And Aaron's on board with all this?"

"Yeah, about that kid. He's kind of a pain in the ass," Kreed said, dodging the answer because Stuart was absolutely *not* on board. His cooperation was grudging at best.

"He's not a kid and I miss playing with him. He's the only one who gives me a run for my money. Don't fuck that up for me."

"When was the last time you talked to him?"

"Probably before Christmas, so four or five days ago." Kreed's brow furrowed. He'd kept a steady pace in the parking lot, but now his eyes cut toward the spa's front door and he stopped dead in his tracks. Had he misunderstood Stuart this morning? Maybe Knox didn't want Cody to know he played every morning… Yeah, but that made no sense. Mitch was the type of guy that did what he wanted, whenever he wanted. He'd have Cody playing alongside him in no time. The front door of the salon opened and the receptionist stood just outside the door, motioning him back in.

"I gotta go." He ended the call and walked forward, then jogged the last few steps with his mind pre-occupied. This morning wasn't a good measure. He was too focused on Aaron's body to remember any of his words correctly. He had to have misunderstood, right? Why would Aaron lie about something like that? Maybe there was another Mitch he played with? Crazier things could happen.

Kreed hit the door, opened it with a hard tug, but came to a stop just inside. His body heated even though he'd been freezing just a second ago. Aaron stood by the counter, his button-down rolled up to the elbows, showing two nicely tattooed forearms. His handsome face was freshly shaven, his blond hair with purple and black tipped strands gone, replaced with dark, rich, silky locks that were clipped into the sexy-ass haircut Kreed had been convinced would look hot—just not this hot. Honestly, the new look took Aaron to a whole new level of sexy. Kreed's entire body tightened in response to the visual stimulation. He hadn't known he would have such a primal reaction to Aaron's makeover. It was just hair, for God's sake.

Kreed's grin grew. "It's perfect. You have to like it."

"It's a little short," Aaron said, making eye contact.

Sergio nailed it; the color certainly made Aaron's blue eyes stand out, so much so that he didn't want to look away. Kreed had figured he was in trouble when it came to Aaron Stuart, but in this moment, he realized just how truly and completely fucked he was.

"But so damn sexy," Kreed added, finally moving forward to appraise the new look up close. "I think I actually like it better than that whole disheveled thing you had going on. I like both, but this… Fuck me. Kid, you're seriously gonna have to fight the dicks off with a stick." Kreed immediately bristled at the jealousy his own words evoked. Where had that possessiveness come from?

Sergio came blasting through the room, a couple of bottles of shaper and gel in his hands. "I explained the importance of the products to achieve the results. The fuck-boy was made for guys like him." Sergio was proud of his creation and placed the products on the counter, turned around, stopped briefly to pat Kreed on the chest, bat his eyes then exited as quickly as he'd arrived.

"I think Sergio has a bit of the fuck-boy attitude."

"Stop calling it that," Aaron grumbled, back to being irritable again.

Hell, the kid was always disgruntled. He hadn't expected anything different with the new package.

"It's the name. The fuck-boy hairstyle. You know, 'Fuck, boy, you look hot.'" Kreed waggled his eyebrows when he got the desired result of a warm blush coloring Aaron's cheeks. He reached back and tugged out his wallet, pulling out his credit card to pay the bill. At least he could expense part of this day, and if he worked it right,

FULL DOMAIN – A *Nice Guys* Novel

they might actually pay for his, which reminded him, he needed to check in with Skinner.

"We need these?" Kreed asked about the shaper and gel.

"Yes, sir. Sergio showed him exactly how to achieve that look." The receptionist ran his totals then his card, before bagging up the hair products. By the time Kreed finished, Aaron had moved closer to the door, his jacket hanging from his hand. Kreed looked him over from behind. Mental images of threading his fingers through the short dark hair and drawing Aaron's head backward for a deep thorough kiss played across his mind. He could almost imagine how those silky strands would feel against his palm. Oh yeah, that would definitely be a fuck-boy moment.

Kreed actually stopped behind Aaron, giving himself a minute to fully absorb that thought. Too bad they hadn't spent their few hours living that fantasy yesterday, but on an upside, when he closed this case, he could test this man's sexual orientation boundaries again and hopefully get him on his knees at least once before they went their separate ways.

"Come on, handsome. We have some clothes to buy and a plane to catch," Kreed said as he reached to push the front doors open, still dwelling on his missed opportunity.

~~~

"All right, you ready? We need to head out," Kreed called through the opened door in their hotel room.

"I already told you that I can't leave until I can ship my shit somewhere." Aaron didn't move from the desk chair where he sat playing *Pay Day*. He focused all his attention on executing the perfect heist. Man, he had to get Mitch on this game. Aaron had always felt like playing games where the bad guys did things like rob banks and plan strategic heists in casinos should be a conflict of interest for a deputy marshal, but having Mitch on his team… They would just kick ass.

"I texted you Colt and Jace's home address. Skinner's working on the details of our stay. It won't take long for him to get us hooked up with a place. He'll have our operation headquarters ready tonight.

Did you load your background information for the job interview yet?" Kreed asked, coming to stand at the door.

"Yep. Done. Ha ha! Oh, man," Aaron exclaimed, his eyes glued to the screen, even though he'd lowered one earbud in order to hear what Kreed was saying. He'd felt, more than heard, Kreed walk up behind him and watch over his shoulder.

"What kind of masks are those?" Kreed asked, bending to better see the laptop's screen.

"Clowns. I'm always Dallas," Aaron said, never stopping the flow of his fingers.

"Huh? Hurry up and do whatever. We gotta go."

"I need to ship my equipment," Aaron repeated, not moving.

"We've already discussed that. Get your ass movin'," Kreed ordered, walking back through the open door. After a minute more, Aaron closed the laptop and moved out from under the fresh scent of Kreed's cologne. How the hell was he going to sit next to that the entire trip to Texas while trying to manage the impending hard-on? If karma were on his side, maybe the flight would be booked and they would be forced to have to sit apart. As Aaron packed his laptop into his bag, he decided he might prefer sitting next to a crying baby over Kreed Sinacola, and he could only pray that would be the case.

Chapter 8

Aaron followed along behind Kreed through the back entrance of the airport. What a seriously better way to enter and deal with an airport. Kreed had managed, through official channels, to book them on the earliest flight out, forcing the airline to bump two passengers to another flight in order to make room for both of them on the plane. Aaron stood ready with his credit card in hand to purchase his ticket, but when he placed the plastic on the counter, Kreed did little more than look down, laugh, and hand his marshal service credentials to the airline employee behind the desk. Apparently she remembered Kreed, because she waved his badge off with a smile as she worked at entering their information.

The attendant never weighed their luggage. Instead, she fastened the ticket around each handle and dropped both on the conveyor belt behind her. She printed and handed over their tickets, and they were moving toward security in a matter of minutes.

When Aaron headed for the standard TSA security line, Kreed grabbed him by the back of the collar, guided him around the long line, and pushed him toward a back entrance. "You're with me," he growled.

"Okay, so you have the traveling pass?" Aaron asked. His parents did the fast-boarding passes, but he didn't realize that it had its own area.

"Nah, it's different than that being a US marshal." Kreed opened a door, waving Aaron through first. Once inside the restricted area, Kreed placed a hand on the middle of his back and guided him to the side. Aaron looked around in amazement; it was a completely different setup.

"I'm Deputy Marshal Kreed Sinacola," Kreed said to a person sitting behind a podium. He pulled his wallet and badge, flipping them open.

"I remember you. You're Deputy Knox's partner," she said, checking his boarding pass and credentials. "How's he doing?"

"Good. Ornery as always, but good."

She gave a cackle as she stuck out her hand for Aaron's information. "He always is. We see so many of you guys coming through here, but he's got such a big personality," she said, doing her thing with Aaron's driver's license before handing it back.

"Don't tell him. He's already got the big head." Kreed laughed.

"Yeah, he's not lacking in ego, I would imagine," she grinned. "Have a good flight."

"Will do," Kreed said. Aaron didn't immediately follow— because, seriously, was that all he had to do to board a flight?

"They aren't even gonna check my bag?"

"Are you gonna bring that to their attention?" Kreed whispered in his ear, lifting a hand to the agent by the back door. "Besides, that's the power of Mitch. He makes friends everywhere he goes. He's this larger-than-life personality. People make allowances for him. They trust him."

"I can see that," Aaron said, feeling the same about Mitch himself. He'd been an unexpected friend since the very beginning.

"The flight's probably boarding now. Let's go." Kreed took off, seeming to automatically know which way to go. Aaron followed, double-timing his steps to keep up.

When Aaron heard the overhead announcement calling their first and last names for final boarding, Kreed took off in a jog, looking over his shoulder to make sure Aaron followed. The flight was loading early, which meant all the seats were taken, and he'd be stuck in the crap seats no one wanted. His earlier hope that he'd sit next to a crying baby over Kreed became more of a reality than he truly cared to consider.

Picking up the pace, Aaron bypassed Kreed, moving quickly toward the gate. As they arrived, he went against his manners, edging past a small crowd still in line as he again heard the last call announcement overhead. Against an angry protest, Aaron stuck his boarding pass in the attendant's face, praying Kreed's tickets might offer preferential treatment. He relaxed some when the woman said, "We were afraid you weren't going to make it."

"Flight full?" he asked as she scanned his ticket. Since Aaron was so tuned in to Kreed, he knew the man had caught up without looking over his shoulder. He could sense his presence anywhere.

"Yes, but they saved you two seats." She winked at Aaron like he was someone important and handed him back his pass. Kreed stuck his out, caging Aaron in as she scanned it. "I think you'll like them. Roddy's flying you out today. When he got the call you were boarding, he worked his magic."

"Good boy," Kreed said, sounding happy by the news. He took off down the jet bridge, leaving Aaron trailing this time.

"Who's Roddy?" Aaron asked, moving slower, still several steps behind Kreed.

"Jealous?" Kreed asked, throwing him that sexy grin over his shoulder. Damn, he hated the way that grin made his heartbeat skip like that.

"Definitely not," Aaron declared, giving Kreed a clear *'you're crazy'* look. Except he kind of was a little jealous. First, Sergio went nuts over Kreed, now Roddy was working magic. "Is he some government employee? Why does he hold seats like that?"

"What? A government employee working as a flight attendant? No. Believe it or not, I'm quite the catch in some circles." Kreed turned around, walking backward, as Aaron caught up to him. He waggled his eyebrows before turning back around and stepping onto the airplane. A man he could only guess to be Roddy stood right at the door entrance. He couldn't have been much taller than five-seven or five-eight with long dreadlocks and a bright smile greeting everyone, but when his eyes landed on Kreed, his grin grew genuine, just irking Aaron that much more.

~~~

Finally some kind of sign! The kid was jealous, no doubt about it. His body language, attitude, and biting tone in the comment he'd made, all rang true for a green-eyed monster. As Kreed waited to board, he knew he shouldn't be so excited that Aaron was at least bi-sexual, but he was. Not that he could do anything about this knowledge, because he couldn't, not while they were partners. But that didn't matter. Someday would come. Eventually he could tap that guy's ass and that was enough of a victory for right now.

"Woo, boy, it made my day to hear you were on my flight!" Roddy declared, reaching up to hug Kreed's neck. Being based close to Dallas—the closest international airport to his home base of Louisiana—both Kreed and Mitch had gotten to know Roddy pretty well over the years. Roddy flew this route regularly. He was older, maybe had twenty years on Kreed, but he never hesitated to reach out, fold Kreed tightly in his arms, always giving him a good-natured, full body hug when he stepped on.

"I saved you each a seat. Who's this?" Roddy asked, his face changing, becoming overly interested in Aaron before moving his excited gaze back to Kreed and giving him a wink. "Well, look at you. He's a cutie. Let's get you two settled."

Probably because they were holding the line, Roddy ushered them both to two seats in first class. "Roddy, meet Aaron. How pissed off are the people you moved to coach?" Kreed asked, reaching up to lift an overhead bin. He placed his backpack inside then reached over to grab Aaron's laptop backpack.

"They'll live. They were very well compensated," Roddy answered, giving a tsk and a solid roll of his eyes before moving his gaze back to Aaron for another onceover. "I like your friend. Is he always this quiet?"

Aaron didn't let go of the strap, instead lifting his backpack to the compartment himself. He was particular about this bag, making sure it lay a certain way, and nothing got in the way, which meant crowding Kreed's carry-on. "Hey, be careful. My Lush products are in there," Kreed said, moving everything in the overhead bin so his backpack wouldn't get too crushed.

"What's Lush?" Aaron asked, shrugging off his coat, shoving it inside the bin as well.

"Boy, you don't know amazing until you've had yourself some Lush," Roddy added, helping Kreed with his coat, before tucking all the straps and things inside the bin.

"That's right. You're the one who introduced me to that stuff." Kreed gestured for Aaron to take the window seat.

"Mmm hmm. You two need to take a seat. Help your boy with his seatbelt. I need to give the green light." Roddy moved around them as Aaron scooted in first and Kreed took the aisle seat. It was far easier to stretch his long legs in the aisle.

"What's Lush? Is it an alcohol?" Aaron asked, pulling the belt around his lap.

"No, bath products. It makes your skin soft," Kreed answered, buckling himself in.

"What?" Aaron stopped in mid click.

"What?" Kreed asked after a minute's pause.

"You're really such a girl. Is that what you were doing when I was trying on all those clothes?"

"Yeah. I usually have to ship the shit in, but there was a store here. It's relaxing. Sue me. Besides, I got you a fizzbanger bath bomb to try. You need to lighten up. Seriously, that scowl you wear all the time's gonna cause premature wrinkles."

Aaron just stared at him for several long seconds before he answered, "I think I heard about that stuff on Rooster Teeth. It was advertised for their mothers for Christmas or Mother's Day or something like that."

Kreed was right on the verge of asking what the hell Rooster Teeth even meant when a female flight attendant bent in toward him. "You need to buckle your seatbelt, sir. Hi, Kreed."

"Hey, honey," he said, but never looked up. He kept his eyes on Aaron's disbelieving face. The flight attendant patted him on the shoulder and continued down the aisle. Aaron's look conveyed the same hard time Mitch always gave him about his hygiene habits. Wait until Kreed took his night off and headed to the bathroom instead of the bar. Aaron was going to flip the fuck out. He slid his gaze to Aaron's hands still holding the buckle. "Need help with that?"

"No…" Aaron still just paused, studying him like he'd never seen him before. After a second or two, he dropped his gaze to buckle himself in as the engines started. Moments later, the plane began to back up. "Everybody on here knows you."

"I fly a lot with this airline," Kreed said, still just watching Aaron. It wasn't a hardship. He was the best-looking thing on this plane.

"It's cool how you got us first-class seats," Aaron said, his head turned away from Kreed, his gaze glued out the small window, forcing Kreed to have to lean in to hear what he said.

"Was that said with a hint of appreciation?" Kreed asked, moving his head back when Aaron turned toward him. It was hard to stay focused on the conversation when those blue eyes landed on his. Kreed forced himself to take a giant mental step backward at the realization he had no idea what he'd just asked that fine-looking man. In his entire life, he'd never had that happen with anyone, male or female.

"I don't scowl all the time," Aaron announced, and Kreed forced a laugh, still trying to remember where he'd left off the conversation. When nothing came to mind, he finally answered with a joke, hoping that saved him.

"I'll remember to mark the day I don't see a frown," Kreed added dryly.

Aaron shook his head. "I just have a lot going on. It's easier to be at home right now."

Aaron could be a politician with that answer. What did that even mean? Every answer the kid gave ended with him wanting to be at home right now. He had a single-minded focus. Though that seemed to be Kreed's problem at the moment too.

"It's cool," Kreed said, still unable to do much more than watch Stuart closely. Aaron's face lost that angry look he usually had, smoothing out in that brief exchange, his hair perfectly combed in the new style. His lips seemed fuller right now, more kissable, and, God, that's exactly what Kreed really wanted to do—kiss Aaron. No matter the desire coursing through him, Kreed forced himself to not move a muscle in Aaron's direction.

"It's the holidays too. It's a tough time to be pulled away. We'll get this wrapped up and get you home soon," Kreed added, hoping to keep Aaron talking.

"It's work right now, not the holidays. I bailed on the family early this year," Aaron said absently, almost like they were about to have a real conversation.

"You and the family close?" Kreed asked.

Aaron was silent several long minutes. Okay, maybe he'd been wrong about the conversation. The plane accelerated then lifted in the air before the kid finally responded.

"It was my first Christmas at home in more years than I could count. I know it seems selfish, especially when you had to leave your parents at such a difficult time. I'm sorry about all that," Aaron finally said. Strangely, the words felt deeply sincere and provided a welcomed comfort to his heart.

"Nah, I get it. I ducked out on the holidays all the time. Besides, my family's not as big as yours."

"I don't wanna talk about them." Aaron shook his head and let out a sigh. He studied his hands in his lap. After a minute, Aaron's gaze lifted and connected again with Kreed's. Unexpected emotion swam in those depths, drawing him in. Kreed stared back, the connection held meaning, but he had no idea what. "It's pretty cool how you get on flights though."

Aaron's voice was smaller right then. Kreed didn't let up on the intensity of his stare, but accepted the change of topic. "I'd like to think it was me, but it's the deputy marshal deal. Airlines let us ride all the time. It makes them feel safer."

"So you have your weapon on right now?" Aaron asked.

"Always," Kreed answered. He never looked away, but lowered his brow, teasing. "Why? Does that turn you on?"

"And nobody checked you?" Aaron seemed content to ignore Kreed's clearly one-track mind. Whatever kind of moment they were sharing had moved on, replaced by a look of shock.

"Not this time. It depends really. They're supposed to, but around DC they get used to people. Mitch helps the security agents remember me. Besides, they'd let us on armed regardless, so it's just a formality."

"I think you're pretty memorable on your own," Aaron confessed quietly.

Kreed tried to contain his smile at that comment and knew he'd failed when he felt his lips twitch upward. He'd almost gotten a compliment. Aaron turned away and reclined his seat, reaching for the earbuds that hung from his neck. He pushed one then the other inside his ears. Kreed figured there was a never-ending supply of entertainment coming from those headphones, because they were always Aaron's go-to device to end a conversation. He watched as Aaron leaned back and closed his eyes, effectively shutting down any further discussion. Kreed reached for the Sky Magazine and started thumbing through the pages. He'd just been given a compliment and effectively put in his place all in one fell swoop. That about summed up every single interaction he'd had with the kid so far.

Chapter 9

"It's fucking Texas, Cody. I thought it was some sort of state law that it has to be warm all the time," Mitch complained, pulling the rental car into Colt and Jace's Preston Hollow home—or estate, depending on who spoke about the house. Mitch gave Colt shit about the size of the house and the area he and his partner lived in before always closing the argument with a win by bringing up President Bush's doorbell only being a few doors down.

"I told you not to wear shorts. It's Dallas. It gets cold up here," Cody shot back, releasing his seatbelt. Mitch put the car in park, leaned over the console toward the passenger seat, and pulled Cody to him.

"It always makes me smile when you refer to anything in Texas being 'up,'" he teased, making air quotes with his fingers. He puckered his lips. Cody had to lean in the rest of the way to kiss him. Without looking, Mitch reached over and turned off the ignition. He kept his gaze on Cody, dropping an arm behind the seat's headrest. Cody wasn't more than a couple of months post-op after taking a bullet to his shoulder. He'd gotten lucky. Actually really lucky, becoming the newest poster boy for Apple products when his iPhone took the second bullet aimed point blank at his chest. Even now, it was a sobering thought and Mitch warred with himself to keep his mood even. Being back in Dallas, in this particular home, had the potential to increase all of their risk, and the panic of this situation left him unsettled. Mitch would have to be on his A-plus game; he couldn't have Cody in any more danger. He searched Cody's eyes before he spoke. "You sure you're good with this? I know it doesn't seem like it, but I can step back and take you somewhere far away from all of this. We could hit a Caribbean island where I could wear these shorts and not freeze my ass off."

There was a pause as Cody searched his face. Mitch knew Cody was nervous. How could he not be? But he could almost see his brave state trooper boyfriend mentally pulling on his big boy Superman Underoos. Mitch needed to do that too. A smile slowly spread across Cody's handsome face. "Are you tryin' to get me out of the country because you wanna marry me?"

Mitch barked out a laugh at that one, leaned back into his own seat, and started to open his driver's side door. Out of the two of them, Mitch was the one rushing them to the altar. Cody had been teasing him about that since he'd proposed on Christmas Eve. A burst of cold wind had him closing the door again, shutting them back inside the still-warm car.

"Hang on." Mitch fished his phone out of his front pocket and dialed Colt. As the phone started to ring, Cody's cell gave a loud chirp. It had to be Kylie. She and her mom had been texting them since Christmas. Cody went for his phone.

"Open your door. It's too cold out here," Mitch instructed when Colt answered his call. He turned just in time to catch Cody shaking his head and smiling from ear to ear. Mitch had to know what put that sweet-silly look in his honey's eyes. "What'd she say?"

"She put the Barbie to bed and thought we should see her sleeping," Cody said, lifting the phone to show the picture Cody's sister had just texted.

"That's sweet. They're wearing matching pajamas." Kylie had a thing for her Uncle Cody. Since Christmas Eve, they'd been getting regular pictures of her Christmas present from them—Barbie eating breakfast, dressing up, playing outside, dressing up again, and now going to sleep. Kylie was overly precious and had turned out to be a little unexpected ray of sunshine in Cody's recovery.

The porch light came on, and Mitch heard Colt's laughter inside the car. He glanced at the phone in his hand and realized he had forgotten to end the call through his and Cody's exchange. *Shit*! He winced and quickly hung up. Bad move on his part. Mitch liked always having the upper-hand, especially after all the shit he'd given Colt over the last year. Now, he'd just given Colt something to hold over his head.

Before Cody opened his door, Mitch placed a hand on Cody's arm, stopping him in mid-motion. "Babe, just so you know, I'm gonna proposition Jace about a three-way at least ninety times over the next few days, so don't let it surprise you. You should know I don't mean it. I gotta get under Colt's skin. You remember what the guy did to me, right?"

Cody's brow lowered. "You two are terrible. I kinda feel obligated to them. I wouldn't've met you if they hadn't brought you to JR's."

"Dammit!" Mitch hissed and turned away. "I forgot about that. Shit. Okay, maybe just once or twice, then." When Cody gave him that look of uncertainty, he tried to quickly explain. "I've got to, Cody. Otherwise, I got nothing other than the bacon to mess with him about. You have to admit it'll drive him crazy. Just don't say anything. Let me do the talking."

"I know. Okay, but remember your dad made me promise that I'd make you be nice," Cody said, opening his door this time. Mitch reached over the seat, grabbing his duffle bag from the backseat. Cody walked around to the back of the car, and knocked on the vehicle's trunk, signaling for him to open the hatch.

Mitch couldn't avoid the cold any longer; he had to get out of the car. He lifted the knob, opening the back then pulled on the handle to his door. Cold swept through the open door, prickling along his exposed skin as he slid out and shivered his way around to the back of the vehicle. His mister was lifting their luggage from the trunk.

"You aren't supposed to lift that much weight," Mitch said, taking the suitcase from Cody in mid tug.

"I'm fine, Mitch. Give it to me," Cody said, giving him a struggle for the handle. Mitch sighed in frustration, but didn't give an inch. They both knew what the doctor had said Cody's restrictions were. Mitch didn't give a shit what Cody thought about his recovery; he wanted him back to a hundred percent, which meant Cody was going to follow every damn instruction the doctor gave.

"You're hardheaded," he thrust his much lighter duffle into Cody's stomach and managed to pull the suitcase handle from Cody's grasp.

"You treat me like I'm an invalid," Cody shot back, catching his bag before it hit the ground.

"Trouble in paradise?"

From behind him, Colt's voice echoed through the chilly air. Mitch jerked, reaching for the weapon that usually sat on his hip. He'd lost track of what they were doing and hadn't heard Colt approach. How good a job could he do at protecting Cody if he just let someone sneak up on them without knowing? To top everything off, Colt's tone matched his expression—both mocking him. Mitch furrowed his brow.

"Who knew we'd be seeing you again so soon." Colt extended his hand toward Cody.

Cody's smile was brighter than the full moon as he accepted the handshake. Colt and Jace had come to his parents' house in upstate New York for Christmas. They'd spent about forty-eight hours there before heading back to Dallas. Mitch had been on his home turf, so he was able to give Colt all the shit he wanted. Now, clearly, by the look on Colt's face, he planned a counter-attack. *Fuck*!

Let the games begin.

While they continued to clasp hands, Colt carefully took the duffel off Cody's shoulder. Mitch scowled even more when Cody didn't utter a word of protest. His guy had argued over handling their luggage since leaving his parents' house. Now, he just handed it over to Michaels without any sort of complaint?

"Thanks for letting us stay here," Cody said, his voice warm and friendly. Colt just looked his way and winked. Mitch knew exactly what Colt was doing, and it wasn't going to work.

"You wanna carry something? Take this, frat boy." Mitch thrust the heavier suitcase toward Colt, and, in the same move, snatched the duffle bag from Colt. Startled, all eyes turned his way, and only then did he realize his monumental mistake. He'd just given Colt more ammunition to use against him. Double damn.

"It's cold out here, guys. Can we go inside?" Jace's voice came from the hood of the car. Mitch had forgotten the cold. Actually he'd grown quite warm with all the testosterone flowing through him. He now understood why Colt acted so crazy and possessive when he and Jace had first started dating.

"Yeah, y'all come inside," Colt echoed, dropping the suitcase until the wheels hit the ground. With the handle extended, he dragged the thing along the driveway toward Jace.

"What was that about?" Cody whispered when Colt moved out of earshot.

"I don't even fucking know, and weirder than that, I don't know if I wanna mess with Colt anymore." Mitch's brow furrowed even further at his words.

"That's what I just said in the car," Cody countered, clearly confused.

"It was a good call. You should've fought me harder on that." Mitch couldn't wait for this honeymoon phase of their relationship to wear off so he could get back to his normal self.

Cody started toward the front, but when Mitch didn't move from his spot, Cody came back, took his arm, and pulled him in the direction Colt and Jace had walked. "You're being weird," Cody finally said.

"I'm always weird. A smart guy like you, I figured you'd have noticed that by now," Mitch replied, finally taking the lead and walking up the front steps. Jace waited outside the front door, arms clutched at his chest to ward off the cold. Colt stood in the foyer, smiling brighter than he'd ever seen him smile. Shit, the guy had figured out Mitch had a jealous streak. Fuck, his life sucked. All of a sudden the thought of staying here the next few days seemed a bit like hell.

~~~

"Cody, I understand you're the grill master," Colt said, carrying two full plates of steaks and hamburgers through the kitchen to a door leading out to a covered patio. Through the window along the back wall, Mitch could see an industrial-size grill pushed close to the house. Jace trailed behind with a second plate loaded with long-cut strips of assorted vegetables. Colt was overly excited about his meat options, and even with the current state of the freezing temperatures outside, he'd lit the grill, planning to cook their dinner outside.

"Leave him alone," Jace scolded. Now that Mitch was a man in love, not single and the instigator he'd always been before, Mitch could see that Jace had always kept peace between the parties—the constant equalizer. It hadn't been more than an hour since they'd arrived, and Colt was already in rare form. He was dishing out the crap, making up for a full year's worth of snarky comments from Mitch.

"What? He grills at home all the time," Colt remarked, acting innocent. Cody jumped up from the kitchen table and opened the door for Colt, pushing it wide to accommodate all the food Colt carried. Mitch watched as fucking Colt Michaels grinned big and winked at Cody. Aggression stewed in his gut.

"Thanks, Cody," Colt murmured, drawing out Cody's name before looking over at Mitch and laughing so hard that the steaks wobbled in his hands. Jace let out a huge sigh and followed his lover, shutting the door behind them. Mitch couldn't make out the words between them but could see the intensity of Jace's words in his expression.

"You're being weird. They're being nice lettin' us stay here. What's your problem?" Cody asked. Cody had moved to the seat directly beside him, speaking low. His honey's eyes implored him to get over whatever was eating so solidly at his good mood.

Colt's teasing was inevitable, but damn it, it made the hair on the back of his neck stand up to have someone flirting so openly with Cody. Worse yet, he hated to admit how it bothered him. And yes, without question, he'd given Colt shit, but that had been in good fun, to give everybody laughs when they'd needed them the most.

Now, Colt wasn't playing fair. Yes, Mitch refused to consider the hypocrisy of that thought. Being on the receiving end sucked when he was just learning how to manage all these protective, possessive emotions bombarding him all the time.

"Stop, okay. He's messing with you on purpose. He'll stop if he sees it's not gettin' to you," Cody reasoned.

"You're hotter than Jace," Mitch grumbled, leaning in to quickly kiss Cody's full lips.

"No, I'm not!" Cody argued, laughing at what he clearly considered absurd.

"To me you are," Mitch countered, proud when Cody beamed at his words and lifted a thumb to his chin, giving his jaw a soft caress. Who could have possibly known how much he'd like these hot moments they shared. They gave him the confidence to continue. "It's not just Michaels. I always remember that night I met you, and you wouldn't tell me anything about yourself, but Michaels walked up and you were all talkie, giving name, rank, and serial number. I don't like that," Mitch said, surprised that moment still bothered him even after all this time.

"I think I might be jealous," he declared. As he said those words, he reached out, fisting Cody's hand in his, needing a lifeline for these stupid insecure thoughts. And he knew how irrational his statement sounded, especially since they'd all shared Christmas day together at his parents' place, where all four of them had gotten along great.

"I talked to him, because I was *not* into him. I was into you. Too much into you. I needed distance. You overwhelmed me. You still overwhelm me, you know. I've told you that before." Cody spoke quietly, his gaze begging him to understand.

Silence lasted several seconds as he stared into Cody's brilliant blue eyes, digesting the entire conversation. "I shouldn't've brought you here. It's still all too fresh. I should've listened to Sinacola. When Michaels walked up on me outside, I never heard him coming. That could've been anyone walking up on us. And I wasn't wearing my weapon. How had I left that in the car? I've brought you into the lion's den, and I was too comfortable and too arrogant to realize just how off my reactions are. It scares me," Mitch admitted, dumping the truth out. If he couldn't be on his A game, Cody needed to be. Well, at least as much as he could be considering he was still recovering.

"We're in this together, Mitch. We're working as a team on this one. You aren't responsible for all of us and we'll be more vigilant. They won't get the drop on us again. We won't let those fuckers win," Cody said, his voice low and assertive. Mitch continued to stare at Cody, letting the words sit between them.

"I know I said we need to follow your treatment plan, but I wanna call your doctor in the morning, see if we can get clearance to practice at a shooting range. We're all the backup we have in this deal. Sinacola's thirty minutes away. Colt and Jace need us to be our best."

"I feel great. I have good range of motion. I feel solid," Cody encouraged, nodding to reaffirm the words.

"I know you keep saying that, but I'd just feel better hearing it was okayed after they look over the latest PT reports. If it's still not a good idea, we need to know the risk so we can make an informed decision. Being here, the threat seems too real to me. I might just feel that way because you're involved. I don't know. I gotta talk to Sinacola. He's the instinct guy. He'll tell me if I'm off base," Mitch said, reaching his free hand behind Cody's neck, drawing him forward for a light but lingering kiss. Cody soothed his heart. He had to stop being balls to the wall and talk to his mister before every knee-jerk reaction.

The door opened and a blast of cold air swept over them.

"Get a room," Colt said cheekily, walking to the sink to wash his hands. Mitch was slower to move away from Cody's full lips, but when he did, he winked at Cody. His guy's soft smile froze and his eyes widened before he immediately shook his head no. Mitch ignored the very clear instruction.

"My guy here's a good one. He's agreed to inviting Jace to join us for a… Well, you know." Mitch waggled his eyebrows at the group now looking his way. He felt lighter already.

"Do you see? If I give him a break, that's the thanks I get. I can't live with that for the next week, Jace," Colt heatedly complained. He'd wheeled around so quickly to face Jace he was dripping water on the floor in front of the sink.

"He's kidding, Colt, and stop getting water all over the floor. You know he's not serious. He loves to yank your chain," Jace said, and Mitch barked out a laugh as Jace and Colt bent in unison to the floor, almost knocking each other in the head to clean up the spilled water. Colt effectively made a bigger mess as his hands continued to drip as he started to step away. "Baby, stop! Don't move. The dirt on your shoes is gettin' the floor muddy. Hands in the sink!"

"Jace, just for the record, I'm not interested in yanking on anything Michaels has to offer, but now you, on the other han…" Cody's elbow went to Mitch's ribs as the comic show of Jace and Colt played out right in front of them. Colt's eyes grew even bigger and his mouth dropped open in silent protest at his last comment. "Okay, okay. That's my one time. Honest. I think I got it out of my system. I swear. I'm willing to call a truce," Mitch announced to the room, lifting his hands in a gesture of surrender.

With a huff, Colt grabbed the paper towels and wiped his hands before dropping them to the floor and scooting them with his foot. Jace was bent over, cleaning the floor with a hand towel and stopped what he was doing as he watched his mister from behind. He looked over at Mitch and Cody, giving them a dramatic eye roll.

"We'll call a truce after I call your pop, Knox. He told me to call him if you got out of hand," Colt added smugly, still pushing the beat-up paper towels with his shoe.

"I'm calling Dr. Knox," Jace said firmly, reaching up to knock Colt off balance to get the paper towels out from under his foot. "He told me to call him when you got out of hand too, mister. Who does this?" Jace said, lifting the dirty, torn paper towels for everyone to see. That had all of them laughing as Jace shook his head and went for the pantry, presumably to throw the mangled paper into the trash.

Chapter 10

"Knox said they fixed enough dinner for us," Kreed mentioned to Aaron as he took a quick turn onto a side road, leading them deeper inside a stately tree-lined neighborhood.

"What're they having?" Aaron asked. He lifted the cover to the mirror on the visor; small lights popped on, and he cupped his fingers to work his hair in place.

"I didn't ask. You don't seem picky," Kreed teased, watching the street addresses on the mailboxes until he found the one he was looking for and pulled into the long driveway. "You don't ever get that pretty for me. I'm butthurt."

"I've heard Knox talk about Jace being a vegan. I generally like some form of meat in my food," Aaron said, completely ignoring Kreed's last remark as he flicked the visor up then reached over the seat to grab his coat. "And you aren't the real MVP. Colt's one of the biggest names in sports history and he came out. He's a game-changer, and besides, Colt and his boyfriend are hot."

Kreed had started to put the gear in place, but abruptly stopped as he listened to Aaron's explanation. He glanced at the man as he finally gave some sort of real clue about his sexual orientation.

"So you're gay? Or at least Bi?" Kreed blurted out, finally asking the question that had been plaguing him for the last two days.

"What's it matter? You don't do your partners, remember?" Aaron repeated Kreed's own words back to him in a teasing way before quickly opening the door and hurrying out of the rental.

For a second, Kreed stared after Aaron, realizing the kid might actually be incapable of answering a direct question. Kreed placed the gear shift in park, and his gaze followed Aaron as he shut the door and moved to the front of the SUV. A smile slowly spread across Kreed's face as he turned the ignition off. A more interesting thought occurred. Aaron was no more intimidated by Kreed than his own parents were. That never happened. His size mixed with all his ink usually got some sort of fear factor going before he ever said a word, but not from Aaron Stuart. With his inability to figure Aaron out, he'd missed they were playing a very strategic game of cat and mouse, and Aaron was the clear victor so far. Damn.

Game on, kid.

Aaron would give him a run for his money; no question there. Hell, the chase was already on. Kreed laughed as he slid out of the vehicle and shut the door behind him.

"You know, this whole I'm-irritable-all-the-time thing you do? It's kind of hot. I like to be put in my place," Kreed called out, taking long strides to catch up as Aaron took the front porch steps.

"I'm certainly not trying to attract you," Aaron retorted, not even bothering to look back as he reached for the doorbell.

"That makes it even better. I like a challenge," Kreed drawled, tucking his hands inside his jacket pockets. "We're in Texas. How the hell's it so cold?"

The front door opened, and Jace stood there, holding a napkin in his hand with a big smile on his face. "You guys made it just in time. Come in."

Though Kreed had seen Jace's picture over and over throughout the entire length of the original investigation, nothing prepared him for the nice-looking man who stood in front of him now. And that smile and demeanor exuded a warm-hearted personality too.

"Jace?" Kreed asked, because he didn't know what else to say.

"I am. You must be Kreed, and this must be Aaron. Please, come in." Jace moved back, holding the door wider as Kreed let Aaron enter first. The door shut behind them as he stepped inside to see a beautiful, open home with a winding staircase right up front. Kreed stuck out a hand, shaking Jace's. "Mitch talks so much about all the effort you two put in to getting this case closed."

"I can't imagine Knox saying too many nice things about anything," Kreed said, and Jace's smile turned into a laugh, changing his face...making it more handsome, if that were possible.

"Let me have your coats. I hope you're hungry and you like meat; Colt insisted you did. I think my cholesterol spiked just breathing the air with all the sizzling beef being served at our dinner table." Jace took Aaron's coat and hung it on the coatrack by the door. Kreed shrugged his off and did the same.

The noise of conversation drew Kreed's attention to the dining room right off the entryway. The first thing Kreed noticed wasn't his best friend standing or Cody wearing a big grin. It was the table filled with steaks, hamburgers, and grilled chicken, all wrapped in bacon. He'd heard the story about the big bacon meltdown the last time Mitch had visited. He guessed, for Colt, having Mitch and the team over meant they could pull out the big guns—a ten-pound slab of bacon.

"Hey, man!" Mitch eased around the table to extend his hand to Kreed. He took it, but got pulled into the brotherly hug they always shared when they were apart for any real length of time. Mitch was family to him, more so than anyone else on this planet.

"Your boy looks good," Kreed said, looking at Cody from over Mitch's shoulder.

"He's doing good. Won't listen to doctor's orders, though."

Kreed separated from Mitch and walked around the table to shake Cody's hand.

"I hear congratulations are in order," Kreed said, grinning at Cody. He'd gone with Mitch the day he bought the ring, not too long after Cody had come home from the hospital. Really, the length of time it took Mitch to ask Cody for his hand surprised him most.

"Yeah, that was pretty big." Cody's smile was as broad as Texas. The happiness reflected there warmed his heart. More than anything, he was really happy for his partner and Cody. They fit well together.

"And who the hell are you?" Mitch's voice boomed from across the room, turning both Kreed and Cody toward the uproar. "I don't even recognize you."

Mitch had moved toward Aaron, who was in the process of meeting Colt. "This was Sinacola's doing. Per him, I look more like a church boy."

"I didn't even know you owned a brush. I thought nonchalant-mess was your signature style. Clean-cut looks good on you," Mitch said, shaking Aaron's hand. "Good to see you outside of a monitor."

"Yeah, we need to talk about that. Helping a friend out's way different than going full-scale undercover. I mean, seriously, what do I know about anything other than killing zombies?" Aaron remarked. A smile split Aaron's lips as he spoke, so different than the irritable guy Kreed had spent the last couple of days with. Aaron's comment had Mitch barking out a real laugh.

As Kreed watched their exchange, another complicating consideration occurred. What if he brought out the worst in Aaron? For some reason, every step forward Kreed made in figuring Aaron out seemed to follow with two steps back and a slap of reality that the kid genuinely didn't like him.

"Yeah, you got Sinacola looking out for you. I think you'll do fine." Mitch gave a good-natured slap on Aaron's shoulder before going back around the table toward his chair.

"Have a seat everybody," Colt suggested from one end of the table. Kreed made his way to the table to officially meet Colt, then turned back to Jace. The stress of the last few months melted away. For the first time, Kreed experienced the driving force in Mitch's determination to solve this case. Instinctively, Kreed felt at ease in their home.

"We don't want to intrude."

"I think Aaron's past the point of caring," Mitch said with a laugh, nodding toward the kid. Aaron had taken one of the two empty chairs at the table, his attention on the food, eyeing one of the steaks while placing his napkin in his lap. No question, the guy had good table manners, but after all these shared meals between them, he understood that was more for respect of the dining experience than anything else. Aaron loved food.

"Smart boy can eat. You might not have enough here for him," Kreed joked. It was a large table, easily seating ten to twelve comfortably, but the shear bulk of muscle took up most of the room. Tall and well-built, Aaron was the leanest man there and Kreed had to squeeze in beside him. The move caused him to brush against

Aaron and he held back his groan at the touch. He liked physical contact. Kreed glanced over to Aaron. The kid didn't move, actually didn't even seem to notice Kreed entering his personal space, so Kreed didn't adjust his chair, he just stayed right there next to Aaron.

"I don't know where he puts it," Mitch answered, reaching across the table to place a T-bone on each of their plates. That was just Mitch's way.

"I didn't expect all this. I've listened to Mitch complain about Jace not letting Colt eat... Wait. Whoa." Aaron stopped in the middle of what he was saying, even throwing out a hand to help stop his words. A blush ignited across his cheeks. Kreed had just picked up a plate of foil-wrapped baked potatoes when an awkward silence fell over the table. Kreed's eyes shot to Mitch's who was looking between Colt and Jace with a giant grin plastered across his face. He then turned his gaze toward Aaron.

"Oh, damn! Aaron has no chill. Why you blasting Knox like that?" Kreed teased, he couldn't help the smile he gave at the huge lack of judgement of Aaron's words. With a thud, he dropped the wrapped potato on Aaron's plate.

"No, I said that all wrong..." Aaron started, but Colt stopped him.

"No, go ahead, I think I'm gonna love this," Colt said, encouraging Aaron to continue.

"I didn't mean it like that might've sounded, and I'm pretty sure I can't finish that thought without possibly making some of the table angry," Aaron reasoned, looking apologetic.

"You won't piss me off," Kreed added. He so wasn't going to let the opportunity to give Aaron shit slip through his fingers.

"You aren't helping," Aaron shot back.

"No really, keep going, Aaron. I think it's probably about the same conversation we have now just about every day," Colt added.

"Why're you putting him on the spot?" Jace asked Colt from across the table.

Uh oh. This just became a little more serious. Kreed and Aaron both glanced back and forth between the couple to make sure Aaron hadn't started a fight between the hosts of their dinner. Jace's smile was too big and Kreed cocked his head toward Colt, who looked positively ready to burst from wanting to say something.

Ah, man, they were cute together.

Not even here for fifteen minutes, and he got why Mitch was so taken with the lives of these two men. Their joy was contagious. In these few short minutes of being inside this house, Kreed now understood why Mitch had started to believe in fairytales.

"I'll say it, to save our *guest* the embarrassment," Jace spoke up as his gaze fixed on Colt's. Probably for dramatic effect, several seconds passed in their little showdown before Jace finally spoke again. "Aaron, last year when Colt came back into my life after dropping me on my ass and leaving me for ten long years…"

"Okay, I don't like the ugly turn this conversation's taken," Colt interjected, interrupting Jace. Colt held the steak knife in the air, pointing the tip in Jace's direction. Jace sat there with his mouth open, clearly waiting to continue, and Mitch was laughing hysterically now. Kreed wasn't sure exactly what was going on at the moment, and judging from their looks, Cody and Aaron weren't either.

"He was so kind and considerate while trying to get his foot back in my door. I would tell him my eating habits were my own. He didn't have to eat what I ate. But I'll have you know, the very same man that picked out several hundred dollars of grade A prime beef for this evening, the same guy who is stupid crazy for bacon… Yes, Colt Michaels insisted he would eat vegan with me. And he actually still does most days." Jace smiled a telling grin at Colt as he spoke.

Mitch pulled out his wallet and placed five one-dollar bills in front of Colt, tapping the center of the stack with his index finger. "That's my portion of dinner."

"Whatever. You know I worried about your protein intake, Jace," Colt said without missing a beat or the chance to pocket Mitch's money.

"I'm not finished. Even though we eat about the same, that refrigerator in there is always filled with meat—all sorts of meat. And most we just throw away because no one eats it." Jace made a show of lowering his brow at Colt. Kreed relaxed a little, deciding this wasn't turning into some earth-shattering fight. With his eyes still drawn to the scene unfolding in front of him, he slowly picked up his silverware and speared a broccoli floret, placing it in his mouth, waiting for Colt's explanation.

"No, our refrigerator's filled with yogurt and fancy fufu tofu that doesn't ever seem to last until expiration. Have I told you I don't really like tofu? It feels like a sponge in my mouth." The knife was back in the air, pointing directly at Jace as Colt spoke. "Now, bacon... That's the good stuff."

"Colt's also trying to move away from vegetables. It's hard to be a vegetarian and not eat vegetables." Jace lifted a glass of water, taking a drink, his eyes still on Colt. Wow, the Montgomery-Michaels duo provided entertainment with their meal. Kreed reached over and handed Aaron the condiment tray for the baked potato, encouraging him to eat.

"What's this then?" Colt motioned to the baked potato on his plate.

"A baked potato filled with artery clogging butter, cheddar cheese, and full-fat sour cream doesn't fall anywhere near the vegetable category. And please don't start on how since the cow eats vegan, it makes the meat vegan," Jace said, turning to Cody now. "He actually argued that point with me once." Jace took a big bite of broccoli. Kreed looked over to see Mitch enjoying the show as much as he was.

"Ha. Ha. Ha. Very funny. Are you finished?" Colt asked, playfully tossing a roll across the table at Jace.

"No." Jace chewed quickly, lifting a finger for everyone to wait. Once he swallowed and took a small sip of water, he continued, "So I keep telling Colt to pick out his funeral plot and make the arrangements before it's too late and the arteries in his chest become solid. Now, I'm finished," Jace said, laughing at his own joke, clearly one that Colt had heard before.

"You aren't getting rid of me for a very long time, so stop planning your single life," Colt added. Kreed got the distinct impression from the way those two were looking at each other, if they were seated closer together, they'd be kissing right now.

"I've had to sit through this for the last year. Normally they have these little spats then they make out until I'm the only one left in the living room," Mitch spoke directly to Kreed. "Oh shit, that reminds me. I have a gift for them."

"Not now," Cody said, shaking his head. As Mitch started to rise, Cody reached for his thigh, but his partner blocked the move.

Mitch was up and out of his chair, almost halfway across the room when he called out, "Don't tell them, Cody. It's a surprise! I'll be right back." Mitch was off; he took the staircase up, two at a time.

"I'm sorry in advance," Cody apologized to Jace.

"Here, Aaron. Try these. Show Colt they're good." Kreed handed a tray of roasted Brussel sprouts and broccoli florets to Aaron, who eagerly took two large spoonfuls.

"Here, Aaron. Try these. Show Jace they're better," Colt said, handing Aaron a bowl of sautéed mushrooms."

"Thank you." Aaron had kept completely quiet after initiating the round of banter between their hosts, but he looked up, a little startled, and took the bowl Colt held out to him. Then he spooned the mushrooms onto his plate.

"Aaron, there's easily a pound of butter in there. I'd be fearful for my arteries if I were you," Jace cautioned. Kreed laughed at Aaron's hesitancy, because seriously, Jace and Colt never gave in. Over time, Kreed could see Aaron easily fitting with these people who seemed to be consumed by the food they ate. He had to hold back his laughter as Aaron looked torn whether to eat the mushrooms since both Colt and Jace were now watching him expectantly. Aaron finally caved and took only a couple of mushrooms from the offered plate.

By then, Mitch had bounded back down the stairs with all the grace of a herd of elephants. Kreed watched Cody, whose face was already tinting a deep shade of red. He began fidgeting in his chair until he completely stopped eating and pushed his almost-full plate out of the way. Based on Cody's size, he clearly didn't miss too many meals. Man, the gift must be something really good.

"Here, buddy. I saw this in New York and figured I should bring you two a thank-you gift for taking us in," Mitch said proudly, handing Colt the gift bag before rounding to his side of the table.

Cody's elbows went to the table and his fingers covered his eyes. "It's inappropriate to do this now."

"Nah, it's good. Go ahead, Michaels." Mitch took his seat, and shoved a big bite of steak into his mouth as Colt dug inside the bag, pulling out a box. Mitch waved his fork around the dinner table. "Eat everyone."

"Bacon condoms?" Colt read from the box, a big shit-eating grin bloomed across his face as he spoke the words. "Make your meat look like meat."

After almost choking on his food, Kreed took a quick sip of water to wash down the rest before he inhaled the wrong way. He swallowed quickly, before saying, "You did not just do that at the dinner table, Knox."

"I did. It gets better," Mitch said, chomping on his steak, a smug expression spreading across his face. Cody just groaned and sat back.

"Eat, babe," Mitch said to Cody, but his entire focus rested on Colt. Kreed turned back to Colt as the ex-quarterback dug farther into the gift bag. It was hard to judge who he should watch, because Mitch's expression was pretty damn funny right now.

"Bacon flavored lube, Jace. He got us bacon flavored lube. *Fuckin' A*! He might be my new best friend," Colt exclaimed, beaming proudly as he lifted the bottle with one hand to show the entire table, while extending a fist to Mitch. Laughing hard, Mitch dropped his fork and reached across the table to meet Colt's knuckle bump.

"You two are too much," Jace said, shaking his head as his eyes danced between Mitch and Colt. "I'm not sure how we'll all coexist for the next few days."

"Eat, babe," Mitch tried again, tapping his fork on Cody's plate. His partner was as happy as Kreed had ever seen him.

"I've had enough," Cody replied, sounding a little embarrassed. He moved his hands up and down on his thighs, rubbing his palms. His face was still bright red.

"You need to eat. You're going to need your energy. I got us some, too." Mitch must have prepared to say those words, because he began laughing before he ever got them all out.

"You'd think I would've learned by now," Cody said, looking up at Kreed. Embarrassment flashing in his eyes.

Kreed laughed so hard at the look on Cody's face that he had to completely stop eating. Out of the corner of his eye, he caught Aaron reaching for another scoop of vegetables. Aaron's plate was almost clean. How did he do that? He'd eaten an entire plate of food, never stopping the flow of the fork to his mouth, while everyone else couldn't manage to eat and laugh at the same time.

"Where do you put it?" Kreed turned to Aaron and asked.

"I told you, fast metabolism," Aaron shot back.

"That reminds me. We have dessert with real pure cane overly processed sugar!" Colt clapped his hands together, pushing back from the table.

Chapter 11

While the house was huge—more space than two people could ever need—the group huddled together around the living room coffee table. The jovial nature of dinner all but gone as they discussed the current plan to infiltrate Redemption Apostle Tabernacle.

Aaron had both his laptop and iPad out as Kreed and Mitch debated the case. If he hadn't just spent the last several months listening to them, he'd be convinced they were fighting. Instead, he knew their process of hashing out possibilities and sat waiting for either one to request information he could access to help substantiate their observation.

In the beginning, Mitch expressed strong doubt when he, Aaron, and Kreed discussed the reason for focusing on this particular church. Mitch had actually argued, believing the better option was the church in the Maryland area that both the CIA agent and his attorney attended. Aaron watched as Mitch became animated and vocal, a total bulldozer when he got something in his head until Kreed raised his voice, stopping his partner with three simple words, "It's this one."

Impressed with how simply Kreed took control, the best Aaron could figure was years of working with Kreed's gut instinct had Mitch slowing his roll. Mitch stared at Kreed for several long seconds before dropping down on his knees beside the coffee table, wanting to see the church layout a little closer from the iPad Aaron used.

Since then, their entire dialogue hinged on this being the spot to stop this particular crime wave in its tracks. Like Aaron, Colt and Jace were little more than bystanders as Cody entered the discussion, adding valuable input as the three talked about the tactical plan they wanted Director Skinner to put in place. As much as the entire group believed in the importance of keeping this quiet, they also believed whole-heartedly in their ability to fully trust Director Skinner.

Kreed finally confessed that, behind everyone's back, Kreed had already set the wheels in motion with his direct supervisor. Even Connors didn't know how in-depth Skinner's involvement had become or the backup he'd put in place to protect Kreed and Aaron while undercover.

They had their undercover space secured already. The government had leased a home, strategically across the street from the massive church complex. The owners, senior citizens, had decided to vacation abroad for the next several months, the government footing their bill. Aaron added the senior citizen couple to his fake bio and updated everyone on the backstory he'd created. He'd pose as their grandson, who had moved to the area after finishing his graduate work at New Hope University. Since Kreed was now divulging the secret of Skinner's full participation, Kreed signed into email on his phone and forwarded a thick file of places, buildings, and professors he needed to associate with in order to pull off years spent there on campus.

"Midlothian looks like a little Podunk town. What if things go bad? How long will it take to get Skinner's team in there?" Aaron questioned as he moved his finger around the screen, looking at the layout of the city.

"Are you doubting my ability to keep you safe?" Kreed asked smugly, effectively not answering the question. The deputy marshal was good at deflecting.

"Well, kind of," Aaron replied, using his finger to pinch the screen back to a more concentrated view, showing the entire size of the compound. Then he returned his gaze to Kreed and waited for his answer.

"I already told you. It's my job to keep you safe. I'll handle those details. Besides, all you're supposed to do is set the place up, get the transmission going with Connors, and keep your head down. We'll handle the rest," Kreed said, patting Aaron's thigh. He didn't doubt Kreed Sinacola could keep him safe, but had the guy just dismissed his value in the outcome of this case? He took a deep breath and let the tension of that thought roll off his shoulders. He and Kreed would be having a talk about that later.

"Is the plan to get Aaron hired a secure one?" Colt questioned. Both he and Jace had remained so quiet throughout most of this exchange that Aaron had almost forgotten they were there. All eyes turned to Colt.

"Yeah, I think so. That's on me, but I have a solid plan. I'll have a job there by the end of the day tomorrow," Aaron answered, not divulging anything more about his strategy. He never talked about the way he manipulated code or the ease of breaking through the most complicated security firewalls. No one needed that information. Not right now. With this group, less was most definitely more. "I need some time, though, before I go over tomorrow. All I've got's my laptop, so it'll take me longer. I need to get into their system and find my triggers."

"No more all night gaming?" Kreed teased, ruffling the back of his hair. He'd pulled that same move a couple of times already today. It was a friendly gesture, maybe a little intimate, and he wasn't entirely sure Kreed even realized he did that. Aaron quickly lifted his hand to finger-comb his hair back in place while he dodged that question.

"This whole thing's put a damper on every part of my life. I'm vested in getting the answers and doing it as quickly as possible," Aaron responded, getting to his feet. He sure didn't want Kreed digging too deeply into his gaming activities. "We should get going. I have a lot to get done in a short amount of time."

"All right," Kreed said, rising a little slower. "I think it's late enough to travel."

"What's that mean?" Aaron asked. He'd begun loading his equipment back in his backpack, but stopped and looked down at his watch. It wasn't that late.

"It's better to show up at the new place at night with less eyes watching. I need to stay out of view," Kreed explained as he stretched his body before reaching for Aaron's iPad then handing it to him. "I just got a text that the remote entry and keys are on the front porch."

"Front porch where?" Aaron asked, feeling a little out of sorts with all the unknowns in his life at the moment. The whole undercover world worked in this fluid dance of secret movements that no one ever seemed to know about.

"Right outside," Mitch answered for Kreed, hooking a thumb toward the front door.

"They delivered those while we were here? Why didn't they just ring the doorbell?" Aaron asked, zipping his case.

"You aren't very bright to be so smart, kid," Kreed teased, bypassing Aaron to head toward the front door. "You'll have to get used to this kind of thing. The idea's not to draw any attention to ourselves. Remember when we came in? Jace didn't turn on the porch light. I'm sure Mitch told him not to. It's little things like that. Not foolproof, but precautionary nonetheless."

"Yeah, I'm not sure that's real effective," Aaron said with a frown, going toward the door and reaching for his jacket.

"I know, but it's the best we got right now. It's early on in reopening this investigation. We're acting fast, and it's a downtime for the bureau. Hopefully if we do have another spy on the inside, no one's been able to tip them off," Mitch explained.

"My equipment's getting delivered here tomorrow. I need that to help pull this off," Aaron said, zipping up his jacket, before slinging his backpack over his shoulder.

Mitch clapped Aaron on the shoulder, walked with him toward the front door, and said, "We'll have a repairman deliver it to your place tomorrow. It's no problem, but listen, this is gonna be hard on Sinacola. He's stuck inside, tracking you from that house. As much as you hate being called into the field, I promise Kreed hates being cooped up even more. This isn't our normal thing. We're used to wide open spaces, so be sensitive to that." Mitch gave his shoulder a little squeeze before letting go.

"I hadn't considered that," Aaron said, and he hadn't. He'd been single-minded, all his focus on getting himself out of there.

"It's only because of Kreed's rep that they didn't stick you with Connors or Brown. Hell, I don't think they could handle everything this is gonna take. You could've had worse than Connors. You could have two of him." Mitch shuddered, but Aaron ignored the joke, stuck on the original thought.

"Yeah, not good. I was just thinking about days on end spent trapped within the same four walls with Special Agent Connors." Aaron frowned. "I just wanna get in there, find what we're looking for, and get out. If it all works out as well as I want it to, Kreed won't be stuck inside more than a day or two."

"Good. If anyone can do it, you can. I appreciate this more than you know." Mitch's voice lowered as he spoke. They were standing in the foyer, closest to the front door, with Kreed about a foot away, somewhat in the conversation, at the very least eavesdropping, but the others seemed to be giving them room.

"It's not a problem, Mitch. You've been a good friend to me. You gave me street cred when I landed the NSA job, when no one else would talk to me," Aaron said, honestly. And he did feel like he owed Mitch for more than just that.

Kreed strode forward, butting into the conversation at that point. "Wait. No. Absolutely not. You've been giving me hell for days now and he got off the hook so easy? Hell no," Kreed said, shrugging on his jacket.

"You're not Knox. I can resent you," Aaron said, casually, defending his actions. Kreed threw up his hands.

"Story of my fucking life. Say goodbye now." Kreed reached over and shook hands with Jace then Colt. "Thanks for having us."

"We're having a small New Year's Eve party here—" Jace started, coming forward to join them at the door.

"Yeah, Bush didn't invite us to the one he's having." Colt interrupted him, a look of abject disappointment flashing across his face.

"And you guys should come. Even if it's late and only for a few hours, we would like to see you," Jace finished, ignoring Colt's outburst, except to reach out and pat his husband's forearm in consolation. Clearly, he'd heard those words before.

"I had the guest list checked out by Connors. It's clean, you'd be safe," Mitch offered.

"Maybe we can. What's the Bush thing?" Kreed asked.

"President Bush lives a few doors down. Colt keeps trying to run into him, get his picture taken. He jogs past his house at least twice a day because he heard the man's a runner. We never see him. Colt takes it personally," Jace explained in a concise and efficient manner. As Jace spoke, Colt's expression changed to aggravation.

"It has to be personal. He used to love the Panthers," Colt explained with a distinct whine in his voice.

Aaron held back a grin at their banter. This was even better than the bacon-flavored lube discussion at the dining room table.

"Babe, I don't think he ever loved New York. He's a former Texas sports owner. He loves this state," Jace explained to Colt, rubbing his back as he spoke. It was like he was talking to a hurt child. "Besides, you don't even like his politics."

"I'll jog with you in the morning, little buddy," Mitch offered sarcastically. Now everyone seemed intent on consoling Colt.

"All right, this just got weird. We're out," Kreed said. He lifted a hand and opened the door, stepping onto the porch. He immediately walked to the side of the concrete landing to a small potted plant near the first step. Kreed casually bent down and picked up a folded manila envelope hidden behind the ceramic container.

"That's my cue, I guess. Good night. Thanks again." Aaron lifted a hand and walked out into the night. No one lingered with the door open. They stayed true to entry—no lights to highlight their exit, just the moonlight guiding their path.

"How far's the drive," Aaron asked, going to the passenger door.

"Hang on," Kreed said as Aaron reached for the door handle. "Step back."

Aaron did as he'd been instructed and watched with growing satisfaction as Kreed rounded the car slowly, examining the ground, before bending forward to look underneath the car. When he got to the tailpipe, he bent low then went for the gas tank, looking before touching the small door and gas cap. Aaron guessed he was satisfied with what he found because he moved to the hood, getting completely on the ground to inspect the undercarriage.

"Is it safe to be standing out here?" Aaron asked after what seemed like a couple of minutes. Was all this truly necessary, and if it was, why had they even stopped here?

"I checked security before we arrived. Because of the former president, the neighborhood has cameras everywhere. The bad guys won't make that mistake again, but they do seem to have a preference for lighting up a vehicle." Kreed walked to the other side and again dropped to his knees, looking underneath the car. After a couple of seconds, Kreed went to the passenger side and unlocked the doors using the key fob.

Kreed reached for the handle, pulled the door open, and Aaron watched him turn his face away. Okay, add another mark to the Kreed Sinacola hotness meter. He'd read enough in Kreed's file to make the deputy marshal very intriguing, but tonight opened his eyes to a whole new side, giving him a front row ticket to some of that SEAL training he'd read about.

Maybe it was the thrill of watching Kreed go all special ops or knowing he could kill a man with his bare hands. Whatever it was, the guy was pretty damn sexy at the moment. Hell, Kreed's hotness invaded every moment, but…this one? Aaron struggled with the need to kiss Kreed, feel the weight of Kreed's body pressed tightly against his and those lethal hands, skillfully roaming over every inch of him. Those mental images had Aaron's body heating in the cold night air, and the overwhelming urge to lower his pants and have Kreed do him right there shocked him. Aaron held back a groan as his jeans grew uncomfortably tight at the thought of that last prospect.

"You take risks?" Kreed asked. The question pulled Aaron from his lewd thoughts and made him laugh. If the guy only knew what he'd been thinking.

"What kind of question is that?" Aaron took another step backward. His risk-taking fell somewhere in the range of masking false IP addresses to conceal his identity and playing Russian roulette with the leftover Chinese takeout in his fridge, and generally never entered the there's-a-bomb-on-the-bus arena.

"I don't see anything askew. Wanna get in while I start it up?" Kreed's smirk gave away his teasing test of Aaron's boundaries.

"Are we gonna go through this every time we get inside the car?" Aaron chose not to answer Kreed's question. At the moment, he truly wasn't certain if he were getting inside.

"Pretty much. I'll have equipment tomorrow to test this car, but we need to be cautious," Kreed answered, making eye contact.

Aaron didn't immediately move. Kreed gave him another smirk as he rounded the hood and opened the driver's side door, easily reading his hesitation. "I didn't see anything out of the ordinary."

Kreed reached inside the car, and Aaron heard the hood latch release. He glanced in that direction as Kreed stepped to the front of the car and opened the hood. He used the flashlight on his cellphone to check the engine.

"Look all right?" Aaron asked, still several feet away.

"Best I can see," Kreed mumbled from under the hood.

"What's your gut say?" Aaron asked.

"We're safe," Kreed answered immediately.

"Oh, well then…" Aaron went for the car. Kreed slammed the hood shut as Aaron closed his door. Honestly, he was still a little freaked out with Kreed's inspection. Out of all the consideration he'd given about this job, it had never occurred to him something like that was needed so early in the game. Aaron read and heard enough that, in theory, he was quite comfortable trusting Kreed's skills as well as his instincts.

"You do know that gut thing everybody says about me is a fallacy, right?" Aaron looked up, startled, and Kreed laughed as he closed his door and stuck the key in the ignition. "You can get out now."

"Just start the car," Aaron said, pulling on his seat belt and buckling himself in place. Kreed didn't hesitate; he immediately turned the key. The car started without a problem. Kreed was clearly messing with him, trying to get a rise out of him, evidently.

"You did all this on purpose," Aaron said as they started to back out. Kreed laughed under his breath, clearly tickled with himself as he backed out onto the street then put the car in drive.

"Only a little on purpose. We need to get in the habit. Besides, with this case, we don't know anything with certainty. They proved they don't have a problem bringing this right to our feet," Kreed justified.

"Okay, be honest, you aren't questioning anyone on the inside of the justice department, are you? I mean, anyone who's in our immediate circle," Aaron clarified. He looked over at Kreed, who kept his eyes on the road in front of him, but tilted his head a little to the side as if truly thinking over the question.

"I don't know. I don't think you're rogue. I don't think anyone in that house we just left is, and I'm certain Skinner's not. He wouldn't have ever hired me or Knox or a quarter of his staff if sexual orientation mattered. Outside of that, well…I'm giving Connors and Brown a free pass. I'm not sensing it in them," Kreed added.

"So you do go by gut?" Aaron asked. For some reason, Kreed checking their vehicle made the danger all too real for him.

"I do, but it doesn't replace logic, and Connors doesn't fit the type. And Brown? Well, he's like Anne. He jumped in to help. He's put in long hours, working right alongside everyone else. I don't see it with him," Kreed said, making a turn, before guiding the car onto the interstate.

"You know where we're going?" Aaron asked.

"Enough to get us in the general area," Kreed answered in that calm, cool, and collected way he had about him. Outside of that brief exchange in the front lobby of the FBI building, it sure didn't seem like anything got to the guy. He needed to take a page from Kreed's book. It would probably help him get through the next few days.

"Okay, wake me up when we get there." Aaron lowered the seat and reached for his headphones. He was tired. All that nervousness of a few minutes ago seemed to reiterate just how little sleep he'd had over the last few days. Besides that, Kreed smelled too good, and the deep, rich sound of his voice seemed to speak directly to his soul. Aaron reclined his seat and put the earphones in then closed his eyes.

Chapter 12

"Cement Capital of Texas," Aaron read a sign in downtown Midlothian as the headlights skimmed across the reflective etchings. "No way. Did that sign really just brag about dumping all those pollutants in the air?"

"Looks like it. There's not much here," Kreed said, following Ninth Street. The roads were barren, and as they passed the small downtown area, Kreed read the signs of the few businesses sprinkled along the route. "We got Chinese food, a bridal shop, a flower shop—they go hand in hand. Wonder what they thought about same sex marriage. We got a Mexican food restaurant, a title company, and a burger joint." As they came to a stoplight, Kreed stopped then looked all around. "Wait, was that it? That's downtown?"

"Looks that way." Aaron leaned forward, searching for something more. Thank God he didn't live here. He turned his head to the right. A small restaurant, a donut shop, and a single stoplight were the only signs of civilization in that direction. *Wow, talk about small towns. If you blinked, you'd miss the damn thing.* Aaron focused his attention to the left. "Besides that Italian place and the donut shop, I see a Sonic, I think, and that's about all they've got."

"What time is it?" Kreed asked.

"It's early still, just after ten," Aaron answered with a glance at the dash and finally sat back in his seat. What kind of place had they landed in? All the way there, they'd passed cities full of progress. Hell, not five minutes up the highway, they had a shopping mall and more restaurants than he could count then this… It almost appeared like the community didn't want to grow. Trying for anything that would help him understand, Aaron finally said, "Maybe the town closed early because it's cold."

"It's not that cold," Kreed said sarcastically. Clearly, he was on the same wave length as Aaron.

The light turned green, and Kreed took the turn as the GPS instructed and got in the right-hand lane to turn again. In the distance, the dimmed sign of a closed CVS Pharmacy caught Aaron's attention, making him feel a little better that at least one chain store had made its way inside the town. He picked up his cellphone and searched the info on Midlothian, Texas.

"I'm feeling very *Back to the Future* here, like we warped back to the seventies. Hell, even Pineville, Louisiana, has more going on than this place," Kreed said.

"Well, you don't wanna go too far back in time. The town has a bad history. Back in the eighty's some kids discovered the identity of an undercover cop at the local high school. They took him to a field and shot him—over a supposed drug deal. That's terrible," Aaron said, reading from his phone.

"Huh," Kreed muttered.

And as much as he hated it, small towns sometimes held the most appalling secrets.

"Yeah, the town's stats don't look so good. Bet there are quite a few hidden secrets," Aaron said, swiping his finger across the screen as Kreed hit another red light, this one with a set of train tracks twenty feet ahead. The crossing signal lit up as they came to a full stop, the safety gate lowering into position. They were the only ones on the road, and both Kreed and Aaron looked one way then the other down the dark tracks, no hint of light to show an oncoming locomotive.

"I saw this once on an episode of the *X-Files*," Aaron said, after a few seconds of nothing but the flashing red lights of the track sign illuminating their car.

"Yeah? What happened?" Kreed asked, drumming his fingers against the steering wheel, still looking one direction then the other for anything that might be coming their way.

"The track was really alerting them of a UFO above them." Aaron reached over and pressed the button, rolling down his window. He stuck his head out and looked up, searching for anything that might be hovering above them. Feeling reasonably secure nothing lurked outside—or maybe it was merely the cold air pushing him back inside the warm vehicle—Aaron sat back in his seat, raising the window. Kreed grunted and kept up the tapping on the steering wheel.

"The town in that episode was almost identical to this one. Real country, not much going on. But we don't have to worry. I don't see any kind of extraterrestrial ship trying to beam us up," he added dryly, his eyes still focused up in the sky through the passenger window as he tried to see as much as he could with the window up. Almost as if he had given an all clear, the crossing signal stopped flashing and the gate lifted. Nothing had crossed in front of them.

"Didn't Mulder and Scully work for the FBI? Connors would have a field day with someone like them," Aaron commented as Kreed continued on and took a right at the next road.

"High school's down there, I think." Kreed pointed straight ahead. In all the darkness, no matter how hard he tried, Aaron couldn't see a thing. Kreed spoke, drawing Aaron's attention the other direction. "Does that sign say Midtowne Senior Citizen Community?"

"Yeah, I think so." Out of nowhere, a neighborhood began with row after row of small, quaint houses. Across the street from there was an extensive set of apartments with another senior community sign in front.

"So we're close." Kreed took the left and drove around the curve to see the only street lights in the area shining down on a massive, sprawling mega church that easily took up acres and acres of land.

"*Damn!*" Aaron muttered at just the sheer size of the place.

"Pretty much my thoughts." Kreed slowed, glancing over at the church before GPS sounded off again telling him to make another right turn.

Aaron quickly searched out info on the church. "It's got a water park, aquarium, convention center, and meeting rooms," Aaron said, reading from his phone again.

"You're fast at getting information out of that thing," Kreed said, giving a quick glance in Aaron's direction.

"It's because I use my thumbs." Aaron waggled his thumbs to prove his point. "You text and work the internet with your forefinger. Makes it slower," he explained, typing again to bring up the church's floorplan.

"Those must be the townhomes we'll be staying in," Kreed said, and Aaron looked up to see that same community style housing from before, now with a long row of attached houses, all perfectly neat and well cared for.

"It looks like that's the entrance of the business office." Aaron pointed to his left as Kreed kept his eyes on the right side of the road until he stopped at a home directly across from the church's office entrance.

"Skinner outdid himself," Kreed said as he took in his surroundings. "You need to know, I never doubted my ability to get to you if something went down, but being right here— Yeah, this is perfect."

"Well, that's reassuring…" Aaron quipped, sarcastically. Kreed might not have doubted himself, but Aaron doubted everything. He'd never planned to put himself in harm's way long enough for Kreed to have to pull a Superman and come save the day. When Kreed started rolling forward again, Aaron looked down the street. "There's an alley."

Kreed drove the length of the street to the entrance of an alley, before looping back around and driving down that dark, small road. He pushed the remote control he'd pulled from the manila envelope, guiding them to the correct garage door. Kreed carefully drove inside and parked the car. He turned off the ignition and reached out to hold Aaron's arm, keeping him from getting out until the overhead door closed again.

"You live here alone, remember. You wouldn't be getting out of the car on that side," Kreed said, letting Aaron's arm go as the last churn of the gears in the overhead garage door unit ceased. Kreed tapped a finger at his temple, looking over at Aaron. "Mental mind-set, like checking the car. You're undercover now."

"So, like Mitch said, you won't really go anywhere until this is done?" Aaron asked. Kreed pushed another button on the remote, plunging the lit garage into darkness.

"If I do, you drive and I stay tucked in the back," he answered, reaching for the manila envelope again. He opened the package, letting the remaining contents drop into the palm of his hand. There was a small note, about the size of a business card, attached to a single key. Kreed lifted his phone, using the light to read the instructions. After another minute, Kreed finally got out and headed toward a backdoor. Aaron wasn't entirely sure if he should follow or stay put, so he did both. He opened his door, stuck a foot out, but stayed seated.

A loud beeping started. Kreed stood as a silhouette at the door. He looked like he was punching a finger into a keypad. The alarm stopped beeping, but Kreed continued to work the keypad. After a few seconds more, Aaron finally got the nerve to get out and stand close by.

"What are you doing?" Aaron asked, watching the long series of numbers and codes being entered into the box.

"I'm connecting this to the bureau. They'll monitor the activity around the house. Remember that senior citizen communities mean that the older adult isn't always working, and they usually don't mind peeping around, poking their nose in your business. I've got to stay hidden at all times. This will help the bureau see who's getting too close to the exterior of the house," Kreed said as they stepped inside the doorway.

Aaron nodded and looked around from where he stood. "It's not a terrible place. Small, but not terrible. Kind of nice." Kreed left him standing there and went to the trunk of the car. He came back with a small device in his hand, edging past Aaron before going deeper inside the house. "So people really live here?"

"Yes. It's really a couple traveling abroad. I'm guessing there are Justice Department eyes in here watching us, but I'm not sure. Usually they leave the bathrooms free of surveillance. Maybe the bedroom for some privacy." Kreed pulled out his device and began scanning parts of every room. Aaron followed for a while but got bored and just stayed in the hallway, waiting for Kreed to finish. It didn't take long. "I'm not detecting any inside cameras, but all the security keypads can become monitors and recording devices if needed, so keep that in mind."

Kreed finally turned on the hall light, before going back to one of the bedrooms. Aaron followed to find a small study with a sofa and a desk. "I think this is the best angle for a full view of the church. I'll set up in here."

As Kreed worked, Aaron walked around to get a closer look at the rest of the house. The home was rather small, perfect for two people and very comfortable. The kitchen, dining room, and living room were essentially one room but had tall ceilings which made it feel a bit more open. The entryway had a half wall that partially blocked the front door from his view. Feeling apprehensive about his new surroundings, Aaron peeked around the corner. There were several large boxes stacked inside. Kreed came up behind him, startling the shit out of him, and walked around the partial wall to pick up a box.

"What's that stuff?" Aaron followed Kreed into the kitchen.

"Probably the surveillance equipment. Your wires, shit like that. I asked for a computer for you. I don't know if they approved that request, but you know, the standard stuff. Grab another box. Let's get it opened. We need to do an inventory." Kreed placed the box he held on the kitchen table, before going back for another. When all three were there, Kreed pulled out his pocket knife and cut through the tape to open each one.

"How'd you get involved in this side of things? I thought the marshals just arrested people," Aaron asked, cocking his head to get a better view as Kreed moved packing peanuts around until he found two large metal briefcases in one box. He pulled each one out.

"Generally, that's all we do. Knox and I are special teams. That usually means we go after the super bad guys, but sometimes we do things like this. Knox got to stay on the case because he'd found all these connections and it had been a senator's kid who'd gotten hurt. Then with Cody's deal…" Kreed said distractedly, lifting the locks on the metal case. "They don't take kindly to having law enforcement shot at, so they're better to stick with the original team as best they can—better continuity for the case. Can you grab the other box?"

"Sure," Aaron said, but didn't move, as he peered over Kreed's shoulder at the contents of the case. "They aren't playing, are they?"

This case held a barrage of weapons. Everything from Glock 9mms, M1911 pistols to an M4 carbine with all the scopes, and the guys at the FBI had even thrown in flash-bang stun grenades, Halligan tools, flexi-cuffs, and all sorts of other tactical accessories. He recognized most of these weapons thanks to his hours of playing *Call of Duty*.

"Nah, they don't normally mess around. The government's stance is to make sure we have what it takes to bring us home alive. From where I'm standing, I can't say that's a bad thing."

Kreed closed the lid, buckling the case, before opening the other one.

"I'm surprised we're here alone then," Aaron said, watching him work. This briefcase was filled with about the same. Kreed closed that lid, put one on top of the other and moved them to the kitchen counter before scooting the few loose peanuts that fell out of the box back inside.

"We won't be alone for too long. By next week, they'll have others involved. It's why we have to get as much done as we can right now. The more involvement, the more red tape and inactivity we'll get." Kreed's brow lifted, and he nodded toward a medium-size box. "You gonna hand me that box?" Kreed asked.

Aaron cringed. *Crap.* He'd gotten distracted by the arsenal housed in those cases and forgotten Kreed's request. "Sorry. My bad."

~~~

Aaron stood almost on top of Kreed, all in his personal space. The kid's eyes shining with interest and excitement.

"This one?" Aaron bent forward, scooting the box closer, then lifted it up on the table. His new partner's surly attitude and the back-off-keep-your-distance stance had diminished. Kreed didn't let himself get too jazzed that maybe they might be able to coexist peacefully, because honestly, these boxes held every little boy's dream come true. Kreed turned away, not letting himself get too worked up with Aaron's close proximity, and smiled, making sure Aaron could see everything he unloaded from the rest of the boxes.

"Do you know how to use all that?" Aaron asked, awe in his voice.

Seeing Aaron's excitement and knowing he was interested in digging through the spyware, Kreed picked up an empty box and shoved it toward Aaron's chest. The guy automatically took it. Kreed grabbed the other two. Playtime would have to wait.

"Yup. Put that in the garage. We need to grab our shit and get settled. You gotta read that intel Skinner's put together for you."

Aaron carried the empty box to the garage as instructed. They unloaded the car, taking all the luggage and their backpacks inside the house. "Which room's mine?"

"The master. I'll take the study. I can keep a better eye on things if I'm in there with the surveillance gear," Kreed said as Aaron trailed behind him.

"I only saw the one bed. The study didn't have a bed," Aaron said, slowing his pace as he got closer to his designated room.

"Is that your subtle way of getting me into your bed?" Kreed teased, giving him a wink as he headed for the bedroom. "If I knew the weapons were such great foreplay…"

"Definitely not that," Aaron scoffed, the indignation creeping back into his voice. That made Kreed smile bigger. For some reason, it was comforting to have the old Aaron back. Kreed shook his head at that thought. The kid could be so adorable when annoyed.

~~~

Burning the candle at both ends was beginning to take its toll. Aaron let out a long, jaw cracking yawn as he sat in the middle of the bed in his pajama pants and T-shirt, working diligently on his laptop. Exhaustion numbed his mind. It was three-thirty in the morning, and he yawned again as he watched code fill the screen. His eyes drooped, and the moment his head fell forward, he jerked, startling himself back awake. He reached up to slap his face, forcing himself to pay attention and keep his eyes open. He had to see this through. He was almost there, close enough to the point he could shut the laptop lid, let the computer work for itself, and he'd finish the rest in the morning. The church systems were insanely easy to break into, thank God for that. He chuckled at his own little unintended joke.

With a few quick keystrokes, Aaron had placed the virus inside their systems, setting it to initiate on cue from his cellphone. The remote activation process had been harder to coordinate than breaking into the church's system, and that said a lot for a group filled with so much hate and secrets. Not a wise call on their part.

A light rap of knuckles on the bedroom door had him looking up as Kreed cracked the door open just enough to look inside, before pushing it all the way open. "I thought you were awake. Did you read the files Skinner sent over?"

"Not yet, but I will before I head over tomorrow. I'm almost done, but this is hour twenty-seven for me. I need some shut-eye," Aaron said as another involuntary yawn tore free.

"Make sure you read it. We need to get everyone straight. They're a little more than I bargained for," Kreed said, propping a shoulder against the doorframe and hooking his thumb in the direction of the church.

"Yeah, I told you they sucked," Aaron replied, watching his screen for a second or two before he lifted his eyes. Kreed Sinacola was exceptional in every way. Ruggedly handsome, perfectly built from head to toe, but more than that, he was such an interesting mix of a man. The SpongeBob pajama bottoms and his white sleeveless undershirt announcing "I Like Dick" in big bold black letters across the chest seemed to fit his personality more than anything else could. Kreed looked vulnerable in the moment with his hair sticking out in various directions as though he'd run a frustrated hand through it repeatedly.

If Aaron hadn't witnessed that hard, unyielding, take-no-shit attitude first hand in the FBI's lobby, he wouldn't believe it was inside this guy standing before him. Aaron couldn't help but give a slight grin at the reminder. Kreed had been prepared to take on all of those armed guards with no doubt he could handle the situation. He was clearly not someone to play with, and Deputy Sinacola was hot as hell when he was all riled-up.

With a mental headshake, Aaron quickly tried to push those images from his mind. They had a job to do, and he had to admit he was somewhat nervous. Okay, a lot nervous about going in that church. "If there really is a spawn of the devil, that pastor over there could be it."

"Agreed. I want you to carry a weapon," Kreed said, and his piercing eyes never strayed from Aaron. It wasn't a question or suggestion, but more a directive as those muscular arms crossed over his broad chest, as though daring Aaron to argue.

"I'm not comfortable with that," Aaron commented and forced his eyes down to the screen. In a matter of a second, Kreed's easygoing manner had turned serious, making Aaron a little intimidated in this moment. He didn't want that to show, so he pasted his irritable mask back in place to hide his response to Kreed's tactic. It seemed the only recourse he could ever muster against the guy.

"Too bad. I can't in good conscience send you in there unarmed," Kreed explained.

"So Skinner's file must be loaded with good shit about them. You didn't know anything about their past before?" Aaron asked, dodging the weapons discussion and turning the conversation in a different direction. Regardless of whether he wore a weapon, he'd be useless with a gun. His weapons training experience didn't go beyond a game controller aimed at a computer monitor. Somehow he didn't think that would help much in a real life situation.

"Not really. I knew they hated homosexuals and blamed the government for cultivating the 'fag propaganda.'" Kreed unfolded his arms to use air quotes over the last few words. "I knew they picketed military deaths and courthouses, shit like that, but I was reading their official doctrine. It's not good," Kreed said with a shake of his head. Aaron had nothing to add to that because he completely agreed. Walking hatemongers filled Redemption Tabernacle. To Aaron, they were the living evil.

Kreed finally shook his head again as if to dispel the silence that had taken over the conversation. Whatever information or images that flitted through his mind in that moment created a pained expression shooting across his face. "I justified their hate based on religious conviction, but hell, that's not godly. They can't even pretend it is. They have to know how evil they are. It's why you have to be protected until I can get to you."

"Well, I can't go in there armed, Kreed."

"Then we need to get someone else in here," Kreed said, pushing himself off the door and making his way farther into the room. Aaron lifted his eyes, watching Kreed close the distance to the side of the bed. Kreed's mannerisms seemed off tonight, different somehow. Something or someone had caused a worried look Aaron had never seen on his face before to show in his eyes and in the lines around his mouth. Maybe his brother? Perhaps his past? Who knew, but those protective vibes were flowing hot and heavy. Aaron felt the care, the concern, and also the apprehensive tension gathering in the air. Aaron's eyes stayed riveted on Kreed as he sat down on the edge of the bed, not facing Aaron. He didn't glance his way or say a word, but looked deep in thought as he bent forward with his elbows on his thighs. Kreed finally sighed, sat up and scrubbed his hands down his face before turning and pegging Aaron with another troubled expression.

Before Kreed could speak again, Aaron said, "Maybe we do need someone else, but that's gonna take time—something we don't have. It's been too long already. These freaks don't believe they'll be caught and your plan has merit. It's been months since an attack. We both know it's time for them to act again. That deacon's in town. I know it. I won't take undue risk. I'll follow the rules and I trust you. We can do this." Aaron tried to infuse his words with positive solidarity. He lowered his laptop screen about midway and placed it on the nightstand, pushing himself up against the headboard. As much as he didn't want to be there, they'd come too far to stop now. Besides, it wasn't going to take long to know if they were barking up the wrong tree or if they'd landed on the mothership.

Kreed didn't respond right away. He stretched out, grabbing one of the pillows next to Aaron and hugged it against that big chest of his as he rested his head in the hand of his bent arm. He scrutinized the bedspread, picking at a thread with his fingers. The weird vibes radiating from Kreed had Aaron narrowing his eyes, trying again to decipher this mood.

Something was really off with Kreed, which was completely out of character from what he'd come to expect. Aaron was far better at reading between the lines in online chatting than reading real people, in real situations. Maybe it was too soon for Kreed to be back in the field in such a high-stakes case, especially since the guy had been secretly leading this case since they'd all been back together.

"I want you wired at all times. You get out of there if anything looks or even feels funky," Kreed finally said, looking up at him.

"Yeah, no problem there. That's pretty much my game plan, but if I can get in there, get their system feeding information back to the bureau, and just be around if something falls through in that connection, I should be fine, right?" Aaron asked.

"In theory, yes."

"You know I trust you or I wouldn't be here," Aaron confessed, wanting to reassure him.

"How much longer do you have?" Kreed didn't respond to that statement. Instead, he changed the subject and pointed to the computer on the nightstand.

"I'm done. I was waiting for the virus to load. I'll test it in the morning, but I think I'm ready."

"Then get some sleep. You need to be sharp." Kreed pushed up and off the bed, tossing the pillow in his direction. Silence fell between them as Kreed stood at the end of the bed, staring down at him. Neither spoke, but Kreed's eyes held a seriousness to them he had only seen at the bureau. Aaron swore something passed between them. He held his breath, waiting for Kreed to make some kind of lewd suggestion, anything to ease the tension, but he never did. Kreed just turned away, padded across the room, and quietly shut the door behind him. Was Aaron disappointed? Had he wanted Kreed to say something more?

A smile bloomed across Aaron's face. Aaron's heart sped up a few beats as he realized how much he liked seeing all the sides of Kreed, and he suspected he might be part of a small select few who got to see the true man. Kreed put value on Aaron's participation in this case—made even stronger since the deputy marshal had hand-picked him to be his temporary partner. Kreed didn't want Aaron getting caught in the crossfire and that care and concern was sexy as hell.

Aaron lifted his T-shirt over his head and tossed it to the floor. He reached for a pillow then tugged at the covers, wrapping them around his body as he lay down. Aaron tried to forget about the tenderness in Kreed's voice, focus only on what had been said and what all of this could mean, but he couldn't pull his mind away from Kreed. For the first time, Kreed hadn't made references to getting inside his pants, but instead he'd been truly concerned. How long had it been since anyone worried about his welfare?

Aaron's body warmed as he let that thought settle on him. Kreed truly did seem to care about him. The look in his eyes told him that much. Aaron curled himself around the pillow Kreed had hugged, and Kreed's scent hit him like a sledgehammer. He buried his nose in the pillow and inhaled the intoxicating aroma as he toyed with his nipple ring, twisting and tweaking the metal loop as he thought about Kreed. All the blood in his brain rushed to his dick. He should focus on getting sleep, but his dick demanded attention and he was too far gone to stop.

Aaron gave in, rolled to his back, and kicked the blanket off his body. He slid his hands down his stomach and into his flannels to fist his cock. His eyes closed and his head filled with images of Kreed, the ones he'd tried so hard to push away. Aaron tightened his fingers. He was hard as a fucking steel pole and leaking like a faucet. It didn't matter that Kreed was in the next room and could possibly hear him or come through that door at any moment. The possibility of Kreed walking in only spurred his excitement and heightened the ache in his balls. All he could concentrate on was easing the need churning through him.

Aaron stroked himself, imagining Kreed's smart mouth and big hands pleasuring, teasing, and torturing him. He imagined he could still smell Kreed's lingering scent in the air. He moved his hand faster, arched his hips, to give his dick more friction. His ass clenched, wanting to be filled. Aaron shoved his pajama bottoms down and out of the way in order to spread his legs, only in his mind it was Kreed's thick legs that held him open wide. Using his other hand, Aaron fondled his aching balls, tugging and rolling them like he wanted Kreed to do. Aaron needed more to push him over the edge. He was on the cusp, hanging in limbo, and he desperately wanted to come.

He brought his fingers to his mouth and sucked them between his lips before shifting both digits to his ass. He toyed with the sensitive skin around his rim before forcefully pushing inside his channel. *Fuck!* The sweet initial burn tightened his balls and made his dick weep with delight. He always liked the feeling of being breached. He screwed his eyes shut tighter and worked his fist and fingers faster. Dark eyes danced behind his, full lips tempted him with that ever-present smirk. Holy damn, he wanted those lips stretched around his dick. Kreed's mouth sucked him… Kreed's fingers in him, working him… The orgasm swamped him, pleasure crashed down on him in breath-stealing waves.

"Kreed." Aaron gasped, calling out the handsome deputy's name as his release painted his chest and chin with thick ropes of creamy warmth. He sucked in air, trying to level out his breathing. Completely spent, he relaxed against the bed, but his body still buzzed with endorphins.

Aaron opened his eyes as his body came back online and his heart quit pounding in his ears. It was so quiet in the house. He stayed frozen, not moving as the last few minutes came into focus. Had he called out Kreed's name?

Fuck!

Embarrassment heated his already hot skin. He removed the fingers from his ass and rolled his body just enough that he could grab a dirty shirt from the floor to wipe the come off his chest and chin. *Damn it!*

He hadn't considered the fact that the security wall mount could be used as a camera. How in the hell was he going to explain that one? Yeah, he could see that playing out right now. Kreed would never let him live it down.

That sated after-sex feeling took over, pushing the fear aside. Aaron snuggled deeper into the warmth of the covers, hugging the pillow that smelled like Kreed tightly against his chest. If anyone heard…well, there was nothing he could do about it now. What was done was done. He'd worry about that if anyone brought it up, which was technically his entire life's motto. Aaron yawned and closed his eyes with Kreed right there in his mind as he fell asleep.

Chapter 13

"Something smells incredible," Aaron said as he came around the corner toward the kitchen. He'd slept later than they had planned. It was already close to eight in the morning. That would mean Aaron had gone approximately twelve hours without eating. Based on the little knowledge he had on smart boy, Kreed didn't figure that happened too many times. As if to validate that thought, Kreed heard Aaron's stomach growl and grumble from across the kitchen. He'd bet the smell of sizzling bacon had Aaron finally rising when he did.

"They hooked us up," Kreed said, reaching for a second coffee cup, refilling his before pouring one for Aaron.

"SpongeBob? I missed my opportunity to give you shit last night. I must've been really tired."

Kreed looked down at his pants as he slid the cup to Aaron across the bar.

"Why? They're comfortable. I bought several pair. I like these because whatever the fabric, they don't shrink and SpongeBob's fucking funny." Kreed picked up his coffee mug and headed back to the stove.

"The ink's impressive," Aaron said as Kreed turned each piece of bacon. Kreed reached up and scratched his bare chest, looking down at the ram's head tattooed there. There was no real story to that particular tattoo, unlike the ones on his arms. He'd started getting the tatts years ago, way before it was the cool, trendy thing to do. After all this time, they were as much a part of him as his extremities.

"Some's fading, I should probably get 'em refreshed," Kreed said, lifting the cup, taking a long drink.

"You have them all over?" Aaron asked as Kreed pulled the crispy pieces from the pan.

"Yeah. I wasn't too smart in placing them strategically. I thought I'd be career military and where I was didn't matter about the ink," Kreed replied with as much detail as he was willing to share. He never, ever talked about his military days, and he refused to let his mind go back to those years. Showing the darkness during that time of his life exposed too much about himself and the lengths he'd go to protect what he loved. The past needed to remain where it belonged—better for everyone that way.

"Why'd you leave?" Aaron asked.

"Things change," Kreed answered absently, breaking open an egg in the full pan of bacon grease. His mom would have a heart attack watching him cook these eggs in all that fat. "How many do you want?"

"Four, if that's okay?" Aaron asked.

Kreed stifled a smirk; as he'd suspected, food had done the trick and changed the course of smart boy's thoughts. That was a handy bit of knowledge about his new partner.

"Sure. Did you get enough sleep?" Kreed asked, adding another egg.

"Yeah, I guess."

Kreed glanced back as Aaron tilted his mug to drain the rest of the coffee then walked over to pour himself another cup. The kid was dressed in his new clothes—a pair of khakis and a striped button-down. He wore a pair of nice dress shoes on his feet. His handsome face was clean shaven, but his hair was still wet from the shower he'd taken.

Kreed looked down at his bare chest and pajama pants hanging low. Well shit, too low. A plumber wouldn't have much on him right now. He reached down and pulled up his pants, tying them at the waistband. Okay, Aaron wasn't Mitch. He and Mitch were comfortable together. He and Aaron? Not so much. A hint of professionalism was probably in order for now. He turned the eggs, removing the ones that were done. He needed to go grab a T-shirt. "I won't be so casual after this morning. I figured it was my last downtime for a while. I'm sorry about this."

"Are you carrying your weapon now?" Aaron asked with a hint of sarcasm. Kreed looked over his shoulder to see Aaron buttering the toast, a teasing smirk on his face as he lifted his head and they made eye contact.

"It's close by," Kreed said, lifting the hand towel on the counter beside him, his pistol sitting underneath.

"I never doubted it." They worked the rest of the meal together in silence. Kreed dished up the bacon and eggs while Aaron added the toast. Before he took his seat, he ran back to his room, grabbed the wife-beater he'd worn last night then decided to toss that one aside in favor of a blank T-shirt instead. "I Like Dick" wasn't professional, no matter how much Mitch had insisted it was.

"OJ, too?" Aaron called out.

"Nah, coffee's fine," Kreed said loudly, tugging the T-shirt over his head as he came back in the kitchen, grabbed his coffee mug, and placed it on the table. Aaron brought the pot over and topped both cups off, giving a quick warmup. Kreed reached for the silverware he'd laid on the counter, but he kept an eye on Aaron the whole time. The kid was different this morning. He'd participated in making breakfast, worked together with Kreed, and that was just plain odd, almost as if the guy forgot to put up the walls he normally placed between them and… That thought caused Kreed to speculate. Whatever had changed, they were oddly comfortable with one another right now—more comfortable than they'd been since he'd picked the kid up at the airport. Kreed liked this easiness they shared.

"It looks good," Aaron commented as Kreed placed the silverware by each place setting before going for the refrigerator and pulling out some fresh fruit he'd found and cut up earlier.

"Do you have enough?" he asked before sitting. Aaron had already taken his seat and was in the process of digging in.

Aaron looked up, confused, his entire focus rested on the food in front of him.

"Not being snarky, just asking. I can make some more. No problem. We can't have you going over there hungry."

"No, I'm good. I like to eat, but I can go without." Aaron gestured with the piece of toast as though it were no big deal, then bit off a big chunk and went back to focusing on his plate. Kreed shook his head and put the bowl of fruit in front of Aaron then sat down.

"You don't miss too many meals. I've seen you get all snippy when you do. Remember I was in the room when you threw a fit over the pizza," Kreed teased as he took a bite of the bacon. Colt's little bacon-wrapped meat show came to mind, and Kreed could physically feel his arteries hardening, but, man, it had tasted good.

"That was more Connors's fault than the lack of pizza. The pizza just got the brunt of it all. But honestly, I think I was figuring out that you had a strategic plan the whole time and there was no way I was escaping."

"All right, I'll give you that one. Are you ready for today?" Kreed asked, trying to keep at a distance the unexpected worry that had him all funky last night.

"I gotta test some things and go over the file, but yeah, I think so," Aaron said between bites.

"And in layman's terms, what's your plan?" Kreed asked. All that techie talk was its own kind of foreign language.

"Layman terms… Okay, well. I'm walking in to apply for a job. I have the takedown ready to activate remotely. Their system's scheduled to stop while I'm there, and I graciously offer to take a look, then fix it. Hopefully, that should secure me a job," Aaron explained. When he stopped talking, he shoved the bite he'd prepared into his mouth. Aaron lifted a finger, holding off any questions.

Kreed waited for him to continue, smiling when he added another bite.

Aaron swallowed and lifted the napkin to wipe his mouth before he continued talking. "While I'm in their system correcting the attack, I'll set the series of spy software for the bureau. It won't take long to infiltrate. The rest happens automatically when they log back in after I shut them down. Pretty standard stuff. I'll just hide what I've done really well, lead anyone looking on a wild goose chase."

"And I'll be here listening and watching," Kreed added. The kid seemed steady and secure, not too nervous, and he wanted to keep him that way. "I feel kind of lame now. You're gettin' to be the Ethan Hunt in this deal. Knox and I always fight for that spot. I just have to sit back and watch you have all the fun."

Aaron chuckled, chewing quickly. "From where I'm standing, it feels like you have the most important part. Goal number one's to get hired. Goal number two is to get them to start me tomorrow so I can do more. If not, it'll probably be after the New Year's holiday."

"Damn, I keep forgetting about that. We have an automatic down day right there," Kreed said, pushing his plate out of the way.

"Yeah, I know," Aaron added, cleaning his plate before he moved it aside. A weird comfortable silence fell between them, which was another first. Kreed wasn't in a mindset to let that go easily. He drained his coffee, thinking about everything Aaron had said. Honestly, it was probably better to get the smart boy in there today, then give their team a day or two to reassess and reevaluate. Let the bureau watch any private activity that might be going on inside the church when no one's around. After a minute more, Kreed pushed back from the table, taking his and Aaron's dishes to the sink.

"Let me take a shower, then I'll wire you up. Don't worry about the dishes. I'll get 'em later." He flipped on the faucet, plugged the drain, and quickly settled several of the dirty dishes inside the sink then left the kitchen to start his day.

~~~

All business, Kreed inspected the equipment spread across the kitchen table while glancing at Aaron as he prepared for being wired. Aaron stood close by where he'd been instructed to stand, his khakis unbuttoned and slightly unzipped; the waistband of his underwear showing while he began working the buttons free of his crisp, highly pressed dress shirt. As the shirt opened, Kreed got a flash of Aaron's nipple rings.

As attractive as that sight might be, and no matter how badly he wanted to tease the silver hoop with his tongue and take the metal between his teeth until Aaron moaned, Kreed conceded there were more pressing obligations to tend to at the moment. But, damn it if Aaron undressing right in front of him wasn't the biggest distraction on this planet. And his dick was straight-up against the notion of anything else taking precedence.

As he worked at the table, Kreed gave a couple of silent prayers. The first one was that he'd get a hold of himself where those nipple rings were concerned. The second? Well, that belonged to the problem of his rock hard cock. He needed the evidence growing inside his jeans to lay the fuck down. This was bad. He had a civilian under his care and protection who was going undercover in dangerous territory. What the fuck was wrong with him?

On a low, disgusted growl, Kreed began an inner reprimand. The mission came first. Whatever he wanted to do with Aaron Stuart should have already happened and, since it hadn't, should be put on the farthest backburner until they were safely on the other side of this particular mission. Kreed had led this whole investigation to this moment. He fucking had to focus.

With a deep breath, Kreed slowly exhaled and channeled his inner secret agent, forcing that man to take over as he began to explain the devices on the table. The blade and ankle holster would come last. He anticipated their biggest fight to be right there. Kreed turned toward Aaron and started from the beginning, as much for himself as for his temporary partner.

"The name of the game's building a case. Our sole purpose is to find the information we're looking for. Get in, get out. Minimal to no collateral damage. If what we're looking for is there like we think, then we build a case that holds up for prosecution. Got it?" Kreed asked, looking at Aaron, who stood there silently staring at him with his shirt now hanging completely open. Kreed swallowed the lump forming in his throat at the sight of a wide-eyed, sexy hot, smart boy looking so unsure and inviting all at the same time.

"I don't know the law on this…" Aaron started, but Kreed cut him off.

"That's not for you to worry about. Undercover work finds the physical evidence that justifies the arrest warrant. Think of this as an accumulation of the last year's work coming down to the next few days. We find the proof we need or move on. It's that simple. Got it?"

Aaron gave a very small nod and said nothing, so Kreed continued.

"Here's what we got." Kreed moved his hand over each section of the equipment on the table as he explained their purposes.

"This is visual. These are the cameras we'll use." Kreed waited until Aaron nodded before he began explaining each device. "These are fixed visuals—the cameras you'll place to monitor everything in a room. Small, easy to hide, but pick up a large range." Kreed picked one up and showed Aaron until he got another nod then put that one down. He grabbed another couple of devices, palming both, and pointed to each one as he spoke. "These are the moving visuals— the ones we place on you and the ones you can apply to moving objects. Got it so far?" Kreed waited a heartbeat for that nod.

"Next is audio. Electronic eavesdropping for the phones. They tap and trace both ingoing and outgoing information." Kreed carefully picked up that device, holding it in his palm. This was the one he planned to have Aaron wear. "For today, it's important you stay contained to one area of the church until we know better what we're working with. Got it? The visuals you capture and create today, helps us map the place out, make sure nothing's changed from the blueprints we've pulled. It's a form of reconnaissance work. It's a critical step in the process. It keeps you safe and gives us a clue how to get in there if everything comes to a head like we think it will. Let me say it again. Your job's twofold today—gettin' your foot in the door and the passive reconnaissance through this device. Got it?"

"Yeah, what's that?" Aaron asked, finally beginning to participate in the conversation as he stared at the pin in Kreed's hand. Kreed extended his palm for a better look.

"We've evolved massively over the last ten years. I don't have to tape anything to your chest today. As nice as all that is to look at," Kreed said, giving a nod toward Aaron's chest. "You can button your shirt back up, though I enjoyed watching you undress. Nice piercing," Kreed added with a grin, feeling a little more on solid ground than when Aaron had first started undressing.

"Dude, are you kidding me?" Aaron asked, automatically buttoning his shirt. The irritation was back, real this time, and Kreed's smile grew.

"You know, you gotta get it where you can. So listen. This's important. We got the newest state of the art…"

"Yeah, whatever, I'm certain the technology's already improved," Aaron said, still disgruntled as hell as he began tucking his shirt back inside his pants.

"As I was saying, this right here is the newest covert recording device, aka a wire, from the bureau." Kreed held his hand out to show the item. Aaron fastened himself back together as he looked down at the device in his palm.

"It looks like a flash drive," Aaron said, sliding his buckle into place.

"Yep. We'll stick this in your front shirt pocket. You don't have to worry about placement. Either way, we'll get whatever's being said around you." Kreed slid the device in Aaron's pocket and reached for a writing pen. "This is the backup. They do the same thing." He put that in the same pocket as the flash drive.

"I thought it'd be bigger than this," Aaron said, pulling out the pen to get a better look. Kreed knew no one would see anything other than a writing pen, even if it was taken apart. "I remember watching movies as a kid where they had to wear all these wires and microphones."

"Yeah, and the recorders taped around their belly, like that would ever work. At this point, I've started both devices, so everything we say's now being recorded." Kreed nodded, staring Aaron straight in the eyes so he would pick up his meaning.

"Next, we have this. It's a cross pin, see? The jewels at each point do something. Video, audio." He lifted the device and showed Aaron. "It's active as well."

Kreed placed the cross on the empty front pocket of Aaron's dress shirt, letting his finger brush lightly across a nipple ring before reaching low to unbuckle his belt. Aaron's breath hitched, his stomach muscles tensing slightly, before he batted Kreed's hands away.

"Hey, what're you doing?" Aaron's eyes met his.

"As if we don't have enough already, consider this backup. If something happens and everything else fails, we'll still be able to get you out." Kreed lifted his palm to show an encasing for his buckle. It didn't replace it, but fit perfectly over the top. Kreed had

FULL DOMAIN – A *Nice Guys* Novel

insisted on this particular belt over all the cooler ones on display for this very reason. Kreed unbuckled the belt, clipped the piece in place, and when he started to re-buckle the belt, Aaron again swatted at his hands.

"I got it." Aaron moved a step away, and Kreed watched as the kid straightened his clothing.

"From this moment forward, we're a team. You blink and I know about it. Teamwork's the only way to properly pull this off. You have your job. I have mine. Connors and Brown have theirs, and they're both listening right now. We're fluid and responsible for one another." Kreed reached over for the ankle holster containing the Glock he'd been saving for last.

"No man left behind?" Aaron asked in a slightly mocking tone, until about halfway through that statement, when it must have occurred to him that he'd be the man left behind in this situation. If this weren't so serious, he might have laughed at Aaron's reaction.

"Something like that."

"You ever left a man behind?" Aaron asked, uncertainty back in his voice.

"Never." Kreed didn't qualify the live or dead factor of that question as he dropped to one knee. The answer was true enough.

"What're you doing?" Aaron started to take another step backward. Kreed stopped him, gripping his trousers.

"Stand still. I'm adding this. It'll make me feel better and give you protection. It's small, lightweight, and can be hidden at the top of your socks. No one's gonna see it," Kreed said, lifting Aaron's pants, relieved when the kid didn't fight him.

"You don't anticipate I'll need that, right?" Aaron asked as Kreed finished, then pulled the leg of his slacks back in place.

"No, not really. It's just to make me feel better." That lie seemed to pacify Aaron for the moment.

"And we can handle this with just us?" Aaron asked. The kid needed reassurance; he'd figured that might be the reason why Aaron had little to no attitude with him today. Kreed patted Aaron on the shoulder before he turned away.

"For now. I'm trusting the process, and honestly, we'll know a lot more once you've gotten on the inside. Until then, Skinner knows we can't bring this down by ourselves. We won't be asked to. But

142 | Kindle Alexander

that's his job in the chain. He'll be ready when we need him," Kreed said, checking the equipment left on the table. There was more he needed to explain, but this was enough to get Aaron started. He had to get hired before any of the rest really mattered anyway.

"What if that time's tomorrow?" Aaron finally asked. The guy was smart; he didn't leave too many stones unturned.

"It won't be," Kreed said, trying for reassurance. He reached for an earpiece then connected it to his ear.

"You don't know that," Aaron immediately replied. All startup jobs were nerve-racking to say the least. He got it; Aaron's anxiety was rising, and he got that, too, but he'd need to calm himself in order to make this work. He had to try to talk the kid down, but supportive reassurance wasn't really his strong suit.

"Maybe not. But I do know it won't be tomorrow. If it were, though, Skinner's a miracle worker. You've got nothing to worry about. I'm not letting you get hurt. Connors, are you getting this?" Kreed lifted a hand to his ear to push the small earbud farther in.

Connors came back with, "Affirmative."

"All right, kid, we're good. You're good and I'm watching you close. Connors just told me in my ear that he's got everything registered. The name of the game for you today's to blend in and be helpful when you can. When you walk in that door, study every single person you see. Become them. Turn and angle yourself so we can see the place, but be natural about it. And for some reason, if they do have a young female staff, you need to stay away from 'em. You're already too good-looking. You'll attract attention, which negates from blending in and being unseen. Stay as quiet and inconspicuous as you can." Kreed stared at Aaron, hoping he'd conveyed everything he could until he had a lightbulb moment. Kreed snapped his fingers, trying to remember that family's name. "Take on the Duggar family persona. Not like that oldest one, but the others. Be like them—naïve to the point of almost dumb, not worldly. And remember, it's against your moral code to be alone with a woman. Right? Isn't that how they are?"

"I have no idea," Aaron said, furrowing his brow, a look of complete confusion crossing his face.

"Well, I think it's something like that. Just do that," he advised, hoping he'd eased some of the fear.

"What if they want me to ride with them somewhere?" Aaron asked.

"Do not get inside a car. I don't care what excuse you give. Shake 'em off. Don't do it under any circumstance. Follow the rules. Drop to your knees and curl into a ball, slapping your head. Don't get inside a car with them. Now, give me your left wrist." Kreed took the wristwatch off the table and placed it on Aaron's arm. "This monitors your vitals and has a GPS tracking device."

In Kreed's ear, Brown whispered, "He's panicked. His heart rate's through the roof." Kreed glanced up at Aaron's face.

Yeah, no news there. While he watched, Aaron began turning slightly pale. Kreed reached up and placed his palms on either side of the kid's head.

"No. You need to stop this. Listen to me. It's *me* against *them*. Stop overthinking. You're safe. Get us in there, and we'll know pretty quickly what we're dealing with. Stop freaking yourself out. I've been in far worse situations and got everyone out alive. This right here is a piece of cake." Kreed stepped closer to Aaron, willing him to understand his words. "You're safe. I swear on my life."

The silence was almost deafening while Kreed waited for some kind of response. Seconds passed and the tension began to lift as he slowly watched calm descend across his partner's face.

"Somehow those scars on your arm make me feel better about the odds," Aaron finally said. Neither moved away, and Kreed remained silent, staring deeply into Aaron's eyes until he felt reasonably sure the kid had a hold of himself.

"You're a smart guy. Assuming you make it past reception, make mental notes of everything. If any church staffer writes a note after something's said, remember that conversation. If something starts an argument, focus and remember the finer details. We do reports every evening. Each member of the team will have different facts, find a different perspective. Connors will gather all the information and those reports go to Skinner for assessment. They'll make sure you have whatever information they assimilate before you ever go back inside that place. Got it?" Kreed asked, taking a step backward when he heard Brown quietly tell him Aaron's vitals were moving back to normal. "What are you thinking?"

"All this is gonna hold up in court? Don't we need a search warrant?" Aaron asked.

"I'm glad you're concerned about staying inside the law. It means you're vested in the case. That's all been taken care of. Skinner's sister in-law's a judge," Kreed advised.

"Okay, I didn't expect that."

"Yeah, the file has been buried under a pile of paperwork, so by the time it becomes a public document, we'll be done here. But right now, don't second-guess any of that. We're on a fact-finding mission. During the end-of-the-day reporting, we'll talk about legalities if we get that far," Kreed added.

"What if they ask me to do something illegal. Do I do it?"

"Yes. Since we're monitoring everything, there's nothing that'll be held against you, if that's what you're asking. Generally, when you're in the field like this, those are little tests to see how you'll respond. Talk about God's grace or just reiterate the kind of jargon they use, but do it. They'll trust you more if they're truly the ones behind this." When no one raised another question, Kreed stepped back several steps and surveyed him. "You look good. I'd think you just came from church camp."

"Thanks." Aaron smoothed his hands down the front of his shirt, taking a deep breath. He abruptly pivoted on his heels, leaving Kreed standing alone in the kitchen. Once he heard him treading down the hall, he moved, following behind, walking slower toward Aaron's room. He'd never worked with anyone so green before, and he had no idea where he stood. If this were Mitch, he'd already be headed over to the church by now. Trying to decide if he'd covered everything, Kreed said from the doorway, "Once you shut their system down, do your thing and stay quiet. Don't talk too much or ask too many questions. It'll tip 'em off that something's not right."

"Yeah, I got that. Outside of that anxiety attack I just had, I'm a big *Five-O* fan. I get what we're trying to do," Aaron said.

"Okay, well then, let me say that I don't want you to do anything you've seen on that show. Just be normal." Kreed watched as he slipped his phone in the front pocket on his slacks and picked up a file folder.

"I was joking with the *Five-O* reference," Aaron said cheekily.

Kreed pushed away from the doorframe and lifted a fist for a quick knuckle bump as Aaron came closer. "Go make me proud."

"Yes, Daddy," Aaron said, the corners of his mouth curling into a smirk. He lifted his fist, bumping Kreed's knuckles as he slid by. Brown barked out a laugh in his ear. *Great.*

"I'm not that old. You're not funny. And shut the fuck up, Brown. You got 'em laughing at the bureau, Stuart," Kreed said, trailing behind as they walked toward the front door. "I'll be listening in the other room. And Connors says you got this."

Aaron got to the entryway and stopped. He took a deep breath and dropped his chin on his chest. As much as Kreed wanted to hover, he gave the kid room. This was a big boy move, one that took some cojones to pull off.

"You got this," he whispered.

"If I fuck this up, I'm sorry," Aaron said, still looking down.

"Well, don't do that either," Kreed teased. He reached up and shoved Aaron between the shoulder blades toward the front door.

"Go get 'em." That was about all the encouragement Kreed had to offer as he metaphorically pushed Aaron out of the nest. He'd been Sally Sunshine for as long as he could. Now Aaron just needed to get his ass over there. Kreed stepped around the entry wall, back into the main part of the house and waited. When he didn't hear the front door open, he peeked around the corner. Aaron stood close to the door but hadn't opened it. Kreed moved back, hiding behind the wall and called out, "Gotta get started in order to fail…"

Several seconds passed again and Kreed came back around the corner. Aaron still hadn't moved. "What's wrong?"

"Dude, chill, you're pushing too much," Aaron shot back. Kreed figured it was an attempt to divert, to keep Aaron from walking out the door by starting a fight.

"Connors says to buck the fuck up and get out the door. And you know, I kinda gotta agree. Reset the alarm." Kreed ducked back out of the way, and even then, Aaron still didn't move right away. Kreed dropped his forehead on the wall and closed his eyes. Everything hinged on Aaron and he was having cold feet. His head shot up when the door opened and the alarm beeped. *Hallelujah!* The code was reset and the front door shut with a hard slam. Kreed looked around the corner knowing there was a fifty-fifty chance Aaron hadn't actually left. When he saw he was gone, Kreed pumped his fist in the air, celebrating his victory before he quickly spun on his feet.

"He's gone," Kreed said out loud, heading toward the surveillance room.

"I'm concerned," Connors answered in his ear.

"Nah, he's got this," Kreed replied, not exactly certain of that, but it was the best they had right now. He went for the study window, lifting the blind a hair to see Aaron walking up the front walkway to the church. He took a seat behind the monitor, checking everything from his end.

"He's in," Connors said.

"I see that, Poindexter," Kreed said, and Brown's soft chuckle came through. Kreed moved to the monitor, the feed coming from the front of Aaron's shirt. Like he'd done several times already, he reached for his weapon and palmed the pistol, checking the barrel. His bad feeling was escalating and they were officially game on now.

Chapter 14

Aaron's heart pounded so hard he thought it might beat right out of his chest as he pulled the front doors of the church offices open. He barely felt the soothing heated air of the lobby entrance greeting him, mainly because he hadn't even registered it was cold outside. He'd been too nervous as he walked across the street to think of anything other than how many different ways he could fuck up this whole operation.

Taking a deep breath, Aaron stepped inside the large white marble entrance hall and saw a single desk sitting to the side about midway across the room. He started for the receptionist, taking in all of his surroundings as he made his way across the marble floor. A large mural ran the length of one wall. His eyes followed the painting up to the intricately etched carvings on the ceiling and over the columns and arches. He kept his eyes up, feigning interest as he looked over the entire length of the church foyer while trying to calm the pounding of his heart.

Honestly, it wasn't like he didn't sneak around all of the time, because he did. He was also very used to hiding. So that couldn't be the reason for all this anxiety coursing through him. So what the hell... *I mean heck...* Was the problem? He waited for the lightning bolt to strike for his bad-word slip in a so-called place of worship. Luckily, it never did.

"Can I help you?" an older woman with a deep Southern accent asked.

"I'm here—" His voice broke while saying those two words. He stopped talking, cleared his throat, and after a second, he tried again. "It's so cold. I wish I had my inhaler."

Okay, where had that come from? Way to improvise, asshole. Inhaler? Really? Way too stereotypical. Exactly what Kreed warned him not to do.

The woman smiled at him and lifted a finger while she answered the phone. To the direct right of the desk stood a white marble statue, and Aaron moved to the side, getting closer to read the name on the bottom. Pastor Gerald Albert Helps. Aaron's eyes shot up to look at the guy's face. A laugh bubbled up, and he had to fight the urge to let it out. Surely if they were going to pay homage to the founder of this extreme right-winged fundamentalist Baptist Church, they would do it with him looking a bit younger, because the guy's image carved into this statue looked eighty-five years old if he were a day. Oh, man, that was funny. He hoped Kreed was getting a good look at this.

"I'm sorry, son. How can I help you?"

"I'm here for an interview for the IT position," Aaron answered, schooling his features before turning back to face the woman.

"Hmm. They didn't tell me they had any interviews today. Who are you interviewin' with?" she asked. Her voice never changed, just very sweet and very Southern.

"His name was hard to pronounce," Aaron said, hedging on that one. Who knew if Thomas Hasselbeck went by Tom or Thomas or if the information in his notes were even correct?

"Well, he's not here this week. That's the problem. I don't know why he would've scheduled an interview when he knew he was on vacation. He took Christmas break off after the big celebration. You should have been here. Were you here?" she asked with a dreamy expression plastered on her face.

"No, ma'am," he said, shaking his head. "I stayed with my church family back home for Christmas. Let me check my email to make sure I got the date right." Aaron reached for his phone in the front pocket of his slacks.

"Let me call our pastor's office. They'll know what to do." She dialed and spoke to someone on the other end as he slid his finger across the screen. He worked quickly, giving the proper command to launch the shutdown.

"Pastor Helps's secretary is on her way over. We only have one person here in the IT department, and he's not in a position of authority, but we regularly can't seem to find him anyway. She'll be right with you, though," the receptionist explained. Aaron glanced over to see her smiling sweetly before looking down at her computer. He'd been dismissed as she went back to typing away. Aaron took a step or two back and waited. One thing he noticed as being a little weird—the front lobby was void of crosses or any real references to or artifacts about a place of worship. The sound of high-heeled shoes clicking on the marble floor grew louder, drawing his attention to the back of the room. Right before the person came into view around the corner, the receptionist gave a very frustrated, "Pooh!"

Aaron stood there a little shocked. This place just got weirder and weirder. The woman came around the corner, wearing a tight-fitting leopard print dress. She had long, bleached blond hair and wore a pair of black patent leather stripper shoes. Her stride reminded him of a model on the catwalk with over-exaggerated steps as she moved forward.

"What's wrong, Stella?" the woman said as she stopped by the desk first.

"I was just finishing the list of new email addresses and the system kicked me out. Now I can't log back in."

So it begins…

Aaron looked down, studying the pattern in the polished marble, kicking at the floor with the tip of his shoe. That had worked faster than he'd even hoped for.

"You know what to do. Restart your computer. It should be fine." The woman dismissed Stella's concerns and turned toward him. "Hi, I'm Julie, Pastor Helps's assistant." She came around the desk, her bright red lips lifting into a giant smile, which, technically, was the only similarity between Julie and Stella.

"Hi, I'm Josiah Smith," Aaron said, taking her hand, giving her that delicate handhold he'd been taught at a very young age to give women. The one that every female he knew absolutely hated receiving in today's business world. Julie didn't seem to mind at all. Her smile even got a little brighter. "I have an interview with Mr. Hasselbeck. I checked my email while I was waiting and he told me to come today. Maybe he's coming in?" Aaron offered, thinking that might be about the worst thing that could happen at this point.

"Why don't you come back with me while we sort this out? I know they're shorthanded in that department. He's always looking for someone. I can give him a call," Julie said, turning to walk back toward the hall she'd come from. "Come this way, and, Stella, let me know if it gives you any more trouble."

Aaron followed a few steps behind, trying to casually turn this way or that, hoping he looked interested in the artwork along the way. Many of the office doors along the hall were closed, but Aaron tried to capture the name-plates as he walked by, in case Connors needed that bit of information. The corridor was long, and from what he could see, only a few people were working. He heard several exasperated sighs as they passed by open doors. The triggers must be working, systematically logging them off.

"Julie, are you having problems getting on?" a man behind a desk asked as they passed by his office.

"I wasn't. No," she said loudly and never stopped her pace. "You can see why Thomas may have scheduled this during his downtime. We aren't very computer literate around here. He's always got his hands full with us." She opened the door to the pastor's suite of offices and extended a hand. He did what every well-mannered man should do, he reached back to take the door, letting her walk in first. She seemed to like that move. Her smile lit up her face as she moved forward. "Thank you!"

"Julie, I can't get on." An older gruff voice came from an office just to the side of her desk. He hoped he'd turned enough and stayed in a decent position to give Kreed and Connors a good layout of this area. He pivoted slowly, seeing two offices and an exit door, the window of which showed it led out to the street they were staying on. He turned his body slowly to make sure they got that shot.

"Have a seat right here. I need to go help him." Julie pointed to a chair at the end of her desk.

"Pastor Helps, there must have been a hiccup in the system. Restart it like Thomas says to do," she explained as she disappeared inside the office where a disgusted grumbling could be heard.

"I don't know why we need these things. They never work right." That sounded like his very own grandfather talking. The generational gap was alive and present in this place, for sure.

"Give it time to reboot and I'll be back. I have to call Thomas anyway." Julie came out of the office a little frazzled, rolling her eyes dramatically, but her smile was still bright.

"Let me get him on the phone. What was your name again?" she asked, taking her seat while picking up her phone. She didn't wait for his answer as she began dialing. The high of moments ago began to fade. Aaron hadn't anticipated the Hasselbeck guy might live close enough to just come on over. He had to remind himself that even if the guy did show up, all that meant was he was back to his original game plan. It would still take a while to figure out what was going on. Aaron was the only one who knew how to quickly override and restore the system. Still, even with that knowledge, he found himself mentally crossing his fingers, hoping Thomas didn't answer.

"Hello, Thomas, it's Julie. I have a couple of things to talk with you about. Call me when you get a minute," she said, that bright smile faltering as she stared at her own monitor. "I got voice mail." She placed the phone back in the cradle as three things happened simultaneously. First, the pastor barked he couldn't log on and he had a deadline to meet. He needed to email Deacon Silas Burns. Aaron prayed the bureau caught that little jewel of information. Second, Julie's phone lines began to light up, and third, the main office door opened.

"The whole place's down, and I can't find Jeb," someone said.

Aaron supposed Jeb was the IT guy they'd mentioned earlier. Aaron weighed his best options. He wasn't supposed to act overeager, so was now a good time to offer his help? Hell, he didn't know. On instinct alone, he finally said out loud, "I could take a look. I have my master's in information technology from New Hope University in Oklahoma."

"I don't know if that's a good idea or not. Let me talk to Thomas first," Julie said, biting her lip as she reached below her desk. Aaron supposed her CPU was there.

"He's taking his grandkids to Oklahoma for the New Year," the guy sticking his head in the door said. Aaron looked back to see several others standing behind him. Probably the entire skeleton crew.

"New Hope in Oklahoma is my alma mater. It might help me get the job if I can fix this problem," Aaron suggested, sliding a hopeful look at Julie.

Aaron fought the shiver skating up his spine as he turned to see Pastor Helps leaving his office and walking toward Julie's desk. Aaron had to school his features as the creepy factor in the room quickly escalated. The guy looked a million times older than the statue outside. The vibe rolling off him wasn't good at all. He couldn't quite put his finger on what caused it, but he knew his blood pressure spiked right then. It took everything for him to stay put and not move away. Aaron looked around to see if any of the others experienced those same sensations and no one seemed to notice, which was odd for how strongly he was picking up the bad juju standing next to him. Aaron narrowed his eyes and looked back at the pastor.

"Let him look at it. I've gotta get this out soon," Pastor Helps snapped.

"Can you call instead of email? You can use my phone," Julie offered. She was clearly the most sensible of the bunch. As much as he wanted this to play out the right way, it was never wise to let anyone off the street in their systems. *Just look at what I'm planning to do if you need proof.*

"You know I can't use your phone for this! Let him try. Can you fix it, son?" A hand clamped down on his shoulder, and the shiver he could no longer hold off rolled down his spine.

"Maybe God had this young man coming in when he did because of the evil in this world always fallin' down upon us, Julie," Stella, the receptionist, piped in from near the doorway.

"Amen, sister Stella," came from someone behind him.

"Can I use your computer, Julie? I need the most up-to-date one you have," Aaron said carefully, wondering if anyone in the room would know how ridiculous that sounded, but he figured the pastor probably had the most updated equipment out of anyone here, just based on his position, and it would kill two birds with one stone if he could get inside that office.

"That would be Pastor Helps. Do you mind, sir?" Julie asked, clearly caving under the pressure.

"Of course not, if you'll get it working," he said, shuffling aside to let Aaron up. Okay, this was working out better than planned. He couldn't believe it. A large part of him had been prepared to walk inside the church offices and be immediately denied, turned away before he got his foot in the door. Instead, this played out in the best-case scenario. Thankfully, the timing helped. Pastor Helps was on a deadline.

Aaron followed the slow moving pastor into his office. Once behind the door, he resisted the urge to do a thumbs up in front of the cross pin clasped to his shirt. He was just so excited to be getting this far inside already.

"What do you need from me?" Pastor Helps growled, drawing him from his thoughts.

"Nothing, sir. Let me just take a look." The pastor stood between him and the computer. When he didn't move, Aaron lifted a hand toward the CPU.

"How long's this gonna take?" Could he use any other tone than that snarled-sounding timbre? Did he preach sermons with that voice?

"There's no way to know until I can sit down and see what's going on, sir." Aaron started forward, scooting around the pastor. He wouldn't let the old man get cold feet now. He needed in their system. That was the only reason he continued talking. "If it's a standard system restore, it won't take thirty minutes."

"Well, don't touch anything on my desk."

Aaron nodded and kept his face passive. The guy sounded more like an extremely old, grumpy grandfather than a motivating godly pastor of such a massive complex.

Aaron sat in the large leather chair and turned toward the monitor. He could see the pastor standing behind him through the darkened screen. Who knew if he planned to move or stand there watching him the whole time, which meant he'd have to hide the paths he took. Centering into himself, Aaron took a deep breath and began. He worked for several minutes before Pastor Helps moved from behind him to a seat at a small table nearby.

"What're you finding?" Even though the sudden noise startled him, the evangelist's voice might not have been so cold and annoying that time.

"It looks like a virus was downloaded, probably in an attachment somewhere. The staff needs to be more careful of things like this. People are too evil in today's world," Aaron said, watching the pastor in the reflective screen.

"I swear computers make the world a worse place. Can you tell who downloaded a virus? We don't allow random searching on the internet. It goes against our doctrine. There's nothing but the homosexual lifestyle of soul-damning, nation-destroying filth out there on the internet," Pastor Helps barked.

"Yes, they do, sir. And yes, I can see if it's traceable." Aaron picked up his pace. He was currently working on creating a virtual tunnel. He kept his eyes down at the keyboard as he registered the webcam's little flicker from the corner of his eye. It would be the only time that happened, but provided the verification he needed that he'd done this right. The screen went dark then wild numbers and letters flashed for a moment before going dark again. Accomplishment washed over him. He'd gotten in.

"Where do you call home?" Pastor Helps asked. Aaron was almost done. He rebooted the system and waited.

"Kansas, sir." Between Kansas, Oklahoma, and Texas, he wasn't sure there was much more of a Bible-beltish area. He hoped that gave him street cred in the religious community.

"I spent some time there. What church were you raised in?" The pastor seemed talkie now which made him a little nervous. He had hoped he could bullshit his way through any conversation thrown his way. The anxiety made his palms sweat, and he brushed his hands down his trousers at the same time the monitor lit up, drawing his attention to the screen. He was surprised they didn't have password protection on this machine. That was a pretty standard requirement in today's world. Actually, that made no sense.

"My parents are fundamentalist, sir. They felt most of the churches in our area didn't teach the true lessons of the Bible. So a few of the families in our area who shared the same belief started a small church in the Topeka area. I went to Oklahoma to finish school. I was hoping I could come up here and fellowship with your branch. They just don't have the fellowship in Oklahoma like you have here." Aaron hoped that lie came off as sincere.

"Hmm," Pastor Helps grunted. "We have parishioners who travel several hundred miles to attend church every Sunday."

"That's how I heard about your church. I'm looking forward to hearing the teachings from the word of God at the worship service this Sunday." Aaron had no idea what that meant compared to what Pastor Helps said, but it was part of the pre-rehearsed call-notes Director Skinner sent over. "My parents homeschooled me and my brothers and sisters, and we had strict Bible study every day. I do miss being able to share the scripture with those around me."

He'd been told over and over that less was more, but he couldn't stop his brain from thinking of his socialite mother, who always had a cocktail in her hand, trying to homeschool any of his brothers or sisters. The thought was almost as comical as the act. She would have called in one of the many household staff to deal with such a trivial task.

"That story sounds very much like many of my flock. Redemption Apostle got its start in much the same way your parents' church did. The lack of preachers to be dutiful watchmen and preach God's judgment is exactly why the world is in such a state of decay today. We have to diligently spread the word. It is up to us to be God's watchmen. Too many men claim to teach the wrath of God, but they are nothing more than false prophets spreading fables—the very reason we're opening congregations in a few other states. It's a slow process. But the children of God need to be vigilant and spread the word. The absolute judgment of God awaits those who fail to repent. I respect your parents' dedication to the Bible and the Lord's teachings," Pastor Helps responded.

"Yes, sir. Thank you, sir." Aaron nodded, not prepared to say anything more. He had no experience with a church like this one. The few times he'd been inside a church in his adult life, he'd felt a sense of love there. This place—and most especially this man—radiated a disturbing creepiness. Aaron tested a few things before he pushed back in the chair. "I think we're good. I should probably check the computers of everyone working today, but it looks like you're back online."

"Well, that didn't take all that long at all." Pastor Helps stood pretty fast for an old man who shuffled when he walked.

"No, sir, it was easy to find. Do you want to make sure you can send your message?" Aaron asked, hoping he could get a visual on the email the man needed to send in all haste.

"I need privacy. Why don't you go check Julie's computer. I'll call you if I have a problem." Pastor Helps quickly pushed behind his desk to sit in the chair Aaron had just vacated, almost running Aaron over in the process.

"Yes, sir." Aaron left the office a little slowly, unsure how to do anything more to stay without coming off as too pushy. Connors would just have to do the rest on his end.

He headed toward Julie's desk as the pastor called out, "Give him a job, Julie."

"Good job! I'm back up, too." She had her hand raised for Aaron to give her a high five.

"I should check your computer. I found a virus known to have crawlers." Same words used on a *CSI* episode he and his buddies made fun of all of the time.

"I wish Thomas would call back in," she said reluctantly, rising from her chair for Aaron.

"Was the pastor serious about hiring me?" Aaron asked, not responding to her statement. Julie rose, and he took her seat and began working quickly on her machine.

"Oh, absolutely, Pastor Helps isn't a big fan of computers. He wouldn't have been happy if no one could get this fixed today." Aaron listened and decided Julie would be his biggest concern. She seemed the most reasonable of them all. When it came time to verify with the quick flash of the webcam, he let out a series of coughs.

"My throat's dry. Must be the cold air," Aaron said, looking over apologetically.

"I'll get you a water bottle." The second she turned away, he hit enter and watched as he got the confirmation he needed to indicate that the bureau had access.

"Here you go." Julie handed him the water as he stood, angling the chair for her to sit.

"I'm glad I checked. It was in your system too. Probably everyone's. I should look," Aaron offered.

"Oh, praise be to Jesus. Josiah, you're a dream. I believe God sent you to us today." Julie swiveled toward him in the chair and looked up at him. Aaron smiled and took a drink from the bottle of water. He'd done what he set out to do. Julie stood abruptly and patted his shoulder. "Come on. I'll show you the way around and get you some paperwork. You should be paid for today. I don't know how much, that's between you and Thomas, but I'll get your new hire paperwork added."

He couldn't help the fist pump he gave and Julie laughed at his excitement.

"Welcome to our family."

Chapter 15

Holding a hand to his ear, Kreed pressed the earbud in to make sure he captured every word Aaron said. Kreed bent forward, watching the screen as Aaron expertly navigated his way through the various offices of the church, creating an opening for the FBI. In a few short hours, Aaron managed to give them visual as well as audio and access to all of the internal workings of the church's administrative headquarters. As he focused on Aaron and his safety, Kreed also had Connors and his team talking in his ear. He heard several 'fuck yeahs' and 'the guy's brilliant' each time Aaron accomplished something new. Without question, Kreed tended to agree, but the darkness he detected while listening to the pastor speak freaked him the fuck out. Something wasn't lying right in Kreed's gut regarding that old man.

Kreed's internal instincts had him tense and reactive. For what, he didn't know, but he'd armed himself as if he were going on a raid and stayed poised to do whatever it took to get to Aaron. The doorbell chimed. Kreed jerked his head in that direction, quickly tugging the earbud free to remove Connors's nonstop voice from his ear. He stared at the wall separating him from the kitchen that led to the entry, like the walls would magically open to show him the answer of who rang the bell.

Seconds passed before he heard some noise in the general vicinity of the front door. He hated moving from the computer screen, but he did, staying along the walls, quietly walking through the house to carefully lift a front window blind, seeing a man carrying a box toward the front door. A moving van was parked at the curb. Kreed relaxed. That was most likely Aaron's delivery.

Kreed swiftly went back to the monitor to see Aaron exiting the building. The relief of him leaving the church drained some of the tension from Kreed's body. He moved back to the window, lifted the edge of a blind, and watched Aaron keep his head down and begin to jog his way across the street toward the house.

He'd managed to get his work done and stay in one piece. *Good job*! Kreed headed back to the entryway as he listened to metal clink against metal as the key unlocked the door. The cold wind swept through the house as he caught the sound of shuffling boxes. Kreed stayed right around the corner of the door, letting Aaron handle the boxes until he heard the door close. He eased around the wall, meeting Aaron, who had a bright smile plastered across his handsome face. The nervousness and anxiety of the last few hours immediately faded away. Aaron was excited and coming straight toward him.

"It was a piece of cake," he said, beaming. He lifted a hand, and Kreed obliged, raising his for a celebratory high five. "What a serious rush."

"You did really well. We got good visual and everything you gave us is working spot-on. Connors is astonished, which is kind of a little weird, but they're already at work, digging in. He's like a kid in a candy store." Kreed trailed behind Aaron as he moved to the kitchen, reaching for a glass then filling it with water from the refrigerator.

"They just bought it. There wasn't any question. That old man needed his shit done and he didn't care how I did it. It probably helped I look like this, but, man, that's cool as shit. I really thought they'd send me packing when I walked in there." Kreed watched as Aaron took a long drink. He was so unguarded right now—animated and excited, clearly very proud of himself. Kreed finally caved and smiled at Aaron's reactions. He propped a shoulder against the small wall that separated the kitchen from the living room. He'd process all that anxiety he'd experienced later. Aaron needed this moment. He'd done better than even he expected.

Aaron's legs were moving before he even finished off the water. He tossed the plastic glass in the sink then turned to pace the room. His smile continued to grow as he came to stand right in front of Kreed. "It's a serious rush."

"I know." Kreed nodded, not able to hide his own growing grin as he crossed his arms over his chest. He wanted so badly to pull Aaron into his arms and just hold him and share in his excitement. Aaron's smile did something magical to his face and made Kreed's knees weak. He couldn't explain the feelings coursing through his body at the moment. They were new and foreign, and frankly, they scared the shit out of him, especially with how worried sick he'd been just a few minutes ago over the guy's safety.

"I get why you do this job. Is it always like this?" Aaron asked, standing an arm's length away, his knee bouncing with excitement.

"Not all the time, but enough," Kreed answered. Aaron nodded.

"I was actually disappointed when they said for me to start on the second. I wanna get in there and get that place wired up. That old pastor's a creep, man. He's like the crypt keeper. Did you see that statue of him? Who does that?" Aaron asked, his eyes going to the weapon on Kreed's hip. "Why are you wearing that?"

Kreed looked down at the holster. That wasn't the only firearm he wore. This being out in the open, on the hip, attested to the serious bad vibes he'd picked up, even as early as seeing that statue in the lobby. Kreed looked back at Aaron and decided to wait to give his honest answer. He didn't want to bust the bubble the kid was riding on.

"I told you I always wear a weapon," he said casually.

"I've never seen it before," Aaron replied and took a step backward, surveying Kreed. He watched as that handsome brow furrowed. Obviously Aaron had checked him out enough to know that he hadn't been wearing his weapon all the time. That thought made Kreed's heart do a little dip.

"That's because we've never needed me to have easy access. If you'd have gotten into a bad spot, you wouldn't want to wait for me to arm up, now would you?" He was still propped with his shoulder against the wall, his thick arms crossed over his chest. Aaron came forward and poked at his chest, then placed both hands on his pecs. A few days ago, he would have loved that move. Today, however, the concern of keeping Stuart safe outweighed everything.

"It's a bulletproof vest." Aaron's confused gaze lifted to his.

"Part of the uniform. You have to know that," Kreed said, mockingly. "If I'm going in, that means shit got bad."

"I guess so." Aaron studied him for a minute more before he turned, leaving the kitchen. "Is Connors still on?"

Kreed turned, watching him walk away until he disappeared inside the study. His grin spread and he looked down at his crossed arms. The kid messed with him. Not five minutes ago he was strumming with pent up energy, now he was smiling. Aaron was giving him mixed signals. One minute he was looking at him like he wanted to eat him, then in less than a second flat, he was back to brooding, keeping him at arm's length. Kreed rolled his eyes at his thoughts and pushed off the wall. He was almost willing to admit he had a crush on Aaron Stuart, and for some reason, that managed to make everything a little bit better. Or did it?

He was a thirty-eight-year-old man crushing on a kid. He regularly ignored the needling fact that Aaron wasn't a child any more than Kreed was an old man. Aaron was twenty-nine, almost thirty.

Kreed thought about last night. God, he only wished he could be certain of what he'd heard coming from the master bedroom. With as fucked up as he'd been over the kid, trying to read all those mixed signals, he could have used the confirmation. But in the end, he hadn't asked. That would have been a dick move at this point in the game, because if, for some wild reason, Aaron was experiencing all this overwhelming attraction, too, then Kreed would be obligated to pull himself from this case. Even now he saw how erratic his thought processes were over the kid—imagine if he knew for sure that Aaron shared the same feelings.

So, that little possible jack-off session that may or may not have ended with his name being said would have to be tucked away for later.

"Sinacola, they need you," Aaron called out. He didn't say anything, just went toward the room, wiping the smile from his face before he entered. He'd keep that revelation to himself. He didn't need to consider that or the absurdity of this situation. He'd give them tonight, let Aaron have his job-well-done moment before Kreed explored what truly happened when he'd laid eyes on that pastor today.

Chapter 16

"We can only go over there for a few hours," Kreed called from the bathroom in the hall. "We need to head back here early."

"Is that because you're getting old, Sinacola, and need to go to bed early?" Aaron asked, coming to stand in the open doorway while Kreed finished shaving in front of the mirror. By now, Aaron should have been prepared for the no-shirt policy. Though that always seemed to be the first thing to go where Kreed was concerned, it still threw him off balance when he walked in to see Kreed's bare chest. He didn't know if it was the broad shoulders, the beautiful ink, or that tight six-pack that robbed him of his thoughts each and every time he came across the unexpected treat, but whatever the case, he was left momentarily speechless.

"It's because you're the church kid. If anyone's watching, they need to see you comin' in early," Kreed said, turning on the warm water. He let it run for several seconds while he grabbed a towel off the counter. The deputy marshal was too tempting to watch, so Aaron tried to avert his eyes, but the tightening in his jeans made him aware it was already too late. Kreed was tough to be around dressed from head to toe, but standing there without his shirt and those well-worn jeans riding way down low on his hips... *Damn.* Yeah, he was too fucking much.

Aaron shoved away from the door, leaving Kreed there to finish up, and went back to his room. For the first time in more years than he could count, he didn't want to sit down at that computer. Actually, he'd barely accomplished more than unboxing his CPU and one monitor. He'd checked in with his team then turned the thing off. He never did things like that.

Not only that but he had been eager to go to Colt and Jace's tonight. Even though they were twenty-four hours out from his first FBI sanctioned undercover adventure, he'd still been riding the high from yesterday, and Kreed had graciously let him. The guy stayed close by and attentive, listening to him turn into Connors as he analyzed everything that had gone down over and over again. Technically, that had been a turn-on too. When did anyone on the planet really give a shit about what he had to say?

Then this morning, it had all started again when he woke to find the bureau's latest remarkable accomplishment. They'd gained access to Helps's private email and were in the process of dissecting mounds of information.

More so, he wasn't worried about or tired of his roommate. Funny, he'd spent all evening then all day with Kreed. They'd talked endlessly. Well, he'd talked as he watched Kreed absently flip a knife in his hand for hours at a time. Kreed's tricks with that blade impressed the hell out of Aaron. The man didn't even flinch when he misjudged a move and nicked himself.

The whole scene was hot as hell. The ease with which he took the pain when he missed on a flip mirrored the strength and determination in everything the man did. When he allowed Aaron to fuss over and take care of the wound when Kreed wouldn't... Well, for the first time since they'd met in person, Aaron felt weirdly satisfied, as though their time together transcended everything.

"I thought you were ready?" Kreed asked from his doorway, tugging a long-sleeve knit shirt over his head. Like most things Kreed wore, it fit like a glove, which was another obstacle for his dick to overcome.

"I am."

"So am I."

"You riding in the back?" Aaron kept his eyes averted. He found that to be one of the only effective ways he could find to deal with the constant threat of an impending hard-on, and honestly, that didn't seem to be helping that much anymore. Aaron grabbed his wallet, tucking it in the back pocket of his jeans before adding his phone to the other side. Kreed disappeared from the doorway, and Aaron followed, turning off the light as he went. Kreed met him in the hallway.

"Yeah. About that. It's the part I hate the most," Kreed said before skirting past him.

"Okay. Do you ride like that the whole way there?" Aaron asked, following Kreed, undecided on where to cast his gaze.

At his hot ass? Nope. How about the freakishly large, broad shoulders… Makes you want to grab on as you sink onto his dick and… Okay, bad idea too. Neither.

Instead, he stopped at the hall closet and grabbed his and Kreed's coats in hopes of giving his mind time to control his libido. What the hell was wrong with him? They were in a dangerous situation. He needed to stay focused on their job then get out of Dodge before anyone caught on to his extracurricular activities.

"I'll check for a tail then I'll move up to the front," he said, doing something in the kitchen.

"Should I lay the rear seats down? I'm not sure you'll fit in the backseat."

"Har, har. Very funny. Get in the vehicle. Wait, are you old enough to drive?"

Okay, well, he'd been serious and Kreed took his words as a joke. Aaron held out Kreed's coat, and he took it as he walked past, flipping off the light switches before heading toward the garage door.

"Real funny, pops," Aaron finally commented. He waited in the dark while Kreed stretched across the entire length of the backseat and, as expected, Kreed's height and bulk didn't fit. Aaron adjusted the rearview mirror and moved the seat up a little before he looked back and said, "I can still see you."

The whole car moved as Kreed readjusted from his side to lying on his back. "Is that better?"

"Now your knees are bent. I told you we should lay the seats down. You'll fit better."

"No. How's this?" Kreed completely ignored him and Aaron rolled his eyes.

He looked in the rearview mirror and didn't see any stray body parts, so he looked over his shoulder. Kreed's angle was all wrong. No way he wouldn't get a cramp in either his neck or leg in that position.

"You can't be comfortable," Aaron finally said.

"I'm good. Get goin'." Aaron sat forward, furrowing his brow. Kreed couldn't be even a little bit comfortable. Damn, the deputy marshal was stubborn.

"All right. Suit yourself." Aaron shrugged and pressed the garage door opener, then he started the SUV and began backing out.

"Shit," Kreed called out, and Aaron slammed on the brakes right in the middle of the alleyway.

"What?" he snapped. With the sudden stop, he heard Kreed shift, but it was too dark to see a thing going on in the backseat.

"I can't see if anyone's tailing us."

"I'll watch for it, but seriously, stop yelling out like that. You freaked me out." Aaron took a deep breath to settle his nerves and continued down the alley to get to the street. A few minutes later, he felt Kreed shift again. He was such a big guy that the vehicle couldn't help but move with him.

"All right, I'm good. I can see a patch out the back window reasonably well. You keep an eye on it too."

"Which way? I can't really remember the different turns. I see the CVS. We turn left, I think, right?" Aaron asked, getting in the left lane.

"Yeah, then right at that burger-slash-Mexican-food place."

"Yeah, okay, and, for the record, the town doesn't look any more inviting than it did when we arrived," Aaron said. It was New Year's Eve. There were more people on the road tonight, but still there was nothing really going on in this small town at all.

"I was reading that they were putting a new bar right next to the nursing home. I got a kick out of that. I bet Pastor Helps is dyin' about that one. Hang on. GPS is tracking." Kreed turned up the volume on his phone, guiding Aaron out to the highway.

~~~

Tired of being cramped up in the backseat, Kreed adjusted his body, trying for anything that bought comfort. Nothing did. Estimating based on time more than scenery, he figured they were about halfway to Colt's place.

Kreed lifted his head again, looking out the back window. It was hard to tell, but surely between the both of them, even with the limited visual he had, they could have detected someone following, especially since the sexy Aaron Stuart in that black leather button-down and the perfectly styled fuck-boy haircut drove like a grandma. The thirty minute drive had already taken at least forty-five. Anyone who followed would have lost interest by now, easily believing this church boy was exactly who he claimed to be. No rebellious sinner would drive ten miles below the speed limit for the entire length of a trip.

Kreed rolled his neck as an unexpected charley horse chose that exact moment to attack his right calf muscle. He kicked his leg out, unintentionally banging his foot against the door, trying to alleviate the sudden agonizing constriction that had momentarily gripped his leg. It didn't work. "Motherfucker!"

"What?" Aaron shouted almost as loud as he had. The car quickly jerked to the left, jostling him as his hands automatically went to the debilitating spasm in hopes of finding some relief. He was at such an angle that he fell backward against the seat when the car shifted, causing the pain to spike straight to level ten status. He grabbed his leg, trying to massage the knotting muscle. "Damn it! What the fuck are you doing?"

When he registered they'd pulled over, he bailed out the door, forcing himself to walk the cramp out while on the side of the road. He let the curse words fly as he shifted his body weight, and forced his heel to the pavement. That shit hurt like a son of a bitch. He could take anything—a punch, broken bones, a blade, a fucking bullet and even torture when necessary—but he couldn't deal with a fucking charley horse for Christ sake. Even at BUD/S, his SEAL training course, he'd been baited about his inability to withstand a 'little' muscle cramp.

"Fuck that and fuck them!" he growled out into the universe. There was no *little* to it. The agony in his leg had just started to ease when he noticed Aaron.

"Why are you out of the car?" Kreed barked. He didn't mean to take his discomfort out on the kid, but fuck, that pain had hit so unexpectedly. As the intensity ebbed, Kreed relaxed a little

"Why are you freaking out and blowing our cover?" Aaron yelled back, now all up in his face.

Could the kid not see the pain he'd endured? For the first time since dumping himself from the vehicle, Kreed registered the cars zooming past. They were on the Dallas North Tollway during a holiday party night, with heavy traffic and cars flying past them at high rates of speed. He was pretty certain even a tail would have had to pass them with how fast traffic was moving. On the tip of his tongue was a quick retort about the kid's driving skill and the obvious fact they should have been there by now, whereby he wouldn't have been cramped up in the back for so long, but a loud honk drowned out his answer.

"Get in the car," Kreed finally commanded. They both headed toward the driver's side. "Hell no, Romeo, I'm driving." Kreed kept moving forward, ignoring Aaron's glare as he rolled his neck and shoulders, not wanting a repeat cramp anywhere else. Kreed was behind the wheel, sealed in, before Aaron even rounded the trunk.

Based on the slamming of the door, Aaron was a little peeved. "What happened to you?"

"You drive like my grandma," Kreed huffed, putting the car in gear.

"So you scream and throw a fit in the backseat?" Aaron asked incredulously.

"What? No! I fuckin' had a cramp," he said, turning on his blinker. He checked his mirror for a safe entry point and picked up speed as he eased into traffic.

"I told you to lower the damn seat." Aaron sat back, tucking his arms over his chest. He was definitely an add-insult-to-injury kind of guy.

"Yeah, and I thought you were fucking with me," he said, still irritated as hell. They were silent several long minutes, so long that Kreed was taking his exit before rational thought filtered back inside his brain. It took two more streetlights and a turn into Colt and Jace's neighborhood before he finally said, "I'm sorry. I'm frustrated with me, not you. I didn't mean to yell at you back there."

"Whatever," Aaron said, staring out the passenger side window.

Great. The cool, irritable prick was back. Damn. He'd liked the peace they'd finally created between them. After another turn of the vehicle, Kreed decided to try again. He had to make this better. He'd gained too much ground with the kid to lose it because of a stupid, fucking cramp that hurt like a motherfucker.

"I shouldn't've gone off like that and I should've listened to you. I was wrong," Kreed admitted, taking a turn onto Colt's street. Aaron stayed quiet, his head turned away, and he didn't acknowledge Kreed in any way. The only thing Kreed got from church boy was a deep sigh. *Damn it!* He'd royally fucked up, but in his defense, he'd been in massive pain at the time. Still, that was no excuse. Right?

Kreed lifted his brow at his internal question. With the degree of agony he'd endured, surely Aaron could find it in his heart to forgive his little outburst.

The sheer volume of vehicles parked one behind the other all the way down the road drew Kreed's attention. It looked like several parties were going on. They drove past Colt's house, with an already-packed driveway, going several houses down before he found a place to park. Kreed pulled over, made sure he wasn't blocking any driveways, and placed the gearshift in park.

"I'll be more careful in the future," he said into the quiet car. Aaron opened the door, got out, and slammed it in his wake. Kreed sighed loudly in the now-empty vehicle then reached for his door handle. Aaron was at least a car's length away by the time Kreed stepped out, shut the door, and hit the lock button. He trailed behind, watching Aaron cut across a lawn toward Colt's house. He could stop him, ask him what the hell he was doing walking away like that in the middle of an active investigation, but he didn't. Instead he felt like a heel for how he'd so completely upset Aaron. He needed to log in his memory how easy it was to hurt the guy's feelings.

Kreed took the steps up to the front porch and joined Aaron, who already stood close to the door. Kreed tucked his fingers in his pockets as Aaron reached for the doorbell. "Don't let me ruin your night."

"Dude, seriously, let it go," Aaron said, but he wouldn't look in Kreed's direction. The front door swung open and Mitch stood there with a huge grin spreading across his face. "Do y'all buy your T-shirts at the same damn store?" Aaron quipped. Mitch was in his usual attire, blue jeans and a T-shirt, but this one read "Ass, The Other Vagina."

"What? This is my special party all night shirt. Get in here, man!" Mitch moved back, barely allowing them inside before he stuck out his hand to Aaron then pulled him into a solid, brotherly hug. "You're a badass, my man."

Kreed watched the tension in Aaron's face fade away as he settled into the hug and gave Mitch one back. Cody was close by, holding two beers, one a Coors Light and the other a Bud Light. Probably one for Mitch. He placed both on the entryway table and shook Aaron's hand as Mitch turned his attention to Kreed.

"You clean up pretty well for a thug," Mitch said teasingly.

"Yeah, I figured I'd be pretty for you tonight," he said jokingly. He'd actually done a little more than that. He'd taken time dressing for tonight's party, styled his thick dark hair, and strapped on every bit of jewelry he owned, which consisted of a few leather straps and a necklace with his brother's dog tags.

"Hey, Kreed," Cody said, his voice slightly slurred. Kreed smiled as he realized Cody must have been drinking for a while now. He was usually very reserved and kept what he considered a respectable distance from his partner. Mitch was the one to always push Cody's space boundaries, but not tonight. He'd sidled up next to Mitch, wrapping an arm around his waist, and worked his big body under Mitch's arm. His partner didn't seem to have much of a problem with Cody being right there next to him. Mitch liked it so much that he lifted Cody's chin and gave him a kiss. Kreed stood near Aaron, both of them smiling while the kiss continued and turned into a full blown make-out session right at the front door.

"Do they do that all the time?" Aaron asked when Kreed just chuckled. He knew Mitch wasn't drinking tonight, not really anyway. He was on high alert, convinced—at least in theory—that they were now the perfect target for the hate crimes. But clearly, since backup had arrived, a drunk Cody was worth exploring, and he wouldn't be surprised if Mitch disappeared for the next hour or so. Lucky guy.

"Probably. It is Knox after all." Kreed turned Aaron by the shoulders away from the potential porn show going on with his partner. There were probably fifteen to twenty people in the living room. If Kreed remembered correctly, the party was an annual event for the coaches and staff at Jace's gym. A quick scan of the guests showed there was a pretty even mix of gay and straight, couples and non-couples. "Want a drink?"

"Is that okay?" Aaron asked, making the same general visual sweep around the room that he'd just made.

"Sure. I can get you home if you wanna drink." Kreed stopped speaking right before he added his next thought. Aaron was back to maybe being semi-friendly again, and he didn't need to freak him by saying how much he liked drunk guys.

"Hey!" Colt called out after spotting them from across the room. He left the conversation he was having with a group of people and headed their way. When he was beside them, he said, "Mitch said he thought that was you two at the door."

"Yeah, Cody side-tracked him," Kreed said, hooking a thumb toward the stairs and glancing in that direction. The couple had just made it to the top and was disappearing down the hall.

"I know I was that sickeningly in love, but hell, they can't keep their hands off each other," Colt said. Kreed knew firsthand the shit Mitch put Colt through when he'd fallen for Jace. This had to be heaven for Colt, finally able to give some shit back.

"You couldn't get all handsy with me because both your arms were in casts, as well as your legs," Jace said, coming up behind Colt.

"I made up for lost time," Colt shot back defensively, drawing Jace close.

"Invite our company in and take their jackets. What can I get you to drink?" Jace asked, reaching for Aaron's coat then handing it to Colt.

"I'll have a beer," Kreed said, shrugging out of his coat and handing it over to Colt.

"Any special kind? We have just about everything," Colt added.

"Heineken?" Kreed asked and Jace gave a firm nod.

"And you, Aaron? We have a full bar." Jace pointed to the kitchen where food filled the center island. Kreed looked down to see Aaron's face light up like a Christmas tree.

"He hasn't eaten," Kreed said.

"I'll come with you," Aaron offered to Jace.

"Well, come on. We have more than can be eaten."

Kreed watched as Aaron trailed away.

"Come on in. Let me introduce you to everyone," Colt said.

Colt held true to his word. He took Kreed around to what had to be every single person at the party. At some point, a cold beer was placed in his hands and an unknown amount of time later Mitch came back downstairs. Cody made an appearance about fifteen minutes after that. Still a little drunk, he was grinning from ear to ear, and had that freshly showered scent going on.

Kreed watched as his always-smooth partner kept it light and friendly with the people at the party, while still tracking Cody's every move, making sure he had everything he needed. Colt and Mitch had that in common—flawless attention toward their partner. Luckily they pulled it off without being smothering. Watching Mitch Knox as a man in love intrigued him.

"You with him?"

Kreed looked down to see a kid standing beside him. Okay, maybe not a kid, but the guy looked young and short. Maybe five-six…or five-seven on a good day. The best he remembered from his whirlwind round of introductions earlier, this guy was a coach in Jace's gym, but Kreed had no idea of his name.

"Who?" Kreed asked.

"If you have to ask, probably not then. Is he single?"

Kreed followed the guy's sight-line as he looked into the kitchen where Aaron had pretty much hovered since their arrival.

"No," Kreed answered automatically, probably a little more forcefully than he should have. He'd been holding that same bottle of beer since he'd arrived, and the irritation of the question had him discarding the bottle on the shelving unit behind him as he tucked his fingers inside his jeans pocket to keep from wrapping them around this guy's throat.

"Is he straight?" The guy's eyes were fixed on Aaron and oblivious to Kreed's reaction. Either that or he didn't care. Surely this coach had to know Kreed could squash him like the bug he was turning out to be.

"Why?" Kreed answered in a low, menacing voice. Finally, the guy took his eyes off Aaron and looked up at Kreed. He was older than Kreed had initially thought. He had crow's feet around his ugly, little beady eyes. So he was clearly a pervert going after younger men. Kreed didn't let the hypocrisy of that statement penetrate his façade, but the jealousy sure did. He didn't give a shit that they were both probably about the same age.

"Hey, no offense. It's why I asked." The coach lifted two hands. The universal sign of no hard feelings, but Kreed didn't feel like accepting that truce as he scowled. "Okkaayyy."

"Hey, everyone! It's on!" Colt had a massive television brought into the middle of the family room in honor of an ESPN special on Jace's cheer gym. This was the first night the special would air, and since just about everyone in the place worked for Jace, the entire room gathered around the screen. Colt stood right up front, remote in hand, raising the volume as he dimmed the lights with another remote.

Mitch came to stand close to Kreed. Cody hadn't slowed in his beer consumption and was hanging out closer to Aaron, who by Kreed's best estimation had just started on his third plate of food. Aaron seemed to be having a good time on the other side of the room, which was technically as far as he could get from Kreed. Smart boy was animated and friendly, surrounded by people closer to his own age, probably the same reason Cody gravitated that direction.

Kreed purposefully kept his distance, wanting Aaron to maintain the happy place he'd developed. A happy that he'd only seen over the last twenty-four hours until he'd blown it with the leg cramp.

"You're quiet," Mitch said softly. They were supposed to be absorbed in the television special. Actually, Jace and his team didn't seem to care so much, but Colt was riveted to the screen.

"I'm good. I get it more now," Kreed answered quietly, staring at the television.

"Get what?" Mitch asked.

"What happened to you," Kreed explained, nodding toward Colt and Jace. He still hadn't made eye contact with Knox.

"Huh. I've been thinking about that. I came to the conclusion it's probably more the whole thing. Them, the case, the hate following so closely. It's kind of life-altering," Mitch replied honestly. Kreed finally looked over at his partner who was focused solely on Cody. Kreed didn't respond.

Mitch lifted his beer to his lips, taking a long drink before a sour look crossed his face. "Ugh. I don't know why I did that. I hate hot beer."

"Yeah, me too," Kreed said, tilting his head to indicate his discarded bottle. It wasn't more than a third gone over the last couple of hours.

"Aaron seems in a better mood."

"He's been pretty up since he did so well yesterday," Kreed answered. His gaze ventured to Aaron before moving back to the television. He'd probably unconsciously sought out Aaron about twenty times over the last thirty minutes. He could tell himself he was only watching his partner's back, but truthfully, that wasn't the only reason he kept an eye on Aaron. Not that he'd admit that to anyone…ever.

"You two getting along?" Mitch asked.

"Sure," Kreed said, a bit guarded.

"It doesn't seem like it," Mitch retorted, now staring at Kreed.

"We're trying. Takes time." Kreed shrugged.

"What're you gonna do when they reassign me?"

Fuck.

He so didn't want to have this conversation right now. In fact, he didn't want to have it at all—ever.

"I'm not thinking about that right now," Kreed answered honestly. Damn, he wished he had a cold beer in his hand.

"It won't be my choice," Mitch said, a darkness underlying his tone. That was something Kreed could relate to. He was happy with his life just the way it had been before all the shit hit the fan.

"I know," he finally added. They were silent for several long minutes. For the first time since he'd entered this house, his focus wasn't on Aaron. Mitch had finally made a real reference to the huge elephant sitting between them. He couldn't have asked for a better partner than Mitch. Honestly, Kreed wasn't entirely certain he wanted to continue with the marshal service without Mitch there by his side, and that just pissed him off that much more. Maybe it was time to reevaluate his life plan. Kreed stared absently at the screen, wishing he could think of any way to stop the inevitability of losing Mitch as a partner.

"Hey, Michaels, how come all those kids jump when Montgomery just looks their way?" Mitch called out in his standard way of diverting attention to escape the heavy conversation they were having.

"I know, right? My baby's a scary guy at work," Colt answered, pride in those words.

"Yeah, right," Jace started, his tone showing his discomfort with that statement.

"No, he is!" It was the girl sitting on a barstool next to Aaron who spoke, drawing all the attention her way. If he remembered correctly, her name was Haley. She was Jace's number two at the gym. "You should see him. He's like this force that no one wants to mess with. He stands there with his arms crossed over his chest and his legs apart and he never smiles."

Haley jumped down and assumed the position, making fun of Jace. She had everyone in the room laughing at the disgruntled look on her face. "Yeah, just like that." She pointed to Jace, who was standing exactly like she'd said, glaring back at her now. "He gets that look, and it just freaks everyone out. No one wants to disappoint him."

"You don't seem to mind," Jace shot back at Haley.

"That's because you love me." She batted her eyes and hopped back on the stool.

"She's right, though. He's like two different guys. Watch this." Colt replayed a specific part where a team was on the mat during a performance, to the right and left of the floor there were darkened figures jumping up and down, cheering the team on. Right in the middle was a man standing there, not moving an inch, even with all that chaos going on around him. "That's Jace. He's the guy in the middle. That's my cheer man. While everyone's jumping all over the place, excited at how well this team did, he's studying them, going over each step in his mind. This team just won Worlds and he never cracked a smile," Colt explained.

"You're making me sound terrible."

"I'm making you sound sexy," Colt countered, sliding both arms around Jace's waist.

"I have seven hundred kids in my care who are tossing themselves or each other through the air. They must be disciplined and have respect for what they're doing. I've never had one serious injury…"

"See how sexy he is? And don't respond to that, Knox," Colt said, causing everyone, including him and Jace, to laugh. Kreed did chuckle. They were fun together, and Mitch clearly felt at home here, but his entire focus remained on Aaron and the young woman sitting close by his side.

It sucked to admit they were pretty together. They had about the same coloring, both dark-headed and tanned, but she accomplished something that Kreed hadn't been able to do. She put Aaron at immediate ease and made him truly smile. Oh man, he wished the kid looked at him like that.

God, Aaron had him all kinds of screwed up.

Kreed lifted a hand to his face, his palm covering his lips as he stood there and watched Aaron interact with Haley. He was confused, uncertain about everything as he watched the two of them together. The kid inclined his head as he listened intently to whatever she had to say. After a few minutes, Aaron's laughter filled the room and Kreed's stomach dropped when Aaron placed his hand on her arm.

Now he was back to contemplating Aaron's sexuality. Maybe he'd only imagined hearing his name in the bedroom that night.

Fingers snapped in front of his face, snagging his attention. He looked over to see Mitch glaring at him. "I'm worried about whatever's going on with you two."

"What're you talking about?" Kreed asked, trying to deflect.

"I thought we agreed, no playing with our partners. It'll fuck you up in the field," Mitch cautioned.

"Who? Stuart? I'm not fucking him." There was no lie there. He absolutely, with deep regret, wasn't fucking the kid.

"But you want to," Mitch countered, stating the obvious.

"Doesn't matter. Look at him. He's not a bit interested in me," Kreed argued defensively. Mitch did look over at Aaron before turning back to Kreed.

"Are you serious?" Mitch's tone seemed a little angry now.

"Is who serious?" Cody asked. He'd come out of nowhere to stand by Mitch's side. Cody draped his arm loosely over Mitch's shoulders.

"He's into you. You're all he looks at and this shit needs to stop. You got my whole life riding in your hands," Mitch lectured, wrapping an arm around Cody's waist as the man swayed a little on his feet.

"Who? Aaron?" Cody asked, trying to follow along. As confused as Kreed was by Mitch's statement, he smiled at Cody's attempt to catch up. His buzzed brain no doubt made things harder. Kreed didn't imagine Cody let loose too often, proving he must feel comfortable here.

"Yeah, you see it too, don't you?" Mitch asked in a softer tone while helping to keep Cody on his feet.

"You don't see it?" Cody asked Kreed.

"No, not at all," he answered honestly. Actually, he was certain they were way off base.

"She's a lesbian," Cody blurted out. The word lesbian came out a little butchered, but he got what Cody was trying to tell him. Huh, that had never occurred to him. He looked up to see her and Aaron laughing again. She didn't give off the lesbian vibe, and he immediately chastised himself at how stupid it was to even think something that stereotypical in the first place.

Could Mitch and Cody know something he didn't?

If so, this piece of information was a complete game changer.

"Stop trying to hide it, ass. He's into you and you're into him, but you need to wait, Sinacola. This case's too important to me, and I've got enough to worry about without adding that to the mix," Mitch said, pulling Cody tighter to his side. Mitch barely paused to give Kreed the evil eye before his face softened as he looked over at Cody. "Are you still my sexy drunk fiancé?"

Cody nodded and leaned closer as he attempted to whisper to Mitch in an octave slightly lower than his normal speaking voice. "Come outside with me. The countdown's startin' soon. Kiss me under the stars." The sweet, somewhat slurred declaration had Kreed smiling as he looked down, wishing he could give them some privacy, but he was trapped between the shelving unit and Mitch.

"Come on." Mitch took Cody's hand, but looked back over at Kreed. There was meaning in that stare, so Kreed did what he did best. He lifted his middle finger and flipped Knox off.

"Worry about yourself. I got me handled."

"Yeah, I'm sure you think you do," Mitch said, turning away. Kreed was back to standing alone. His arms were crossed over his chest and he purposely kept his head lowered just enough that he could watch Aaron without anyone noticing. He'd never once caught Aaron looking his way, and he'd done more than his fair share of hoping. Mitch would definitely be the one to mess with him, give him shit, and laugh when he crashed and burned with Aaron. Mitch always joked around, but tonight his tone held warning, not encouragement. Kreed could understand that given the circumstances, but he wouldn't put them in danger…any of them.

Feeling very much like a teenager, Kreed couldn't help but glance in Aaron's direction every chance he got. The kid was beautiful. Of course, Aaron would probably argue that a man couldn't be beautiful. Kreed smiled to himself, because he knew Aaron would be wrong. Everything about the guy was beautiful— his lips, his skin, the gentle curve of his jaw, the way his eyes lit up when he smiled.

Man, he was so dumb. Why the fuck was he sneaking peeks like a teenager in a classroom? Kreed lifted his head and blatantly stared in Aaron's direction, startled when their gazes collided. Curiosity flashed across Aaron's face seconds before he dropped eye contact and looked down at his shoes. Kreed watched as Aaron's head lifted and those piercing blue eyes shifted back toward him again.

"Twelve. Eleven. Ten."

Somewhere in the back of his mind he registered the countdown beginning. With his heart pounding wildly in his chest, he watched as Aaron diverted his gaze for a second time, but this time, didn't look back.

They'd been playing this dumb cat-and-mouse game for the last week. It was too much. Fuck the consequences. He wanted Aaron Stuart. Hell, he couldn't even think straight anymore, because every single thought he had was centered on that man who was back to pretending to ignore him.

"Nine. Eight. Seven."

The voices rang out in unison. Kreed pushed away from the wall and stalked across the room. He had a single-minded purpose, barely noticing all the happy couples waiting for the stroke of midnight as he passed them by.

"Six. Five. Four."

Aaron held a plate in one hand and a drink in the other. The guy sat on the barstool, his head turned, facing the television as he chomped on a piece of ice. Kreed kept going. Within a foot of his target, Kreed reached for the plate, startling Aaron, who looked at him but didn't move. He dropped it on the counter behind Aaron as he threaded his fingers through Aaron's hair.

"Three. Two. One. Happy New Year!"

Loud cheers erupted throughout the house. Out of the corner of his eye he caught the fireworks on the TV in the distance. The symbolism wasn't lost on him. He had a feeling those fireworks were about to explode inside his own head. Kreed didn't give caution to anyone around him, his only focus was on Aaron.

He pulled Aaron's head back and stared deeply into his startled eyes. Kreed knew the exact moment when surprise shifted to hunger, and Kreed descended, crushing his mouth to Aaron's. The big bang came seconds later when Aaron's cup slipped to the floor, his lips parted, and he slid his tongue forward. The ice cube Aaron had been chewing melted quickly as their tongues met and tangled. The sensation of Aaron's cold tongue exploring his heated mouth sent a wave of excitement through Kreed as he deepened the kiss.

Chapter 17

The whoops and hollers registered once he came up for air. His mouth moved from Kreed's lips, along that prominent jaw, to his neck. God, Kreed smelled so good. Aaron was on his feet, not exactly sure how that had happened. But he'd never forget the look in Kreed's eyes as those strong fingers had gripped his hair the moment before Kreed's full lips pressed against his. The kiss had been so unexpected, searing and intense. Aaron hadn't had time to do anything but accept it. Welcome it.

Kreed's lips were possessive and demanding, everything he'd dreamed they'd be and so much more. Aaron didn't know if he should move or remain in place. He pressed his mouth to Kreed's neck, giving him another kiss while inhaling his intoxicatingly spicy scent before pulling back. Or at least he tried. Kreed had wrapped around him so completely Aaron could do little more than hold on. Kreed had him trapped in place, pressing him backward over the counter as his tongue slid around the shell of his ear.

"Don't stop, church boy. I like your mouth on me," Kreed whispered in the ear he'd just licked, his hot breath cooling rapidly against Aaron's wet skin. A shiver slid down his spine and landed in his balls. His cock jumped at Kreed's words, eager for him to keep doing just as Kreed insisted. Aaron had no intention of stopping. He could explore Kreed and sample his skin forever. His hips rolled forward, grinding firmly into Kreed, who was hard and ready. The growl Kreed let loose was wicked and full of tempting promises, much like the man in his arms. From the small taste he'd gotten, he knew precisely why Kreed's nickname was Sin.

Jesus, why had he denied himself this? *What a fool.*

"Get a room. Midnight kisses ended like…fifteen minutes ago." That was Colt's voice and Aaron didn't give a fuck where they were, he never wanted this to end, but Kreed went rigid in his arms. No, not in the way he would have liked, but instead the deputy marshal stopped the exploration of lips on his neck and loosened his hold, pulling Aaron to an upright position. Kreed hadn't backed away when he withdrew from the kiss. His handsome face remained close to Aaron's, not even an inch of space separated them as Kreed's eyes searched his. Aaron felt desire pouring off Kreed, and this time, he didn't shy away. He took in the need swirling in Kreed's eyes and allowed the emotion to burrow deep inside his heart. In this minute, with that kiss… Yeah, this was a game changer—one he didn't want to fight. Aaron lifted his hand, running his palm over Kreed's cheek, caressing across those full, soft lips with his thumb.

"We should go," Kreed said quietly, still staring at him. Oh hell yeah, they should go. As far as he was concerned, they were wasting time. He nodded his agreement. It had been so long since he'd had sex. As Aaron moved his hands toward Kreed's waist, his fingers lightly skimmed that hard, well-defined stomach he'd seen earlier that day. Yeah, they absolutely needed to go—maybe as far as the closest hotel room.

Kreed finally turned his head, breaking that mesmerizing bond, though his body was still pressed tightly against Aaron's, keeping him in place. The entire party became unusually quiet. Aaron moved his head to the side, angling to look around Kreed.

Maybe he'd acted a little overeager. Every eye in the place was locked on them. His grip on Kreed's waist tightened as he fought the incredible desire coursing through his veins.

Haley was still near him. He'd liked her so much and she was smiling at him. Heat creeped up his face, but he shouldn't feel embarrassed. She'd been encouraging this very thing for about the last hour and a half.

"I need to talk to him in private before we leave. Do you have an office, something like that?" Kreed asked. Aaron didn't know if

Kreed's question was directed at either Colt or Jace, because they were both standing side by side nearby. Aaron felt Mitch standing close by as well, but he couldn't quite make eye contact with him yet. He was pretty sure Mitch wouldn't be too happy about him playing tonsil hockey with his partner.

"You guys can stay the night. We have room," Jace offered.

"No. We need to go. I just need to talk to him first," Kreed said. He stepped back this time, and Aaron felt an instant loss as the deputy marshal released him. Then Kreed made everything right by taking his hand and threading their fingers together.

"My office is to the right when you walk in the front door. Come on. I'll show you." Jace led the way while Kreed pulled him along. That was fine by him, because he would gladly follow Deputy US Marshal Kreed Sinacola anywhere he wanted. Every bit of desire and craving he'd tried to deny over the last week of living with this man, had hit him like a freight train with that game-changing kiss. He hadn't been prepared for the emotional assault that accompanied just a few swipes of Kreed Sinacola's tongue.

Jace turned on the light and moved aside. Kreed tugged Aaron inside, shut the door, and had him pinned against the wall in less than a second. This time he was ready, opening for Kreed before their mouths even collided. This kiss conveyed every bit of yearning he'd felt since the second he'd spotted Kreed across the airport's baggage claim.

He laved Kreed's mouth, melting against him while his hands roamed freely over every single inch of that irresistible body. Aaron dropped his hands lower, cupping Kreed's ass before moving around to grip that hard cock confined in those tight-fitting jeans. Kreed's chest rumbled on a low growl as he urgently responded by grinding against Aaron's palm. Tearing free of Kreed's insistent mouth, Aaron's breaths came in small bursts as he spoke. "Let's go back to our place."

Kreed had him panting, his heart hammered in his chest. Aaron wanted this. He wanted Kreed. Fuck the consequences. The guy had him so primed, and Kreed's hands never stopped exploring his body. Those fingers toyed with one nipple ring then ghosted firmly over his dick, giving him a small glimpse of how spectacular this night was truly going to be.

Oh yeah, happy fucking New Year!

"Why did I ever say no in the first place? We should've been doing this from the beginning." Aaron made a fist and stroked the length of Kreed's hard cock.

"Aaron, I want you. Lord help me, but I do. We need to wait." Kreed's breath puffed against his ear as he spoke, then he nipped at his lobe. God, it was such a turn-on to be so wanted.

"It's fine. I can wait. We don't have to stay here tonight. It's only like a thirty minute drive." Aaron moved his face back up to kiss Kreed again. This kiss was swift and hot, something to tide him over for the drive home. "It's been a while for me."

Aaron worried his lip, and Kreed gave him a tender smile as he leaned down and kissed Aaron until the lip he'd bit was now in Kreed's mouth. There was no doubt in his mind Kreed would be an attentive lover.

"God, I'm sorry, Aaron." Kreed lifted both his hands to Aaron's cheeks, caging him right there as he continued to speak, his voice low and gravelly. "It's gonna be a little longer. I can't... We can't...until this is done. We'll close this case as quickly as we can, then I'll take you somewhere—just the two of us. I'm gonna take my time with you, smart boy. Explore every last inch of your body until you squirm and beg, then I'm gonna do it again and again." Kreed leaned in, pressing a soft kiss to the corner of Aaron's mouth.

"Oh, fuck yes." Aaron's knees grew weak; he wanted that too. But more than that, he wanted to feel Kreed inside him, thrusting with all that caged strength.

"So I'm your type after all then?" Kreed's voice was low and mesmerizing; the smirk lifting the corner of his mouth, sexy as hell.

"Yes." Aaron nodded as Kreed pressed against him again. Aaron could feel Kreed's hardness pushing against his own, and damn, it felt so good all he could do was pant and say, "So my type."

"I'd hoped so," Kreed replied, rubbing his nose along Aaron's cheek. "You smell incredible, and I fucking want you so damn bad. Have for a while now. But we really have to wait."

"I want you, too." Aaron kissed Kreed again, taking his mouth with such force that he hoped Kreed wouldn't be able to mistake his intentions, confirming that, absolutely, Kreed was his type and Aaron wanted everything the man had to offer.

Kreed held him tightly, their bodies rocking together, kissing him back with as much passion. Their tongues tangled, dancing in unison. Kreed sighed into his mouth and lightened the kiss incrementally. He slowly regained his senses. He tore his mouth free when his brain finally caught up with Kreed's words—words that didn't match the need coursing through every part of his body. "I'm not sure I understand. Are you saying we aren't going home to have sex tonight?"

"Yes, that's what I'm saying. I can't have sex with you. I'm afraid it'll fuck things up. We can't take that chance right now. When this case is over, you can have me any way you want me. I want exactly what you want. I promise," Kreed said, leaning in to inhale his scent.

"Wait. What? You were the one that fucking kissed me," Aaron said a little desperately. Hell, he didn't care who did what at this point as long as Kreed made him come. "You got me all worked up." Lifting his hands, he pushed at Kreed's chest, but the guy didn't budge. "Let me get this straight. You wanna fuck me. I want you to fuck me. And your response to that is to put on the brakes?"

"Nothing's changed. I want you so fucking bad, Aaron, but we can't. It doesn't work. I've seen it over and over. We have too much riding on this case. It'll put everyone in greater danger, and there's already too much of that." Aaron started to move away from this crazy man who'd turned him on, more so than he'd ever been in his life, then ripped it all away, but Kreed caged him in against the wall. "Please, don't be mad."

"I'm not mad. I'm disappointed and confused." He glanced up into Kreed's stormy eyes, his hands fisted in Kreed's shirt, and his dick implored him to change Kreed's mind.

"I am too." Kreed sighed and leaned even farther into his personal space. His proximity, heat, and scent made coherent thought impossible. Aaron put his hands on Kreed's shoulders, resting them there for a moment before taking a deep breath and shoving the man away. Kreed released him and Aaron took several steps back as he pushed his fingers through his hair. He was sure the disheveled mess he'd created was symbolic to the chaos running through his body. Thought, reason, even speech, were almost impossible to coordinate at the moment. Kreed had gotten him so worked up, so ready. Hell, he would have blown him right there, but instead, Kreed had dumped him on his ass. That shit wasn't cool.

Finding a semblance of calm, Aaron reached inside his jeans and adjusted his dick. Stupid traitorous thing wanted Kreed's hand to be doing all the touching and caressing right now. He ignored that and willed himself to settle down. It wasn't going to work, but he had to try. He'd ignited at Kreed's kiss and could only imagine the flames he'd have gone up in if they had done more. Fuck, he wasn't sure he could jack himself enough to make this right.

He sensed Kreed hovering close behind him. He hadn't touched Aaron since he'd released him, but that damn cologne enveloped him like a caress, and he had to take another step away, then another. Aaron didn't think it would work, but he rolled his shoulders and tried to shake off the embrace of that alluring scent. He needed a workout, something to burn this energy off before he did something stupid like beg Kreed to fuck him.

No, he couldn't do that.

"I wish you wouldn't've started this," he said quietly, looking down at his shaking hands. He clenched his fists tight and closed his eyes, working on evening out his breath.

"I don't. You were making me crazy. Now at least I know that when we get the information we need, I'll get more than just a taste." Kreed stood directly behind him again and gentle hands came to his shoulders. Aaron immediately moved out from under the touch, swiveled around, and headed toward the door. He combed his fingers through his hair, hoping to settle the pieces back down. There was no way to get the style back, but at least he could appear to have his shit somewhat together.

With the doorknob in hand, he looked back over his shoulder at Kreed. "We need to leave. It's already past midnight."

"Don't be like that," Kreed said, coming toward him. No way could he have that. Kreed needed to keep his distance at all cost. He extended a hand as he jerked open the door and moved out into the foyer.

"No... Just no." He always wore his feelings in his eyes for anyone keen enough to see; he'd been told that before by a few very observant people. But most people never saw past themselves, otherwise they'd know exactly what he was thinking. Of course Kreed would see. He'd read Aaron like an open book from the very beginning. That was why he'd tried so hard to mask his feelings and hide his true self.

There wasn't much privacy at this point, but Aaron looked around the open space leading inside the living room, all eyes were on him. *Shit*. He turned on his heel and went toward the bathroom off the kitchen. He needed a minute before he got inside the car with that man who still hovered too close. He could feel Kreed behind him. Man, Kreed needed to learn the lessons of personal space.

Whatever, Aaron thought, somewhat defeated. It wouldn't matter if he did know those boundaries. If Kreed was anywhere in the vicinity, he'd sense him, and shit, if that didn't make this whole situation harder.

~~~

Kreed stood by the front door, holding both his and Aaron's jackets, waiting for the kid who was most definitely not a child but acting like one right now, to come out of the bathroom. Mitch was in his face, talking low and quietly, with the rest of the party silently keeping their distance. Somehow he and Aaron had squashed the vibe of the entire gathering. They had become the sore spot, and with the tension floating off him in waves, he got why. They needed to split.

Damn it, he'd managed to kill the fun with one impulsive action. He didn't regret kissing Aaron, not even a little bit, but he should have had enough control to wait. Aaron made him weak. He was more pissed at himself for fucking up the balance that he and Aaron had created, possibly jeopardizing the outcome of this case, than he was at anything else. Well, except Knox, who wouldn't leave him the fuck alone.

"Don't come at me, Knox. Get the fuck out of my face," Kreed said menacingly. He didn't need the *'we-have-a-lot-at-stake'* speech right now. Kreed knew what the fuck he was doing; it was the reason Aaron wasn't bent over the desk in that office right this minute.

Mitch did what he did best. He not only moved, but he also slightly bumped Kreed in the chest when he did. It was classic Mitch. He was diverting attention, giving Kreed something to think about other than Aaron's sweet lips. Knowing what Mitch was doing and responding accordingly didn't seem to go hand in hand at the moment. Kreed lifted his gaze and stared with blazing eyes into Mitch's equally angry glare. Kreed was pissed at Knox for trying to warn him off Aaron. He lifted both palms and pushed at the guy's chest. Mitch barely budged.

"Wait, guys, wait!" Colt yelled out. Out of his peripheral vision Kreed saw Colt bounding over the sofa, running toward them. "Hang on. Not in the house!"

"I've got this, Michaels," Mitch said, his face right in Kreed's.

"Not in the house." The front door opened, and with a surprising amount of strength, Colt bulldozed Mitch from the back, forcing him into Kreed who was driven out the opened front door. Kreed couldn't help but fall when his feet tangled with Mitch's. The fight was gone from his mind as he reached for anything that might soften the blow of his body hitting concrete. Nothing did.

"Colton!" Jace yelled as Kreed tucked his head and landed flat on his back. Mitch followed him down, his friend's weight knocking the wind out of him. As the air left his lungs, Mitch's elbow landed in his gut and his palm slid across his face. Those two moves were done on purpose. They were the moves they used all the time in aggressive arrests. So even though the anger had left Kreed's body during the fall, just for the hell of it, he executed a perfect wedding tackle assault, effectively kneeing Mitch in the balls as he thrust his lower body forward, gripping Mitch's shirt. He tossed Mitch over his body.

Regret flooded him as soon as he heard the sound of planters breaking, but then the thuds of Mitch tumbling down the steps lifted his spirits and soothed the worry. He'd send over replacement planters tomorrow for Jace and Colt's front porch.

"You're a fuckin' douche," Mitch mumbled from the bottom of the steps.

"Yeah, takes one to know one, princess." Okay, that was what eight-year-olds said, but it was the only thing that came to mind in the moment.

"Jace, this would've happened inside our house if I hadn't gotten them out. Don't be mad." He heard Colt explaining from above. His coat was dropped on his body and part of it covered his face.

"Jace, be mad. I'm hurt real bad," Mitch called out. Kreed pushed the jacket away from his face and rolled to his side to see many of the guests standing at the door. The rest were watching from the windows. Aaron fought his way through the crowd and came out on the porch. Kreed stumbled to his feet but looked down to see Mitch rising at a much slower pace, his hand cupping his crotch. It probably wasn't fair; Mitch had been off work for a few months, but whatever… He'd started it.

"I'm sorry." Kreed started toward Colt and Jace, but the sound of metal scraping across concrete followed by a loud thud, drew his attention back to the stairs. Knox had fallen again. He lay sprawled across the ground. From the looks of it, he'd used the rail to help climb the steps and that gave way under his weight. Kreed couldn't help the belly-laugh that burst out. Served the guy right. Kreed's back was sore. Certainly there was some road-rash going on. His clothing was probably ready for the trash bin, but he went down the steps and extended a hand to Knox. It took a second, but his buddy took it and scrambled to his feet.

"Where's Cody?" Mitch asked, looking over his shoulder toward the group.

"If you were in there taking care of him instead of putting your nose in my business, you would know, right?" Kreed said, looking through the crowd at the door, not seeing Cody at all.

"What happened?" Aaron asked, rushing down the steps. "Did you tear up their front porch like that?"

"Knox did," Kreed said.

"Fuck you. Where's Cody?" Mitch asked again.

"He's passed out on the couch. He's been there for a while," Colt answered, lifting his hands as he turned toward the partygoers behind him. "Show's over, folks. Everyone back inside."

Mitch held his back, probably where Colt's shoulder rammed him, and said, "How the hell weren't you a defensive end? You can fuckin' tackle."

"You're paying for all this," Colt responded over his shoulder as he shooed everyone back inside.

"No. Sinacola is," Mitch tossed out toward Kreed as he moved across the front porch, his hand still on his back.

"No, Colton is. Why would you shove them out the door like that? They were talking," Jace said, kicking the broken pots out of the walkway.

"Babe, when chest bumps and hand shoves begin, it's all downhill from there," Colt replied, picking up the handrail and placing it in a corner of the front porch.

"Knox, clean this up in the morning," Kreed called out when Mitch was at the front door.

"Yeah, about that. Fuck you." Mitch never turned back. He just lifted his hand and shot him the finger as he shut the front door behind him.

"Are you okay?" Jace asked, making his way to where Kreed stood in the front yard. Aaron stayed quiet, but remained close by. He held both their jackets in his hand. Like always, Kreed was drawn to him. The moonlight filtered through the clouds, lighting his face just enough so Kreed could see Aaron's eyes were wide with trepidation. Maybe a little shocked in what was going on, but Aaron was still beautifully handsome, more so than maybe ever before.

"I'm fine. I'll get this all replaced. I'm sorry," Kreed apologized.

"No, it's not a problem. I'm just sorry things got out of hand with Colt. I think he misses all that on-field aggression at times. To be honest, we were all so relieved you finally took matters in your own hands," Jace said, giving Kreed that smile that lit up his face. He was almost as handsome as Aaron in that few seconds.

Kreed didn't turn to gauge Aaron's reaction to Jace's words. "We should go."

He stretched a hand out, placing it on Aaron's lower back. He shouldn't touch him in public like this, and he wouldn't continue to. He just needed the contact, even if only for a second. "Thank you for tonight. Good night."

Jace was silent as he walked back up the porch. Even though Colt was right there, Kreed made sure they got inside before he left the yard. This was why he didn't mix business with pleasure. They were in an active case and all these men had to keep them safe were Mitch and him. And now their two protectors had fought like adolescent boys in a schoolyard over some pimple-faced little girl. Except Aaron wasn't a pimple-faced teenage girl. No, he was sexy as hell and exactly what Kreed wanted. They probably wouldn't have come to blows; Mitch was right about some of the things he'd said. But what-the-fuck-ever. Mitch couldn't even follow his own advice when it came to Cody. Why should Kreed start following it now?

"What happened?" Aaron asked as they got closer to the car. He stopped several steps away, and Kreed turned to ask him why. "Don't you have to check it?"

"I can, but it's not necessary. That's the former president's house." He pointed to the house they had parked in front of.

"He's a private citizen now," Aaron said, confused.

"Yeah, but his security's solid," Kreed said, moving closer to the car.

"How do you know?" Aaron asked, remaining a few steps back.

"I can see the checkpoints." Kreed moved back to Aaron's side. He clicked the key fob, unlocking the door. "And they asked me to head it up."

"No way." That seemed to impress Aaron. Out of everything he'd done in his life somehow that one job instantly became the most important because Aaron seemed truly fascinated.

"I'm not a slouch. I'm good at my job," Kreed said, taking Aaron's arm, drawing him closer to the car. He pushed Aaron toward his side as he opened the driver's door, resting his forearms on the top as he waited for Aaron to make his way around the vehicle.

"I know you aren't a slouch. That's obvious. So we can just get in?" Aaron asked, trailing slowly around to his side.

"Yeah, see?" Kreed lowered to his seat and started the engine with Aaron still back a few steps. After a second more, smart boy came forward and climbed inside the rental.

"Okay, so does that rule out his security as possible suspects in the case?" Aaron asked after closing the door.

"Good question. Probably. Who knows? But it makes it harder to act when other eyes are watching." Kreed put his hand on the gearshift, but didn't drop the lever into drive. Instead, he turned toward Aaron and asked, "Are we okay?"

"Yeah. I just needed time. I'm not usually like this," Aaron answered.

"What's that mean?" Besides the few expressions he'd caught on the kid's face, Kreed had a hard time reading Aaron.

"Maybe it's the situation. I don't know."

Great. Non-answers. Fan-fucking-tastic. "What's that mean?" Kreed tried again.

"I was into the kiss," Aaron confessed sweetly, keeping his eyes focused out the front windshield.

"Me too." Kreed reached over and took Aaron by the chin, turning his head until Kreed could look him in the eyes. "I'm honestly into you. I have been since I first saw you back when we were in Kentucky. My interest never faded. You're hot. More so in person, but you're also smart. It's a pretty damn sexy combination to me."

Aaron didn't say anything, but he did smile as he moved out from under Kreed's hold and looked down at his hands.

"It's just like that fight though. In a case like this, we don't need distractions. You're a big ole six foot, gorgeous distraction and I've gotta stay focused. You understand, right?" Kreed reached over again, this time threading his fingers with Aaron's, pulling their joined hands to the center console.

"Yeah," Aaron finally answered, tightening his fingers around Kreed's. "Shouldn't I drive?"

"Probably, but when we get closer, you can duck down. It's dark and after midnight. No one should question or realize it's not you if there's only a single occupant," Kreed said, relieved they'd been able to work this out, because honestly, staying away from Aaron Stuart might be about the hardest thing he'd ever do. Definitely an incentive to get this case wrapped up as quickly and safely as possible. Aaron's safety had never meant more than it did at this moment.

Chapter 18

Not entirely sure if the pull-out sofa could be more uncomfortable, Kreed lay sprawled out, staring up at the ceiling. His arm was tucked behind his head, trying to make the old, flat pillow a little more appealing. He held a blade in his other hand. Sleep wasn't coming easily tonight. Three forty-five in the morning and no amount of sheep had been able to lull him to sleep.

He'd been a jerk tonight, and he was better than how he'd acted. After they'd gotten back to Midlothian, he'd sent Colt and Jace quick messages of apology, and also one to Knox. His phone lit up with several reply messages from Mitch, but he'd never looked at any of them. He knew what Mitch had to say, and more so, he also knew the guy was right, but it didn't change anything. His attraction to Aaron was too strong, and if he were smart, he'd remove himself from this case and get someone else in here that had a clearer perspective.

The problem was, he wasn't a very smart guy—never had been. This case was too personal. Someone new might miss something, and his gut told him they were in the right place to find the answers they'd been looking for.

Besides, he had intimate knowledge of gay bashing and the extent people went to in order to express their hate—a hatred that knew no bounds, especially in the ignorant and biased teachings of extreme religion. It was something a person could never fully comprehend unless they'd lived it. That had to give him an edge in searching out the facts.

Kreed closed his eyes and forced them to remain shut. Images of Aaron's handsome face appeared. He replayed that moment of surprise right before Kreed had first kissed him. Yeah, that was a good moment. He'd never really considered how fluid the two of them truly were. They weren't awkward at all. They'd connected on the first press of the lips then moved as if they'd been together for years. That was hard to find, and Kreed wondered if that would have continued had they been somewhere a little more private.

Fuckin' shit. He'd gone there again. His eyes popped open and a small groan slipped free. His dick tented the blanket. He'd given up an hour ago on trying to get that irritating thing to lie down. A creak drew Kreed's attention to his bedroom door as it opened. The blade in his hand stilled and his grip tightened in preparation for attack until he saw Aaron's head peek around the corner.

"Are you asleep?" Aaron asked. Kreed contemplated not answering. "I see your eyes open." Kreed sighed inwardly as he pushed up slightly on the couch.

"Yeah. It's not a good idea for you to come in here." Aaron didn't pay any attention to him. That was another thing he liked, since he intimidated almost everyone he came in contact with—but not Aaron.

"See? I was lying in bed, thinking about you, and I realized, no matter what we do, this attraction is gonna be a big huge distraction between us now." Aaron pushed his way fully inside the room and Kreed narrowed his eyes. Aaron held something in his hands and his stride was purposeful. "We have a better chance if we give in to it, fuck, and get it out of our system than we do by ignoring it."

Kreed held out his hand to stop Aaron as he lifted the blanket. He watched as Aaron dropped several packets on the desk, probably condoms and perhaps lube.

"Stop, Stuart. It's not gonna work that way with us and you know it. It's not gonna be enough, because once I get a taste of you, I'm not gonna wanna stop." Kreed jerked the covers back and scrambled from the makeshift bed as Aaron quickly pushed his pajama pants down. Kreed froze and almost swallowed his tongue when Aaron's beautiful erect cock sprang free and bounced against the bottom of that firm, tan belly. He let out a defeated groan; the kid was fucking killing him. Him and Aaron? Such a bad idea—a terribly, stupid idea in fact.

"This between us will only complicate things." Kreed gestured between himself and Aaron as he spoke. He needed to walk out of the room right now, needed to leave while he still could. Kreed's legs were rooted in place, and he couldn't move. His heart hammered in his ears, and all of a sudden, he lost all ability to speak. Aaron climbed on the pull-out bed and crawled to the middle on his knees as Kreed stood on the other side of the bed watching, completely dumbfounded. Need flared, and hunger possessed him.

Fuck! His dick began to push its way out of his underwear while questioning why he'd made these stupid rules in the first place.

"You don't know that." Aaron sat up on his knees and gave his erect cock a long, slow tug. *Double fuck!* All Kreed could do was watch, his gaze transfixed. The kid was fucking gorgeous. The light glinted off the silver rings in Aaron's nipples and the straining of his muscles made his tattoos come to life and dance across his skin as he stroked himself. Kreed's mouth watered. He could feel his defenses slipping away with every pass of Aaron's hand. Fuck, the guy was sexy. Kreed reached down to adjust his cock, which was as hard as a fucking chromium rod and demanding him to go to Aaron at once.

Aaron bit his bottom lip and jacked himself a little faster and a lot bolder. "I want to feel you slide inside me."

Aww shit! That was all it took. Kreed stepped forward, never breaking eye contact.

"I'll regret this in the morning," Kreed hissed as he shoved his briefs down his thighs, almost tripping on them before getting them completely off his legs.

"You don't know that either," Aaron repeated, hand still working his dick.

"But I absolutely do," Kreed said, wrapping an arm around Aaron, drawing him up against his body as he leaned in for an intense but swift kiss. Aaron's hands clutched at him, fingers sliding through his hair. He had no doubt this was a bad decision, but he was selfish and foolish and he wanted exactly what Aaron was offering, consequences be damned.

"You're gonna be my demise, church boy." Kreed broke free, resisting even as Aaron tried to pull his head back to his lips. "Not here. This bed's too uncomfortable."

Kreed stepped away, reached for the packets Aaron had tossed on the desk, scooped them up, and turned back to Aaron. "Come on. Your room has a bigger and more comfortable mattress."

Aaron climbed off the bed and shot past him before they hit the doorway.

They made it as far as the hallway when Aaron spun around, took Kreed's face between the palms of his hands and fused their mouths together. Aaron's tongue was down his throat before he could react. Kreed hadn't ever been kissed as passionately as Aaron kissed him. The kiss was aggressive and raw and full of need.

Aaron hoisted himself up Kreed's body, his knees almost buckling when the kid wrapped those long muscular thighs around his waist and began to rock his hips back and forth. Aaron's cock slid up and down his stomach, leaving a wet trail of pre-come along his skin. Kreed turned them and pressed Aaron's back against the wall, holding him in place so he could plunder that seductive mouth. Jesus, he'd never experienced anything as seriously hot as this moment.

Kreed dropped the foil packages in his hand and slid his palms under Aaron's ass, pressing his fingers into the flesh as he squeezed and kneaded the firm globes. God, Aaron had the most magnificent ass. The need to breathe made him tear his mouth away from Aaron's. Demanding fingers tightened in his hair and pulled his head back. Soft lips nibbled along his jaw. Hot breath ghosted across his neck. "Fuck me, Sin."

Kreed's dick jerked at the name as desire spread through his veins.

"Yes." The strangled word escaped Kreed's lips.

~~~

Kreed carried him down the hall to the master bedroom, their mouths fused together in a hungry kiss. Their tongues twisting and tangling, their breath mingling as they swallowed down the other's needy sounds. Aaron couldn't have pressed any harder against this man if he tried. He groaned at the sensation of Kreed's cock sliding up and down his crack with every step, tempting him with each and every stroke. Aaron wanted nothing more in this moment than to feel Kreed's thickness sliding into him inch by inch, stretching him wide and making him burn. He wiggled his hips, increasing the friction on his own leaking cock caught deliciously between their bodies.

"I want you in me now, Sin," he panted. Kreed's breath hitched, and his grip tightened. Aaron smiled at Kreed's reaction. Just knowing he could cause that kind of response with no more than a few words was a heady feeling. He loved the way Kreed's nickname danced in his mouth and rolled so easily off the tip of his tongue.

Sin... Tempting, illicit, seductive. It fit the man so well. From the minute his eyes had locked with Kreed's in the airport, Aaron had known sex with this guy would be like a drug, intense and addicting. He'd be hooked from the first taste. So far he'd been right. He craved Kreed, even though sex with the deputy marshal could lead him down the path to possible ruin. He'd tried to resist, for everyone's sake, but Aaron really couldn't find it in himself to care at the moment.

Kreed held him close as they tumbled down onto the king-size mattress. His back hit the cool material of the sheets, contrasting deliciously with the heated wall of man pressing into his front. Kreed's body lay half on his and half not as they continued to probe each other's mouths with their tongues. Kreed abruptly pulled back from the kiss.

"Fuck! The condoms." Kreed jumped off the bed with a curse, then leaned back over for a peck to the lips. "Hold that thought, church boy. I'll be right back," Kreed said breathlessly, before rushing out of the room.

"What the...?" Aaron's brain played catch-up as he propped up on his elbows to watch the doorway. Damn it, as the man had done at Jace's house, it was full steam ahead one minute and brick wall the next. He was starting to worry Kreed had changed his mind again, but the deputy marshal bounded back into the bedroom, waving condoms and lube in the air before jumping on the bed.

"They were in the hall." Kreed's grin lifted at the corners of his mouth, and his eyes twinkled with wickedness as he dropped the bottle and foil packets on the bed. "Now, where were we?" Kreed crawled on top of him, picking up right where they'd left off. The deputy marshal kissed him deeply, their cock's rubbing and bumping hard, creating the perfect amount of friction as their bodies slid together.

"You were gonna fuck me." Aaron rolled his hips and ground them into Kreed's groin as he slowly licked across Kreed's lips. He slid his hands down Kreed's back and over the taut globes of his ass before gripping them. A low growl rumbled from Kreed's chest. Their mouths fused together, locked in a sizzling kiss. Aaron mapped the muscles of Kreed's body with his hands as they rutted desperately against each other. After several minutes, Kreed broke from the kiss, trailed his lips over Aaron's cheek then nipped at his lobe.

"Gonna take care of you, sweetheart. Give you what you need."

Aaron melted at Kreed's words. He loved Kreed's nicknames for him and that one just might be the most endearing.

"Promises, promises," Aaron managed as Kreed's full weight rocked between his thighs. Aaron groaned and lifted his hips, pushing his groin up against Kreed in an effort to spur him on. He wrapped his legs around Kreed's waist and ground hard as he squeezed his thighs together.

"So demanding." Kreed chuckled and kissed his neck. Hot breath fanned across Aaron's skin as their cocks slid roughly against each other, pre-come wetting the tips. Kreed dragged his tongue along Aaron's collarbone then dipped his dark head to suck a nipple into his mouth to flick the ring with that talented tongue.

Hell fire! Kreed wasn't playing fair. He'd always had sensitive nipples; that's why he'd gotten them pierced, but nothing had ever compared to the friction of Kreed's tongue sending currents of need straight to his already-aching balls.

"Fuck yes. Harder. Bite me." Aaron spread his thighs wider and slid his fingers through Kreed's hair, gripping tightly before urging that mouth against his chest. Kreed licked across his nipple, took the ring between his teeth and tugged before nipping, then blowing a cool breath across his wet, stinging skin.

"More." He was being a needy bitch. He knew it. He usually wasn't so open about what he wanted, but it had been forever since he'd had sex and the stakes felt higher. His need pushed him; he didn't have time to be shy. He wanted to come, so it was all or nothing tonight.

Aaron slid his hand down Kreed's body to wrap it around that hot dick, hoping the touch would move things along. Not surprisingly, Kreed quickly slapped his hand away. The deputy marshal clearly enjoyed torture with all the self-restraint he'd used at keeping them apart to this point.

"Not tonight, church boy. It'll be over before we even start if you do that." Kreed's hand lifted to Aaron's other nipple, toying with the piercing, before sliding down his stomach and wrapping around his dick, stroking him. The deputy's tongue followed the same path his hand had taken. Kreed's lips pressed against his hipbone, nuzzling and nipping. Kreed lay between his legs and used the hand not wrapped around his cock to hold his thigh in place as he nosed the spot between his hipbone and groin.

Aaron lifted his head to watch Kreed stroke him. Desire simmered in his eyes as he licked a path from his hip, down the line of his inner thigh before sucking his balls in that wicked mouth. Kreed mouthed his sac then licked up the underside of his dick. His soft tongue swiped across Aaron's crown right before he swallowed his dick down to the root.

"Oh fuck." Aaron's fingers twisted in Kreed's hair as warm moist heat engulfed him. "God, so fucking good." Aaron's eyes rolled back in his head as he closed them and arched up into that hot wicked suction to fuck Kreed's mouth. Aaron held Kreed's head tightly and pushed his prick to the back of that throat over and over. And holy hell, the sexy man took everything he gave him.

The feeling of Kreed's throat constricting around his dick almost had him blowing. He slowed his thrusts and gave himself over to the feeling of Kreed's mouth on him. His hips rolled and his orgasm built, but then Kreed pulled his mouth away, and with it, that wondrous suction, causing Aaron to let a deep, protesting groan slip free. He moaned at the loss of Kreed's warm mouth and at the cool air on his wet dick. Before Aaron could gather himself enough to figure out what had happened, he heard a lid snap shut then his legs were pushed back and strong fingers found his hole then plunged inside.

"Fuuuck. Yesss!" he hissed and pushed back against the sudden invasion, loving the burn as Kreed urgently worked his ass, stretching him. Aaron gripped the back of his thighs, drawing his legs up higher, holding them open as Kreed scissored his fingers a few more times then added a third.

Chills raced over his heated skin when Kreed's digits curled and brushed across his prostate. Kreed twisted and pumped in and out of his body, fast and hard each and every time. Aaron lowered his feet to the mattress and dug in, fucking himself on Kreed's hand. If something didn't happen, he was going to blow, tumble over the cliff before Kreed ever put his dick inside him.

"Please... Don't wanna come... Need to feel you in..." He couldn't draw the air in his lungs to finish the thought. Not with Kreed's fingers pressing and probing, taking him closer to the edge.

Suddenly, Kreed's pressure disappeared, leaving him empty. Aaron propped up enough to watch as Kreed tore the foil packet and rolled the condom down his thick length. His ass clenched as Kreed drizzled the lube on that covered cock, then tossed the bottle to the side. Aaron reached for the back of his knees and hugged them against his chest, opening himself for Kreed. His body vibrated with anticipation as the blunt head dragged up his crack then pressed at his entrance. He looked up to find Kreed's gaze right on his face. Those dark brown eyes bore into him as the man slid in deep, stretching and filling him, giving him exactly what he needed.

"Ahh, yesss." Aaron's legs shook. The pressure along his passage bordered between pain and pleasure. He loved that initial burn of muscles being forced open.

"You okay?" Kreed stilled, not moving, his voice deep and intimate, concern swimming in his eyes.

"I'm fine." Aaron bit his lip and smiled. He could feel the tension coiling in Kreed's muscles. Whether the tremble was from the strain of holding back or the fear of hurting him, he wasn't sure, but he wanted to reassure Kreed that they were in this together. Aaron released one knee and brought his fingers to Kreed's cheek, stroking gently. "Actually, never better. I want more."

Kreed's face relaxed at his words and the deputy marshal slowly pulled back, his thick cock dragging along Aaron's passage, waking every nerve ending along the way.

"I don't wanna hurt you," Kreed said, then dipped his head and pressed a soft kiss to his lips.

"You won't. Now show me why they call you Sin." The glint in Kreed's eyes showed the challenge had been accepted. Kreed thrust forward—hard—and Aaron dropped his head back to the bed as his eyes slid closed, the sensations consuming him. Bright white spots danced behind his eyes. Kreed's mouth descended on his, kissing him hard and long as he wrapped his legs around the deputy marshal's waist.

Aaron had no choice but to hang on. He dug his fingers into Kreed's shoulders, drawing his nails down Kreed's back, wanting everything Sin could give him. Kreed moaned against his lips then angled his hips just right, hitting against Aaron's gland every single time he drove forward. *Good God in heaven!* Kreed pulled out before slamming back inside, driving him higher and higher, right where he wanted to be.

"Yes, Sin…fuck me." He untangled his legs from around the deputy marshal, and Aaron tilted his hips, taking everything Kreed gave him. Kreed buried his head in his neck and switched things up, fucking him in short, quick jabs, then slow, deep strokes. Sin teased him mercilessly. Aaron clenched the muscles in his ass and pushed against the cock inside him.

"You feel so fucking good wrapped around my dick," Kreed growled against his skin. "I can feel you working me." Hot breaths lingered on his neck, sending chills down his spine.

The sound of Kreed's flesh slapping against his… Loud grunts and soft moans peppered the air. The heady smell of their need, mixed with leather, cinnamon, and wild spices saturated the space surrounding Aaron as Kreed filled him. He was in heaven.

Aaron grabbed Kreed's firm ass and pushed, wanting the man deeper in his body. Kreed rose up on a knee, gripped Aaron's leg at the shin then pushed it back. Kreed's hips never lost rhythm as he pistoned in and out.

Their breaths mingled and their groans filled his ears. Aaron drew his free leg back farther as Kreed settled on both knees…fucking him harder. Kreed's warm palm curled around Aaron's dick as the deputy marshal took him in hand and stroked him roughly.

"Yes… I need…"

Kreed slammed up against his gland one last time, and Aaron lost it, shooting his load all over his chest and Kreed's hand.

"Aaron!" Kreed cried out as his body tensed.

Kreed's dick twitched hard in his ass, drawing one last shudder from his body before Kreed released his shin, carefully pulled out, then collapsed on the mattress next to him. They both lay there, breathing heavily. Kreed's hot hand on his belly, thumb idly stroking his skin.

Who knew how much time passed? Aaron's body was spent and so fucking blissed out. He covered his eyes with his arm and tried to regulate his breathing as he floated in the aftermath of ecstasy. The mattress dipped, and he peeked out from under his arm. Kreed sat on the side of the bed, staring down at him with a huge grin on his face as he tied off the condom and tossed it carelessly to the nightstand.

"That was hot, church boy." Kreed reached out and stroked his face, before leaning down to brush a kiss across his lips.

"I thought so, too," Aaron answered, his voice still a little haggard from all the recent strenuous activity. He managed to smile up at Kreed. "I'm covered in jizz and I can't fucking move."

"Jizz, huh? Can't have that, now, can we?" Kreed winked as he dipped his head and licked the come off Aaron's chin then moved down his chest and stomach, before bringing his hand to his mouth and sucking what remained of Aaron's orgasm from his long fingers. Aaron's dick started to regain consciousness.

"Okay, that had to be the hottest thing I've ever seen," Aaron said and pushed his dick back down.

"Oh, yeah? I love doing it." Kreed chuckled then leaned in and took his mouth in another searing kiss. Aaron opened, and Kreed's tongue slid inside, brushing against his. Kreed took his face between his palms and drew him closer, deepening the kiss. He could still taste his bitter release on Kreed's tongue. This guy was amazing, but now that the orgasm had released some of the tension of the moment, the needling thoughts in the back of his mind kept trying to push to the front and warn him that there was a reason for those cautionary barriers he'd failed to maintain. Kreed Sinacola was still a life-altering complication.

Damn it!

He was screwed. Aaron slid his hands to the back of Kreed's neck then up into his thick, dark hair and kissed Kreed passionately, letting his feelings rather than rational thought take control of his actions.

After a few minutes, the kiss turned into a soft, sweet sampling of lips. Several more minutes passed before Kreed's head lifted and that dark gaze held his. Kreed moved his fingers along Aaron's neck and his thumb stroked back and forth across his jaw, his sinful lips curling into a smile.

"We need to get some rest. I have plans for you tomorrow." Kreed dipped his head and kissed him again. Aaron nodded; he was completely spent and couldn't hold his eyes open any longer. Aaron rolled to his side and smiled when he felt Kreed draw the covers up and over them. Aaron snuggled into his pillow, pressing his ass against Kreed as the deputy marshal curled around him from behind. Kreed pressed his big body tightly against Aaron's back and surrounded him with those strong arms. He felt safe and secure as he listened to the cadence of Kreed's even breaths, and Aaron drifted off to sleep.

Chapter 19

A smile slowly spread along Kreed's lips as his eyes blinked open. Aaron's scent held him in place as he breathed his lover in, only moving to roll his head to the side and glance at the alarm clock on the nightstand in Aaron's bedroom. Happy New Year to him. They'd shared a night to remember. Epic. One for the record books.

Mind-blowing, hard-core, body-bruising sex with a hot, wickedly naughty partner then falling asleep curled tightly around the same guy seemed one of the best possible ways to start this year off right.

Kreed never slept in this late. Not that they hadn't drifted off too much before sunup. So technically, sleeping in till ten was in reality only a few hours' sleep, not necessarily the self-indulgent act it sounded like when you heard words like, "sleeping in till ten o'clock." Last night had been amazing and Kreed could honestly say with his whole heart that he wanted more.

Normally, he didn't do repeat sessions with the guys he fucked either, let alone waking up in the same bed with them. He really liked Aaron—more than liked him—but could he have a relationship with this man? Who knew for sure, because he had no idea how the dynamics of that worked. Relationships had never been in his vocabulary.

Of course, he'd have to factor in Mitch. Yeah, he and Mitch had had a brief fling for a short time, going out, getting drunk, and fucking each other. Not committed by any means and it happened when they were much younger. But nothing compared to this feeling. He'd woken with fucking butterflies in his stomach, for Christ's sake. Yeah, nothing compared remotely to Aaron.

His short-lived time with Mitch had been what they'd both needed at that particular stage in their lives. He and Mitch would have never ended up as a couple. They just didn't fit that way. Most definitely better as brothers-in-arms than lovers. That strong bond was probably the main reason Skinner had enough sense to assign them as permanent partners.

But him and Aaron? Yeah, he could see himself with Aaron Stuart…for the long haul. Kreed shifted his position to get a better look, but with Aaron's body spread across his, he couldn't move much without disturbing him.

Stubborn, smart-mouthed, hard to get along with Aaron Stuart was an extreme snuggler. Who would have known? Actually Aaron was a lot of things that he hadn't appeared to be at first glance. Warm, compassionate, caring… Smart, funny, and a phenomenal lover… Chatty, too. When he'd opened up last night, he'd been animated and talkative. Words like adorable, fun, and caring also seemed to apply.

Aaron knew about world events, cared about the human race more than any other person he'd ever known, and was shockingly a political activist. More surprisingly, they actually agreed on most parts of the political spectrum. Honestly, Aaron hadn't come right out and taken a progressive stand, but his thoughts on moving society forward in a positive, protective way were a part of every unguarded conversation they'd had during the night.

Those open discussions had given Kreed pause, made him look at Aaron in a whole new light. Those were all very attractive qualities to someone like Kreed, who had spent his whole adult life working as a public servant, who believed in protecting society.

Kreed had chosen to ignore the little prickling needles of concern when it came to Aaron. Based on his own jaded past, he knew the lessons of how easily ethical lines could blur while working for the greater good. And whatever Aaron did, he seemed to truly believe in his life's work, focused on making the world a little better. One thing for certain, Aaron hadn't been tainted. Life hadn't beaten the hell out of him yet. He was idealistic and determined, which was incredibly refreshing, and a little arousing. He wasn't sure he knew anyone who still believed they could make a difference, and Aaron had no doubts that he could.

Running a palm lightly across Aaron's bedhead, Kreed decided breakfast would be a necessity after the intensity of last night. He grinned at the thought of the workout they'd had. The kid would no doubt wake up starving this morning. Kreed carefully managed to shift his position and lift his head to stare down at the guy sleeping so soundly on his chest. Aaron looked so much younger than his twenty-nine years. As expected, a small twinge of guilt spiked through Kreed for allowing himself to give in to his desires. He should have been stronger. Business never mixed well with pleasure, and now the stakes were so much higher, if that were even possible.

With the pad of his finger, he brushed over Aaron's lip and a wave of emotion flooded his heart. He had to protect this beautiful man. If Kreed wasn't level-headed and diligent, he could end up getting them both hurt—or even killed—not to mention the other four men he cared about across town. He needed to get his head back in the game. But all he could think of at the moment was how sweet those perfect lips tasted.

Fuck! He laid his head back against the pillow and stared up at the ceiling with a sigh. He was in so deep, and it had happened so quickly.

He needed to stick to his rules. Kreed placed a soft kiss on the top of Aaron's head before carefully untangling himself from the sleeping guy. Aaron stirred and turned to his side, allowing for an easier escape.

Rolling out of bed, Kreed walked quietly across the floor toward the door, his muscles protesting the action. Oh yeah, he would be feeling the little reminders of last night's activities…hopefully for a few days. He smiled to himself as he left the bedroom, softly shutting the door behind him.

Making a pit stop by the hall bathroom, he brushed his teeth and worked at taming the hair sticking up in all directions. He ran a hand over the stubble on his face and decided to leave it, since Aaron had confessed he liked the five-o'clock shadow.

Kreed chose commando as he pulled up his athletic shorts and headed for the kitchen. They'd have to make a store run, meaning Aaron would have to go to the grocery store, but they were good for today. He started the coffee before pulling out the bacon and eggs. Kreed had always liked to cook. He wasn't Chef Ramsey by any stretch of the imagination, but he liked the idea of cooking and trying out new things. That was another thing that made him the yin to Aaron's yang. He could prepare food and Aaron could sure put it away.

Thrown off guard at the random thought, Kreed took a giant mental step backward. His only focus needed to be on the here and now. That was it. What was going on today, that was all he could allow. If the kid was interested, he'd give them the next twenty-hours. He craved a new life, but right now, he had a case to solve and people relying on both of them to execute that with precision.

Since both situations—this case and his personal, fucked-up emotional crossroads that had started even before his brother's death—required his full attention, he had to concentrate on this case first and put the rest on the back burner until they had that wrapped up tightly.

"Hey," Aaron said from behind him. Kreed looked over his shoulder, and all the internal debate he'd suffered through faded. Aaron was there with him, and he looked amazing. Bed-rumpled, sleepy-eyed, hair sticking up in every direction, and deliciously naked, trying in vain to tug on some jeans. He kept missing the opening with his foot, stumbling several times before he managed to get his foot inside the leg hole. There was no underwear, he'd obviously gotten out of bed and come straight to the kitchen, probably absently grabbing at his jeans on the way out of the bedroom. Kreed would have been fine having him remain naked throughout the day. A twinge of disappointment rippled through him when Aaron gave a small jump, pulling his pants up and tucking his package inside.

"Hey. Coffee's ready." Kreed pointed toward the pot. While the bacon sizzled, he went for a bowl to break the eggs. "You hungry?"

"Always," Aaron said, still standing in the middle of the kitchen. Since he couldn't seem to keep his eyes to himself, Kreed turned back and caught a look crossing Aaron's face, some emotion passing quickly over his features. Maybe regret? Uncertainty? That had Kreed's brow furrowing a bit. He wasn't entirely sure what that look meant, but something wasn't right, and he damn sure didn't want to see regret, especially since he was on board with testing the theory of a possible future for them after this case ended. Kreed left the bowl on the counter and walked across the kitchen.

"Good Morning." Kreed pulled Aaron to him.

"Good Morning." The lines on Aaron's face relaxed as he tilted his head and lifted enough to kiss Kreed's lips. He liked that move and countered with one of his own, wrapping both his arms around Aaron, drawing him up tightly against his body. They fit well together, and he lowered his head, adding tongue this time. The kiss was swift, and to his surprise, Aaron broke away first.

"The bacon's burning," Aaron said, pointing toward the stovetop. Kreed hid his smirk. Of course the kid would notice the food, effectively ending the intimate greeting Kreed had tried to give. Another thought occurred, and Kreed darted around a little panicked. He wanted Aaron secure in what they'd shared, but he also needed to stretch out their rations to make the food they had last another day, and burning breakfast, even for a passionate kiss, wouldn't help matters. Luckily, their breakfast wasn't burning, only ready to be turned. "I've got to get online. I have something working that I need to take care of. Is that a problem?"

"Nah, I got this. Go ahead," Kreed said over his shoulder, turning the bacon.

"I'll do the dishes." Aaron was beside him, offering him a cup of coffee.

"I don't mind doing the dishes. I need to wash some clothes today. Anything you need washed, bring it out. I'll get it started." Kreed took the offered coffee and brought it to his lips for a long drink. "Thanks, I needed that."

"No one I know likes cleaning," Aaron replied, resting a hip against the counter close to Kreed as he took a drink from his mug.

Kreed eyed him as he reached over and began breaking the eggs into a bowl. He didn't know what it was about this guy, but damn, the kid just drew Kreed in. Absently tossing an egg shell in the sink, Kreed moved, leaning in to kiss Aaron quickly on the lips.

"I've been on my own for the last twenty years. I don't mind doing this. I like to cook, and that requires cleaning afterward," he said and went back to turning the bacon.

"Yeah, I don't feel that way at all. I'll take you up on the laundry." Aaron left the coffee cup on the counter before leaving him standing there and disappearing from the kitchen. The kid was back by the time the eggs were poured into the skillet with a laundry basket half full of dirty clothes. He'd changed into a loose pair of gray workout shorts.

"Church boys wear lots of clothes," Aaron teased, dropping the basket on the floor over in a corner of the living room.

"Wanna eat in here or do you need to go work?" Kreed asked, pulling two plates down from the cabinet.

"In here's good. I sent a message to my team that I'll be on in about an hour," Aaron said, going for the drawer that held the silverware.

"What team's that?" Kreed asked absently, making two plates of food. Aaron seemed to have a group of people he worked with at the NSA, a group of gamer friends, then another group that...well, Kreed didn't actually understand what they did.

"Just a small group that works together on some things when any of us needs help," Aaron replied, setting the table. Kreed nodded. Made sense. Still incredibly vague. Admittedly, he wasn't a techie by any stretch of the imagination, so he had no frame of reference to decipher what the words actually meant.

"Like what kind of things?" Kreed asked and reached for the coffee pot to refresh their cups.

"Nothing really important. Just stuff." Okay, that was a complete non-answer, and Kreed stopped what he was doing, looked over his shoulder, and waited for an explanation of what '*just stuff*' really entailed. His chatty partner of the last twelve hours had clammed up. Apparently he'd run up against a topic Aaron didn't discuss. After last night, Kreed learned that was a short list. Aaron didn't discuss his family or much about his personal life in general and, now, his online community. Since Kreed had his own list of non-negotiable discussion topics, he let it go.

Kreed refilled their cups then put both plates on the table in their usual spots across from one another. Looking down at the distance between the place settings and still riding high on what had to be some of the best sex he'd ever had and the pleasant mood he still carried from last night, Kreed moved his plate to Aaron's side of the table. He caught the pleasant hint of surprise on Aaron's face as he went to grab the OJ from the refrigerator.

"My original plan was to make you breakfast in bed," Kreed confessed, moving closer to Aaron, running a hand down that still-bare chest, grinning at the blush of embarrassment skating across Aaron's cheeks. "I really enjoyed last night."

"Me too. I'm a light sleeper most of the time," Aaron said. Their food was getting cold, but Kreed enjoyed being in Aaron's personal space, breathing the kid in.

"Not that light of a sleeper," Kreed teased, remembering how deeply Aaron slept while wrapped around his body. He'd never slept so near anyone in his life, and he liked the intimacy and closeness of that act. A blush flamed across Aaron's handsome face at Kreed's words. He grinned again as Aaron ducked away and moved toward his seat.

"Wait. We didn't cover this last night. Do you have somebody at home?" Kreed asked when jealousy spiked through him at the unexpected thought. It made sense to ask. Aaron had slept so hard in his arms, like a man accustomed to being held. *Shit!* How had he never thought to ask that question before now, especially after all the possible relationship planning he'd been doing this morning? Maybe that was why Aaron didn't talk about his personal life.

"No, not at all. Do you?" Aaron asked, infusing those last words with the same defensiveness he suspected had been in his own question.

"No. I'm single." The surge of tense jealousy then overwhelming relief was a heady mixture. Kreed moved to his seat next to Aaron and his cocky grin slid in place. He liked the confirmation of Aaron's possessiveness he'd heard in that tone, because he sure as hell felt it too. "Remember, lived alone for twenty years."

That seemed to settle things. "Good, I don't need anyone that might look like you gunning for me."

That had Kreed barking out a laugh. He grabbed the kid's head, and pulled Aaron in again, kissing his lips as he picked up his fork to eat. The move clearly surprised Aaron as much as it did him, but Kreed let that go. Whatever. This whole deal had amazed him since the very beginning. He promised himself one day with this guy was what he needed to get all this out of his system then it would be back to business as usual until the case ended. It had to be that way. He waited before taking a bite, watching as the napkin went to Aaron's lap. For some reason, he loved the little moves that telegraphed Aaron's exquisite manners. He dropped his napkin to his lap too.

~~~

"You're so fucking sexy with those fuck-me-I'm-so-smart glasses on and that intense look on your face."

Aaron glanced up and narrowed his eyes as he shoved the glasses off to the top of his head and stretched out his back. There was just something about the big, gorgeous deputy marshal growling those words at him that made his dick want to come out and play. A tired yawn from hours of sitting behind his laptop slipped free as he rubbed his eyes.

"And those noises you make are a complete turn-on."

"I have a feeling it doesn't take much to turn you on. A slight gust of wind would probably have you at full mast," Aaron teased, lowering the lid to his laptop. He'd done as much as he could with this computer. He needed to move to the bedroom, work on his system in there, but he liked being in the living room. It was close to everything Kreed had going on today.

From this vantage point, he'd watched Kreed clean the kitchen and put a pot of New Year's good luck black-eyed peas on for dinner—something the guy seemed pretty excited to have found in the cupboard. He now stood across the room at the kitchen table—sexy as hell—folding the laundry that had been spread all across the top. Domesticated. Who knew that'd be so hot to watch? The tension of the case they'd been working was gone, not even hanging over their heads. They were totally comfortable with one another. It was incredibly rare to find this level of ease with anyone, especially this man—a deputy US marshal.

"With you it doesn't take much to get me hot." Kreed's voice was deeper now and Aaron moved the laptop to the coffee table. He couldn't see the front of Kreed's shorts, but since his own dick had taken notice of the deputy marshal's tone, he suspected he'd find Kreed's in the same state of eagerness.

"We could both use some rest." Aaron had decided he should probably play a little harder to get. He figured guys like Kreed had no shortage of ass at their disposal. He saw it all the time. Hot, good-looking guy needs distraction then moves on to the next distraction, over and over again. And to be honest, that was exactly the kind of man Aaron sought out. Relationships were complicated and always ended messily. But with Kreed, his feelings were all over the place. He couldn't get a handle on what he really wanted from Sinacola. Actually, on one hand, he wanted it all. On the other hand, he knew without question they would only have the length of this case to fuck each other raw then they would have to go their separate ways. That thought made him a little sad.

Aaron pushed himself off the sofa, not bothering to adjust the erection tenting the tight cotton sweats he had thrown on. He wanted Kreed to get a good look at the condition he'd been working in. "I'll probably go rest for a little while. You good with that?"

Aaron never looked back as he walked past Kreed. He made it as far as the bedroom door before he heard heavy footsteps following behind him. Aaron lowered his head, smiling to himself. After spending the last few years closed up, dodging relationships, never letting anyone too close, it felt good to be wanted. He always masked his identity and his activities from everyone around him. Surprisingly, being forced into this case hadn't caused his life to fall apart like he'd originally thought it might. Actually, quite the opposite.

Thinking fast, he moved quickly, stepping into the bedroom and pressing himself against the inside wall. Kreed, as usual, had established rules early on last night that today was it as far as them hooking up while on this case. Aaron wasn't certain about those boundaries because they fit too well together; their chemistry was off-the-fucking-charts hot.

As Kreed rounded the corner and stepped through the doorway, Aaron jumped out. He got the surprised response he was hoping for as Kreed wrapped him in his arms, pulling him tightly against his body.

"Are you really going to rest, church boy?" Kreed growled in his ear.

"Not at all. I hoped you'd follow." God, it felt so good to be held in this man's strong arms. He lifted up on his toes, threaded his fingers in Kreed's hair, and drew Kreed's mouth to his for a kiss.

"And why's that?" Kreed asked, the first to pull back from the kiss.

"Because I'm gonna bury myself in your ass, deputy marshal, and fuck the hell out of you," he answered confidently. Kreed's arms tightened, drawing him closer if that were even possible. The deputy marshal's dick twitched against his, making Aaron's smile a little broader. Kreed seemed into the possibilities.

"That's some dirty mouth you've got on you, church boy." Kreed's grin was predatory and somewhat wicked as he ground against Aaron. "And what makes you think I'll give you my ass?"

"Because of all the dirty things I can do with my mouth and…" Aaron used Kreed's words back on him and slid his hand between their bodies, directly into the waistband of Kreed's athletic shorts, then slowly dragged his fingertips over the deputy marshal's wet-tipped cock.

"Mmm…and?" Kreed licked at the seam of Aaron's lips and slid against him.

"And…because you're leaking for me." Aaron pressed his thumb into the moisture collecting on the head of Kreed's cock and spread it across the crown, then gripped the hard length roughly in his palm. Kreed's eyes dilated, and his breathing picked up as he pushed into Aaron's fist.

"Fuck, yes. Anything you want." Kreed reached up and tweaked a nipple ring, sending sparks of electricity down Aaron's spine and firing into his balls. With his free arm, Aaron pulled Kreed's head to his and forced his tongue between Kreed's lips. Kreed's body shook and his fingers moved to Aaron's waist, skimming down to his ass.

"You're so fucking hot." Kreed moaned against his lips.

His own dick jerked, the thin material of his sweat shorts amplified the heat of Kreed's cock rubbing against his own. Kreed's tongue pushed into his mouth again, and he opened, wanting more. He slid his tongue over Kreed's teeth, exploring his mouth. They rocked against each other's bodies. Kreed's cock slipped in and out of his fist, hard and insistent.

Aaron tore away from Kreed's mouth. "Wanna suck you, taste you on my tongue." He pushed at Kreed's shorts, working them down his muscular legs.

"Bed, now!" Kreed gripped his wrists, spun him around, and swatted his ass. The sting of Kreed's palm warmed his skin beneath his shorts and made his dick twitch in response.

Kreed moved to the nightstand and placed the supplies within easy reach before he took a seat on the edge of the bed, spreading his legs as he watched Aaron with lust-hooded eyes. Aaron pushed his shorts down his legs, stepped out of them, and left the cotton material abandoned on the floor. He gripped his aching dick and stroked himself for Kreed's greedy eyes.

"Stop making me wait." Kreed had his dick in his hand, jacking himself as Aaron closed the distance to the king-size bed.

Aaron went to his knees between Kreed's open thighs, inhaling the man's scent as he pressed his lips to the tender skin between his inner thigh and groin. Kreed's fingers lightly rested on the back of his neck. Aaron ran his palms up the insides of Kreed's legs before taking his rigid cock in his hand, the thick head blushing and swollen and leaking. He hungered for a taste.

The salty taste of pre-come and the heavy feel of Kreed's length against his tongue made his dick drip. Kreed threw his head back and moaned, his hips lifting and rolling into Aaron's mouth. The smell of Kreed's arousal made him dizzy with need. Aaron flattened his tongue down the underside of Kreed's cock, licking along the vein as Kreed's hands moved in his hair.

Aaron sucked at the crown, opening his mouth to let Kreed push farther inside. He bobbed his head, taking Kreed deeper and deeper until the thick head hit the back of his throat. Then Aaron glanced up and swallowed around him.

"Ahh fuck, kid." Kreed's fingers tightened in his hair, holding his head in place as Kreed fucked his mouth. The muscles in Kreed's thighs tensed as his dick's thickness filled his throat, only pulling back for the need to breathe.

Aaron used his hand, working Kreed, stroking him as he nibbled down Kreed's shaft and moved lower to mouth Kreed's balls. Aaron inhaled the heady scent of Kreed's musk and sucked a testicle into his mouth before moving to the other, manipulating them with his tongue. Kreed moaned and dropped back on his elbows.

Aaron flicked his tongue over the sensitive area between Kreed's balls and ass. He used a hand on the back of Kreed's thighs to push the deputy marshal's leg back and began to devour his ass. He worked Kreed with his tongue and nibbled around that quivering hole as Kreed squirmed under his assault.

"God, yes." Kreed writhed on the bed. Aaron spit on Kreed's pucker and pressed a slick finger inside the deputy marshal's tight ass and they both hissed at the contact. Kreed was so fucking hot.

"You like my finger in your ass, Deputy Marshal? Do you want more?" Aaron moved up on his knees and took Kreed's dick to the back of his throat again as he pressed another finger into Kreed. Aaron worked his digits in and out, stretching Kreed nice and slowly. He pulled his mouth off Kreed's dick and buried his face back in his ass, licking and sucking around his own pumping fingers.

"So fucking good... Love your taste and the way you squeeze my fingers so tight." Aaron used his spit as lube and forced a third finger into Kreed's tightness.

"Ahh, fuck, church boy. That feels amazing."

He drove his fingers in and out of Kreed, curling them till he hit his mark. "I want your cock... Want you in me," Kreed begged. Aaron removed his fingers, slowly pushing to his feet.

Kreed tossed a condom and lube toward Aaron. He quickly ripped into the condom and rolled the thin latex on before popping the top on the lube, slicking up his fingers and dick.

His stomach did a flip, his heart hammering in his chest when Kreed lay back against the bed and regarded him with those lust-hooded eyes. Aaron took hold of Kreed's legs and pulled him so the gorgeous man's ass was right at the edge of the bed.

"You're gonna feel so good in me." Kreed held his legs open wide as Aaron took his cock in hand, positioned himself, and surged forward, his eyes never straying from Kreed's dark stare.

"So fucking good, Sin." Heat swamped him as the tip of his cock slipped past the tight ring of muscle that kept him from heaven. The coolness of the comforter brushed against his knees as he bent forward and kissed Kreed, long and unhurriedly. Kreed's ass fluttered wildly around his dick as he pressed in inch by inch until his groin met the back of Kreed's thighs. He moved slowly in and out, letting Kreed adjust to being breached.

Kreed arched his back and moaned. Aaron fought every urge in his body that demanded he pound into the man below him. He gradually drew his hips back and eased forward until he was as deep in the deputy marshal as he could be. The way Kreed moved on the bed had Aaron picking up the pace and thrusting his hips, each movement building into a sweet, steady rhythm. Not too fast but just enough to make them both squirm for more.

"Harder... Let me feel you." Kreed threw his head back and rolled his hips. Aaron didn't hold back. He gripped the front of Kreed's bent thighs and used them to wedge Kreed's ass against him as he shoved deeply into his body. Their current position, with Aaron standing at the end of the bed and Kreed on his back, legs spread wide and ass barely off the edge, put Aaron in the perfect position to hammer into Kreed.

Aaron thrust into that mind-blowing heat a few more times before grabbing Kreed's legs and placing them on his shoulders, changing the angle of penetration. "Right there... Yes, church boy, fuck me," Kreed gasped. Pleasure etched over his face as he ground the words out through clenched teeth. Aaron did exactly as instructed and pounded into Kreed with all he had. Sweat beaded his forehead as his hips pistoned in and out of the deputy. Aaron was close to losing it. If Kreed didn't come soon, he wasn't sure he could hold his orgasm back any longer.

He took over stroking Kreed in time with his thrusts, his fist working up and down the thick length as he rocked wildly into Kreed's quivering body.

Refusing to come before Kreed had Aaron's balls aching from the pressure of holding back. With every press of his hips, he slipped a little closer to the point of no return. Kreed's ass clenched snuggly around him. Fire ignited at the base of his spine and burned like acid through his body. The feeling was too much. Their moans and heavy pants filled the room. His balls drew tightly against his body.

"Come for me, Sin," Aaron commanded and sped up his hips, thrusting faster and deeper.

"Yes. Need... Fuucck, Aaron," Kreed shouted, his whole body rigid, then his cock swelled and jerked in Aaron's fist as he came. Hot come ran over Aaron's fingers and ribbons of cream splattered on Kreed's stomach and chest.

"Sin," Aaron hissed when strong muscles rippled around him, squeezing him so tight he lost his rhythm. Aaron's thighs burned as he wedged himself deep in Kreed's quivering body and came with such a force that he doubled over from the pleasure. His muscles ached from the strain of his release, his body completely limp from his orgasm. Kreed's legs were the only thing that held him upright.

Air. He needed air. He held on to Kreed's shins as he floated back to earth. Aaron sucked in a breath, his head still spinning from the strength of his release. Damn, losing his breath like that was a first for him. So much of everything he experienced with Kreed fell in that category—something he told himself he could get used to.

As much as he hated pulling out of Kreed's heat, he gripped the back of the condom and eased his softening cock from the deputy. Kreed's legs slid off his shoulders, but he didn't move except to throw an arm across his eyes.

"Damn, church boy, you fucked me right into the mattress." Kreed peeked at him from under his arm.

"Yeah, that was fucking amazing. Let me grab us a towel. I'll be right back." He winked at Kreed then bent forward and gave the deputy a quick peck on the lips. Aaron removed the rubber and tied it off on his way to the bathroom. After tossing the condom into the trash, he grabbed a towel, wet it, and headed back to the bedroom to take care of Kreed. When he finished cleaning Kreed, he dropped the towel beside the bed.

"Honestly, I'm surprised I can still move. Scoot over. I want to lie down beside you," he said and smiled down at Kreed.

"Not sure I can move, but I'm not complaining." Kreed laughed and scooted back, giving him room as he crawled onto the bed and between the deputy's legs. Aaron let his full weight settle on Kreed's chest and the man immediately wrapped strong arms around him. Their breathing fell into a mirrored tempo. Kreed's nose nuzzled into his hair. He felt complete, and so close to Kreed in this moment, despite every alarm in his body warning him not to get too comfortable and let his guard down.

Chapter 20

Aaron lay in the dark bedroom in the early morning hours, combing his fingers through Kreed's silky strands as the man slept. Kreed lay propped up on two pillows, Aaron's head resting on Kreed's shoulder. Their position was perfect. Aaron leaned slightly forward and pressed his lips against the stubble on Kreed's jaw as he listened to the deep sounds of Kreed's rhythmic breathing. He couldn't quit touching this gorgeous man who had been so exposed and honest, even caring, through their hours of lovemaking.

Out of the corner of his eye, he caught his monitor lighting up again. The code to let him know he was needed online. He'd set up the offsite remote notification a few years ago. The all-access never really bothered him before because he put the interruption down to the greater good of what they were trying to accomplish, but right now—or, technically, over the last twenty-five or thirty minutes—the thing had steadily blinked, and yet, he hadn't moved from his spot. Kreed sleeping underneath him felt too right to step away from. He couldn't find the mind-set to budge, even though the delay would cost him credibility. An inner groan slipped free.

"What's wrong?" That small noise was enough to wake Kreed. The guy slept very lightly.

"Nothing. I've gotta get up. I need to go help a friend," he said, trying to talk himself into shifting away from Kreed's warm body.

"With what?" Kreed asked, obviously forgetting their unspoken rule about not digging too closely into each other's lives.

"A coding issue," Aaron answered vaguely. That was enough reality to have him untangling himself from Kreed's hold, which only made the deputy marshal clutch him tighter.

"You need to sleep. Tomorrow's a big day," Kreed said, nuzzling against his neck. As much as he wanted to stay in this position with Kreed and never leave, Aaron tried again to get up. Aaron scooted away and placed his feet on the floor as Kreed yawned big, but his discerning eyes didn't close like Aaron had suspected would be the case. Instead, Kreed tracked Aaron as he went to the computer on a makeshift desk in the bedroom.

"It's not video games, is it?" Kreed asked. His tone clear that he'd be interrupting Aaron's game.

"No, not at all." Aaron sat down at the computer. He'd changed his mechanical keyboard out for a standard one he'd found in the house when they'd moved in. A few minutes passed before Kreed spoke again.

"You're not really a big gamer, are you?"

"Not really," Aaron admitted, bringing his system up. Taking the chance that his honest admission might set off some warning bells, he turned the monitor, hopefully away from Kreed's line of sight. "The keyboard's quieter. I'm sorry if it keeps you awake."

"I like watching you," Kreed finally said. Aaron looked over, and Kreed had scooted up in bed. He was propping himself up against several pillows now, getting comfortable against the headboard. His chest muscles flexed as he positioned the pillows behind him. His flat dark nipples stood out starkly, even against all the beautiful ink. The blanket was draped low, exposing way too much deliciously decorated skin. Aaron loved watching Kreed too. "You don't have the standard nerd look."

Aaron wasn't sure what to say to that, so he didn't. He just forced himself to center in and open the program. He quickly scanned the message and hid his inner turmoil. Kreed's presence in his life inspired a good-versus-evil attitude, and all of a sudden, his current activities seemed to be coasting right on the line between the two. This hack job was a favor to a guy who'd jumped in and helped him when he'd needed. He didn't really have much of a choice this time. He'd agreed to this when he'd asked for help the last time.

Scolding himself, Aaron closed his eyes. What the hell was wrong with him? He did this all the time. With two or three calming breaths, he opened them again, staring at the flashing cursor on the screen, forcing Kreed from his thoughts. Aaron read the messages, catching himself up, and began working. He was so centered inside himself that he startled when Kreed ran his fingers over the top of his head, ruffling his hair.

"We only have about an hour before we had to get up anyway. I'll make coffee," Kreed said from behind him.

"Okay," he tossed out, eyes on the monitor, trying to stay focused.

"One last kiss?" Kreed whispered against his ear.

One of their last conversations before Kreed fell asleep had the deputy marshal set on cooling this thing between them for the duration of the investigation. Kreed wanted to resume the possibilities between them more fully once the case was closed. Of course, only if Aaron was interested. Kreed placed the ball in his court to decide if he wanted to pick this up when they were done.

After the last thirty-six hours, it seemed that the gallant and probably smart thing to do would be to put this off, but now Aaron wasn't entirely sure about anything anymore. He couldn't deny the connection between him and Kreed, and he was quite certain if given the chance, he wouldn't ever get enough of Kreed Sinacola.

They'd been pretty damn hot for one another. Once they'd made it back inside the bedroom yesterday, they'd only left the bed to eat, and even after all the sex of the afternoon, Aaron had ended up getting a blow job in the kitchen, then he returned that favor in the living room, before spending the rest of the night in Kreed's arms. Aaron wished he could figure out a way to keep Kreed and his secrets too. But how?

Damn it to hell, he was so fucking screwed. He had done what he said he wouldn't. He'd let Kreed get under his skin and he still wanted more.

Aaron darkened the screen with the stroke of a key, pretty certain Kreed wouldn't understand what he might see displayed on the monitor, but he was sure the investigator inside the man was smart enough to retain innocuously gathered information and examine it later. Aaron turned and tipped his head back, sighing as Kreed's mouth slid against his. He opened, allowing Kreed to deepen the kiss. When Kreed's fingers pulled against his waistband to slide inside, Aaron had to stop him. Reaching for his wrist, he regretfully ended what he wanted so badly.

"Give me an hour?" Aaron asked. Kreed didn't hide the disappointment spreading across his face.

"You're right. We shouldn't. I just… Kissing you makes me forget everything. As much as I want you, we can't," Kreed said, not moving his hand, but not pushing him either.

"We could if you weren't so damn hardheaded." Aaron tried for teasing, but he meant those words. He truly believed they could balance the case and whatever all this was going on between them. That "Sinacola resolve" Aaron was learning all too well flashed in Kreed's eyes, and he shook his head as he stood.

"I better go make some coffee before we both have to repent for our sins, church boy." Kreed reached out, ruffling his hair again. The words and the tone were all off compared to the hungry lover who'd fucked him senseless last night.

"Yeah, coffee sounds good," Aaron replied, placing the keyboard on the desk. The look in Kreed's eyes worried him. They certainly weren't to the point that he could easily read Kreed, and he was torn over pushing Kreed to talk or letting him go.

"Get to work. I've gotta call Skinner. He called last night," Kreed said from the door.

"What time did he call?" Aaron didn't remember anything but his few hours online interrupting them yesterday.

"I'm pretty certain it was somewhere between you bent over the couch or you on your knees in the shower. I'm not exactly sure," Kreed said coyly, snickering as he left the room. Aaron hesitated. He hated seeing Kreed thrown off his game, and from the tone of his voice, the deputy definitely left the room a little concerned he'd missed the call. The urgent blinking of the screen drew him back. After considering his options for a minute more, he decided to get this over with before going after Kreed. He picked up the keyboard and dropped it back in his lap to finish what he'd started.

~~~

Quickly, Kreed dressed for the day. He grabbed a cup of coffee and dialed Director Skinner's personal cell number as he headed back to the study. When the phone began to ring, Kreed used his foot to close the bedroom door behind him. Nothing about the room had changed since he'd left the bed twenty-four hours earlier. He set the coffee cup on the desk and made his way to the pull-out sofa, lifting the end of the bed and folding it back in on itself. After returning the cushions to their proper place, he dropped the pillows on each end of the couch.

Out of sight, out of mind. It was no longer the giant red flag reminder of his inability to stay away from Stuart. But damn, they were good together. He wanted Stuart, no question there. What surprised him more than anything was that Aaron was a demanding and aggressive lover. The kid knew exactly what he wanted and how he wanted it. Kreed didn't have any complaints. He was more than happy to see to Aaron's every whim. The guy had this way of getting him off and immediately making him rock hard again. Aaron had him acting like a teenage boy in his prime. They'd most definitely fucked like bunnies for the last twenty-four hours. His tender ass was proof of that. On that thought, he smiled and reached for the couch throw, draping it over the back of the cushions.

"I know you're there. I can hear you breathing," Skinner yelled into the phone.

"I'm here. Sorry, I was lost in thought," Kreed answered, not really sure how long he'd made Skinner wait.

"I tried to call you several times yesterday, Sinacola." Skinner's tone was scolding, and he should be in trouble for missing those calls.

"I saw that, but it was too late to call you back," he answered honestly.

"Are you sure you're good with this assignment?" Skinner asked, his tone still irritated.

"You aren't getting rid of me. I didn't answer the fucking phone. My bad," Kreed said, frustrated with his lapse and Skinner's attitude. Already, he was slipping. Last night, he easily justified the mess up, deciding he could call Skinner this morning. Why had he ever thought that might be acceptable?

"Knox is concerned about you," Skinner informed him.

"Knox is an asshole who's trapped inside a house, waiting for something to happen, no different than me."

"I can see that. Sinacola, I don't normally worry about you. If you need out of there, just tell me." Skinner's voice had changed, not quite to the level of 'pissed off' it had held before, but Kreed wouldn't call it warm and fuzzy either.

"Of course I will. Why'd you call?"

"I've got Thomas Hasselbeck, the head of the IT Department at Redemption Apostle Tabernacle, in custody. We've been productive on our end. The dots are starting to connect. What Stuart was able to give us put the church in front of several sets of very well-connected eyes. We're elevating this to a domestic terrorist cell, Sinacola. Bottom line, Hasselbeck comes with a stronger IT background than we realized. There's concern that if he showed up onsite, he could jeopardize what Stuart's accomplished. It appears the church searched him out to protect their systems. I've got interrogators in with him now. He's showing signs of breaking, but he's hanging on longer than I thought. I'd hoped we'd know more before Stuart went back in today," Skinner explained.

"All right," Kreed said as he stopped pacing in the middle of the room to take in the new information. That changed everything.

"Explain the threat level change to domestic terrorist cell. That's a pretty big leap in such a short amount of time. What did you uncover?" Kreed tried to understand the steps Skinner had taken over the last twenty-four hours. His brow furrowed at the implications. All of a sudden this case hit way too close to home for more reasons than just the hate associated with sexual orientation. His eyes closed, and he listened intently to every word Skinner said.

"It's a cell, Sinacola. It's organized and there are several. These people use religion to hide behind and single out the victims to prove their point. Your gut's right. Special Agent Langley didn't work alone, regardless of his claims in his confession. Now we need to see how far this goes," Skinner said.

"And you're following all legalities to make this stick?"

"It's why you're staying onsite," Skinner advised.

"But I'm not alone here, am I?" Of course he wasn't.

"No, you have backup. They're close by."

No way would Skinner leave him alone with that threat. It had to give him hope, even as the dread of the next question filled his soul.

"But Stuart's alone in there?" The silence that came back said more than anything. Damn it. Aaron wasn't equipped to handle this kind of situation. Kreed absolutely didn't fucking want Aaron back inside that church. A terrorist cell? About damn time someone paid attention to those extreme freaks who hid behind the Bible. With his mind racing, Kreed cocked a brow. He was surprised the church had flown under the radar for this long with their vile propaganda and hate-filled picketing.

Think, Sinacola. Stop and think.

What makes this different than any other case? Nothing. Aaron's green, but solid. Just lay it all out to the kid. He'll be fine.

But, more than anything, Kreed didn't want Stuart back inside that church. The church targeted homosexual men and made horrific examples out of them. Fear gripped his heart.

Seriously, he couldn't lose anyone else right now, especially not Aaron. It would be too much. He wanted a future with him in it. Damn it! What they had would never be just a hookup. Clearly defined emotion was now involved, and he didn't want his guy walking back into that church this morning.

The minute he'd walked across Colt's living room and kissed Stuart, everything had changed. This was Mitch-fucking-Knox's fault. All up in his face, telling him the kid had had eyes for him all night long... Kreed's jaw clenched as he sneered at the memories in his head. Man, if he hadn't already thrown Knox off the porch, he'd fucking do it again. This wasn't even his damn case to worry about. Fucking Mitch Knox! People got hurt every day. That was life.

Kreed steeled his spine and forced all this unwanted sentiment out of his head and his heart. It was harder to do than he'd ever thought possible.

"Sinacola, answer the fucking question," Skinner said, forcing him to tune into the conversation again.

"Repeat," he fired back, having no idea what question he'd missed.

"Are you sure you can handle this? There's no shame in walking away. It might even be for the best," Skinner added quietly. He was the one person on this planet who knew everything there was to know about Kreed Sinacola. Knox didn't even know as much as Skinner did.

"If I bail, it'll derail things. I'm not leaving Aaron without someone to watch his back. The kid and I have things worked out. We don't have time to get acquainted with new partners. He trusts me, and you need the kid," Kreed reasoned.

"Aaron needs to trust you, but the kid phrase bothers me. He's almost thirty. Are you using him to fill the void from the loss of your brother?" Skinner asked boldly, and it took all Kreed had not to bark out a laugh at that one.

"Hell no, not at all." *Fuck no!* Aaron was the light in all the darkness that had surrounded his life. Hell, it didn't just surround him, it had consumed him until Aaron Stuart worked his magic. Kreed's eyes darted toward the door as he realized the magnitude of that thought. Aaron had come into his life and chased the shadows away. There was silence from Skinner, and he had no idea what to say. His director was savvy enough to put two and two together, and if he did, he'd pull Kreed from this case in a matter of minutes. He had to think of something—anything—to help qualify his statement.

"He looks like a kid. Stuart looks real young. That's all I'm saying. He's not a kid, and he's vested in this case just like I am. It took us a few days to get things right. He's not overly social. He doesn't do well with all this, but I think he trusts me now. It'd drag out this case if we brought someone else in." When Skinner didn't respond, Kreed changed his tactic. "I truly believed this was small potatoes. I thought at best we'd find someone here that knew what Agent Langley was doing and tie this case up. It's bigger than that. I want to see this through for Knox. Don't take it away from me."

Silence continued until Skinner finally spoke. "All right. Watch your back. I'll be in touch. If this goes down like I'm thinking, we'll have minutes to get Stuart out of there. Tell him the procedure if we storm in. I don't want him hurt."

"I will. Stay in touch." Kreed ended the call. His nerves were getting to him. He looked down at the floor, unable to escape the frustration building inside him. He was so unbelievably angry at himself. Why in the world had he crossed the line? Ignored his rules? Just missing Skinner's call yesterday spoke volumes to his state of mind. All he could think about was Aaron Stuart, and that could get them both killed.

Rage boiled below the surface at the stupidity of his choices. He fisted his hand, trying to hold off the burst of anger that usually followed. Aaron wouldn't understand if he went out there and laid into him for no reason. It wasn't Aaron's fault Kreed had broken his own rules. Even now, as mad at himself as he was, he still wanted the kid on a level he'd never experienced before.

Apprehension settled in. Kreed was working in uncharted territory. He sat on the edge of the sofa and hung his head. Minutes passed before he was able to move his thoughts from something ugly and destructive to finding a common ground in this new turn of events. So what was the bottom line? Kreed lifted a hand to tick off the points with his fingers.

Aaron meant something to him. That was a fact.

He didn't want to leave this case. That was a fact.

But why didn't he want to leave this case? Was it a sound reason? That took a little longer to answer. He didn't want to leave the case because he didn't want Aaron's welfare left to anyone else.

Decision made.

He stood at the same moment Aaron knocked on his door and pushed it open to stick his head inside. They were now officially past the private boundary stage if the kid was comfortable enough with Kreed to open the door regardless of what he might be doing.

"What's wrong?" Aaron asked, and Kreed furrowed his brow at the question. Aaron shoved the door open all the way and stepped inside with a wet head and wearing his khakis and a white undershirt. "What happened?"

"What'd you want when you came in here?" Kreed asked, trying to skirt around Aaron's question.

"You go first." Aaron stood in front of him with his hands on his hips. Kreed liked Aaron's height, but resisted the urge to lean in and kiss those upturned lips. He wasn't sure where to draw the line now, especially after determining he really liked Aaron, but he needed to figure that all out before he made too many more moves forward.

"I'll tell you over breakfast. I need some coffee." Kreed extended his hand and began to step forward, but Aaron didn't move. That concern on his beautiful face twisted Kreed's stomach.

Kreed bent forward, almost as if compelled, and kissed those pouty lips he couldn't resist. The worry in Aaron's eyes had been too overpowering. Kreed only wanted to comfort him. Out of all the players in this game, Aaron needed to be the one with the least concern as he went back inside that church today. Kreed reached out, wrapped an arm around Aaron's shoulder, and began turning him toward the door. "We're good. The case's moving forward. It's gonna be fine. I promise."

Aaron stayed rooted in his spot, clearly not believing him. Kreed went for the door before turning back, forcing all the emotion from his face and voice. "Food's in the kitchen. You've gotta be starving; it's been at least eight hours since your last feeding." He smirked at Aaron before turning and leaving the room on that joke. Hopefully that would reduce Aaron's unease with whatever expression he'd seen on Kreed's face when he'd barged in the room. Eventually, he heard Aaron following behind him. Now, he just needed to decide how much to say.

~~~

Aaron sat across the kitchen table, watching Kreed push his breakfast around his plate. Before the last thirty-six or so hours, he would have said that might be usual for the man. Back then, Aaron's sole focus had been on finding ways to remain aloof and unengaged, but now he knew there were too many sides to Kreed. One telltale sign things weren't right had to be when Kreed took the seat across the table from him. They'd been eating every meal together side by side since yesterday morning.

Beyond that, Kreed's face was way too passive, as though he was controlling his movements and his words. The lack of sarcasm and snarky remarks leaving his lips should be enough to concern anyone who'd been in Kreed's presence more than a few hours. Honestly, it was kind of freaking Aaron out a little bit. At first, he thought the new, aloof attitude was Kreed's attempt at creating distance. That was fine. Kreed could try, but Aaron wasn't entirely certain of the reason behind his actions, meaning something may have changed from the time Kreed left the bedroom until Aaron followed. That couldn't have been more than twenty minutes at the most.

Looking down at his watch, Aaron estimated he had about an hour before he had to be across the street, reporting in for work. That didn't give them much time, which meant Kreed needed to start talking.

Not quite finished with his food, Aaron laid his fork down on his plate. He picked up his napkin and wiped his mouth before laying that out on the table. He pushed the plate back a little dramatically. "Spill it, Sin." Relief seemed the most dominant look on Kreed's face, but he held firm to the quiet. "So you're just gonna let me go over there blind and not tell me whatever's eating at you?"

"I texted Connors. He's checking on a few things. I need an update from him before I know for sure," Kreed said vaguely.

"Tell me what you know," Aaron demanded, placing both elbows on the table as he leaned forward, going for the tough-guy routine.

"I only know enough that it sounds dangerous," Kreed said as he seemed to look over Aaron's intimidation tactic. Amusement flashed in Kreed's eyes, but the handsome deputy marshal quickly covered it with a smile. Aaron rolled his eyes. So much for being the tough guy.

"Well, isn't that what the alphabet boys do best? Make everything way more dire than it really is?" He tried to bait Kreed into telling him what he still wouldn't say.

"Not this time, Stuart." Kreed stood, picking up both their plates and taking them to the sink. He rinsed them and wiped down the counter before turning to face him again. Kreed rested back against the sink, crossing those brawny arms over his chest. "They're escalating the church's status from hate group to a domestic terrorist cell. That's significant. Hate group implies verbal spewing. A terror cell indicates desire to harm. That tells me that it's not only isolated to the single agent and perhaps someone rogue on the inside. And it's probably not isolated to that building across the street. But while I have thought of them as homegrown terrorists, now everyone's on the same page, and the intel points to it starting there. From what they've been able to glean from the access you were able to grant them, they had enough to take the IT manager into custody. They'll hold him and his family until this case's resolved, but it sounds like he's part of the problem, and they felt, with his background, he could figure out what you're doing."

"So Hasselbeck won't be there today?" Aaron asked, trying to follow all the information given. Once the term terror cell was mentioned, he wasn't certain he'd heard much else Kreed had said.

"No, he'll be on medical leave with no access to the church. Those calls have been made to excuse his absence. He's in federal custody under lock and key. His background reports are shady at best. He knows his shit. Skinner compared him to your skill level. They feel like he was hired for the specific purpose of keeping people out of the church's shit. Regardless of all that, you've been an unexpected asset. They're afraid he'll catch what you've done, and they want to protect against that for as long as possible," Kreed explained a little further. Now he got why Kreed had been so weird this morning.

"He wouldn't," Aaron said absently, looking down at his hands. A terror cell. Wow. Okay.

"You don't know that," Kreed started, and Aaron lifted his head.

"Kind of I do." He wasn't being cocky when he said that. There weren't too many people on this planet that did things like he did.

"That cocky attitude's my biggest concern." Kreed sighed and ran a hand through his hair. "At this point, we assume nothing." Kreed shoved off the sink counter and paced into the living room. Aaron had noticed Kreed's pent-up energy during the meal and knew the man needed a direction for it. He seemed larger than life right now as Aaron watched the guy walk across the room.

"It's not arrogance that leads me to say that. In really basic terms, I set it up and masked the hell out of it—actually several times. It appears somewhat simple to remove, kind of basic. So if they search, it just looks like the breach is a little better than an amateur move. If I found it, I wouldn't look further," Aaron said, trying to explain while also trying to calm Kreed's nerves. "I don't take any of this for granted. Trust me on that. I'm not trying to play hero here."

"That's what I wanted to hear." Kreed spun around and headed back his way. "I assured Skinner we're solid."

"We *are* solid," Aaron said, confused. Where had that come from out of everything just said?

"But without being in DC, I can't know for sure what they're looking at. I only get bits and pieces of information that they feel are important. There's too much left unsaid, but what they think they've found is big. You're green, and I'm fresh off bereavement leave. We aren't ideal," Kreed explained.

Yeah, okay, so he got that. He'd argued that exact point before they threw him into the middle of all this.

"The terrorist thing's weird to me, but I always had a feeling it was big." Aaron pushed his fingers through his hair, the weight of the situation starting to take hold. These people killed because they hated another group of people that they saw as an abomination to their God. Those were extremely archaic and barbaric ideals and spoke volumes toward the findings he'd uncovered so far from that church.

"I honestly downplayed it in my head. I'm pretty certain Connors did too. I had a feeling we would find answers here, but I didn't realize how far this thing actually reached and how organized it truly is. We've got backup, but my first thought was that I didn't want you back in there," Kreed said quietly, now standing less than a foot away from him.

Kreed extended a hand to touch his face, but stopped mid-reach and dropped his hand to his side. It didn't matter that Kreed didn't follow through with the touch, Aaron had caught the flash of intense concern in his eyes before Kreed took a step backward. Aaron realized that was Kreed's way of putting barriers back between them, and that was okay. He could deal with that. It seemed crazy, but if Kreed had grown attached to him over the last twenty-four hours, Aaron needed to allow him to create distance, at least for the time being. Kreed needed his mind on the case and not on Aaron. It seemed a reasonable coping mechanism.

"So really nothing's changed on our end. Everything's different from the bureau standpoint, but we're in the same place we were. Right?" Aaron asked.

"I guess. You just have to keep your ears open," Kreed reinforced.

"Exactly what I've been doing."

"Listen to me. If anything feels off, you get your ass out of there. I'll be tracking you every step of the way, but it's on you to keep your guard up. You hear the wrong thing and you take off for the closest exit," Kreed stressed.

"Of course I will."

Kreed stared at him long and hard, the deputy marshal's dark eyes searching his.

"I promise I will get out of there, Kreed." Aaron saw some of the tension ease from Kreed's face as he made his oath. Kreed didn't say anything, just nodded once and turned to leave.

"I think this freaks you out more than it does me," Aaron called after Kreed.

"Probably. I'm gonna shower. We need to talk about your goals for today before you head back over there." He heard the bathroom door shut after he spoke, but Aaron didn't move until he heard the water in the shower. He wasn't exactly sure how to take Kreed right now. Kreed was unsteady, and he'd never seen that before. Aaron didn't doubt Kreed's ability to keep him safe; he wasn't certain why Kreed did. Besides, there was no indication Aaron had given that he was a risk taker and he wasn't going to be in this situation. Behind the computer? Absolutely, but not in this. He'd get the hell out of there way before anything went down. Kreed could bet his ass on that.

Chapter 21

Not thirty minutes later, Aaron was wired up, dressed in proper church-boy clothes and fully briefed by Connors on everything that had gone down in the last two days. Kreed's guilt over not taking part in whatever information they'd found yesterday came through loud and clear. The problem was, he didn't see how Kreed could have helped. What was the big deal? He'd missed a phone call from Skinner. Not even Connors had included Kreed until this morning.

It seemed to Aaron, Kreed was doing exactly what he was supposed to. No slacking at all on his part. Maybe this was an after-sex guilt thing and Aaron absolutely hated that idea. He didn't want Kreed to have any regrets about being with him. But he just didn't see Kreed as the kind of guy who had guilt over spilling his load. If so, that was fucked up, and he needed to know that sooner rather than later.

Right now, though, he had to push all of that out of his mind and concentrate on his task like Kreed wanted him to do.

"Keep your head down today, Stuart. Be as available as you can, but blend in," Connors instructed from the speaker of Kreed's cellphone.

"All right. That's pretty much been my plan this whole time. I should get going. It's close to eight," Aaron said, hoping that would end the call with Connors.

"Give me a minute to get him out the door," Kreed said, completely back in super-serious mode.

"Can you see me out?" Aaron asked. He knew no matter how quiet he got, the wires would catch everything he said now. He hooked a thumb over his shoulder and left the room. He went for the kitchen and covered the cross pin on his shirt with his left hand before going for the pad of paper by the phone. He scribbled a note quickly as Kreed trailed in behind him.

Nothing's changed. We've got this. He pointed to the pad on the table before he went for his coat. He zipped up his jacket, covering the cross altogether as Kreed read the note and nodded. He wasn't certain if the buckle wrap had a camera so he pulled his bomber jacket down, covering his belt as he walked back to Kreed, lifting a finger to his lips. Aaron pushed up on his tiptoes and pressed his lips to Kreed's, knowing he was committing a major no-no.

He tried not to take offense when Kreed's eyes grew to the size of saucers, and he immediately backed away, shaking his head. Aaron smiled at his reaction; poor guy looked like a deer caught in headlights. Where was all the bravado now? Aaron ran his tongue across his lips, hoping to hide the smile tugging at the corners of his mouth.

On second thought, he couldn't resist and stepped in to brush his lips over Kreed's one last time before turning toward the front door.

Kreed wasn't the only one that had a vested interest in what they'd done or the job they had to accomplish. It was time Kreed got on Aaron's page. He was tired of playing on his partner's. Besides, Kreed's page wasn't any fun. Kreed had all those rules he lived by, and Aaron just wanted to make it through life reasonably unscathed.

Aaron never looked back as he grabbed his well-used Bible—a prop that had come by mail after they'd arrived. He headed out the door. Man, what a difference a few days made. He was ready and eager to bring this church down.

~~~

Kreed couldn't deny Aaron had done an outstanding job. Seven hours into the day and Aaron had made it to every computer in the place. He'd moved so swiftly and so casually that Kreed wasn't completely certain of what Aaron had accomplished until Connors team gave the occasional "atta boy" into the earpiece. Aaron had managed to place listening devices all over the administrative offices, including inside the pastor's personal cellphone. That had caused a round of back-patting from DC, because Aaron had subtly had the pastor hand him the phone. Aaron skillfully added the device right there in the open while listening to Bible verses being tossed his way and the angry pastor standing directly in front of him.

Aaron Stuart was damn good at this sneaking around shit. Kreed sat back from the monitor where he'd been stationed all day long and scrubbed a hand over his face. Aaron was too good at all this… Like he'd done this before. Keeping his eyes on the monitor, Kreed silenced his connection with the bureau and called Mitch. His buddy picked up on the first ring.

"Skinner get a hold of you?" Kreed asked when Mitch answered.

"Last night. He was looking for you."

Kreed didn't respond or acknowledge that statement. The less his partner knew about him and Aaron, the better. Knox had made his thoughts more than clear where he and Stuart were concerned.

"What do you know about Stuart?" Kreed asked.

"Why do you wanna know?" Mitch shot back. Great, they were playing twenty questions, and Mitch was still defensive about the kid.

"Don't be a pain in the ass, Knox." Kreed leaned back in his chair.

"That's what I do…" Silence held between them as Kreed kept a constant eye on everything he could see from Aaron's angle. He'd just wait Knox out. It took longer than expected. "I met him online in a *Call of Duty* chat room like years ago. He was active and on and knew his shit, so we built a friendship."

"Hmmm. When was he hired with NSA?" Kreed asked.

"I don't remember. It was a year or so after that," Mitch answered.

"But he had a record," Kreed replied. That had always been the weird part about Aaron getting hired.

"It wasn't a solid record. It was like a fraternity prank...maybe. The government hired him to test their systems in place of sending him to prison. I helped where I could in giving him credibility," Mitch added.

"Hmmm..."

"Why, Sinacola? Is he rogue?" There was a small amount of confusion in Mitch's voice, but he could tell by Mitch's tone that his long-time partner was having a hard time believing those words he'd just asked.

"No. I don't think so. Actually, not at all. He's given too much to this case, but there's something going on. He's just very smooth for someone that's never done this before."

"Really? Are you watching?" Mitch asked.

"Every move he makes." There was silence between the both of them. "I heard some chatter today that you were possibly going out in public tonight."

"Yeah, it's firmed up. We're puttin' on a big show, taking Cody out on the town. Keep an eye on Aaron, Sinacola," Mitch said. Kreed nodded as if Mitch could see him. He'd heard they were enlisting Mitch and Cody to help try and flush these guys out, get them so riled that they might make an error. Aaron's thoroughness in wiring that office today helped. Skinner had to be getting some solid intel if he were to the point of baiting.

"Watch yourself. I'm hanging up now," Kreed said and turned the volume back up on the feed he shared with Connors. They hadn't really spoken in hours, but he wanted direct access if they were able to get the IT manager talking.

His eyes stayed on the screen. Aaron hadn't mastered going to the bathroom yet. He couldn't quite keep covered while unzipping and freeing himself. Kreed smiled a little while turning away to give the guy some privacy. He thought over what Mitch told him and waited a minute or two after he heard the flush before he turned back.

Aaron washed and dried his hands before checking his appearance. To Kreed, he looked fine. Actually more than fine and he smiled at the screen. Seconds later, Aaron's eyes dropped down to the cross on his shirt and he gave a small smile back. There was absolutely no way that the kid could have known what Kreed had just done, but it felt personal and the sweet gesture made Kreed smile bigger.

"Watch your six," he said to the monitor.

"What?" It wasn't Connors's voice, but someone on the other end, causing Kreed to look down at the small box in the corner of his screen.

"Nothing." Kreed shook his head, momentarily forgetting he wasn't alone. "I wanna blow by blow of Knox. There better be an army watching them."

Several seconds went by before Connors answered. "There is. I wasn't so much into that plan, but I've seen the surveillance following them. Brody Masters is heading it up himself tonight. I know you worked with him before."

"Yeah," Kreed said. He liked Brody. They'd worked together for years, and it did ease some of the concern he had. He just wished he could be there himself to have Mitch's back, but his loyalties were divided now. He had Aaron to consider. He watched on the monitor as Aaron walked back into the IT office. The kid sat at his assigned desk, which happened to be catty-cornered to a wall mirror. He could see Aaron's reflection perfectly. Aaron meant something to him, and for the first time, Kreed couldn't immediately blame all these soft sentiments on the sex, although that was amazing. The problem? He and Aaron connected outside of sex, which meant so much more.

Besides that, this case stressed him the fuck out. He palmed his phone and pulled up the contacts to send Brody a quick message, telling him to watch that group closely, since he couldn't be there. He got an immediate text back assuring him they were set. Kreed had to let it go and let the process play out. It was already so personal before he ever factored in the relationships he had with all the people involved in bringing this cell down. Kreed rolled his shoulders, trying to force the tension from his neck and back. God, he hoped this would all be over soon.

Chapter 22

Aaron kicked back at the desk in his bedroom, the keyboard propped in his lap. He was almost done helping his buddy. He'd completed as much as he could for the night, and now he was just tinkering around, surfing the web. In reality, his sole focus rested on listening to the activity across the hall.

Disappointment had swamped him when Kreed had sat parked inside the study directly across from his bedroom since the time he'd gotten off work. After a while, Aaron managed to find things to keep himself busy. After the initial moment of sadness when Aaron realized the night wasn't theirs, he decided to catch up on a few projects he'd put off. Kreed kept his distance and stayed in the study. Since this little fucked-up town had three Subways, two Whataburgers, about a million pizza places and not much else, Aaron ordered in pizza and left Kreed alone. Kreed's whole demeanor radiated intensity. His total concentration was focused on Mitch and Cody.

It hadn't taken long for Aaron to open a link for Kreed to watch everything going on with Mitch and Cody, and that was where the deputy marshal had stationed himself ever since. While Aaron worked at the church today, Kreed seemed to have locked himself tightly back up, hid behind the same walls he had placed between them from the beginning. He understood Kreed was worried about this whole situation. And he had played right into Kreed's hands this morning by letting him pull away and allowing him the opportunity to put those barriers back in place. Aaron should have stopped Kreed in his tracks, because now he felt like they were starting things back at square one.

Aaron put the keyboard on the makeshift desk and turned the power off on his monitor like he'd done more times than not since he'd met Kreed. He went for Kreed's door, first standing in the open doorway then, after being ignored, he moved to the sofa, sitting on the edge, watching the screen that had kept Kreed's attention all night.

"How's it going?" Aaron finally asked after a few minutes. Just as he finished asking his question, Kreed's phone rang. He held up a finger and answered it on the second ring.

"Hey." He watched Kreed's features visibly soften. "Watch yourself." Kreed disconnected the call and let out a deep exhale before turning a worried gaze Aaron's way. "They're in a secure location."

"Not at Colt's place."

"No. They made the news tonight. Colt got on air on WFAA and did the sport's report with Dale Hanson. He apparently supports equality. A photo of them out tonight made it in the segment. They're calling tonight a success," Kreed explained.

"You aren't?" Aaron asked. Kreed was still bowed up tight with stress.

"No, I am. They got what they wanted out of it. Now we've gotta keep a closer eye on you. If it's gonna happen, it'll be in the next few days. I don't know how long they'll need to plan a hit, but I'm thinking it'll be like the agent in Washington, enough to send them over the edge if we're in the right place," Kreed said, looking down at his hands. "If we're barking up the wrong tree, maybe we can get a better direction."

"Can the alphabet boys see us?" Aaron pointed to the screen, and Kreed reached over, turning the monitor off. "Is that the only feed in here?"

"Everything else's off."

"Good." Aaron stood and strode across the room, stopping right behind Kreed's back, he lifted his hands to Kreed's shoulders and the deputy marshal shifted in his chair to look at him. "Turn around. You're too wound up."

"Aaron, I don't know if you touching me right now's such a good idea."

"It's just a massage. Your virtue's safe for the moment. I promise. Now spin around." Aaron made a twirling motion with his fingers, signaling for Kreed to follow his directions.

Kreed let out a huff, but he finally faced the other way. Aaron started with his thumbs, digging into the tight muscles in Kreed's upper back and shoulders. Several minutes passed with Aaron using as much strength as he had in his fingers to work Kreed's muscles before he heard a relaxed sigh. He leaned in and kissed the top of Kreed's head. It was interesting how all this distance Kreed kept putting between them hadn't affected Aaron. Normally, he'd have his feelings hurt by now, especially since he'd done little more than think about the guy all day long, counting the hours until he could cross the street and just be with Kreed. But Aaron understood this standoff thing Kreed had going on. All this distance was really Kreed's way of coping with the situation. Kreed wouldn't be pushing him away if his head wasn't confused about what they'd done.

Aaron moved his hands, kneading the muscles along Kreed's spine. He reached for the hem of Kreed's T-shirt and pulled it up. Kreed fought him, grabbing for the cotton fabric to hold it down.

"We can't." Kreed spoke so softly his voice sounded strained, husky with need. Aaron got it; he was needy too. Kreed turned him on. There was no doubt about that. But right now, he just wanted to comfort Kreed—build him up again, make him steady.

"No sex, I promise," he whispered in Kreed's ear. "Come sleep in the comfortable bed. Get some real rest."

Kreed looked back at him, vulnerability and desire playing across his face. After a minute, whatever sign he searched for in Aaron's eyes, he must have found. Kreed lifted his hand and threaded those long fingers through Aaron's hair, tugging his head down until he was close enough to press those warm lips against his. The kiss was soft and sweet. Kreed lingered.

When Aaron slipped his tongue past Kreed's lips, the deputy marshal pulled him closer and held him tighter. Regretfully, Aaron pulled back from the kiss. He'd made promises, after all. He honestly didn't want to spook Kreed. He slowly pulled Kreed's shirt over his head before returning to massage his shoulders for several more minutes. His eyes slid down Kreed's broad back, admiring all the beautiful designs and marks along his skin. His eyes moved lower, taking in Kreed's perfect form. That was when he saw them—a weapon at Kreed's back and a knife on his hip.

He was learning Kreed's habits, and when he thought there was a possibility things could get rough, Kreed's weapons were never too far out of reach. Kreed always carried a gun—Aaron got that; it was Kreed's job—but, all the rest, he just didn't fully understand. The weapons were just scary for Aaron. He'd never been around guns, knives, or anyone quite so rugged and possibly deadly in his life. Those deadly abilities kind of freaked him out. He tried to ignore it. At least to Kreed he wanted to appear unaffected by the weapons.

He moved around, picked up Kreed's hand, and tugged him off the chair. He walked backward to face Kreed as he pulled him from the study. Luckily, Kreed followed, reaching for his phone before they'd exited. They made it as far as the middle of the bedroom before Kreed stopped and again took Aaron's face between his big palms. Kreed's thumbs stroked lightly across his cheeks and jaw. The deputy marshal's eyes met his.

"I want you. You have to know I do," Kreed said quietly.

Aaron reached up, placing his hands on top of Kreed's. "I know…just not right now. I understand you need your head in the game. Let me hold you tonight." Aaron watched as Kreed thought over what he'd said. Kreed finally nodded, and Aaron pressed a chaste kiss to Kreed's lips, then turned and walked toward the bed.

Aaron pulled the bedcovers back. He left his pajama bottoms and T-shirt on. He clicked on a lamp, and when he decided Kreed wouldn't bolt, he left him standing there to turn off the overhead lights. Kreed slowly began to undress. He placed the long knife at his hip on the nightstand, along with his phone, then he checked his service weapon's safety before placing it between the mattresses. The guy must really be spooked. Aaron crawled into bed from the other side and stretched out on his side. Kreed placed the blade he had strapped to his leg under his pillow before sitting on the edge, untying his boots.

"I hate feeling off, like there's something I'm missing. I'm stuck inside this house and it's killing me. I need to be out there doing more," Kreed confessed with his back to Aaron.

"I figured as much, but there's nothing else you can do. Mitch must feel the same," Aaron said, not knowing what else to say. Kreed kicked off his boots and rose from the bed. He tugged down his jeans, stepped out of them then tossed them over a nearby chair. Kreed turned toward him wearing just his dark blue briefs. He kept those on as he climbed in bed. Kreed rolled to his side and pushed his feet under the blankets, facing him.

"You did good today," Kreed said.

Aaron smiled at that. When he was little, his mom and dad would talk before they fell asleep, and for some reason, this reminded him of that, finding comfort in the moment. That was before everything got so fucked up with his family.

"You've told me that once already."

"I know, but I'm proud of you. You know, you don't have to sleep so far over there," Kreed added.

"I didn't want you to think I was pushing you into anything."

"No, it's good," Kreed replied.

Aaron began scooting over. Kreed met him halfway, drawing him in closer until he was able to lay his head on Kreed's shoulder. It was weird sleeping with someone like this. The few times he'd actually slept in bed with guys, he was usually the biggest guy, so the men would try and cuddle up against him. Kreed's body was huge and didn't give, his chest was rock hard and Aaron tried to find a comfortable position on all the muscle. "I really like having sex with you, but if you're anywhere close to where I am, what we shared was more than just a fuck to me."

"That was an honest statement," Kreed said, moving around until he was looking at Aaron. Kreed adjusted his pillow, giving some to Aaron as he stared at him, studying his face. "You aren't normally so forthcoming with information. Usually it's like pulling teeth to get you to open up about anything."

"Am I putting too much thought into it? Was I wrong?" Aaron asked, tucking his hands under his face.

"No, not wrong. Just finally honest without being pushed. And I would be lying if I said you were just a fuck," Kreed said, regarding him curiously.

"So I get why we need to hold off. It messes with your head," Aaron added, staying away from the honesty subject.

"I told you that."

"I know you did. When this case is over, do you think we will see each other again?" Aaron asked. If Kreed didn't want anything more with him, he needed to know, rein in all this runaway sentiment racing through him. He wanted to be with Kreed, but the stupid voice in the back of his head kept telling him he needed to stop before he got in too deep and ended up in prison. Why did he always want what he couldn't have?

"It's definitely something I'd like to explore. Depending on what they'll need from me once this wraps up, I have vacation time I can use to take you somewhere," Kreed answered. That was new too—someone wanting to take him somewhere as opposed to him being the one to take his guys places. How cool was that? His heart warmed.

"I'd like that," he finally said. God, he would like that so much. He would just have to figure out how in the hell he could keep his other activities off Kreed's radar. Kreed's palm came up and tenderly cupped his face.

"You're unexpected," Kreed said, and Aaron stayed silent. If Kreed only knew the truth. And how long would it take for this newfound attraction to turn against him if Kreed ever found out?

"Where do you call home?" Kreed asked. For the first time in a long time, he didn't want to lie. He lifted his head and searched Kreed's face, knowing he was taking too long to answer but he couldn't help it. He wanted to be honest. "It's not a hard question," Kreed said teasingly, but the laughter wasn't reaching the deputy's eyes. He knew Kreed was picking up that things weren't exactly right with Aaron. There were holes in his story and he knew it. Kreed saw things that no one else did. He hated having to hide himself from Kreed. Aaron had made a habit out of making himself inconsequential, but Kreed wasn't letting him slip through the cracks like he tried so hard to do.

"I have a place in Florida," he finally said and quickly tried to change the subject. He wasn't lying; he did have a place in Florida. "Where do you live?"

"I have an apartment in Louisiana that holds my stuff, but I travel all the time," Kreed said quietly. "You don't really live in Florida, do you?"

That hit way too close to home. "I do. It's just family's a touchy subject." He tried to deflect and started to turn over so Kreed could spoon against him. If he gave Kreed his back, maybe Kreed would drop the subject. This conversation had gotten too personal and Kreed was too perceptive.

"You'll learn soon enough that you can be honest with me. I know what I do for a living, but I also get it's not cut and dry out there in the real world. I could help with whatever you're running from," Kreed offered, keeping him from turning away as he pushed up on his elbow, changing his position. Kreed placed his fingers under Aaron's chin and forced his gaze up. Aaron shifted on his back and stared up at the deputy marshal as his stomach roiled at Kreed's comment. Did he know or was he just trying to piece together what he didn't know? Sin leaned forward and pressed a kiss to his forehead.

The tenderness was such an incredibly sweet gesture. One that was endearing and heartfelt, and he was absolutely certain Kreed meant those words with his whole heart. But would Kreed still feel the same if he ever found out the truth?

Now wasn't the time to open all this up. Aaron lifted to kiss him lightly on the lips, which was sort of new for him. He didn't make it a habit of kissing all that much. He'd probably kissed Kreed more than he'd kissed anyone in his entire life, and he was quickly becoming addicted to the man's sinful lips.

Aaron remained silent. Kreed gathered him in his arms, drawing Aaron against a warm hard chest. Aaron felt Kreed lightly kiss the top of his head as he wrapped a big arm around his waist and draped a leg across his. Kreed tugged on the covers again, covering him completely. He snuggled closer. His body fit so perfectly against Kreed's.

"Goodnight."

"Goodnight," Kreed responded. They both laid there at least an hour before Aaron finally heard Kreed's breathing even out. He started to pull away, let Kreed sleep in peace, but Kreed's big arm tightened and held him in place.

"Stay. I sleep better with you here." Kreed held on to Aaron like an anchor in the storm. It was comforting, and Aaron finally closed his eyes and let himself drift off.

Chapter 23

The warm body plastered completely against the front of Kreed stirred him awake, his morning hard-on trapped beneath a heavy thigh draped temptingly across his groin. If he didn't have to pee so bad, he'd be tempted to rub one off quickly, and with the way Aaron pressed enticingly against him, it wouldn't take a second.

On that thought, Kreed turned his head to the side. Aaron looked peaceful and innocent, the sight of that vulnerability made Kreed smile. That funny, warm feeling in his belly spiked again as he watched Aaron sleep. He could wake like this every single day and never have it grow old.

Those thoughts of waking up next to Aaron for the rest of his life should have had him clamoring for the hills. But lying there with this man's body tightly wrapped around him only intrigued Kreed, which was a completely foreign concept to him. At this point, he'd be a fool if he didn't admit his feelings were growing more and more profound the more time he spent with Aaron.

Guilt made Kreed hate himself for not taking better care of Aaron last night. Aaron had been attentive, kind, and comforting and kept true to his word. Not one time did he try to take advantage of the moment. Kreed was beginning to understand Aaron didn't play by any set of rules. The guy's life seemed to dance on the outskirts of authority, taking risks once he deemed the situation appropriate and safe. Case in point—yesterday morning Aaron had reached up and boldly kissed his lips, showing Kreed exactly what he thought about the boundaries he'd put back between them. Aaron hadn't been worried about himself, even though minutes later the kid walked across the street into the living evil of this world. Instead, he'd been worried about Kreed's anxiety levels.

Last night, Aaron had respected Kreed's rules and tried to find a way to be there for him without pushing too hard. Kreed couldn't remember a time in his adult life when anyone had ever wanted to take care of him. His heart seized at the prospect of finally having someone there for him.

Oh damn, church boy was a keeper. There was absolutely no hiding from the fact he had developed very deep feelings for the kid. He wasn't sure what any of that meant in terms of a relationship after this case was over, but he wanted to pursue the possibility.

On that thought, Kreed shifted his position. He really needed to get out of this bed before he lost the struggle with his own rules and bulldozed through the obstacles they presented. Kreed desperately wanted to live in a world where he could have relieved the tension of yesterday by making love to Aaron last night. And now, waking next to him with a fucking boner didn't help his resolve either.

He left Aaron sleeping. There wasn't any reason to wake him, especially not in the state Kreed was in. Aaron had chipped away at his will and he didn't have a whole hell of a lot of it left anyway. No one had ever swayed his resolve...ever...except Aaron.

Quietly, Kreed made his way to the hall bathroom, flipped on the light, and then slid out of his briefs. His hard-on stood out like a motherfucking pole, but the pressure in his bladder demanded a more immediate release. Kreed pushed his dick down and leaned over the toilet and waited. Fucking thing wasn't making this easy. Seconds later, Kreed had a nearly unending flow of curse words running through his head. His motherfucking prick wouldn't give, and he was determined to ignore it. Kreed finally finished his business, despite his dick's attempt to derail the situation. He reached over and turned on the shower faucets, allowing the water to heat.

He grabbed a towel and tossed it on the counter, then, looking down at his dick, he sighed before stepping into the shower. "Not gonna happen today, buddy. Get used to it."

Unfortunately the thing had a mind of its own and refused to go down. The steamy mist swirled around him and the heat of the water penetrated his skin. Trying for a moment of meditation, Kreed took a deep breath, inhaling warm vapors into his lungs, then slowly exhaled. The cleansing breath actually helped to take some of the edge off his fucking frayed emotions.

With monumental effort, he tried not to think about Aaron. Kreed turned, putting his back under the hot spray, letting the water pound against his shoulders as he grabbed the body scrub and poured the soap into his hand. The hard force of the water on his muscles made him do exactly what he hadn't wanted to, think about Aaron and last night. *Damn it!* He continued to ignore his cock. Mind over matter, he repeated in his head. He should just turn on the cold water, but he seriously doubted it would help much. Kreed lathered himself, scrubbing his upper body and back the best he could, then washed his balls and between his legs.

His hand slid over his stomach and brushed down along his dick. Kreed closed his eyes and let his mind drift to the man sleeping in the bed just on the other side of the door. He shouldn't, because just thinking about the kid made his balls ache for release.

Damn it! Just give in and get it over with, Sinacola. You're gonna be worthless otherwise.

Apparently that was all the encouragement he needed. Kreed closed his palm around his aching cock and began to stroke. Images of Aaron instantly filled his head; he couldn't get away from him. Last night when Aaron's strong fingers massaged his shoulders, it had taken every bit of self-control he had not to carry the guy to the bed, roll Aaron underneath him, and make passionate love to him. He wanted to drive Aaron insane with pleasure, make him scream his name as he pounded into that tight ass, show Aaron exactly how much he appreciated the care he'd shown.

Kreed stroked faster. He leaned back against the shower wall, biting his lip, being as quiet as possible. He screwed his eyes shut tighter, seeing Aaron's gray eyes staring into him, as Kreed fucked his soapy palm. Thoughts of Aaron filled his mind, his delicious scent, his contagious laugh, the way his lips lifted and lit up his whole face when he smiled, the sinful way Aaron's long lean body moved against his when they made love. Fuck, he wanted Aaron Stuart more than he wanted anything in his life.

"I can help with that." Kreed's eyes popped open at the husky sound of Aaron's voice echoing over the water. His hand all but stopped the workout he was giving his cock. His mouth gaped open as a completely naked Aaron stepped boldly into the shower with him.

"Aaron?" Kreed's tongue was heavy and thick in his mouth.

"The one and only, at your service," Aaron drawled the same words Kreed had used when they'd met. His blue-gray eyes danced with mirth as he stepped closer. Droplets of water gathered on Aaron's skin, rolling down the brightly colored tattoo draped across his shoulder and chest. Kreed's heart pumped double time as Aaron wrapped his fingers around his own cock and worked it while staring at Kreed with that double-dog-dare-you grin. *Shit!* "Looks like I'm just in time. Seems like you could use a hand. And just so happens I have a free one at the moment." Aaron stalked closer. "I'm really very good at double tasking, Deputy Marshal."

"Ah, fuck," Kreed cursed. His mental walls were falling fast. No, screw that. They were being blown the hell away.

"Only if you ask nicely." Aaron winked at him. The fucker actually winked. Here he was trying to do the right thing because he and Aaron were partners now. Well, temporary partners, but still. He had rules. His dick jerked, ready to argue that point, and he gripped the base tighter. Aaron's eyes dropped to his cock and the kid licked his lips.

"Fuck my stupid rules," Kreed growled and hauled Aaron against him. Their lips met, wet and open. Kreed took Aaron's mouth with his, hard and bruising. They both groaned, needy and hungry. Aaron pressed against his body, and his long fingers slid into Kreed's hair, rubbing against his scalp as the kid kissed him back.

He palmed Aaron's ass and dug his fingers into the firm, muscular flesh, rocking their erections together. Kreed broke from the kiss.

"You penetrate my defenses. What is it about you? " Kreed muttered against the side of Aaron's mouth.

"Don't know, but I like getting my way." Aaron nipped his lip then grabbed both of their erections in his hand and started to jack them. Kreed moaned and took Aaron's face between his palms and kissed him. The friction that Aaron's slick hand created on his dick had his hips bucking.

"Want you under me."

"Then we both want the same thing," Aaron continued to stroke them. And damn it felt so good that Kreed almost didn't have the strength to pull Aaron's hand away. He clutched Aaron's face in his palms, his church boy's beautiful face, and kissed him.

He was so fucking going to hell for this, but he couldn't fight it any longer. Kreed had had every intention of sticking to his rules, adhering to his plan, but that had been blown to smithereens. Deep, growing feelings for Aaron made it impossible to resist him. Kreed pulled back from the kiss.

"Hold that thought." He turned off the shower and reached for the towel on the counter, wrapping it around Aaron to quickly dry him, then hurriedly used it to dry himself.

Aaron followed him into the bedroom then lay back on the bed. Kreed grabbed the supplies out of the nightstand and tossed them within easy reach. His dick jerked and his balls grew heavier between his legs as Aaron spread his thighs and began stroking himself.

"You're incorrigible."

"And you're taking too long. I want you in me now," Aaron whined and cupped his balls.

"Be patient, church boy. I'm definitely going to be in you. I promise." Kreed flipped Aaron onto his stomach and swatted his ass, grinning when Aaron let out a surprised yelp.

"Ooh yes! I do like it when you make naughty promises." Aaron immediately lifted his body off the bed as he scrambled to his hands and knees and positioned himself in front of Kreed.

"Why can't I resist you?" Kreed stood at the edge of the bed, admiring the view—Aaron on all fours, begging to be taken. His palms slid over Aaron's warm skin, caressing all that perfect flesh. He smoothed his hand along the globes of Aaron's uplifted ass then down the back of his thighs and back up again. Beautiful. Aaron glanced back at him over his shoulder, a coy smirk playing across his lips.

"You are resisting! I'm waiting and you're talking. Now stop talking and fuck me already," came Aaron's smartass reply. Kreed had to chuckle at the kid's lack of patience.

"In due time. I'm going to savor this." If he was breaking the rules, he was going to enjoy the ride. And he had no intention of rushing through any of it. He slowly nibbled his way down Aaron's back and placed a tender kiss at the base of his spine, before spreading Aaron's ass cheeks with his palms and licking across the pink pucker.

The heady scent of his musk and the feel of Aaron's warm flesh against his tongue shot straight to Kreed's dick. He slid his hands to the front of Aaron's hips to draw him back to his mouth. Kreed kissed and mouthed Aaron's hole. Aaron's essence slid across his palate, sweeter and more addicting with every swipe of his tongue.

"Oh, God, Sin." Aaron pressed his ass into Kreed's face. Using his thumbs to hold Aaron open, Kreed pointed his tongue and began to fuck Aaron with it. After a few more prods and passes of his tongue, he pulled back and sucked his fingers into his mouth, wetting them. Kreed tapped softly at Aaron's entrance with the pad of his index finger then lightly ghosted over the tender flesh before sliding inside. Quickly adding a second, then third, he started pumping them in and out of Aaron, enjoying the way they disappeared into Aaron's body with little resistance.

"That's it… Fuck yourself on my fingers," Kreed growled, and Aaron rolled his hips, forcing the fingers deeper into his clenching passage. He pushed in even farther and twisted his wrist, curling his fingers before pulling back.

"I need more, Sin. Want to feel your cock stretching me. Please." Aaron rocked forward and backward, impaling himself wantonly on Kreed's digits.

Kreed pulled his fingers from Aaron's ass, purposely scraping across that spot that made Aaron shudder and his ass contract.

"You're so fucking evil," Aaron murmured.

"And you love it," Kreed chuckled as he opened the condom, his fingers twitching with anticipation. Just the thought of being balls deep in Aaron Stuart had him shaking with need. He had sworn he wouldn't do this, would keep his professional distance, but damn it to hell, the kid pressed every button he had and in exactly the right order.

Kreed squeezed the lube along his dick and used his hand to spread it evenly over himself before aligning his length with Aaron's entrance. Aaron swiveled his hips.

"Please," Aaron groaned and pressed back. The friction of sliding his dick up and down Aaron's crack caused him to shudder.

"Gonna fill you up, church boy." His balls ached to be inside Aaron.

"I'm starting to think you're all tal— Ahh fuck!" Aaron gasped when Kreed pressed forward, pushing past the outer ring of muscle, and slipped inside. Fire engulfed him. Aaron's tightness held him like a glove as he sank deeper and deeper into heaven. He fought to keep on his feet and hold back his need to pound into the embracing heat.

"Feels so good. Tell me what you need."

Aaron's muscles clenched around him, drawing him deeper until his groin pressed tightly against Aaron's ass.

"Fuck me, and I want to feel it for the next week."

And he wanted to do just that. Kreed dug his fingers into Aaron's hips and slowly started to move, pulling out until only the tip remained then sinking forward until their bodies meeting stopped him.

"Feel good?" He reached around to stroke Aaron's erection, spreading the slick pre-come across the head then dipping his nail into the leaking slit.

"Fuuucck yes, Sin." Aaron bucked into his fist.

When Aaron relaxed even more, he picked up the pace and began fucking him harder. His knees grew weak, his legs were wobbly like cooked spaghetti noodles, but he kept on pounding, his hips thrusting of their own accord. Kreed palmed Aaron's neck, drawing him fully up on his knees and back against his chest. His fingers tightened on Aaron's neck, holding him in place with his hand as he mouthed the salty skin just under his ear.

"I can't last. Gonna come too fast," he confessed against Aaron's heated skin, his body moving in and out of Aaron. So fucking right. Kreed continued to stroke the thick cock in his hand in time with the frantic rhythm of his thrusts. Heavy pants and the sound of naked flesh slapping against naked flesh filled the room. Whatever this was with Aaron, he never wanted it to end. No other man could ever make him feel this out of control, this reckless with such purpose. He was helpless against this brilliant kid.

"You feel so good in me." Aaron groaned and his hips stuttered as he pressed back, grinding on Kreed's dick. Aaron's hot channel gripped him like a fucking vise, making it hard to think.

"Need to see your face when you come. Please." He released his hold on Aaron, and withdrew from his warmth. Aaron rolled to his back and scooted to the middle of the bed. Kreed followed him, stopping to bend forward and lick across the flat brown nipple then flick the nipple ring with the tip of his tongue. He fucking loved Aaron's nipple rings.

"Oh, God." Aaron's breath hitched as Kreed captured the tightening bud between his teeth. Aaron's fingers dug into his shoulders as he continued to toy with the metal ring. Kreed gave the other nipple an equal amount of attention then settled himself between Aaron's spread legs.

"Where were we?" Aaron bit his lip and pulled his legs to his chest, his eyes hooded with lust as he purred the words. Kreed leaned over his church boy and brushed his finger across his brow, moving a stray strand of dark hair that had fallen close to his blue eyes. Aaron smiled up at him.

"Losing myself in you." Kreed's eyes locked with Aaron's as he positioned himself and pushed into his lover's constricting heat. Kreed held himself up on his forearms to gaze down at Aaron.

Aaron's eyes glazed over and his lips parted on a sigh. Kreed's heart fluttered as he watched an unmistakable look of pleasure cross the kid's face.

"Mmm...fuck. Sin," Aaron rumbled, licking his lips. Kreed loved the way his nickname flowed off Aaron's tongue. Warm hands slid up Kreed's back, lingering at the nape of his neck before sifting through his hair and urging him down.

Kreed took Aaron's mouth, thrusting his tongue into the warm recesses, probing, tasting everything that was Aaron. He licked across the kid's teeth then sucked his tongue. Aaron responded by digging his fingernails deep into his scalp. Kreed stiffened his tongue, mouth-fucking him while he drove his cock deep into Aaron's body. Aaron returned the heated kiss with abandon, his hips lifting to meet every thrust.

Tearing his mouth from the kiss, he nipped at Aaron's neck and shoulders, tasting his salty, sweat-dampened skin as his dick slid in and out of Aaron's tightness. The hot, delicious, and forbidden feeling blanketed him.

"Make me come, Sin," Aaron pleaded.

"My pleasure," he growled against Aaron's ear. Balancing on an elbow, he sped up his thrust, aiming for that sensitive bundle of nerves that made Aaron squirm. He worked his hand between their heated bodies, took Aaron in his grip, and stroked him in earnest. His hips pounded out the perfect rhythm as hot skin slid against hot skin. Damn, he was so close, and the small sounds of pleasure coming from Aaron made it hard to concentrate on his own movement. The pressure built in his spine and rolled up to the base of his skull. He was holding on by a thread.

"Let me feel you come around my dick." His words were breathy, needy, and commanding, but he was rewarded when Aaron's ass tightened around him.

"Aaah gah...yes." Aaron panted, shook violently, then turned rigid as hot come spread between their joined bodies. Kreed pushed in deep, burying himself to the hilt as Aaron thrashed beneath him.

"Ah, fuck, church boy." The wild contractions in Aaron's ass pushed him completely over. The force of his orgasm took his breath, and everything went black except the burst of white spots that danced behind his eyes.

Kreed threw his head back and shouted through his release. Their pleasure-filled groans mingled, saturating the otherwise silent room. Riding the waves of his climax, his body bowed and his cock twitched as his seed filled the latex in Aaron's passage. Spent, he collapsed on Aaron's chest.

Awareness slowly trickled into his brain. At this moment, his body was so relaxed it felt heavy. His heart still thundered in his chest but his wasn't the only one. He could feel Aaron's beating out the same rhythm. He lifted his head and upper body then pressed his lips to Aaron's forehead, drawing him as close as he could, before kissing his eye, nose, and cheek. Their bodies fused together with sweat and cooling come, and he wouldn't want it any other way.

"You know we have to get up, right?" Kreed smiled at Aaron, stroking his cheek with his thumb, trying to soften the news. They had a job to do today; people were counting on them. Kreed wanted every part of this case closed and behind them so he could spend his days wrapped up with Aaron just like this.

"I know. I just don't want to," Aaron whispered, his fingers lazily roaming up and down Kreed's back as they held each other. The smell of sweat and sex hung heavy in the air, a pleasant reminder of what they'd shared.

"Come on. We need another shower then we have to get you dressed for church." Kreed shifted positions, and his softening cock slipped from Aaron's body, making him groan.

"What if I said I would rather stay right here in bed with you and forget about those religious freaks?"

"I'd say you have the best ideas. But you know we can't." He kissed Aaron and rolled to his side.

As much as he hated leaving the warmth of the man next to him, he forced himself to get up, making it as far as placing his feet on the floor and standing, before turning back to his church boy.

"First one to the shower gets a blow job!"

Chapter 24

A warm front blew through, making the weather not only bearable, but nice. Aaron left his jacket at the house and found he was in a great mood, actually happy this morning, as he walked across the street with a little kick in his step. He couldn't hide the smile plastered across his face and had to lower his head to keep from looking like an idiot. What a strange reaction with the heavy weight of this case looming over his head.

He hadn't been expecting the breakthrough he and Kreed had had this morning. It was a welcome surprise, one he was reminded of with every step he took. They'd had earth-moving, toe-curling, better-than-chocolate sex. Well, he had kind of initiated that, but who started what didn't matter right now. For the first time in his life, he wasn't concerned about whatever system he planned to hack or about this case Mitch dropped in his lap; he was focused on a guy and that felt amazing.

Aaron entered the church a little before starting time. Stella was already at the front desk. Today he was finally prepared to meet her normal bubbly, religiously over-the-top greeting with one of his own. Instead, she looked up with a firm frown stretched across her round face, not the always pleasant person he'd grown to expect. This morning all she could do was shake her head before lowering her eyes and looking away as he passed by.

Okay, that was odd. His smile faded. The vibe he got chilled him to his bones. The whole attitude here was wrong. The place felt off. That self-righteous air that seeped from the walls of this building was upset this morning. Aaron lowered his brow and took a step backward toward the desk. With his safety being top of mind, he shouldn't get too far in without knowing what was going on.

"Is there something wrong today?" he asked the secretary before remembering to turn his body so the cross pin could capture the image and conversation.

"They're flaunting their sin. Pastor Helps is very unhappy this morning," she said, as if that explained everything.

"I'm not sure what happened. I stayed up late reading my Bible." Aaron repeated the words he'd heard over and over since starting his job at the church. That seemed to be a perfect excuse for anything not done around this place. It excused everything.

"Those homosexuals keep making the news. It's disgraceful and utterly disgusting," she whispered angrily. Aaron assumed she referred to Colt Michaels. He suspected the guy got regular coverage around here, being too popular to fade away easily.

So that meant their night out had worked. He hoped Kreed and the alphabet boys got that little piece of intel. His phone vibrated in his pocket, and he suspected that was Kreed confirming his thought.

"I didn't see. I don't watch that much TV. It's the devil's tool," Aaron said, unsure really what else to say in order to keep her talking.

"It's disturbing. They are abominations before the Lord. The Bible says they are to be put to death and their blood will be on their own heads. Leviticus 20:13." Aaron was sickened by her words, but he just nodded, tried to look upset, and left the entryway. On the way back to his office, everyone who had already arrived had about that same attitude. These people were absolutely certifiable. The mood of the building was dark and totally creeped him out, sending a shiver racing down his spine.

The lone guy who now made up the entire IT department with him was actually in this morning, typing away on his computer. That was a little bit of a surprise. He never spoke, and Aaron wasn't entirely certain of his name. Maybe something like Jeb, but the not-speaking part was nothing new. Techie guys weren't usually known for their sparkling personalities. He'd learned Jeb's absence came from spending lots of time in the chapel, on his knees. Prayer seemed the other acceptable excuse as to why the staff didn't get their daily tasks completed. Aaron had only really seen Jeb a couple of times in passing since he'd started.

"I can't get a video to play on my computer," Pastor Helps barked at the door to their office. Aaron was the first to respond, moving in the direction of the pastor, who might have been a little more surly than normal, but it was honestly hard to tell.

"I'll be happy to take a look for you," Aaron offered, and Pastor Helps grumbled something unintelligible. The old preacher was slow on his feet, and Aaron stayed a step or two behind as they entered the administration office. Julie had about the same disposition as Stella, with her face all pinched up in disgust. No one around the place appeared pleased this morning. Mitch must have outdone himself last night. Aaron was kind of sorry he'd missed their little show. Again, his phone vibrated in his slacks, and after a second or two, he decided against checking who texted. If it were Kreed or Connors, surely they could see he was occupied. "What's it doing?"

"It's not playing," Pastor Helps barked.

"Yes, sir. I mean, does it open?" Aaron asked.

"I don't know. See for yourself." The older man didn't hover this morning, and that was odd. Instead, he took a seat across the desk while Aaron made himself comfortable in the one behind Pastor Helps's computer. His guess was that there was a simple update that needed to be done, but he sat there longer than normal, trying to see if there was anything else he could get off this computer.

"I'm tired," the pastor finally said, breaking the silence. Aaron looked over to see his head lowered; he was rubbing his eyes with his thumb and forefinger.

"Yes, sir. You work hard." He had no idea what to say but wanted to keep him talking.

"You came from New Hope University, right? I remember a pastor there. He was a true fundamentalist to the core. Professor Lehman. Was he still there?" Aaron hated those kinds of questions because, while he'd schooled himself on the faculty, he had no idea who'd come and gone over the years.

Thankfully he was saved from answering the question when the door to the outer office flew open making a terrible racket as it banged against the wall. Aaron looked up as a tall, well-dressed man came barreling into the room. His insides ran cold. He knew the voice. Deacon Silas Burns. Julie barely got a greeting out before the Deacon began raging.

Hours of schooling himself on everyone involved had paid off. This was actually the first time he'd seen the deacon in person, since the man was supposedly in Mexico. He was as scary as his pictures looked. The disfigurement of his face came by way of a scar that ran from the center of his forehead down across the right eye, all the way to his ear. His face contorted with anger, his stance volatile and threatening.

The deacon came at the pastor in such a way that Aaron involuntarily scooted back in his chair, reaching for the weapon strapped to his calf inside his slacks. What he thought he'd do with it against the likes of this clearly evil man, he had no idea, but Pastor Helps was an old man. He had to try. When Aaron's eyes moved back to the pastor, the realization hit him, stopping him in his tracks. Helps was just as enraged as the deacon.

"The sodomites are brazenly flaunting themselves in front of God. The expression on their faces bears witness against them, and they display their sin like Sodom; they do not even conceal it. Woe to them! For they have brought evil on themselves. Isaiah 3:9," the deacon shouted.

Aaron's heart began to race as he realized what was going down. He lowered his head and put his hands on the keyboard as the pastor's voice echoed the deacon's sentiment when he said, "We are to be diligent watchmen, my brethren. It is our duty to sound the alarm. Ezekiel 33:6 says, *'But if the watchman see the sword come, and blow not the trumpet, and the people be not warned; if the sword come, and take any person from among them, he is taken away in his iniquity; but his blood I will require from the watchman's hand.'* Brother Langley gave his life for shooting that detestable homosexual who paraded around as a highway patrol officer, flaunting his unnatural desire, and for punishing the other wicked sodomites for their ungodly sins. He was a true disciple and did as commanded by the Lord. The filthy fags will be held accountable for their inequities. Sodomy is punishable by death. We must finish

Brother Langley's work and do as we've been instructed and exact the wrath of God for their flagrant displays of homosexuality."

Aaron's stomach roiled at the hate coming from these men's mouths. He rose quietly from the chair, careful not to draw attention to himself as he headed around the other side of the desk and out of the room. He kept his head down as he walked; his entire body shook under the fear of those words.

Luckily, he'd checked the connection to the alphabet boys a moment ago. The computer was recording, and the pastor had just acknowledged knowing what happened to Cody. Hopefully if he left, they would give a full confession in their anger. Aaron had barely made it out of the office, before the pastor's door slammed shut, closing the two men inside the room behind him. His eyes had to be as big as saucers as he rushed away from that office.

"Josiah!" Julie whispered harshly, catching his attention, motioning him over to her desk. He lifted his eyes to the side outside door, estimating maybe twenty steps to that door. His heart pounded so hard and the blood rushed to his head so fast he couldn't think straight as he moved toward Julie's desk. Surely, he could deal with her. He was just so relieved he wasn't trapped in that room with those radical freaks any longer.

"You *must* keep what you've heard to yourself, Josiah. It's very important. You wouldn't have been hired if they didn't trust you completely."

Aaron nodded, freaking out a little more, because in his mind, she'd just admitted to knowing what was going on too. He nodded again, turned on his heel and headed for the administration office door. It took everything inside him to walk down the hall—not run—toward the reception area and outside the front doors of the church. As he got closer, Aaron couldn't resist the urge to bolt any longer. All the hate and malevolence oozing from those supposed men of God freaked him the fuck out. In the battle of good versus evil, Deacon Burns was a vile and malicious force and completely supported by the members of this church office.

Aaron took off running toward the house as Kreed busted through the front door with his weapon drawn. That justified his fear; Kreed would never break cover so completely without a verifiable threat. Kreed never looked his way, his entire being laser-focused on the church. Aaron barely made it up the front porch steps before he saw two large tactical vehicles flying down the street from opposite directions. As he ran past, Kreed backed away, coming inside, slamming the door shut with his foot. Only then did he turn around.

"What the fuck happened? Was that enough information? I tried to get everything I could!" Aaron yelled as his heart raced in his chest. Everything had happened so quickly that his adrenalin pumped, making him a little frantic. Kreed thrust a walkie-talkie and a pistol in his hands, and he accepted them without an argument, gripping the handle of the pistol tightly in his fingers.

"Stay put. Keep the doors locked. Stay away from the windows." Kreed turned to leave, but Aaron grabbed his hand.

"What's happening?"

"Whatever you did gave the visual. Helps told Burns to go after Mitch, to take him down and any others standing in their way because they were no more than abominations that needed to be cast into the lake of fire, but Hasselbeck had broken a few minutes before. He confessed what was going on. It all came together at the same time. I gotta go." Kreed shook Aaron off, yelling a quick "Lock the door" before he left.

~~~

The Midlothian Police Department cruisers turned on the street with sirens blaring about the same time that Kreed ran across the church's front lawn toward the building. The church was already surrounded with bureau agents and USMS deputies, all swarming both the interior and outer buildings. He stopped by a bureau truck, badge in hand as he identified himself. He pointed his finger toward the house they'd used and quickly yelled, "I need you to watch that house."

In all his panic to get out here, Kreed had barely tugged the official marshal jacket on, identifying him as a deputy US marshal. The volume of screams coming from inside the building had him ducking while running toward the front doors, weapon still drawn, pointed toward the ground with each step he took.

The scene inside was chaotic at best. Staff members were already handcuffed and sitting or lying on the ground, depending on how much they'd resisted arrest. Kreed was cautious as he walked through the room. He looked down the hall before he continued. Vicious words echoed off the walls, drowning everything else out. The pastor was in rare form, spewing vile Bible verses of hellfire and brimstone. Kreed saw more agents than should have been needed, making him move more swiftly toward the main office. Brody Masters came out the door when Kreed was about halfway down the hall. He was talking into a handheld radio, only pausing when he saw Kreed.

"Deacon Burns got away. He got past us somehow."

Fuck! He'd left Aaron alone in the house with no one really. What if the lunatic followed Aaron? Fear coiled in his gut, and Kreed's heart wedged in his throat.

Kreed didn't say a word. He spun on his heels and took off running as fast as he could toward the house. He could hear Masters's booming voice instructing others to set up perimeters and search each and every house near the church's complex, but Kreed never slowed as he sprinted across the street. Burns could have seen the way he'd covered Aaron as he'd left the church and figured out Aaron was involved in this somehow. He hadn't considered the consequences when he'd busted out of the house; he knew what Aaron didn't, and his only goal was getting Stuart to safety.

The house was across the street, no more than three hundred feet, but the last hundred feet felt like miles. His legs and lungs burned with worry as he sprinted up the walkway.

Kreed kicked open the door, knowing it would be locked if Burns did indeed have Aaron. He barreled through, barely pausing as he rounded the corner, prepared to fire. Aaron came rushing through the office door. Fear, then surprise, crossed his face. Aaron's eyes went straight to the gun in Kreed's hands, and he stepped back as his hands went in the air. "What the hell?"

"Are you alone?" Kreed bellowed.

"Of course," Aaron answered, taking another step backward, clearly unnerved. Kreed moved, his eyes sweeping the room as he stalked toward Aaron. He wanted to touch him, draw him into his arms just to make sure Aaron was truly okay.

"Has he been here? Did you see the deacon leaving the building?" Kreed asked. He stopped at the entrance of the hall and finally lowered his weapon.

"No. You guys didn't get him?"

Kreed shook his head and, feeling someone's presence raised the weapon until he verified it was an agent behind him. An unspoken faith had him moving forward, turning toward the study, hoping the agent behind him moved toward Aaron's bedroom.

"No," Kreed finally said. He turned to speak to the small team forming in the living room. "Sweep the place," Kreed instructed as he went for Aaron, only stopping about a foot from him, forcing himself not to draw the guy against him like he wanted. Instead, he holstered his weapon.

"How'd he get away? Is he going after Mitch?" Aaron asked, moving toward him with the same fear and concern clouding his eyes that Kreed had felt only moments before.

"You two can relax." The deputy marshal who checked Aaron's room came out, pointing to his earpiece as he spoke. He had a direct line of information filtering through his ear. "They've got an eye on the suspect. He's headed down Midlothian Parkway. He's on the run, but they'll get him. There's nowhere to go."

"Keep me posted on that." The front door was still wide open, and Kreed heard several vehicles taking off from across the street. Probably Masters heading toward the chase. Reaching out, he took Aaron by the neck, guiding him inside the office, away from prying eyes. Kreed closed the door behind them, before pulling Aaron to his chest.

"You scared the shit out of me," he whispered on a haggard breath, burying his face in the crook of Aaron's neck.

"I was scared. That guy was off the charts," Aaron said, wrapping his arms tighter around Kreed.

"I didn't know if you'd get out of there. I was texting you, telling you to leave. It felt off from the minute you walked inside the place," Kreed said, pressing his lips against the heartbeat pulsing in Aaron's neck, still clutching him like a vise, so thankful he was safe in his arms.

"I didn't have a chance to check my phone." Aaron relaxed against him.

"I need to check on Knox. Find out what's going on. Are you good here? I'll have someone stay." Kreed started to pull away, but Aaron's hands fisted in his jacket. There was a hint of panic hidden in their blue-gray depths. He looked down to see Aaron's hands shaking as he clenched them closed. His calm, cool, collected guy that pushed every boundary Kreed put in place had anxiety rolling off him in waves. Kreed covered Aaron's fists with his palms. "You're okay, Aaron. It's over. You did good, exactly what we needed. You don't have to go back there again."

"I'll be all right. It's just a lot," Aaron said quietly. Kreed watched as Aaron visibly tried to pull himself together. Even with the uncertainty of the deacon on the run, Kreed waited several long moments before he lifted Aaron's chin with the tips of his fingers, studying his face. Aaron was freaked, but had worked himself out of meltdown mode. That said a lot for a situation like this and the man Aaron truly was.

"We'll be leaving here tonight. Pack up, but plan on staying with me for the next few days while they decide how much they need from us." Kreed tried for reassuring as he kept his eyes on Aaron's. Giving a small smile, he wanted to convey the pride he had for the job Aaron had accomplished. The kid had done everything he was supposed to. While Kreed sat at the monitor, watching, he'd been going a little nuts wanting Stuart to abandon the job and get his ass out of there, but church boy pressed on, closing this case up tight.

Not completely certain they weren't being heard, Kreed still leaned in and kissed those slightly upturned lips. "You did so good today. Stay put for me."

"Call Mitch. Make sure they're okay." Aaron nodded.

"They are. I'm going to call and check on them, but they're at a secure location," Kreed confirmed, bending in to kiss Aaron again, this time he lingered for a second or two longer.

"This has to be bigger than just here," Aaron added. The kid was thinking now, surely that was a good sign. Except when Aaron started using that brain, they ended up in situations like this. Maybe the kid could contain the thought process until they got this part of the investigation closed.

"I'm sure it is, but Connors is all over that. Our job's done." Kreed lifted his hand for a high five, and Aaron smiled a little, giving his hand a soft slap, before running his fingers through his hair.

"We really did it."

"Yes, we did." Kreed followed Aaron's lead, running his fingers through Aaron's hair while wrapping an arm around his waist, drawing him against his chest. Kreed kissed him thoroughly and swiftly. All the tension he'd held, the worry over keeping his church boy safe, faded. They'd done it.

Chapter 25

Both Mitch and Kreed stood side by side in front of the one-way mirrored window, watching as two of the bureau's agents interrogated Pastor Helps. He answered every question asked of him with a tirade of hellfire and damnation Bible verses that Kreed wasn't entirely sure were word for word from the scripture. He suspected Helps added and deleted as he needed to drive his point home.

"I just got word that Burns didn't make it," Brody said, coming inside the small room to stand next to Kreed.

"I didn't see how he could," Mitch said. Kreed silently agreed. The car chase had ended almost as quickly as it had begun, with a cement truck pulling out onto the parkway, clearly unable to anticipate the fleeing man's high rate of speed. The deacon, with no way to avoid the impact, lost control of his vehicle and slammed into the side of the truck. Even though the fire rescue team had arrived quickly, it took a solid hour to remove him from the wreckage, and he'd been barely alive at that point. "He's pissed off," Mitch added, cocking his head toward the pastor.

"Yeah, but his staff members are singing like canaries," Brody replied, tucking his hands into his slacks pockets. The pastor sure was putting on such a show that it was kind of hard to turn away. To be so old, he was going strong. For many reasons, Kreed would hate to be at one of this guy's sermons, because he could see hours spent waiting for him to finish on the pulpit. "We've got more than enough to file charges. They're just trying to get information now about the satellite churches—how much they knew. He's gonna be the one to have that information."

"You think that vein in his forehead's gonna explode?" Kreed asked, shoving his fingers into his jeans pocket, not able to tear his eyes away from the scene playing out in front of him.

"I've been watching it but decided only the good die young," Mitch stated.

"Seriously, he looks like the crypt keeper. Did you notice that?" Kreed asked Mitch, knocking him in the arm with his elbow.

"More like the crypt keeper's weird grandfather." Mitch chuckled.

"You guys are too much," Brody said, laughing a little.

"Has he cracked yet?" Skinner asked, coming inside the office. His arrival was the only thing that had all three men turning from the window.

"He's close to a confession or blowing a vessel. It's hard to know which one," Kreed answered. Skinner shook each of their hands before patting Mitch then Kreed on the shoulder.

"Job well done. If you hadn't stuck with this, we might not have ever known. Most certainly more men would have lost their lives," Skinner said, taking a spot next to Brody, looking in on the pastor.

This case was Mitch's baby. He deserved that credit, but he'd never take it. Kreed was certain his buddy just felt like it was all in a day's work.

"Where's Stuart? He needs some recognition in this," Skinner asked.

"He's still in Midlothian. I need to get back there," Kreed said, thinking about the look in Aaron's eyes just before he'd left.

"Montgomery invited you to stay at their house," Knox said, and as anticipated, he never acknowledged the compliment Skinner had just given him. That was so fucking Knox. Kreed nodded, having turned back to continue staring inside the small interrogation room. He decided he'd probably take Jace up on that offer. The kid seemed to really like Jace and Colt. Aaron would probably feel better staying in Dallas with someone he knew than waiting alone in a hotel or even waiting in some stale room here at the station for when he might be needed.

"I really need to go check on Aaron," Kreed finally said, forcing himself to turn away from the window once again.

"We need to talk to Stuart," Skinner said, but he didn't move. The director couldn't seem to stop staring at the freak show playing out in the other room. Kreed understood. It was like watching really bad reality TV but knowing, for sure, this was completely real. No script could be this fucked up.

"I'll bring him in, but give me a few hours," Kreed said to Director Skinner, then turned his attention to Mitch. "Do I just call Jace?" He kept his eyes averted from the interrogation, not wanting to be drawn back in to the crazy, fucked up performance going on behind the glass divider.

"Yeah...or I will," Mitch said, finally turning away. The guy followed Kreed out the door and walked with him down the hall. As they stepped out of the front doors of the office, Mitch walked all the way to the parking lot. In the silence they shared, Kreed could tell his partner was trying to get out from under the contact surveillance cameras surrounding the building. From this vantage point, they'd still be seen but not necessarily heard. Mitch swiftly pulled off the sunglasses hooked to his T-shirt collar and put them in place before he turned to Kreed, stopping him about ten feet from his rental car.

"Thank you for this," Mitch said, holding open his arms and hands. Mitch was a little awkward in his movements, his brow furrowed. Aww, damn, his partner was emotional.

"You did this, man. I just helped out when you needed me." Kreed swallowed the lump in his throat at Mitch's sentiment. Nothing more was said. They stood there, staring at one another until Mitch drew Kreed in for a hug, and Kreed accepted it, wrapping his arms tightly around his partner. It felt so good to have those crazy people off the streets. There would always be more like them, but just knowing this cell was shut down made the moment a little more special. "I wanted you to have this finished so you wouldn't always be looking over your shoulder. I know it killed you not being right in the middle of this after what they did to Cody."

When Mitch pulled away, he lowered his head, digging his fingers in his eyes underneath his glasses. After a second or two, he finally said, "You saw it through for me, and between you and Skinner, y'all kept me involved and gave me purpose in the case."

Kreed nodded and silence settled between them again. "I've gotta go. Aaron's alone. I figured I'd take Montgomery up on his offer."

"Cool. They're ready to extend their appreciation too," Mitch said, kicking at something unknown on the pavement. "You've been a little weird. Is there something goin' on with you?"

"The kid and I started something. I don't know where it's going, but if it's a problem, we can stay at a hotel," Kreed stated, just laying it out there. Mitch deserved the high coming his way from closing this case. Kreed didn't want to be the downer, but he also didn't want to wait to explore what might or might not be between him and Aaron.

"So one room, then. I'll tell Montgomery. Aaron, huh? You know, all this time, I really thought Stuart was straight." Mitch chuckled before he turned and left Kreed standing alone. He grinned as he watched his buddy walk away. Kreed sighed deeply, so glad that had gone as well as it had. His heart was lighter than it had been in a while. He pulled the keys from his pocket as he headed toward his truck. Aaron would be waiting for him.

Chapter 26

Two days later, Kreed backed out of the Michaels-Montgomery driveway with a scheduled fourteen days off. Aaron sat in the passenger seat with his phone in hand, texting, his thumbs moving faster than Kreed had ever seen anyone before as he worked the small keyboard on the screen. That alone highlighted the generation gap between them. Kreed wasn't a texter, and when forced, he punched at the screen with his forefinger, much like he did with a computer keyboard. That was just never his thing.

Although Kreed was almost completely free for the next fourteen days—only being available if something with the case came up—Aaron apparently had work. If he'd heard it once, he'd heard it a hundred times—smart boy was far behind in whatever his job required.

It had taken quite a bit of talking to get Aaron to agree to come to Hawaii once Jace had offered up his place for a little extended R and R. In the end, Kreed conceded on all points in order to get Aaron alone for an obstacle-free vacation. He had a shit load of the kid's traveling computer gear bundled up and shipped out so he could complete his work from the island. Kreed had even promised he wouldn't interfere when Aaron sat down to do his job.

The whole Aaron-slash-work situation needled at him. Kreed only now realized the kid might not be as into him as before, and he didn't know exactly how to get them back there or what had happened to make the change.

Jace and Colt stood on the front porch, waving them off. Both Mitch and Cody were downtown, helping Masters put the final touches on the case that had exploded over the last forty-eight hours. Twenty-five arrests had already been made, most of them being people with knowledge of the church's activities.

With all the focus on this case, Kreed was certain they'd have those few apprehended in no time. This particular hate ring was far reaching—bigger than anyone had thought—and Mitch was being hailed as a hero for sticking with the case when no one else would.

"They're nice," Aaron said, never lifting his head. Kreed reached for his sunglasses on the visor and slid them on as he drove down the street. "Offering up their place in Hawaii was pretty unexpected."

"Yeah, you sure you want to go?" Kreed finally asked, braking as he came to a stop sign. He kept his voice neutral, trying to hide the disappointment those words caused. He should probably give the kid an out before they were stuck on an island together with him hearing the dreaded words, "It's not you, it's me."

The bigger problem? Part of him just wanted to take whatever time Aaron offered. The irritating other part wanted him to dig deeper and find out what had caused Aaron's hesitation.

"Yeah, why?" Aaron responded, his head still bent toward the phone.

"You've just been weird. We don't have to do this," Kreed interjected, navigating another turn onto a busy street.

"Why? Is that what you want?" Aaron stopped texting, lifting his head as he turned toward him. Kreed cut his eyes over to Aaron then focused back on the road.

"No, not at all. I wouldn't be going if I didn't want this," Kreed said.

"Me either. I just need to make sure I have time to do my thing. I committed way before all of this." Aaron explained his mystery business deal again for the third or fourth time over the last two days. As the silence settled between them, Aaron didn't look back down at his phone. Instead, he tucked the device in his back pocket, eyes trained in his direction. Kreed reached down to take his hand, threading their fingers together. The one thing they had never really been was awkward, but the last twenty-four hours may have tested that theory.

"I thought we were on the same page about seeing what this is between us."

"We were," Aaron said a little defensively, but gave Kreed the reassurance of gripping his hand tighter. That was really all he needed to get his heart right again. "We *are*, I mean. You just got distant."

"No, not really. I was just giving you the space you needed to work," Kreed said, alternating his focus between Aaron and the road. "I get funky when I'm filling out all that paperwork. I hate that shit, but you were in all those meetings with me then coming back to Jace's place and working all night. I didn't want to smother you. I was trying to give you room."

"Room for what?" Aaron asked, his tone now completely uncertain. "Like to change my mind or for you to change yours?"

At first, the words made Kreed immediately defensive. He didn't feel like he'd created any distance between them for any reason, and if he had, he'd just explained why. He'd certainly never wanted space. He liked the kid. Just being around Aaron made him relax. Why would he want that to change?

Being innately self-reflective sucked, especially right now. Okay, so maybe he did put some space between them. Kreed knew he totally had that whole attitude of 'an island to himself' thing going on. He'd developed that during his years in the military. He pushed everyone away, kept even Knox at arm's length most of the time.

That just made Aaron's point crystal clear. The kid was remarkably intuitive at reading his moods, more so than anyone ever before. Maybe he did have an ulterior motive behind his actions. He did keep himself at the bureau offices until late into the night. He hadn't sat next to Aaron when they ate together, and he'd left the house usually before Aaron woke.

Okay, so he had put space between them. What could that mean?

Kreed tightened his hold on Aaron's hand. No matter what, whatever he'd done over the last few days was definitely not him changing his mind.

"I didn't want you to feel like I was forcing you into anything. You've been through a lot over the last few weeks. It was all a new experience for both of us. I didn't want you to feel like you had to stick with anything you said under all that stress. I want you to want this as much as I do." The words were the truth, and his raw honesty even surprised Kreed himself. He hadn't even realized that had been an issue for him until right that minute.

"I'm not weak, Kreed," Aaron replied, frustration in his tone.

He'd been blaming Aaron for all the barriers between them when it was clearly him pulling away.

"I didn't say you were," Kreed said immediately.

"I'm not a kid," Aaron responded in that same irritated tone.

"Okay. I do call you that, but I don't think you're that either. I called you that in the beginning to try and give you a place other than the one I wanted you in. Believe me, I know better than anyone you're not a kid. It just stuck. It's now a term of endearment, just like church boy. I call you that and you don't go to fucking church," Kreed added, trying to figure out where Aaron was going with all that.

There was silence between them for several long minutes. Kreed navigated onto the highway. They had gotten a call to stop by the house in Midlothian to pick up a few things left behind, then they needed to make a quick trip by the store before heading to the airport.

"I don't want it to get weird between us," Kreed finally said in all the silence between them.

"Then quit pulling away and making it weird," Aaron countered. The kid had spunk. The only person on the planet who talked to him that way was Mitch, and he regularly put Mitch on the mat.

"Okay." Kreed nodded to confirm that thought before adding quickly, "Then don't let me."

And the silence was back again between them.

Kreed had made it as far as South Dallas, almost to the suburbs, before Aaron responded, "I haven't ever done the relationship thing before, not even tested the waters. I guess this is probably part of it."

"Probably," Kreed replied. He'd had what he'd thought at the time was a relationship, but it was a long time ago and mostly, as it turned out, was just in his head. The fantasy of finding 'the one' became a casualty of war when the guy ended up having a wife and a baby on the way. "So you're taking us up a notch and shooting for a relationship?"

"Well, no…" His always-confident Aaron stumbled on that question, and Kreed laughed out loud.

"I'm totally kidding. I couldn't help it. It's all good and I agree," Kreed said, still chuckling.

"I just know that, back when we were staying at the house, you said we'd go away and see if this was real. I was just emphasizing that thought." Aaron tried to correct his slip.

"No, church boy, I got it. Truly. I was teasing you. Things got so tense with us the last few days…" Kreed drew Aaron's knuckles up for a kiss. "I'm sorry. I didn't know what to say or do. I didn't mean to cause doubt between us."

The kid got silent for a minute before he gave a little laugh.

"Which is actually kind of funny. The last two days should have been a breeze. The case was over. And when we decided to go away somewhere, that shit we were dealing with was way more serious." Aaron's grin was infectious.

"Yeah, I know, but you're pretty hot. It's hard for me to keep my head straight when you're around. My brain gets all jacked up."

There was a moment of silence again while Aaron's expression turned softer, smoothing out his handsome face.

"That was a real good answer there, Sinacola. Keep that up and I'm pretty sure you'll get lucky tonight," Aaron teased.

"Mile high club? Oh man, this nine hour plane flight just started looking up."

"Yeah…" Aaron started, then stopped before adding, "I'm not sure I want to be arrested today."

"I'll be the air marshal on the flight. I guarantee I won't arrest you," Kreed added, grinning broadly.

"That was pretty impressive—how you got us on that flight for nothing."

"Yeah, you need to stick with me, kid. I got the hookup."

Aaron barked out a laugh at that one. Whatever tension had built between them seemed to fade away once they were alone again. Maybe Kreed had caused this uncertainty between them, but it sure seemed like Aaron had also pulled away, at least a little. Regardless, the kid didn't want to cancel the trip, and Kreed certainly wasn't ready to end whatever they had going on. This time the silence between them wasn't terrible. They drove the rest of the way to Midlothian, pulling off the highway in the same way the deacon had chosen to leave town. Kreed passed the site of the crash, right around the railroad tracks. The skid marks and soot stains from the fire still marred the road.

"The town doesn't seem so bad from this vantage point," Aaron said. Kreed's head was turned toward the accident, studying the marks on the pavement, and he couldn't help but tease Aaron.

"We have some extra time. Wanna grab lunch?" Kreed kept his head turned away to hide the smile.

"Hell no!" Aaron had been propped up in his seat, leaning across the console to see out the driver window, but dropped dramatically back into his seat. "How does a town this size not grow? It makes no sense. There are more churches in this city than places to eat."

Kreed chuckled. That had been a sore spot for Aaron the whole time they'd been there. "It's how lots of parts of Texas work. You have all these progressive cities surrounding this one tiny town, and you drive in there and it's like the sixties. It's all designed to help keep the cities' values intact or some shit like that." Kreed rolled his eyes at that one.

"Yeah. I'm not buying it. I bet that undercover officer from the eighty's family doesn't think it's too great a town."

"I didn't say they were good values they were trying so hard to protect."

The church came into view. The whole place looked to be still under lock down. The local law enforcement was stationed out front and also at every available entrance into the building. That was one great thing about Midlothian. Kreed did have lots of respect for the local police force. Even getting involved late in that game, they'd been right on it, eager to help and lend a hand wherever they were needed. Apparently the church had been a thorn in their side for quite some time. Kreed pulled the car as close as he could to the house they'd used. Many other federal vehicles were parked out front.

"How long will they be out here?" Aaron asked as Kreed rounded the hood where Aaron stood waiting for him. He reached inside his jacket to pull out his badge and extended a hand, motioning for Aaron to walk up the sidewalk in front of him. There was lots of activity in the house they'd used, probably a cleaning crew and someone removing the surveillance equipment. The bureau's security guard out front, along with all the police presence, let Kreed know some agency still considered this a hot spot of activity.

"They'll probably stay like this until the rest are caught or they feel like they collected all the required evidence. Even then, it'll stay locked down." Kreed lifted his badge to the suit by the door, but the guy never looked down.

"I know who you are, Deputy Sinacola. We've got a bag for you. It's a few things they found left behind. A couple of shirts and a keyboard they don't think belong here." Kreed glanced to the bag at the guard's feet. This wasn't his first time packing quickly for an assignment, so he knew he had everything he'd brought to the house, and they weren't usually this nice. Typically, if it was left behind, it got tossed. Kreed reached for the bag and looked inside. Yep, it was all Aaron's things. His partner had clearly been more shaken than he'd admitted to not at least grab the keyboard. The shirts he'd probably left on purpose. They were Aaron's church-boy clothes. Kreed would take those; Aaron made a hot church boy. But the kid treated his computer equipment like gold, so he was glad they'd bagged the leftover belongings.

Kreed handed Aaron the bag and shook the agent's hand. "Thank you."

"Sir, can I speak frankly?" The formality of the FBI always made him a little nervous. He rarely liked what he heard when explanations started this way.

"Maybe," Kreed hesitated, furrowing his brow behind his sunglasses.

"It's not bad, sir." The agent lifted his sunglasses.

He wasn't dressed in the standard issue men-in-black suit, but he suspected it was close underneath the long coat the guy wore. Also, he was younger than Kreed had originally suspected. His face turned handsome as he grinned at his words.

"I followed your career for a couple of years now after I watched you make an arrest in Virginia."

The agent paused, looking deeply at Kreed, if that were even possible. For him, he'd made so many arrests that he had no idea what the agent might have seen so he said nothing, instead politely inclined his head, nodding as he waited. There was still a long pause before he finished.

"You make things better for us, sir."

There was a slight stutter in the agent's words. He must be gay but didn't feel comfortable enough to even say the words to Kreed. Kreed nodded again, making sure he gave the signal that he understood. He did get it. Although lots had changed for gay men, it was still hard to function normally in their chosen industry. Kreed hadn't fully come out until he was well into his twenties, and it had taken years to get to this point. Sometimes he still felt like he had to work harder and longer, perhaps even a little smarter, than his straight counterparts in order to be treated as an equal. He lifted a hand to pat the agent's arm.

"Thanks, man. We are who we are." It was Kreed's standard response, because honestly, words weren't needed. Enough had been said.

"Thank you, sir."

Kreed turned toward the car, lifted a hand in acknowledgement, and found he had to reach back, grab Aaron by the collar, and tug him in order to get him moving.

"Do people do that to you a lot?" Aaron asked, immediately falling in step with Kreed.

"It's not always an easy path to find your way out, especially in this job," Kreed said quietly a few steps away. "It's funny though… Even in today's world, when I meet straight guys in this field, they almost always have that look that you just know they're thinking, 'I wonder if he tops or bottoms.' My record, then, doesn't matter anymore. They just wonder if I take it up my ass."

Kreed dug his keys from his pocket, going around the hood to the driver's seat. Once inside the car, he put the key in the ignition and waited for Aaron to get settled in the passenger seat.

"How was your coming out?" Kreed asked.

Aaron laughed a humorless chuckle. "I never hid it. My parents knew before I did, but they still don't really think it's real. They call me rebellious."

"Really? That surprises me," Kreed said, putting the car in drive, but he didn't pull away. Aaron didn't talk about his family, but he assumed with as confident as Aaron was that he'd have been supported.

"Why?" Aaron kept his eyes forward and pointed out the front windshield. "Shouldn't you be driving?"

"You don't seem destructive. You seem self-assured and strong in who you are." Kreed finally did start driving forward, his gaze shifting between the road and Aaron.

"I guess I am. I don't know. My family's pretty accomplished."

Kreed picked up the hint of pain in Aaron's words. That was even more surprising. Aaron was so bold. Hell, he'd had blond spikey hair tipped with black and purple when he'd picked him up from the airport. He seemed fine with who he was as a man. After making a quick U-turn in the road, Kreed took Aaron's hand again, drawing those knuckles to his lips.

"Well, I've got a special treat. You get to go to a small town Walmart. Lucky," Kreed teased.

"I keep telling you this town isn't that small," Aaron shot back. No matter what he'd said earlier, Aaron wasn't a fan of the area.

"And I keep saying it's not the people count that matters. The town thinks they're small. That's enough." They drove the rest of the way to Walmart in silence. The store was right off the highway in a prime location. He'd been in enough of these kinds of places to know the Walmart was everything to a town—a social meeting spot, a political hotbed, or a place people gathered to get the latest gossip. Like normal, the parking lot was packed.

Kreed parked and headed inside with Aaron right on his heels.

"Now, why are we here?"

"I need to grab something," Kreed said vaguely, looking around the store until he saw the signs for the electronics department.

"I'm going to the health and beauty section," Aaron said, studying the signs at the ceiling.

"No, you gotta come with me first." He grabbed Aaron's arm and took off toward the area he intended. Aaron trailed a little behind, looking around amazed. Clearly the kid hadn't spent too much time in a super-store, but Kreed was at home here. He grew up going to Walmart. He took a turn and went to the back of the store, scanning the aisles until he found what he was looking for.

"Pick what you want," Kreed said, once he got to the row of earphones.

"What do you mean?" Aaron asked, somewhat confused. He'd been so busy people-watching that he hadn't paid attention to anything else.

"What headphones do you use?" Kreed asked patiently, pointing to the brightly colored packages, drawing Aaron's eyes to the selection.

"Bose, why?" Aaron asked, his brow furrowing as his gaze drifted back to Kreed.

"Okay. Well, I don't think Walmart carries those. What can get you by until I can get some of those?" Kreed asked, lifting the most expensive ones he could find. Of course, the kid would have something pricey instead of just the five dollar earbuds off the shelf. "Will these work?"

"Still asking, why?" Aaron said, his eyes on Kreed, waiting for an explanation.

"I was making the bed this morning and they fell off as I was moving. They didn't hold up too well under my boot. I tried to put them back together, but, yeah...just get something here and I'll replace those. It's cheaper than a store at the airport." Kreed gave a small smile and tried again to hand Aaron the earphone box.

Aaron just stared at him. He didn't look too happy, especially not with the scowl that was slowly forming on his usually handsome face.

"I'm sorry, but I'm trying to make up for it, so that should count." Kreed gave him his biggest smile and nodded his encouragement for Aaron to agree.

"Do you have any idea how much those cost?"

"Umm...probably not, but I said I'd replace them."

It still took a second, but Aaron finally turned away and scanned the choices, grabbing a cheaper version than Kreed had in his hand. Okay, maybe those Bose weren't so expensive. He placed his choice back on the rack and followed Aaron, catching him just as he turned out of the aisle. His guy was angry, leaving Kreed confused. It was just a stupid pair of earbuds.

"You should've told me when it happened," Aaron said over his shoulder. Kreed trailed behind him, staying quiet. Of course he should have told Aaron, but they were in that tense place and he didn't want to add to it.

"I'll replace what I broke," Kreed finally grumbled. "Where can I get them? Maybe we can stop some place on the way up."

"They were a thousand dollars and custom made," Aaron tossed back over his shoulder.

"A thousand dollars for earbuds? Are you kidding me?" Kreed barked out, stopping in the middle of the main aisle, blocking traffic. It took Aaron a few seconds to realize Kreed wasn't following him. A thousand freaking dollars for earbuds that break so easily? Who did that? Those would have lasted about a day in his life before he tore the hell out of them. It was just too shocking to continue to move.

"Come on," Aaron called out, motioning him forward. "I've got a backup pair. I just packed them with my equipment so I'll need these for the flight."

"You have two pair of thousand-dollar earbuds?" Kreed called out, barely able to move one foot in front of the other. Could the guy be serious?

"They're the best," Aaron said once Kreed had caught up. "Come on. I need hair dye."

"What color are you going for now?" Kreed finally asked after he processed the amount of money being spent on something so ridiculous. Thank God his subconscious was working, and he was able to add, "I like the dark."

"You do?" Aaron asked, looking back over his shoulder. He wished he had a camera to capture that look. All thoughts of expensive earphones left as his dick plumped.

"What's your natural hair color?" Kreed asked. The kid was just gorgeous, stunningly handsome. Aaron would look amazing with any color hair.

"Dark. I can keep it like that. Maybe add some purple. Purple looks good with black." Aaron was looking down all the aisles, passing several before he turned.

"You do this yourself?" Kreed asked, following along.

"You're gonna help," Aaron added, looking at the rows and rows of hair color. An overhead announcement interrupted his thought before he had time to answer. Although he loved spa day, the activities of the spa always stayed there. He had no idea how to dye hair.

"Chasity Clover, your car is ready in Automotive," a woman's voice drawled over the store's paging system. Her voice had a deeply Southern accent tinged with a bit of Roz from *Monsters, Inc*.

Aaron's face lit up, his excited gaze shooting up to the ceiling, his smile bigger than anything Kreed had seen before. Yes, Aaron Stuart was absolutely beautiful, but Kreed wasn't entirely sure what had him so excited.

"Chasity Clover, your car is ready in Automotive." Aaron quietly mimicked her last word. "Oh my God, that's golden," Aaron cackled, bending over, grabbing his belly, laughing hysterically.

"What?" Kreed found himself chuckling because Aaron's laughter was contagious, but he had no idea what was so funny.

"*Ootttoomoottiiivvve!*" Aaron mimicked her sound. "She was so country. Oh my God. When she said automotive, that was like twenty fucking syllables."

Kreed did laugh at that. He lived in Louisiana, making him used to that slow Southern twang, but Aaron had a point. That particular woman's voice had taken the accent to a whole new level. As if on cue, there she came again, saying something new, yet long and drawn out. Aaron went into a second giggling fit. This time he held on to the shelves, trying to keep himself on his feet. He was almost as funny as the woman speaking overhead.

"Quit throwin' shade," Kreed said, still laughing, trying hard to mimic her as he spoke. "Grab what you need. We need to get goin'."

Chapter 27

Aaron sat in first class, looking out the small window with his new earbuds in, but they did little to drown out the noise around him. They were about twenty minutes outside of Kauai, and the fasten-your-seat-belt sign had just flashed on the display screen above his head. Kreed had been up, stretching his legs, before disappearing inside the bathroom. The man was so big and muscular that he didn't fit well in cramped surroundings, so when he exited the small door and had to twist awkwardly to navigate that part of the cabin, the action captured Aaron's attention…and Aaron noticed he wasn't the only one drawn to the sight.

The heat of Kreed's gaze landed right on him, his dark brow lifted and a knowing smirk curled the corners of his beautiful lips. Since he'd spent the last nine hours dodging the suggestion of joining the mile high club, Kreed must have been checking out the space possibilities for the flight home. What did it mean that he was so in tune with Kreed that he instinctively knew what was on the deputy's mind?

The weight of that thought made him instantly antsy, so he mentally shoved it aside and concentrated on the new look. Kreed had managed to change his clothes and was now wearing a pair of walking shorts and a T-shirt. He wondered where Kreed might have hidden his weapon under that tight-fitting shirt. He carried his backpack and boots in his hands in front of him as he squeezed down the aisle toward his seat. Kreed's eyes continued to hold him transfixed with that small grin in place as he lifted his beefy arms to open the overhead bin to place his items inside before taking his seat.

"Seatbelt on, Kreed," a flight attendant said absently as she passed by on a final sweep through the cabin. It seemed Kreed had close to free rein, able to do just about anything he wanted on any flight he took. The rules barely applied, and by extension, they were easier on Aaron through most of the flight.

"Sure thing," Kreed mumbled as he leaned over, angling his head until he was in Aaron's direct line of vision and reached up to tug the earbud free from Aaron's ear. Kreed had performed that move five or six times during the trip. "Just so you know, we would've fit."

Seriously, the guy had a one-track mind. "No, we wouldn't. I saw you have to turn those big ole' muscles to the side to enter the bathroom." Aaron used that Southern accent, imitating the lady from Walmart to describe the width of his shoulders and making Kreed's smile grow.

"We would've fit. There was enough room. I measured. No more excuses. We're doing it on the way home," Kreed declared.

"Pretty sure of yourself," Aaron replied, placing the earbud back in his ear. Kreed reached up to pull it out again.

"Don't be tryin' to get out of it."

Kreed's face was right in his, the ever-present, sexy little smirk in place. Aaron actually liked that Kreed didn't allow him to divert the conversation, and he smiled back.

"I'm fucking you," Aaron whispered and winked.

"Whatever you want. You know I'm up for anything. Just want to join that club so I can get the T-shirt. Mitch has the hookup, but there's gotta be some kind of proof." Kreed finally reached for his seatbelt as the plane began its descent. Aaron had no idea if Kreed was serious or what kind of proof would be necessary. Man, he was in serious trouble with this guy.

~~~

Aaron opted to drive, forcing Kreed to sit idly in the passenger seat of the rental car, watching out the side window, with his cellphone stuck to his ear. Aaron continued to cement his grandma-driver status as Brody Masters efficiently caught Kreed up on everything they'd missed since leaving Dallas nine hours earlier. He gave several muttered yeahs and yeses, but as a whole, he just listened. Four of the five fugitives had been apprehended and a nationwide manhunt was in place to execute that final arrest. They were tying up the pieces with the entire Department of Justice focused on nailing this terrorist cell to eliminate any lingering threat they might pose to American citizens.

The closer they got to Jace's place, the more beautiful the scenery became, drawing him into an automatic peacefulness. Between Aaron's driving pace, Brody's voice, and the water churning in the distance, Kreed relaxed, paying less attention to Masters and more to the tropical paradise surrounding him, only tuning back in when Brody got to the last point that seemed to frustrate the boys at the bureau as much as anything that might have happened with the case.

For the first time since the call had started, Kreed turned away from the breathtaking view outside his window and spoke directly to Aaron to relay the new information they had.

"Some group took over the church's website today. They redirected it to a website with the words '*God hates no one*,' before then redirecting it to a human rights group. There's a big video posted, already received millions of views, and this one got a lot of public help. It's fucking everything up for Connors."

"How so?" Aaron asked, and Kreed lifted a single finger as he continued listening to Brody before he spoke.

"Okay, call me in the morning," Kreed said and lowered the phone, swiping a finger to end the call before turning to Aaron. "Right now, the FBI thinks that for the time being they've managed to downplay the arrests to the media. You know, to keep status quo—at least their considered normal state of affairs. But everything with the bureau has a spin. They feel like the church has a solid following, and they wanted to control how all this information got out to the public, swing the propaganda in their favor, make the FBI look like heroes instead of an agency that refused to even consider all this evidence for a good solid year. Now that the national news has the story, everything will slowly be leaked. The media keeps doing breaking news reports over and over, reporting on the case. To Connors, he's saying it'll stop the progression of the case, and Masters said the bureau's already preparing for damage control."

"Huh," Aaron said, seemingly unaffected. He was a young techie, so he'd probably agree with the hack, maybe even wish he'd been able to take part in it all instead of flying to Hawaii. "I wondered how long it would take. I bet it was Protector. They can't stand stuff like this. They hate Redemption Apostle Tabernacle Church. They've targeted that church for years. They'll probably track the hack down to a farmhouse somewhere in Nebraska."

"Yeah, I guess. I get what they're doing in trying to keep society informed, but they're a giant pain in the ass. They always pop up at the worst possible times. I just can't figure out how they know shit so quick. They're on it, and don't hesitate to jump right in there. Sometimes they do it before we even know," Kreed said as he turned back in his seat, taking in more of the picturesque view of the ocean. The water seemed to go on forever.

"The deal about Protector… It's really anyone who wants to be involved. Sure, it's organized by a few, but we can all jump in and clog up the different systems," Aaron explained casually.

"You and I both know that statement's a load of crap. There's a small cell of people orchestrating the attacks, guiding the outcome," Kreed shot back.

"Regardless, it wouldn't work if it weren't for everyone playing a part. I was reading on the marshals' internal network that a couple of those guys in Protector made it to the top fifty most wanted list. They think it's two or three guys that started it. But they don't really know who they are so it's real open-ended. No name, no face, not even a clue as to how to find them. How's that gonna work for those in the field?" Aaron asked, appearing somewhat distracted by the traffic forming on the road.

"It's more about the reward that gets attached to each person. Somebody'll turn them in. Somebody in that inner circle knows what's going on and will eventually get greedy," Kreed said, but on a happier note, he turned back to Aaron. "Then, I'll go get 'em. Keeps me employed."

Aaron gave a humorless laugh, but didn't comment. Kreed decided to keep it light where Protector was concerned. Now wasn't the time for a discussion on such a monumental difference in point of view. Protector had fucked up many a raid he'd been on over the last few years. They were absolutely a huge pain in the ass, and Kreed had to make a mental note to remember to tell Aaron not to show his support out loud again if others were around. No division in the Justice Department appreciated those hackers or their so-called social conscience. Better that no one knew Stuart was a Protector sympathizer. "Do you know any of them?"

"Not that I know of, but there's a possibility. Those hacktivists that orchestrate all that, they keep that shit quiet. I could see it just being one or two people and no one else knowing," Aaron said. GPS sounded off and Aaron followed the instructions off the highway.

"It's just a matter of time. It always goes bad," Kreed said absently, looking out over the ocean again. "It's beautiful here."

Work wasn't even on the top million list of things he wanted to be thinking about right now. He'd been impressed with how easily he'd been able to keep work back on the mainland and mentally move on as a man on vacation. Kreed would receive daily updates and worst-case scenarios. He might even have to head back to Dallas or DC if something broke, but that just meant he needed to make the most of every single day.

Man, it felt good to get away and completely relax. He wasn't in a frame of mind to let that easily slip away. Months of intense stress had made being on this island with Aaron that much more appealing. After Aaron made the turn onto a sand-covered road into a residential area, Kreed reached over to entwine Aaron's hand with his. The act of holding this man's hand balanced him. Aaron made him feel lighter, and that thought settled inside his heart. It might have been years since he'd experienced this much inner peace, and Aaron seemed to be clueless at the power he held.

"This is where they met?" Kreed asked, trying to remember the story Colt had told them as they turned down a long street that ran alongside the ocean.

"Nah, I don't think so. I think they came here on vacation when they were younger and Jace bought the place years later when it came up for sale."

"Who would've known cheerleading paid so well," Kreed added, watching the houses as they passed by. The farther they got on the street, the more space separated each home.

"I know, right? That's all I kept thinking in Dallas." GPS interrupted them again, so they paid closer attention to the house numbers until they came to a stop in front of a very nice cottage-style home.

"Man, it was nice to have them offer this up," Kreed said, unbuckling his seatbelt. Aaron hopped from the driver's side. The tropical backdrop stood in stark contrast against the kid's dark, winter wardrobe of jeans and long-sleeve shirt. Kreed worked his feet back inside his flip-flops he'd shoved to the corner of the floorboard then opened his door. He stepped out, breathing in the clean, salty air. No doubt the place was beautiful.

Kreed headed toward the trunk as Aaron clicked the key fob to open the latch. He grabbed both the heavy bags, letting Aaron get his backpack and laptop. Those two items were always the first things cared for in any trip they made.

"I need to change," Aaron said, standing near the front porch, waiting for Kreed to make his way up the sidewalk by the driveway.

"Yeah, I checked the temperature on the way here. It's close to eighty degrees."

Aaron reached for the handle of one of the bags Kreed carried, trying to take his own luggage, but Kreed held on tight, nodding in the direction of the house to get Aaron moving. Of course, Aaron was more than capable of carrying his own heavy shit, but Kreed just liked doing it for his guy.

Aaron finally relented, moving forward, walking first toward the house, fishing something out of his front pocket. The closer they got to the front door, Kreed saw some of the repairs Jace and Colt said they'd made. The porch looked pretty new, though the house appeared to be in need of a new paint job.

"They haven't been here since the accident?" Kreed asked, taking the steps up to the front door. "Didn't they say Michaels repaired the roof?"

"Yeah, that's pretty funny. Jace put him straight to work, didn't even give him a chance to breathe. Colt must've been trying hard to get his foot back in the door." Aaron swung the front door open, showing an entry that looked right in the middle of a remodel. Colt's accident had stopped the progress they'd made while trying to spruce the place up. The kitchen sat right off the entry with the dining room and living room straight ahead. Curtains were drawn shut along the back wall, and Kreed supposed that was a sliding glass door, but instead of looking for himself, he headed toward a hall located to the side of the living room.

He found one small bedroom, a bathroom, and the door at the end of the hall leading into the master bedroom. He opened the door all the way and stepped inside the large, nicely decorated room. The master suite had a modern feel, decorated in soothing island colors. If he ever owned his own place, this would be exactly what he wanted. His senses relaxed even further. The room looked very much like one you'd find in a high-end, expensive spa. Right up his alley! Man, he was going to love this place.

After looking around, Kreed placed both suitcases in the closet before going back in search of Aaron. The living room curtains were now open and Aaron stood at the back porch railing, looking out over the ocean.

"It's peaceful here," Aaron said, never looking back. Kreed smiled as he came through the door, wondering if Aaron knew how telling that move was. They were truly in sync with one another if Aaron could sense when he was around.

"Yeah, I was thinking that driving up," Kreed confirmed, moving in behind Aaron and wrapping his arms around his waist. He didn't stop pressing against Aaron until they touched from head to toe. Aaron's body relaxed into his, his back resting against Kreed's chest. Several minutes passed as Kreed got lost in the churning white and blue of the water as the waves broke over the surface of the ocean. He needed a place just like this in his life. Maybe someday.

"This is so beautiful. I can't believe I'm here with you. That day at the airport when I first saw you in person, I never imagined I would be in Hawaii, let alone wrapped in the hot leather god's arms, staring out at the Pacific. You're unexpected," Aaron said quietly, seemingly just as lost to the lure of the ocean as Kreed.

"You too. I knew I wanted you when you shot me down in front of Mitch on Skype, but that was something different. I don't know how many times I jacked off with thoughts of fucking that smart mouth of yours fueling my fantasies. And when I saw you at the airport in person, you confused the hell out of me. So yeah, you're unexpected in the best way," Kreed responded, whispering the words before brushing his lips against the sensitive spot on Aaron's neck right behind his ear. "Change clothes. Let's make a quick store run so we can go down to the beach and stay there. I see a fire pit. We can cook and eat down there tonight."

Aaron nodded, but didn't really move. Instead, he began to unbutton the front of his long-sleeve shirt before undoing his wrist buttons. "That's a good plan. We need to add condoms to the grocery list; we're almost out. But I was thinking a swim wouldn't be bad. The water looks so tempting."

Aaron took a step from the embrace and peeled his shirt off, dropping it before quickly unfastening his jeans. Kreed's mouth gaped open when those pants hit the steps, then Aaron's underwear was lost in the sand a few feet from the water's edge as Aaron ran into the surf and motioned for Kreed to join him seconds before disappearing under the water. That cute bouncing butt held his gaze until it disappeared into the surf.

Kreed shook his head and pulled off his shirt. He dropped the worn cotton on top of Aaron's. His shorts carrying his cell and his wallet made a heavy thump on the wooden deck. Kreed jogged down the steps, losing his underwear about the same place Aaron had shed his. Aaron broke the surface just as Kreed hit the water wearing nothing but a smile. As he plunged under, then up again, he decided Aaron might be the death of him, and if that were the case, then it would be a spectacular way to go.

Kreed swam to where Aaron floated. One strong tug had Aaron against him with his lips descending as he captured his mouth, lazy and slow. Yeah, the kid was going to be the death of him... Aaron encouraged Kreed by wrapping his legs around Kreed's waist and kissing him back. Kreed loved that fucking move. Aaron was so in tune with him. The kid read his mood and body language like a fucking book, knew exactly how to get him riled up.

"Fuck, you're a bad boy, aren't you?" Kreed panted against Aaron's mouth.

"If you only knew the truth about me, Deputy Marshal, you'd be hauling me into custody."

"That can be arranged. I do have handcuffs."

"Mmm...tempting." Aaron licked at his lips and ran his fingers down then up his back before cupping the back of his head.

Kreed melted when Aaron's swollen cock ground against his. He slid his fingers between Aaron's ass cheeks and pressed the pad of his pinky finger against the tightly puckered flesh of his entrance.

"We'll have time for handcuffs and toys later." Aaron groaned, tilted his hips, and pressed back against his finger. "I want you in me. Now."

"Not here. The condom and lube are in my short's pocket." Wet sand gave under his feet as he started moving them toward the shore.

They hit the beach, hot and heavy, naked and horny. Aaron's thick erection stood out from his lean body, a tempting distraction from the beautiful backdrop surrounding them.

After grabbing the condom and packet of lube out of his shorts, he tossed his clothing back down. Kreed couldn't keep his eyes off Aaron's ass as he followed his guy toward the little alcove at the end of an outcropping of lava rocks that started at the base of a heavily bent coconut tree. Luckily for him, the spot was hidden out of view from the open beach by tropical plants, plumeria trees, and hibiscus bushes.

Aaron stopped and turned just as Kreed stepped into the tropical enclosure. Kreed savored the sight in front of him. His gaze slowly dropped from the beautiful dragon tattooed over the kid's shoulder and down his chest, lingering briefly on those tempting piercings before it fixed on what his church boy was doing with his hand. Aaron stroked himself, hard and ready, and the thick head glistened with pre-come that Kreed was tempted to taste. Kreed's gaze flicked back up to Aaron's face to watch his pink tongue dart out to lick across full lips that now captured Kreed's attention.

"Fuck, I don't know where I wanna start."

"Kissing's always good." Aaron smirked. Kreed didn't waste any time pushing Aaron against the base of the coconut tree, kissing him, hard and demanding. Aaron's warm palm curled around his dick, and he thrust into the tight fist. Aaron took the condom out of his hand and tore the small package with his teeth. His lust-clouded blue gaze never left Kreed's as the cool latex rolled down his length.

"Turn around." His voice sounded a little rushed and desperate. It wasn't his fault he was so needy; Aaron made him that way.

"Here, you'll need this." Aaron opened the package of lube, coating two of his fingers before offering the package to Kreed who watched with mixed emotions as Aaron reached behind and started to prepare himself. Fuckin' A, that was hot as hell. He loved watching the kid open himself, but right now, he wanted to be the one stretching Aaron. He quickly spread the lube on his dick and fingers.

"Please. Let me," he said, turning Aaron around to face the tree. Kreed smoothed his hand up Aaron's back, watching the way Aaron's muscles bunched under his palm as he urged him to lean forward. He slid his knuckles between that dark crease where Aaron's fingers had disappeared and eased them from his hole. A groan rumbled from Aaron's chest and a shudder racked his body when he pushed two slick fingers in Aaron's ass. He'd caught on quickly that Aaron craved the burn and the stretch of penetration. Tight muscles seized his fingers, gripping them, drawing them in.

"More," Aaron hissed as he sucked in a breath and widened his stance.

"So fucking tight." Kreed twisted his fingers, pumping them in and out, stretching Aaron before deliberately, curling his digits and pressing on that spongy gland he knew would send Aaron into a frenzy.

"Fuck... Fuck!" Aaron bucked against Kreed's hand, humping on the fingers in his ass. "Don't make me wait, Sin."

Widening his stance, Kreed splayed his hand across the small of Aaron's back then slid it up and pressed down on the top of Aaron's shoulder blade, digging his fingertips into the top of his church boy's shoulder. Aaron spread his legs wider and tilted his ass up. Electricity shot through Kreed's body and sparked in his balls at the sight of Aaron open for him. He took his dick in hand and pressed it to Aaron's opening, pushing past the outer tight ring of muscle, completely seating himself in Aaron in a long, slow thrust.

He stopped his movement the moment his groin met Aaron's ass, allowing him time to adjust. The fine hairs on the back of Aaron's thighs rubbed against the front of his. Aaron's hot passage immediately clamped down on him, the tight heat driving him insane with the need to claim what was his. But he remained still.

"Move. Fuck me, Sin." Aaron's weight pressed back against him, and he slid in a fraction of an inch more...and swore the angels sang.

"Yeah. Just need to hear you say it, sweetheart." With those words, he gripped Aaron's hips and pulled almost all the way out then thrust fully back in, holding his cock deep in his lover's ass before pulling out and pressing in again. He dug his fingers into Aaron's skin, firming his hold, increasing the speed of his hips.

"Harder, baby," Aaron growled, his knuckles turning white from the grip he had on the tree trunk.

"Jesus Christ, you feel so fucking good." He canted his hips, changing his angle as he kept plunging in and out of Aaron's searing heat.

"Need you deeper. Make me come." Aaron lifted his leg and placed his foot on a large lava rock, allowing him better access.

Kreed took full advantage of the position and slammed wildly into his church boy's body. "Fuck! I can't last."

He palmed Aaron's cock and stroked the rigid length in time to his thrusts. Aaron's ass tightened and clenched around him. *So fucking good!*

"Oh shit! Oh shit! Yess…right there, Sin." Aaron cried out as he came, his ass fluttering, sucking Kreed in, squeezing and milking his orgasm from him as his lover's release warmed his fingers and hand. Kreed slammed into Aaron one last time, pulling his lover back on his cock at the same time he thrust forward.

"So fucking deep in you, Aaron." Heat ignited in his spine and burned up the base of his skull before detonating in his balls with such force Kreed saw fireworks. Kreed's jaw clenched, his thighs stiffened, and knees wobbled as he emptied his load deep in Aaron's contracting ass. He kept thrusting through his release, his legs threatening to collapse under him.

The pounding in his ears quieted. The birds and sounds of the ocean grew louder as he calmed from his orgasm and his body recovered. He gripped the end of the condom and withdrew from Aaron, who immediately turned and embraced him.

"This is paradise." Aaron squirmed against him as Kreed tied off the condom. The guy was insatiable.

"Having you here to share it with makes it paradise." Kreed dipped his head, kissing Aaron.

"You always say the sweetest things, Deputy," Aaron said and smiled up at him.

"I hate to spoil the mood, but if we want to enjoy paradise, we need to get cleaned up and head to the store before it gets too late." Kreed kissed the tip of Aaron's nose then took a step back, holding out his hand for Aaron.

"Can I have a blow job in the shower?" Aaron asked, taking his hand.

"Whatever you want, church boy." He chuckled as they turned toward the house.

Chapter 28

With his mind filled with coding possibilities, Aaron came out of the bedroom he'd designated as a small office, digging his thumb and forefinger into his tired eyes. A yawn slipped out as he went in search of Kreed. He checked the kitchen then turned toward the living room. The curtains were wide open, and he was surprised to find it was actually dark outside. Time had gotten away from him again, and it was later than he'd originally thought.

The frown he wore turned to a grin as he got closer to the sliding glass door. Kreed clearly had no problem being left to his own devices. After they'd come home from the grocery store and a small clothing store, Aaron had forced himself to the back room to work. Only about an hour into catching up did he really see how far he'd let things go. He hadn't stood a chance, though. Both the church and Kreed Sinacola had turned out to be monumental concentration zappers and the sheer volume of his uncompleted workload was a little overwhelming. That was hours ago, and true to his word, Kreed hadn't bothered him one time since he'd closed himself up inside the bedroom.

Based on what he saw as he stood at the back door, he knew why he hadn't been interrupted this evening. Kreed was sitting outside, close to the edge of the water in a low reclining beach chair facing a dark churning ocean. The moon was bright and lit up the ocean just enough that he could see the white of the wave break rolling along the top of the surf.

A blazing fire wasn't more than a few feet away in the fire pit he'd spotted earlier. Kreed had positioned himself close enough between the wood pile and the fire to easily reach over and pitch a fresh log on when needed. That made Aaron smile.

There were so many things about Kreed that made him smile.

Kreed had anchored a large beer cooler in the sand between himself and an empty chair. He supposed that was there for him, and his heart leapt as it connected with that thought. He'd really like to always be the one Kreed wanted to join him.

Aaron slid open the glass door and stepped out onto the deck. The wind blew softly, fragrant with the smell of salt, tropical flowers, and campfire. Aaron sank barefoot into the cool sand. A row of lit tiki torches had been strategically placed in the sand and lined his path down to the chairs. Kreed had to have filled and lit each one of those, which must have taken some time. Aaron paused to take in the sweet gesture.

All the little things the guy did made Aaron feel cared for and wanted. They happened all the time with Kreed. From remembering his deep dislike of having cheese on his burger and returning his lunch today without a second thought, to stopping at the FedEx store without being asked in order to gather his computer equipment— something that Kreed clearly didn't understand, but that didn't matter. He did those things without being asked, just for him. And Kreed held his hand.

How long had it been since anyone had held his hand?

After allowing himself a minute of reflection, Aaron pushed those thoughts aside in a desperate attempt to keep perspective, reminding himself the man he was sharing his bed with was a well-trained, special teams deputy US marshal. Those type men didn't knowingly hang with criminals. They arrested them.

No matter what happened between him and Kreed, no matter where all this emotion stemmed from or how genuine this felt, there was no way they could continue past this vacation. He couldn't risk it. And what would crush him more would be the disappointment in Kreed's eyes if he ever found out the truth.

Mitch's case was closed. The adrenaline had already started to ebb and life was slowly settling back to normal. The key reasons he kept people at a distance were back in play. He'd made those decisions a long time ago. Too many people depended on him. Aaron closed his eyes at the pressure building in his heart. Guy's like Kreed didn't just stumble into your life every day. They were a once-in-a-lifetime deal.

The irony of a deputy marshal being the first person in his life to stir all these feelings hadn't gone unnoticed. Life was a cruel bitch. Pain gripped his heart at the thought of having to say goodbye to Kreed and never being able to see him again. Aaron reached up and held his chest. No matter how badly he hurt, he would do what must be done when the time came. But right now he could focus on the here and now and enjoy his time with Kreed. Build memories to last a lifetime. Aaron took a deep breath and headed to Kreed.

"It's paradise," Kreed called out, looking over his shoulder as Aaron got closer. It was a little chilly out tonight, but the closer he got to the fire, or perhaps Kreed, the warmer he became.

"Sure beats Midlothian, Texas," Aaron quipped, trying to be cheeky. Kreed had the music up as he walked toward the beach. "Call Me" by Shinedown was playing on the radio. Just fucking perfect. The sadness started to settle back in his chest as the verse played loudly in the background. How could he ever give Kreed up? How was he going to just walk away and go back to his life and pretend Kreed hadn't changed him? He took a deep breath and forced those thoughts from his head. It wasn't the time to worry about saying goodbye.

With a soft brush of his hand, Aaron's fingers slid across Kreed's shoulder as he passed by. The need to just touch him, connect with him in some small way, was overwhelming. Those fast reflexes had Kreed grabbing his fingers before he sat.

"Did you get done?" Kreed asked, drawing Aaron's hand to his lips, kissing his knuckles before turning and kissing his palm. It was a sweet move that effectively zapped the melancholy messing with his head. He had right now and needed to live in this moment, worry about life later.

"Nah, not really, but it's hard to concentrate when all this is waiting for me." Aaron gestured toward the ocean before leaning in for a soft kiss and dropping down in the recliner next to Kreed.

Kreed reached inside the cooler, pulled out an ice cold beer, and handed it to him.

"I got us a bottle of whisky along with beer. Shots with beer chasers. That's always a good time waiting to happen. Colt texted me the name of a club he said we need to hit," Kreed said, tossing his empty beer bottle in a bucket and grabbing a new one, along with the whisky and shot glass. He twisted the top and flipped the cap in the trash bucket. He sat the beer between his legs and poured a shot. Kreed downed it then poured another shot. "Here. Your turn," Kreed said as he handed over the small glass.

Aaron took the glass. "If I wasn't already a sure thing, I'd think you were trying to get me drunk so you could get in my pants," he said and gave Kreed a wink as he tossed back the shot. The amber liquid burned as it slid down his throat. He quickly grabbed his beer and tipped it back, letting it chase the burn down to his stomach.

Kreed lifted his brow. "Drunk sex could be fun."

"Yeah, it could." Any kind of sex with Kreed was fun. Why did he have to like this guy so damn much? Aaron took another sip of his beer and dug his toes into the cool sand, trying to force the tension from his body.

"The weather's nice here, isn't it?" Aaron picked at the label on his beer.

"Yeah. Are we gettin' weird again?" Kreed asked. He was so good at picking up moods. Aaron needed to always remember that about Kreed. He could tune in to the most subtle emotions with no words spoken. He was just too intuitive. Kreed reached across the armrest and took his hand, threading his fingers through Aaron's. "I don't want us to get weird."

"We don't have a lot in common, Kreed," Aaron finally replied, trying to find something easy to say to help validate what Kreed might be picking up on. He certainly couldn't say what he was really thinking at the moment—that he was falling hard and it was killing him that he had to fight it tooth and nail because he wasn't who Kreed thought.

Just the thought made Aaron squeeze Kreed's hand a little tighter. Man, he fucking wished things were different and he could stay with this guy.

"We have to build our common," Kreed said, giving him a sideways glance, taking a long drink.

"You know, that sounds like someone who's been in a relationship before." Aaron tried to change the subject, surprised at the jealousy that one sentence evoked.

Kreed gave a sharp grunt kind of laugh. Okay, that laugh spiked his jealousy to a whole new level. Maybe the deputy marshal *had* been in a relationship before. He turned fully toward Kreed and watched as the man took another drink. How had this never been fully discussed? Possessiveness slithered up his spine and coiled around his heart. All this time, he'd worried about hiding himself from Kreed, when he had no idea what was really going on with the guy.

When Kreed didn't respond, Aaron pushed. "Tell me."

Kreed's face twisted in thought before he lifted his beer for another drink, then said, "I wouldn't call it a relationship. Even if I would, he didn't. It was one-sided—brief. I was in the navy. Of course I wasn't out yet, because back then you didn't come out, and he was on a different team. It was the first time I had emotions with sex, so I figured that meant a relationship—you know, all that was in my head; I never said it out loud. He definitely never said it. Then he got deployed and didn't come back for me. That's it, end of story."

"How long ago was this?" Aaron asked after absorbing all the information.

"Are you trying to make me feel old?" Kreed released Aaron's hand to pour them another round of shots.

"Definitely not, but you've been out of the military for like ten years, right?" Kreed had tried to gloss over the details, but this was too important—at least to Aaron, who had again made a huge error in his line of thinking as he realized he'd assumed because these emotions were new to him that they'd be new to Kreed. How had he allowed himself to be so self-absorbed that he'd never asked these questions?

"Yeah, I left when I was about your age. How old are you?" Kreed asked. He must really want out of this conversation; he was trying hard to move the dialog to another topic.

"You know how old I am. Quit changing the subject." Frustrated with the lack of response, he figured he'd just start asking very direct questions. "So he meant something to you? Did he hurt you?"

"I don't know. I guess at the time it hurt," Kreed said, shrugging it off.

"Enough for you to remember him," Aaron pointed out, and Kreed tipped his beer bottle in Aaron's direction in a toasting gesture.

"You're smart, kid. Why're we still talking about this?" Kreed teased and poured two more shots of whisky.

"I'm not a kid, remember?" Aaron downed his shot and stared at Kreed. Jealousy didn't suit Aaron at all, but he couldn't help it. He was jealous about a man he didn't even know and who was no longer in Kreed's life…and over someone he couldn't even have, which was incredibly stupid.

Kreed watched him for several long seconds. Everything went quiet between them. The radio played in the background and the sound of the waves hitting the shoreline just a few feet away harmonized with the occasional crackling of the fire, making that moment feel surreal. Aaron wouldn't give, and Kreed finally spoke, a grin growing with each word. "I know you're not. You're anything but. Stop getting all defensive." Kreed opened the top on another beer and handed it to him.

Aaron could only stare at him as he accepted the bottle, because Kreed was right. He had gotten defensive, but that had happened way before Kreed had called him a kid.

"You're jealous," Kreed announced matter-of-factly.

"I'm not." Aaron denied the clear truth and downed the beer. Of course, he was jealous. That wasn't rocket science. But he didn't have a right to be, and that was what made him even crazier.

"You are too. That's sweet," Kreed started. The smile was there, but Aaron could tell he was thinking as he spoke. "All right, let's see. That was a long time ago. I wasn't trying to be vague. I just honestly don't remember a lot about it all. I wasn't much more than twenty years old, and it was more than just a fuck for me, but at that point, I hadn't been with a lot of guys. When he never came back for me, it fucked me up a little. No calls, no letters, not even a fuck you. He was older. My head got a little crazy, so I looked him up—

to make sure he hadn't gotten hurt, even though back then all the teams were close, so I would have heard if he went down. Then I found out he had a wife and a bunch of little kids. He was just using me."

"Have you ever spoken to him since? Do you know where he is now?" Aaron immediately asked.

"No. I've never looked for him again. I don't actually really care anymore."

"And there's no current significant other in your life?" Aaron pelted him with questions.

"We've talked about that already. Finish that shot and the beer and have a couple more. You've got some catching up to do. I like my guys youngish, cute, and drunk," Kreed said, taking his hand again. Aaron sat there silently contemplating what he'd heard, and after a second, he took the shot and swallowed down the beer. Kreed watched him, a knowing little grin in place, the firelight dancing in his dark eyes. He supposed there was some unspoken meaning in that look. Kreed broke eye contact and reached inside the cooler for another beer and twisted off the cap.

"Man, I like being with you. Makes me feel good. Here." Kreed handed Aaron the beer. "Scoot closer. You're all right. You know that, Stuart?"

"Huh." Aaron eyed Kreed curiously as the guy pushed the heavy cooler from in between their chairs then gripped the side of his chair and started to pull him closer. Kreed's strength was pretty amazing. Aaron actually moved a little before he finally got up and helped Kreed scoot the chair in the sand. After he picked up another log from the stack and threw it on the fire, Kreed reached for him again and hung on to his hand a little tighter this time, not letting him go.

Instead of sitting back in his chair, Aaron moved to Kreed, straddling his lap. The unexpected move caused the deputy marshal to release his hand and immediately grip Aaron's hips. Aaron tested the sturdiness of the chaise, surprised and thankful the chair held their combined weight.

"Okay, I'm amending my statement. I like my guy's youngish, cute, drunk, jealous, and in my lap when I spend time with them." Kreed waggled his brows as he spoke.

Lifting a hand, Aaron threaded his fingers through Kreed's hair, before tipping up his bottle and taking a long drink. He wouldn't let himself get too drunk—that could be dangerous—but he did have some drinking to do. Swallowing the mouthful, he leaned forward, dipped his head then pressed his lips against Kreed's. Kreed opened for him, their tongues meeting and tangling. He could taste the mix of alcohol on Kreed's tongue, so fucking good. Kreed's hands left his hips and toyed with the hem of his shirt before dragging it over his head.

Surreal was the only way he could describe the moment. Aaron was feeling good and relaxed, truly wanted. He was pretty sure he was in over his head with Kreed. If things were different, he could see himself building a life with this man.

No sense in denying it, he was skating on thin ice where his feelings for the deputy were concerned, but there was something so special about being in paradise and sharing this moment with Kreed that he let himself dream. The tropical breeze blowing against his skin, the feel of cool wet sand under his toes, and Kreed Sinacola between his thighs, that hard erection rubbing against his own... Yeah, he could get used to this, if only. *Stop dwelling on it and enjoy the time you do have.*

He recognized "Closer" by Nine Inch Nails the moment the first bass beat played on the radio. The thumping, seductive tones drove him to push himself off Kreed and stand in front of the sexy deputy marshal. The way Kreed sat in his chair, legs spread, arms resting across his stomach watching him with hooded eyes, sent a jolt of electricity through his balls.

"I love this song. Makes me want to dance." He hadn't felt this tipsy, this free, in such a long time. He swayed his hips back and forth to the rhythm of the song and leveled his eyes on Kreed. "Ever had a lap dance, Deputy?" Aaron ran his hand down the front of his shorts and squeezed his cock through the material. Biting his bottom lip, he slowly undid the buttons, giving Kreed a wink as he slid the zipper down.

"Probably nothing like the one I'm hoping to get." Kreed grinned up at him, the firelight giving his eyes a wicked glow.

The way Kreed watched him so expectantly made him want to shove his hands in his pants and relieve the pressure churning in his balls. Kreed was a fucking sight to behold as he removed his shirt;

his dark nipples stood out against the lighter color of his skin. Aaron knew exactly how it felt to have them pebble against his tongue. There would be plenty of time for that after.

"You say all the right things, Deputy." He began to move his hips in circles, catching the rhythm of the song in his movements, sliding his fingers along the top of his chino shorts. He turned his back to Kreed, letting him get an eyeful as he hooked his thumbs in the waistband of his shorts and pushed them low on his hips.

"You're so fucking hot." Kreed's gaze slid slowly up and down his body as Aaron turned around and stepped out of his shorts. That stare lingered on his cock then moved up to meet his eyes. "Very nice. Don't stop on my account."

Kreed watched him intently. He didn't know what his deputy was thinking, but a smile teased the corners of his lips as Kreed unfastened his shorts and scooted them down far enough to put that gorgeous dick and balls on display.

Aaron's mouth watered at the sight of Kreed's erect length straining against his belly. Aaron ran his hands over his body while he danced, enjoying the effect he had on Kreed.

"I love the way you move. I could watch you for days. You undo me, make me insane with need." Kreed's words sent shivers of delight up his spine. The man always seemed to have everything under control, so calm, cool, and collected.

He stepped closer to Kreed, tugging slowly on his swollen prick as he continued to move his hips to the music and inch closer to the gorgeous sight before him.

"I fucking want you." Kreed slid an arm around Aaron's waist and pulled him back down to his lap. Aaron straddled him, his legs spread wide across Kreed's thighs, their cocks bumping together as he used the sultry beat of the song to dance on Kreed's lap. Kreed sucked two fingers into his mouth then reached around behind Aaron. The deputy marshal's hand slid down his spine, and Aaron lifted his hips. With a dip of his head, he took Kreed's mouth with his as Kreed pressed those slick fingers against his hole and then slipped in his ass.

"Mmm…" Aaron moaned into the kiss, their tongues dancing slow and measured then hard and demanding. He wiggled on the fingers in his ass then lifted himself off Kreed's digits before sinking back down with agonizing slowness, then doing it all over again. His body quivered as Kreed's long, firm fingers dragged along his passage.

"That's it, baby. Need to be in you." Kreed thrust his hand up with those words, driving Aaron to heaven with every brush of his prostate.

Aaron dropped down to meet Kreed's flexing and twitching fingers, increasing the sensation inside. When Kreed withdrew his fingers, Aaron managed to somehow get his legs under him and stand, which was a miracle because his legs were fucking jelly.

After reaching into the pocket of his shorts, Kreed pulled two foil packets out and waved them in the air. Aaron grinned at that and stroked his dick harder. His ass clenched as he watched Kreed rip open the package and roll the condom on that beautiful, thick cock. He stood mesmerized as Kreed kicked his shorts off the rest of the way and crooked his finger at him.

"Want to feel you around me."

Aaron wanted that too, as quickly as possible, so he turned around, situated himself between Kreed's open thighs and bent forward, tilting his ass up, giving Kreed a good view of his backside. Kreed's fingers ran down the crevice of his ass, sliding between his cheeks to tease and press against his hole.

"Fuck me," Aaron groaned.

Strong fingers kneaded his ass then slid to his hips before pulling him back. Kreed held himself in the perfect position as Aaron spread his ass cheeks and sat back until the blunt head of Kreed's cock pressed exactly where he wanted it. He lowered himself, working Kreed into his ass, lifting and lowering, enjoying the burn of being stretched and the pure bliss of being penetrated.

"So perfect." He moaned as he sank down, driving Kreed's cock deep. The sudden feeling of fullness drove him to grab his dick and tug.

"Son of a mother fucking bitch." Kreed hissed and ran his hand up Aaron's back to his neck, sliding long fingers against his scalp, curling them in his hair, then pulling his head back roughly. Sin bit and licked at his neck while making slow circles with his hips. Kreed's dick moved deep inside him as he curled his toes into the sand and stroked himself. Fuck, this was so good, too good.

His back rested against Sin's chest as he writhed to the music while Kreed fucked him. Kreed found his nipple and pinched, toying and tugging on the sensitive metal ring as he gave himself over to every pleasure Sin offered.

Kreed's hand slid up, ghosting lightly over his collarbone, before those long fingers wrapped securely around his neck, and pressed his head against his lover's shoulder. Aaron was held firmly in place while dominant fingers moved possessively against his jaw as Kreed ground up into him.

"You fuck me so good, church boy." Kreed's mouth pressed against his ear, and the hot puffs of breaths dancing across his skin turned him on even further.

Kreed moved a hand down Aaron's torso to wrap strong fingers around his dick and grip him roughly before beginning to stroke. He squeezed his internal muscles, tightening and releasing Kreed's dick as he took advantage of his position and bounced up and down, riding the cock in his ass.

"Agh…Fuck yes! Not gonna last." Kreed growled and thrust up into him, bumping his prostate. Aaron saw stars, almost lost the delicious rhythm he'd built. He was so fucking close. He was caught between needing to come and wanting it to last forever as Kreed's grip tightened on his cock.

"Fuck me harder." Aaron reached behind him, threading his fingers in Kreed's hair to anchor himself and let Kreed take over. Every thrust drove the breath from Aaron's burning lungs. He slammed down on Kreed's dick and worked his hips back and forth. Pressure built in his spine and his balls. Sin's steady strokes on his prick drove him to the brink. That thick cock pushing against his prostate… Lips grazed the side of his neck right before Kreed sealed his mouth against Aaron's skin and bit. *Fuck yes!* He bucked, his ass clenching as his orgasm flamed through his body and drew his balls up tight.

"God, yes…Sin!" Hot come hit his stomach and chest as he struggled to draw air into his lungs. The rhythm of Kreed's thrusts increased. The hand on his dick stroked faster, harder, drawing out his release.

"Ahh. So close…gonna…fuck!" Kreed gasped when his body stiffened. The cock in his ass jerked as the deputy came. Heavy breaths ghosted over his ear as he melted back against Kreed to catch his breath. Kreed released his dick and wrapped strong arms around him, holding him tightly in the cool night air, as their breathing returned to normal. Firm lips pressed against his temple.

"You were amazing. And I was right about one thing."

"Hmm…what's that?" Aaron tilted his head to the side as he turned to look at Kreed.

"I've never had a lap dance like that." Kreed waggled his brows and pushed his hips up, his half-erect cock sending a twinge of electric energy through Aaron's ass, making him clench again in response.

"It's a first for me too." He lifted his chin, and Kreed captured his lips in a slow drawn-out kiss. Aaron groaned when Kreed's softening cock slid out of him as he shifted positions.

"Can you stand?" Kreed helped him up then picked up his shirt off the beach and used it to clean the come off Aaron's stomach and chest. He removed the condom, tied it off, and pushed it into an empty beer bottle before dropping down in the sand and tugging Aaron down too.

They both settled on an oversized beach towel in front of the fire. Kreed wrapped protectively around him, holding him as if his life depended on the contact. Nothing felt as good as being in this moment with this man.

~~~

The big arm draped over Aaron's body held tighter as he tried to roll over. His half executed turn had him wedged against Kreed's warm chest. Normally, that was a sexy as hell move, one that would keep him there and lull him back to sleep, but not this morning. His head slid from Kreed's chest, and his face pressed into the deputy's armpit. All that hair tickled his skin and made it impossible to breathe.

Aaron pulled his head away only to have Kreed force him back, moving in such a way that he became Kreed's body pillow. Those beefy arms and legs embraced him tighter, and Kreed nuzzled into Aaron's hair. He arched his large, hard body, grinding his rigid cock against the front of Aaron's thigh before a soft snore made him smile.

He wasn't sure if it were his extreme cotton mouth or the squawking of the birds that was the final straw. Aaron rolled onto his back, trying to shift away from Kreed, who was still snoring loudly. He squinted, forcing his eyes partially open. The sun was almost too much to bear. He lifted a palm, shielding his eyes, and tried again. His eyes wouldn't cooperate and remained nothing more than slits as he looked around. Shit, they were still outside.

"What's wrong? Why are you moving so much?" Kreed asked, finally waking up and turning toward him. Aaron rolled to his side to look at Kreed, his movement happened to be too fast and made his queasy stomach roil.

"What the hell happened last night?" Aaron asked, fully pushing at Kreed, who fought to keep him there.

"Why are you leaving?" Kreed grumbled again, flopping onto his back, throwing his arm over his eyes.

"We're outside." Aaron stated the obvious as he moved to a sitting position, still trying to adjust his eyesight. The annoying birds sang overhead, the ocean lapped against the shore but it sounded more like pounding in his head, which he didn't need at the moment. Aaron concentrated on just breathing; his stomach felt nauseous and he had sand in his fucking ass, for God's sake. Not the way he had intended to wake up on his first day in paradise.

"I know," Kreed barked on a chuckle. His tone made it clear what he thought about Aaron's declaration.

"And naked," Aaron added the next obvious point. How had he let things get so far out of control?

"Even better," Kreed teased and reached his arms out, becoming octopus-worthy. Aaron had to struggle and dodge to rise. He finally scrambled enough to stand, while covering his cock with his hand as he reached and jerked the large beach towel off Kreed that they'd obviously used as a blanket last night. He quickly tied it around his waist, tucking the ends inside the towel as he scanned the beach. "There are people out here!"

That made Kreed finally lift his head and look around before dropping it back on the towel. "They're on the other side of the beach. They can't see us."

"Get up. If we can see them, they can see us. What happened last night? How did we not make it to bed?" Aaron asked, a little dumbfounded. He'd never let himself drink that much. With a solid grunt, Kreed rolled to his side before lifting to his feet. He dragged the towel up with him. He, of course, didn't wrap it around his body; instead, he tossed it over his shoulder, reached his arms up in the air, and stretched out his long body.

"You started dancing. Remember that?" Kreed teased.

"We don't need to talk about that." Aaron winced. Kreed was most definitely a bad influence. He'd completely let go last night, lost his inhibitions, and done a little strip tease for Kreed. He couldn't remember a lot about the execution of it, but Kreed seemed to like the dance.

"I didn't think you'd remember," Kreed said with a smirk as he passed by Aaron and headed up to the porch. Aaron's eyes followed him up each step.

"I can't remember what we danced to," Aaron said, trailing behind him.

"I think you started off dancing to "Closer" by Nine Inch Nails then ended up with "Fuck You Betta" from the stripper playlist on your phone. You were too good at it, even though you said it was your first time. That wasn't your first lap dance," Kreed added, opening the back door. His statement didn't come in the form of a question.

"You're just jealous you don't have my moves," Aaron called out, following along through the back door. The alcohol must have affected him more than he'd realized. Just like with everything else, Kreed had Aaron breaking long-standing rules. He knew how he got when he drank too much. Clothing always became optional. Actually the clothes came off and he became Magic Mike—if only in his own head. Lord, he wondered how red his cheeks had just gotten thinking about the possibility of last night's show.

"Hang on. I got something for the headache." Kreed went for the kitchen, and Aaron re-tied the knots holding his towel in place. He watched Kreed pull out several bottles from the cabinet.

"I'm not a Bloody Mary drinker," Aaron said. He'd just suffer through.

"You haven't had mine." Kreed worked at the counter while Aaron went for a handful of Advil and a glass of water. He swallowed, relieved when they stayed down.

"Here. Try this," Kreed said, handing him a tall, filled glass.

"I don't think I can." Aaron held his stomach, scrunching up his face, shaking his head no, but Kreed was having none of that.

"I promise it helps." Kreed walked Aaron back against the cabinet, reached up, and pinched Aaron's nose closed, making him swallow some of the drink. Aaron's stomach roiled as he lifted his hand, taking the glass before moving from under Kreed's hold, trying to keep from wearing the Bloody Mary.

"Stop!" he yelled. Kreed laughed as he reached over and grabbed his own glass, doing about the same as he'd done to Aaron. He plugged his nose and drank several large gulps. Kreed kept his eyes on Aaron, using his finger to motion for him to start drinking. Once he realized he did feel a little better, he took another drink, only having one moment of worry that maybe everything was coming back up. By the time he got to the bottom of the glass, Kreed had managed to put everything away and was rinsing his glass. He reached for Aaron's to wash and rinse his too.

"I need a shower. I have sand in terrible places and my ass is sore." Aaron left the kitchen.

"It should be. What can I say? I'm such a stud," Kreed called out.

"You could have shown some mercy," Aaron shot back, walking down the hall.

"You're the one that used me like a pole," Kreed called out loudly. Aaron stopped dead in his tracks. He had very little memory of that. He spun around as Kreed turned down the hall. "You gave the words lap dance a whole new meaning."

"I did not." But from the sweet twinge in his ass, Aaron figured he probably had.

"And you promised a repeat," Kreed said suggestively, bypassing Aaron and ducking into the master bath first. Kreed turned on the shower faucet before he started brushing his teeth. Aaron stood in the doorway, waiting for his turn at the sink.

"I'm embarrassed," he finally admitted.

When Kreed finished, he gathered Aaron up, kissing him lightly on the lips. His breath probably wasn't in the best condition right now, and he tried to push some distance between them.

"First, I honestly doubt your level of embarrassment. You'll do anything, anytime, anywhere, and I've seen that shit with my own eyes, so I'm calling bullshit. Second, best night of my life, and I'm not sore at all." Kreed paused as if he contemplated that statement. Then he looked Aaron directly in the eyes and said, "I think you need to change that at some point today."

Kreed patted him on the ass and ducked inside the shower. That made Aaron smile and eased his tension a little. He shook his head and made his way to the sink to brush his teeth. Kreed yelped—probably at the scalding hot water from the sink faucet he'd just turned on. Aaron quickly turned the faucet off, waited about a minute then flipped it back on. Kreed hollered out again. Yep. That was good to know.

"You did that on purpose," Kreed yelled, his head popping out around the shower curtain. Aaron only laughed as he finished brushing his teeth before joining Kreed.

~~~

"You mad?" A cool burst of air chilled his skin as Aaron slipped into the shower. The steam rose up around them, along with the smell of cinnamon and evergreen. Aaron brushed against him and his dick grew stiff.

"Nope, but payback is a bitch," Kreed replied as Aaron stepped under the spray and tipped his head back, wetting himself. Aaron's nipples pebbled, the little silver rings drawing Kreed's attention. Kreed slid his fingers up Aaron's waist, the water rolling down Aaron's skin as Kreed's fingers moved higher to touch the dragon tattoo. "So beautiful."

Aaron opened his blue-gray eyes, capturing Kreed's gaze with the heated promise they held. He slipped the tip of his pinky finger in the silver loop and tugged, drawing a groan from Aaron's lips. Kreed bent his head and flicked the ring with his tongue then took Aaron's nipple between his teeth.

"Kiss me." Aaron's voice was ragged and filled with need. He slid strong fingers to the nape of Kreed's neck and cupped his head.

He spun Aaron around and pushed him against the tiles of the shower wall and kicked his legs apart. He ran a hand up the back of

Aaron's thighs, smoothing them over the perfect roundness of his butt. Aaron tipped his ass back and widened his stance even more. Kreed used his hands to spread Aaron's ass cheeks and stroked the pink pucker with his thumbs.

Water ran down Aaron's crease and Kreed leaned down to chase it hungrily with his tongue. Aaron groaned. Kreed dropped to his knees, getting in a better position, and buried his face between those firm round globes to lap at Aaron's hole. Aaron shuddered as Kreed held him open, licking and lapping. His own erection was heavy and bobbing as he found a comfortable spot on the decorative tiles.

The sound of Aaron's groans and moans echoed sweetly off the shower walls. He stuck his tongue against Aaron's entrance, stiffening it. The outer muscle gave way as he pressed inside and began fucking Aaron with his tongue. He used his thumbs and worked them deeper into Aaron as he ate his ass. His lover squirmed against his face and on his tongue, the steam of the shower adding to the heat in Kreed's balls. He slid his thumbs from Aaron and swatted his ass cheeks. Aaron groaned.

"You like that, don't you?" He reached between Aaron's legs and fondled his balls. Kreed grabbed Aaron's hips, turned him around, and deep-throated him, taking his church boy so deep his lips touched the close-trimmed hair at his root. He held him there then slowly pulled back, only to do it again, drawing a moan from Aaron.

Kreed gripped Aaron at the base and licked at the vein running along Aaron's shaft, paying special attention to the cockhead and the sensitive underside with the flat of his tongue.

"Put your leg on the side of the ledge." Aaron did as told, and Kreed picked up the body wash sitting nearby and poured it into his hand. He set the brightly-colored bottle back down, careful not to spill the soap he held in his other hand. He reached behind Aaron and spread the soap on his hole, dipping his pinky inside before using his free hand to capture Aaron's dick and begin stroking him.

The water ran down his face as he used his slicked-up fingers to tenderly tease Aaron's entrance. Kreed replaced the hand on Aaron's cock with his mouth then gripped his own cock when Aaron's hips set the rhythm.

Kreed pumped himself faster, the hard shower floor cutting into his knees as Aaron's cock hit the back of his throat and he struggled not to gag around him. Constricting heat wrapped around his fingers as he worked Aaron's hole, slow and deep. He twisted and curled his fingers to give Aaron the greatest pleasure he could without pressing hard enough to truly hurt. Aaron's thigh shook on his shoulder. His thrusts became uncoordinated and jerky.

"I'm close." Aaron panted above him as his fingers tightened against Kreed's scalp. He slacked his jaw and let his lover fuck his face. Pushing his fingers deeper, he hooked them and pressed against his church boy's prostate. He swore Aaron's cock swelled against his lips.

"Kreed," Aaron shouted. His name echoed off the shower walls. His lover's salty release hit the back of his throat. He swallowed every last drop, his own orgasm one stroke away.

"C'mere," Aaron said, pulling him up off the floor so quickly he fought to retain his balance. Aaron pushed against his chest, and his back hit the warm tile wall. Everything happened so fast he didn't process it until Aaron dropped to his knees and inhaled him with a dip of his head. Hot suction on his cock blinded him. Electricity charged in his balls and rolled through his body. Kreed was already so close that he welcomed the onslaught of pleasure. He fisted Aaron's hair and thrust his hips forward, fucking into that amazing mouth.

"Mmm….fuck." His hands slid down the sides of Aaron's face, holding his head in place as his release bowed his spine and he spilled his load down his lover's welcoming throat.

After the fog cleared in his brain and he regained his senses, Kreed tugged Aaron against him and just held him as the water fell around them.

Chapter 29

After spending the last five days in Hawaii, Kreed knew without question, all the fuss about this place growing old was absolutely nuts. Kreed was pretty certain he could get used to living on this island. This little slice of heaven was nothing short of paradise—not too hot, definitely not too cold, just perfect.

The rental car's windows were rolled down, allowing the sea-scented air to wash over them as Aaron drove down the street. He liked that Aaron enjoyed the island breeze blowing in his hair as much as he did. As they got going, Kreed lifted his phone and saw he'd missed a call. He put his window up about half way and reached over to lower the radio volume as he touched the icon to return the call.

"I missed a call from Mitch," Kreed said to Aaron as he lifted his cell to his ear, listening as it rang.

"When? I never heard it ring," Aaron questioned, looking over at him. His guy looked nice tonight, dressed up for their first official date night. They'd decided to go back into town, hit up the dinner-slash-dancing joint Colt had suggested. Based on Jace's warning that his mister couldn't keep his hands to himself while they were there, Kreed knew it would be a place made for him.

Even before he'd seen how good his guy looked all dressed up, Kreed had planned to pull Aaron out on the dance floor and pretty much molest him for the next couple of hours. He wanted Aaron plastered against him, head to toe, with some sexy music keeping them tightly together. Yeah, and he also wanted the other men to see exactly who he would be taking home tonight.

The thought had Kreed smiling as he reached up, running his thumb across Aaron's cheek when he looked over at Kreed, probably waiting on him to answer whatever question he hadn't paid attention to. Aaron was just too fucking hot for him to be able to think straight tonight.

"I hear you breathing, ass-lick. Did you butt dial me?" Mitch's voice pulled Kreed from his wayward musing.

"Sorry," Kreed said, forcing his eyes from Aaron. He rolled the window the rest of the way up so he could hear.

"You know it's midnight," Mitch grumbled, and no, Kreed hadn't considered that when he'd called, but that did make it better that he'd missed the call earlier.

"No amount of beauty sleep's gonna help, princess," he shot back.

"Har, har, har. What do you want, Sinacola?"

"I'm returning your call."

"That was like…five hours ago. Clearly, it's not urgent. I'd be dead by now if I'd needed you. Just call me when you get wherever you're going," Mitch shot back and Kreed smiled. Mitch just never gave him any kind of break at all.

"Nah man, tell me. My guy's driving. We're going to dinner. It'll be a late night. What's going on?" Kreed asked. Aaron reached down to raise his window, helping to plunge the car into silence.

"Your guy, huh?" Mitch chuckled at him. Of course that would be what Mitch caught on to.

"Yeah, you got a problem with that?" Kreed questioned, looking over at Aaron, hoping he couldn't hear Mitch's words. Aaron was just coming around, opening up to the idea of them in a relationship, and he didn't want him to close back up because of some ill-timed words, not understanding this was just the way he and Knox communicated with each other.

"I got a bigger problem with you calling so late and waking my ass up." Mitch let out a loud yawn.

"Then get on with it; we're almost to town. What's going on? Catch me up."

"Let's see. Okay, well, the bureau's upped security on the victims. They're worried about copycats. It hit the news, and the fanatics are coming out in droves, so watch yourself. We're gonna stick around Dallas for a while longer."

"That was only a matter of time. I haven't turned on the news, so I haven't seen it."

"It's all over the place. It's taken on a life of its own. Every station's clamoring for information. People hate that church, but some are playing devil's advocate. Shit's getting touchy."

"Hey, Kreed," he heard Colt's voice in the background.

"Where are you at that Colt's in bed with you? What the hell's going on there? Now I know why you wanted to stick around a little longer," Kreed teased.

"Fuck you. I came downstairs when you called. I didn't wanna wake up Cody, ass."

"Tell him I'm sending him a text," Colt hollered.

"Don't," Mitch yelled.

"Too late. I just sent it." Colt sounded smug.

"I'm telling Jace about your bacon fetish," Mitch threatened.

"Fetish now? You already sold me out. That ship's sailed, Knox," Colt said in the background.

Kreed's phone vibrated, and he pulled the phone away from his ear long enough to open the attachment which turned out to be a selfie of Colt with Cody, both with big smiles. Colt had his arm slung around Cody and his fingers spread to give a peace sign. The most interesting thing about the whole picture was Mitch's image captured several feet behind Colt, scowling toward the duo. Kreed chuckled, knowing exactly why Colt wanted him to see that picture.

He put the phone back to his ear quickly and could feel the giant smile on his face as he said, "Put Colt on the phone."

"Fuck you. Call him yourself," Mitch said and hung up on him. Kreed lowered the phone, laughing.

"What happened?" Aaron asked.

"Mitch and Colt have that love-hate thing going on. They get so possessive. You saw it while we were there. Well, Colt took a picture with Cody where they were all huddled up together. Mitch is in the background, and his pissed off, jealous face is captured in the photo. Photographic evidence that Colt won that round." Kreed's phone started ringing, and he glanced down to see Colt's name come up on caller ID. He answered to Colt's hysterical laughter.

"That's greatness," Kreed said.

"Yeah. I might have to blow it up and hang it in my house or save it for special occasions when I know Knox is coming over."

"What were you doing?"

"I just took a selfie with Cody for his family. They're big football fans. Then I saw Mitch's face when I was scrolling through the pictures. Oh my God. It was too much," Colt explained between laughing fits. The guy was really tickled, and it was contagious. Kreed was solidly laughing now while trying to listen and holding off a curious Aaron's attempts to find out what was being said.

"Y'all laugh all you want. I'm going back to fuckin' bed. I need my sleep since I'm the one keeping you safe," Mitch called out, his voice trailing off at the end as though he were leaving the room.

"No way. Did he just take his toys and go home? *And* still try to use the protection card?" Kreed asked.

"Yeah, he gets his panties in a wad every time I show that picture. It might be my most prized possession now."

"Yeah, that's too funny. Make copies of that. Don't lose it. I gotta roll. We just pulled into the parking lot of that bar."

"Y'all have a good time."

"Thanks for the laugh. That's awesome." Kreed opened his door.

Aaron was already out and rounding the car. He was there, wanting to know what was going on. Colt disconnected the call, and Kreed switched back to the picture, lifted the phone, and showed Aaron, because that picture was worth a thousand words. It took about as long as it took him to slam the door shut and move around Aaron before his guy burst out a laugh.

"Colt's giving him hell, isn't he?"

"Seems like. Deserved though. Come on. Let's get this date started." Kreed placed his hands on Aaron's hips and turned him toward the door. Dinner needed to come first because Aaron's mood definitely adjusted when there was food placed in front of him. Then they'd be dancing. If he got lucky and used his words correctly, maybe he could even talk his guy into some dark corner or bathroom sex.

~~~

"You're sexy," Kreed whispered in Aaron's ear as he cupped Aaron's ass, grinding him against his hardened arousal.

"You're the sexy one," Aaron tossed back, offering his neck, enjoying the small kisses Kreed kept giving him. He was under sensual assault with Kreed doing his best to talk him into doing the naughty right here in the bar. God, it was getting harder and harder to resist this man.

The dance floor was dark enough that Aaron, with the few drinks he'd had tonight, felt reasonably secure that the way Kreed was grinding on his body wouldn't be noticed by anyone in the bar. It was late and the place seemed open to almost anything, even if borderline inappropriate.

Aaron rolled his hips as Kreed nibbled along his neck with evil lips. But now, as he swayed to the song with Kreed's big body wrapped around his, Aaron was so fucking horny, his ass clenched each time Kreed ran his hands over his butt cheeks.

"I need you." Kreed's warm breath cooled the wet path his tongue had left on Aaron's skin as he whispered against his ear.

Aaron shivered and again rolled his hips against Kreed's.

"You're bad," Aaron replied. Kreed tightened his hold on Aaron, forcing him to arch his back as Kreed leaned in to him.

"I'm really into you." Kreed nibbled along his jaw.

"I like you too," Aaron confessed, wrapping his arms around Kreed's neck.

"But you're not gonna let me do you here, are you?" Kreed asked, his lips by his ear again. He loved that move. Hell, he loved any move where Kreed's lips were on him. But who would have known how much he'd love having someone whispering in his ear like that.

"Not here." Aaron brushed his lips along the length of Kreed's neck.

"I tried to get you drunk so I could have my way with you," Kreed replied.

"I know you tried. You get an A for effort."

Kreed lifted his head and looked deeply into his eyes. Aaron could lose himself in that dark chestnut gaze and had many times over. Aaron resisted the urge to kiss the tipsy deputy marshal. He glanced up and caught a rare moment of vulnerability crossing Kreed's handsome face. The look so intense, he drew back, but Kreed locked him tightly in place with strong arms.

"I'm falling, Stuart. If you're not there with me, you should probably say something before I make a fool of myself," Kreed confessed.

Aaron's pulse jumped at Kreed's words. He lifted his hands to Kreed's face and continued to stare deeply in those beautiful eyes he couldn't resist. Absolutely he was falling. Hell, he had already tumbled head over heels.

He didn't know when it had happened. Despite his best efforts to avoid it—to keep it purely physical and temporary—he'd let Kreed in and there was no denying that to himself any longer. Man, he wanted to say it, especially right then. Kreed had made this night so special; no one had ever done anything like this for him. He had been wined and dined. Kreed ordered just about everything on the menu because he knew Aaron liked food. Then came the dancing… Damn, the dancing was hot. Kreed made him feel wanted and they connected in a way he'd never connected with another person. He could sway on this dancefloor with this man forever. Aaron swallowed hard.

For the first time in his life, he wished he was just a guy that worked for the NSA. When he'd made the decision to do what he did, he hadn't understood how much he would truly have to give up. He hated the fact that he couldn't ever be completely honest with Kreed. Lying to this man ate at him every day, and that feeling only intensified as he got to know more of him and wished he could be so much more for Kreed.

"You're intoxicated," Aaron finally answered. Kreed glanced down to Aaron's mouth as he said the words.

"You're intoxicating," Kreed whispered before taking his lips.

He opened for Kreed, and tilted his head to deepen the kiss. The kiss was the most intense of his life, so intimate and raw. Kreed made love to him through that kiss, and Aaron could only wrap himself tighter around Kreed and try to hang on as the emotions he tried to deny wrenched his heart wide open.

When Kreed broke away and pulled back, he captured Aaron's eyes again with his penetrating gaze. Aaron had no trouble spotting Kreed's intuitive side in that look as the deputy marshal kept trying to read him. Aaron should have learned by now he couldn't hide behind words with Kreed; the man was too savvy.

"I'll give you more time, but you need to be honest with me. Every day I'm falling a little deeper. We're close to no turning back. You need to stop what's happening and spare me from the hurt later on if you're not feeling it now."

No question, Kreed had been good to him—so willing to explore the depths of their attraction, never hiding behind the pain of the past. He was more open than any person he'd ever met. Even now, when he was certain to be hurt if Aaron pulled away, Kreed was willing to give him time to explore his feelings. The honesty and goodness this man shared with him gave Aaron a rare moment of certainty, and he spoke from the heart.

"I'm caught up in you, Sin, but I can't see how any of this can continue past this week. Life's gonna complicate this. *I'm* gonna complicate this."

"You're putting the cart before the horse. Right now is all I'm asking for. It's enough to know you're experiencing this with me. We'll cross that other bridge when it's time," Kreed spoke softly, his gaze dropping to Aaron's lips. "I'm so fucking addicted to your mouth."

Aaron lifted his lips for a kiss and slid his lids closed as Kreed met him halfway. Aaron threaded his fingers in Kreed's short hair, trying to press as much of himself against Kreed as he could. Swept away, Aaron deepened the kiss, but Kreed cut him off, placing both hands on his face to create distance. That commanding and deeply intense look settled back in Kreed's eyes. What was he trying to figure out now?

Seconds later, Kreed had Aaron by the hand, dragging him off the dancefloor and down the dark hallway of the club. In the background, the odor of stale smoke, booze, and arousal hung heavily in the dark corridor.

"You get me so fucking hard." Kreed shoved him against the wall, buried his face in Aaron's neck, and sucked at his skin. A hard powerful body anchored him to the chipping plaster, strength and muscle held him in place. The way Kreed pinned him didn't give him any choice but to submit to Kreed's demands. The deputy's mouth brushed against his neck, alternating between sweet kisses and heated licks. Aaron's dick jerked at the sting of Kreed's teeth sinking into his flesh. *Oh, fucking hell!*

"Sin…" Aaron dropped his head against the wall, giving Kreed full access to his neck, and dug his fingers into that firm ass. Kreed pushed a knee between his thighs, and he widened his stance. Eager hands skimmed his sides then gripped his cock roughly through his pants. Fingers pressed against his dick then slid to his hip and around to cup his ass.

Aaron smiled into Kreed's hair when the deputy tensed the moment his hands finally discovered Aaron hadn't worn any underwear.

"You fucker," Kreed said against his neck. Aaron chuckled and nuzzled in closer. Kreed's scent engulfed him, made him shudder and go weak in the knees. The smell of leather, cinnamon, and cloves permeated the air around him. Kreed kept him on his feet with that big muscular body anchoring him to the wall.

"Thought you might like it." Aaron pressed his groin into Kreed's hand and twisted his hips, searching for more friction. Anyone could walk down the hall and see them, but he didn't give a fuck. It only added to the intensity of the moment. Kreed pressed a palm hard against him and Aaron's hips arched into the touch on their own accord.

"You have no idea."

Kreed's low, husky voice caressed his skin. The pressure of Kreed's palm grew stronger, his strokes steadily rougher. Electricity rushed through his veins and charged through his groin. He tipped his head back and looked into Kreed's dark eyes.

"Make me come, Sin." He ground his hips against Kreed's palm as Kreed's mouth once again devoured his.

"Fuck yeah, sweetheart." Kreed's lips brushed against the corner of his mouth. Aaron heard the distinct hiss of a zipper, but it wasn't his. He ran his hands down Kreed's body, smiling when he realized where this was headed.

Impatient fingers fumbled with the buttons on his pants, so Aaron pressed against his lover's hand, hoping that would help Kreed get them undone faster. Aaron pushed his hand inside Kreed's underwear, palming Kreed's erection and squeezed before drawing his hand up and down its length, making Kreed groan.

Kreed worked his pants down his hips just enough to gain the access he wanted.

Cool air hit his dick right before warm rough fingers wrapped around him. His hips immediately thrust forward, driving his cock deeper into Kreed's tightened fist.

"Mmm...you're leaking. So fucking hot." Kreed's thumb slid over his cockhead and spread the pre-come across the crown, his finger dipping into the slit with every pass. Hot need coursed through Aaron's veins as they stroked each other in the corner of a darkened hallway.

Kreed let go of him, spit in his hand, then angled his hips. Their cocks rubbed together as Kreed took them both in hand and began to stroke. The friction of Kreed's cock and fist sliding against him sent a "hello" and "hell yeah" straight to his balls.

Kreed greedily took his mouth again, tongue sliding against tongue, lips pressing against lips, as he rocked into Kreed's fist. The sweet constant pressure on his dick had his hips stuttering, searching for the right rhythm. He held Kreed's head in his hands, his fingers lost in his hair as he desperately tried to draw the man closer. Kreed's tongue dipped in and out of his mouth in time with the delicious strokes on his cock.

"Looking for a third? I'll suck both your cocks."

Aaron's eyes flew open. He'd been so into the hand job that he'd forgotten about being in the hallway of a gay club. He had no idea how long the guy had been standing there, stroking his own cock and leering at them. Kreed pressed a kiss to the side of Aaron's mouth, using his body to shield the continuing motion of his hand.

"You need to keep moving. We're not interested. You hear me?" Kreed's voice took on a deep growl as he spoke against Aaron's lips, never turning to look at the guy or slowing the strokes of his fist.

"Loud and clear. You didn't have to go all caveman," the guy said and continued to stroke himself as he walked away.

"Mmm…staking your claim, Deputy Marshal?" Aaron's body tightened at how possessively Kreed's body molded around him. Surprised at how turned on he'd become at the thought of the deputy going all caveman on him. But that kind of taking would have to wait till they got home. Aaron slid a hand between their bodies to join Kreed's, whose lips pressed against his ear.

"I'm fucking you when we get home. Claiming what's mine." Kreed's growled words sped up Aaron's hips and drew up his balls. The fire started at the base of his spine and flamed up, sending liquid heat coursing through his veins.

"Yesss…Sin." His orgasm engulfed him so quickly he almost doubled over from the force of his release. Kreed sank his teeth into Aaron's neck as they both came, hot come mixing on their slowing fists. Kreed pressed his forehead against Aaron's as their ragged breathing calmed.

"You having any regrets over getting a hand job in a gay club?"

"No fucking way. Not even a little. That was hot as hell. I do have one problem, though. My hand is covered in spunk." Aaron lifted his hand, not really sure what he should do with it.

Kreed turned to look at his hand and laughed. "Yeah, it was hot. But nothing compared to what I've got planned for you at home, church boy. Good thing the bathroom is around the corner. Come on. Let's get cleaned up and go home." Kreed kissed his forehead, then his nose, before capturing his mouth in a slow, sweet kiss.

Chapter 30

Happiness filtered through Kreed on a cosmic level, something he hadn't experienced in a very long time, maybe made a little bit better because Aaron hadn't flat out told him to fuck off when he'd laid his heart on the line. Without question, Kreed could sense Aaron was holding back; he just couldn't figure out why, and for some reason, that wasn't limiting how deeply Kreed's connection developed. The sorrow he'd experienced over the last few months about his brother had really done a number on him. Kreed flipped on the master bathroom lights while working to free the buttons of his dress shirt. Thoughts of his brother threatened to squash his good mood.

"You're really gonna share? I feel pretty special," Aaron joked, coming in behind him. Strong insistent arms wrapped around Kreed's waist, halting the process of removing his shirt. It was remarkable how quickly Aaron zapped the funky mood he was developing.

"You're pretty special. I might even get you hooked. You might have to start sending Lush products along with your computer equipment everywhere you go."

Kreed chuckled, turning in Aaron's arms in order to peel off his shirt. "You know, I'm not sure I realized how happy you are after you come."

Aaron tilted that smiling face up, making it easy to lean forward and softly kiss those perfect lips. "You make me do things I wouldn't normally do."

"I like watching you do things you wouldn't normally do, but I doubt you wouldn't normally do them. I just think you let me think it's my idea." Kreed tugged free of his hold, going for the drawer that held all his spa products. He'd gotten shit for years from Knox over this stuff; he'd grown accustom to guys thinking it was weird. But he was certain, if they'd ever tried it, he'd have to fist-fight over his stash.

The old tub looked roomie for a bathtub made in the seventies. As he reached for the faucet, he dropped the plug in the drain and turned the water on. The thing had jets. There was a switch for those, and he flipped it on briefly, listening to see if the motor turned on. Score! Who would have thought they would still work after all this time?

He turned them off, waiting until the tub filled. Kreed reached for his belt buckle, but stopped as he spotted Aaron tugging off his clothes. It was becoming one of his favorite things to watch his guy undress. Kreed's eyes fixed on Aaron as he pushed down his jeans. He knew Aaron was commando from the earlier hand job at the club. His church boy hadn't bothered to wear any underwear on their date. He smiled. Aaron was full of little surprises, and damn if that shit didn't turn him the fuck on.

Wet dreams weren't as good as Aaron Stuart. His long torso, perfect ass, and strong muscular legs made Kreed want to run his hands up and down all that beautiful, naked flesh.

If it were up to him, he'd have his guy naked all the time. But that was all in due time. He would have that and more someday with Aaron, because he wasn't going to easily let him go. There were obstacles to that dream, but he just had to figure out the barriers Aaron kept placing between them and remove them one by one.

Those decisions were made, and his heart clung to the hope they presented. He liked the contentment and hope Aaron offered, and it had been far too long since he'd experienced either one of those emotions. Now it was time to up his game and make Aaron realize they could get through anything, as long as they were together.

Aaron tossed his clothes aside, looking over the things Kreed pulled out of the drawer.

"Which are we using?" Aaron asked, moving the condoms he had in his hand to the bathtub. "Do they smell good. Is that it?"

"They smell amazing and make your skin feel fantastic. Some of the scents relax you, things like that."

"Like aromatherapy?"

"Pretty much." Kreed laughed at Aaron's need to understand all the angles of the brilliance of these bath products. Lush wasn't meant to be understood; it was meant to be enjoyed. Tossing his clothes on top of Aaron's, Kreed lowered his foot into the water to test the temperature. He pulled his foot back quickly and adjusted the knobs to cool things off a little then went for the spice bomb—hell, anything named bomb surely was meant for a guy. He dropped it inside and watched it begin to fizzle. The scent of cinnamon and cloves instantly filled the entire room.

"You're hot," Aaron commented, coming to stand beside the tub as they watched the thing bubble apart. "Your body's incredible, and I haven't seen you work out."

Kreed tested the water again, turned the faucet off, and stepped inside. It was hot, and like always, immediately began to soothe him. He lowered himself, reaching for Aaron's hand and tugged.

"I'm gonna crowd you," Aaron said, resisting a little.

"Good. That's the plan," Kreed encouraged again, pulling a little harder this time. Aaron stepped in, shuffling around a little until Kreed reached up and guided him down.

"I don't take baths—and never with someone else," Aaron said, moving awkwardly.

"Stick with me, church boy, and we'll change that. I love taking baths. I do it all the time, especially after a hard workout. I'd rather sit in here than a sauna any day." Kreed coaxed Aaron back, spreading his thighs wide, lifting his knees, helping Aaron get comfortable until his back rested against Kreed's chest, that silky, dark head now close enough for him to kiss. So he did. "See? It feels incredible."

"Am I hurting you?" Aaron asked. Kreed barked out a laugh at that one.

"Of course not," he said, pushing water up Aaron's chest. "Your skin's gonna be soft when we get out."

Kreed trailed small kisses along Aaron's neck, lapping at the drops of water on his skin, but his guy was still tense. "What's wrong? You need to relax."

"I'm worried I'm squishing you," Aaron said, and Kreed grinned as he ran his nose through those silky strands. He liked Aaron worrying about him. Proved he cared.

"You'll never squish me. In fact, I love the feeling of your weight against me," Kreed said and lifted his hands to rub Aaron's shoulders. "Relax. It's supposed to be soothing, remember?"

"Talk to me," Aaron said and started to relax against him.

"About what?" He slid his hands along Aaron's shoulders, down to his chest, stopping to tease the small metal ring in his nipple.

Aaron inhaled sharply. "Stop trying to distract me. Tell me about your life." Aaron leaned his head back on Kreed's shoulder.

The request confused him, and he narrowed his eyes and tilted his head to get a closer look at Aaron. The kid's eyes were closed, but he opened them and gave a sideways glance in Kreed's direction.

"You're fascinating. Sue me for being curious."

That earned Aaron points right there. Very nice comment. He liked knowing Aaron was into him enough to want to know more.

"Let's see. I don't really know where to start. No one's ever asked me that question before." He sat back against the tub to think, his hands manipulating Aaron's strong shoulders again.

"What kind of kid were you?" Aaron lightly brushed his fingertips up and down Kreed's thighs.

"Normal, I guess." Kreed continued to rub Aaron's shoulders, moving down to his upper arms, then back up again, losing himself in the question. He hadn't thought about his childhood in more years than he could remember.

"Let's see. Well, I was an only child for most of my formative years. My brother didn't come along until I was starting my teens. So I guess the best way to describe my childhood was that I was bad when I was little. My mom was kind of a pushover. I'd get in trouble, but she'd let me off the hook. Then I was the definition of bad when I was a teenager because they weren't paying any attention to me after they had Derek. They tried for a long time to get that boy." The thoughts of his brother caused a dark void that he wasn't strong enough to face right now, so he quickly changed the subject. "What was your life like?"

"No, we're not changing the subject. Bad, like how?" The conversation seemed to loosen Aaron up, or at least redirect his thoughts, because he rolled over in the water, Aaron's chest now pressed to his. Kreed looked down at Aaron's upturned face, then bent in to kiss his full lips.

"Like bad enough that it was go into the military or one of those six-month boot camps. I chose the military," Kreed answered. When Aaron stayed silent, Kreed figured he wanted more of that story. Since he wasn't too proud of that time in his life, he didn't want to rehash the events. "I wasn't always comfortable being gay. Or wait, it wasn't necessarily that back then. I didn't understand it. I wasn't exposed to too many homosexuals in my life. I didn't get why I was so focused on cocks while my buddies kept talking about all the girls they were hittin'. I acted out some. Did you ever go through that?" Kreed asked.

"Stop changing the subject. You're fascinating. Keep going. So you went in the military..." Aaron prompted. Kreed stared for a couple of long seconds, but Aaron looked truly interested. Kreed lifted a foot and flipped the switch to turn on the jets. The water came to life in a gentle roll of soothing air bubbles.

"I did. I enlisted, and it was perfect for me. Gave me something to think about besides men, which is weird because I was around nothing but hot as hell guys. It should have been just more of the same as high school, but it wasn't. I came into my own there."

"And you moved around a lot. I read that in one of your reports."

"I love that you were digging around to find out things about me. I knew you were into me," Kreed said smugly, lifting Aaron slightly so he could scoot lower in the tub, aligning their chests. Kreed grabbed Aaron's thick hard-on and urged him to shift positions so both their cocks slid deliciously together between their bodies in the slick water.

"Keep going, big guy," Aaron encouraged, moving Kreed's hand from between their bodies. Kreed barked out a laugh at the double meaning, but Aaron kept going, "Your career's fascinating. It's like a real life *Call of Duty*."

"There's a reason that information isn't anywhere," Kreed explained, and when it looked like Aaron was going to persist, he put his fingers to his guy's lips. "I really can't talk about it, for my safety as well as my family's. Even you, Stuart. Everybody in my life. But I did leave the military about ten years ago. It wasn't necessarily my decision, but it was time to go. I left with an honorable discharge and chose the marshal service. I moved up quickly. It was Skinner who talked to me about the US Marshals Service Special Operations Group—SOG for short. He introduced me to Mitch. By then, I had calmed down quite a bit." When he felt the vibration against his chest, he goosed the man on top of him. "Stop laughing. I did, and Mitch was up-and-coming. Skinner couldn't say to us that we fit because of the gay thing, but it definitely helped to pair us up. We did better with the staff. It was important, I guess. Skinner's a good guy."

"Did you ever doubt him in the Redemption Tabernacle deal? Because you had to suspect everybody once Agent Langley's involvement came out."

"Never him. I was talking to Skinner behind everyone's back almost from the beginning. Well, at least since the Grayson kid went down. I never doubted him one time," Kreed said.

"What about Connors or Brown. Did they set off any red flags?"

"Of course. What about you? What did you think?"

"I had insider information, but I trusted you. You're too honest not to, if that makes any sense." The words coming out of Aaron's mouth didn't quite match the look in his eyes.

"Yeah, it makes sense," Kreed agreed, but he couldn't shake the feeling Aaron was hiding something. From the moment he'd met Aaron, he sensed the kid was trying to skate under the radar. At first he thought it was because Aaron didn't like him, but that clearly wasn't the case. As it turned out, they had amazing chemistry. Everything felt right with Aaron. He had fallen hard for his best friend's gaming buddy, and if he were reading all the signals correctly, he was certain Aaron felt the same way about him. But none of that changed the fact that he was certain Aaron was keeping something from him. Kreed sat forward, turning the faucet on, warming the water before sitting back against the tub.

"Did you ever think we'd be working together?" Kreed lightly traced circles up and down Aaron's back.

"No, but I'm glad we did," Aaron answered, turning his head so that his chin rested on Kreed's chest.

"I still can't believe you shot me down like that. I think it's because you wanted me," Kreed teased, grabbing Aaron's ass and sliding their bodies together to pull him up for a kiss.

Aaron broke the kiss and lifted his head, smirking at him. "If I remember correctly, it was more you wanting me," Aaron teased back.

Kreed pushed his hand between them again and ran his fingers along the sides of their erections as he spoke.

"I want to know everything about you. Things like, whether you like Oreos or Tim Tams, beaches or mountains, dogs or cats? I wanna be the one you share your dreams with. The one you tell your secrets to. I wanna discover all the things that make you, who you are." Kreed felt Aaron's body tense as soon as the words left his mouth, so he quickly added, "What was your childhood like? What kind of kid were you like growing up? Tell me about your job with the NSA. That sounds like it might be interesting."

Kreed didn't care what Aaron had done in his past, or what he may be hiding. Hell, there wasn't anything the kid could say or do to change all this deep emotion developing inside him. But evidently he was doing a piss-poor job of getting that point across and getting Aaron to level with him.

"Nah, it's not that interesting working for the NSA. And there's really not much to tell. What you see is what you get with me." Aaron shrugged as a determined smile spread across his face. "My life isn't near as exciting as yours. Besides, I'd much rather talk about how I plan on taking care of you right now." Aaron's gaze drifted down their bodies and locked on his cock.

Desire and need flared in the pit of his belly when Aaron brushed persistent fingers against his length. The kid nudged Kreed's hand away and firmly took hold of his aching erection. He still hadn't gotten any more answers out of Aaron. Now it seemed his questions would have to wait, because Aaron's grip was currently scrambling his brain.

"You aren't playing fair, church boy."

"Just leveling the playing field, Deputy." The fragrant water sloshed against the side of the overly large tub as Aaron shifted his position and started to stroke him with purpose. Kreed was helpless against Aaron's deflecting techniques, and he'd effectively derailed his Q&A session.

The kid was good. So good in fact that Kreed's eyes rolled back in his head as the thumb circling the head of his dick pressed into his slit. He couldn't think straight, not with Aaron teasing him like he was.

"Fuck that feels amazing," he half said, half groaned. "But I've caught on to your game."

"What's that?" Aaron stroked him a few more times.

"Distracting me with sex," Kreed answered as he thrust up into Aaron's fist.

"We can always talk later. I just want to make you feel good," Aaron reasoned.

Kreed gave in. "Yes, later. And just so you know, what you're doing right now feels just fine to me."

"I'm gonna try to make it so much better." Aaron smiled at him then released the grip on his cock before pushing up and off him.

"Just relax against the tub," Aaron ordered, nudging him as he inched between Kreed's open legs. The back of his thighs rested lightly across the top of Aaron's. The kid used his hand and tugged him closer before fully rising up on his knees, the warm water rolling down Aaron's body, splashing between his spread legs. In this position, Aaron's balls pressed against his as he bent forward, and took both of their dicks in hand and started stroking again.

The feel of Aaron's hard-as-steel cock firmly pressed along the length of his sent a jolt of electricity straight to his balls. Kreed drank in the sight in front of him. Aaron was one hot motherfucker. His gunmetal blue eyes stood out against his dark hair and tan skin. And those damn nipple rings made Kreed's mouth fucking water.

The sensation of Aaron's fist gliding up and down his length and the feel of Aaron's hot sac against his almost pushed him past the point of no return, and he was already dangerously close to losing his load. Aaron slowed his rhythm and swept his thumb across Kreed's swollen head spreading the pre-come leaking from his cock. There was so much tenderness in his touch. Aaron's fist tightened around him, moving up and down his shaft in long lazy strokes that had him arching his hips in search of more friction.

"Ahh, fuck!" Kreed gasped. Aaron continued to pump their cocks with one hand while teasing his balls with the other, those mischievous fingers pushing him to the brink.

Aaron's rhythm sped up. That brilliant gaze locked on his. He could feel the air around them charge with electricity. The strong fist pumping his cock tightened and twisted wickedly on the upstroke. Fuck! The kid knew exactly what he was doing. And when Aaron licked his lips then pulled that plump piece of flesh between his teeth and smirked, he almost came. He hadn't ever imagined he would find someone so perfectly suited for him, but he had in Aaron.

Kreed reached out, his hand joining with Aaron's on their wet cocks as the kid leaned in and their lips touched. The way Aaron kissed him—soft and unhurried, almost reverent as he pushed his tongue into Kreed's mouth and stroked, tongue against tongue, firm lips moving in tandem with his—made his knees week. Kreed tightened his grip on their pricks while still following Aaron's lead, jacking them hard and reckless. The sweetness of the kiss didn't match the intense stroking rhythm Aaron was orchestrating on their cocks and that unexpected variance combined with the feel of the water fucking amazed him.

"I'm almost there." Kreed's balls drew tight against his body and fire raced up his spine. He was completely helpless against the pleasure that seized his movement and made him moan.

"Fuck. Yeah. Aaron…" Kreed's release flooded through him, and he came on a strangled cry. His dick twitched wildly as ribbons of come splattered on his stomach and chest.

Soft grunts filled his ears as Aaron followed right behind him. His lover's body grew rigid but his guy's hand never slowed as he continued to stroke their cocks through their release, and Aaron's essence mixed with Kreed's on his stomach. Kreed let go of their cocks to run his fingers through the warm come coating his skin as he caught his breath and allowed his racing heart to slow.

"Fuck! That was good!" Aaron collapsed on top of him, kissing him thoroughly and deeply. Kreed wrapped his church boy in his arms and closed his eyes, completely contented, drinking in everything that was Aaron. They stayed encased in each other's arms till the water started to cool. Kreed pressed a kiss against Aaron's hair.

"The water's getting cold and we're gonna turn into prunes if we don't get out," Kreed finally said after a few minutes. He would have stayed locked comfortably in Aaron's embrace all night if the bath water hadn't cooled so quickly.

"Oreos. I like Oreos," Aaron mumbled.

"What?" Kreed asked, unsure he'd heard right.

"You wanted to know if I liked Oreos or Tim Tams. I like Tim Tams, but Oreos with a cup of ice cold milk is one of my all-time favorites. And just so you know, I don't think I can move from this spot. I'm way too comfortable," Aaron said, snuggling closer.

"I knew you were an Oreo guy. Me too. We'll have to pick up a package and get some milk too." Kreed shifted his position and trailed his fingers up and down Aaron's spine. Goose bumps broke out across Aaron's skin and his lover shivered. "Come on. The water's cold and I have a promise to keep."

"What's that?" Aaron asked.

"I believe I told you earlier, at the club, that I was gonna claim what was mine, and I always keep my word. But first, I want to be claimed by you. That is, if you're up for it. You seem a little tired."

"Is that a challenge, Deputy?" Aaron's head lifted and his eyes met Kreed's.

"I do believe it is." Kreed grinned then kissed the tip of Aaron's nose.

"In that case, challenge accepted."

Chapter 31

Something had changed tonight. Aaron wasn't entirely sure what, but that didn't alter the facts. Kreed had been so into him—at least it seemed that way—and he was so into Kreed. Aaron tucked his pillow under his head. They were facing each other in bed and had managed to scoot as close to each other as possible. They pushed their hips together, tangled their legs, and Kreed rested one arm across his hip with the other shoved under his pillow. It was late or early, however you wanted to say it—somewhere around four in the morning—but neither wanted the night to end.

Honestly, the idea of letting this man go didn't seem possible, but he had to. There was too much at stake. Besides, if Kreed found out, he wouldn't want anything to do with him anyway. Tough, hard-nosed, incorruptible public servants didn't mess around with people like him. That thought made him sad, so he pushed it aside like he'd done since he'd met Kreed.

"We've been talking like teenage girls," Kreed said and let a yawn slip free. Once that one completed, another much bigger one came.

"Stop it. You're making me yawn." Aaron's eyes watered as he yawned again. Kreed laughed and pulled him closer. It felt so good to have this time with Kreed, to be wrapped in his arms, to be wanted by this extraordinary man.

"You're very comfortable just being you," Aaron continued after a bit.

"I can't be anything different. Besides, I learned that in high school. I've got to just own me," Kreed said and shifted. In one swift move, Aaron was laying against Kreed's side, who was now on his back. "We need to sleep."

"Yeah," Aaron agreed.

Another loud yawn came from above. "I don't want this to end between us after we leave the island."

Aaron didn't say a word. He took a deep breath and shut his eyes, trying to block the pain that suddenly squeezed his chest.

"You don't agree?" Kreed lifted his head.

Aaron opened his eyes and looked at Kreed. "I didn't say that."

"Good. Then what's the problem?" Kreed gathered him closer, his fingers brushing lightly up and down his back.

"Logistics."

Kreed cut him off. "We're a global world. Long-distance relationships work now."

"Yeah, maybe."

"Yeah, maybe, like absolutely they do. Besides, I can live anywhere. Not that I'm packing up right now and moving closer, but if it works, I can. At least I'd be willing to try."

Aaron was quiet again. His heart actually hurt. God, he wanted that, wanted it so much. How did he tell Kreed he didn't live where he'd said he did? How did he tell him he wasn't who Kreed thought he was? Better yet, how did this ever end with Kreed not arresting him on the spot when his secret activities came out? Karma was a bitch, making him fall for a man who swore to uphold the law while he spent his days breaking it, even if it was with the best of intentions.

"Stop being so head issue-y. One day at a time, as long as all your days are spent thinking about me." Kreed gave that sexy chuckle that made Aaron snicker too. "Kiss me. I can't keep my eyes open."

Aaron lifted his head and had to push up on Kreed's chest to get close enough to kiss him. He placed a small kiss on the deputy marshal's lips. Kreed's eyes didn't open again. A few minutes ago, he'd been tired too, but not anymore. Worry was stronger than caffeine at keeping a person awake. Aaron moved his arm and Kreed tightened his embrace. He was beginning to expect that from Kreed; it was sweet and a little smothering as his face got buried in Kreed's shoulder. He wiggled around, fought the hold until he was looking down at a sleeping Kreed, trying to etch his gorgeous relaxed face deep in his memory.

The sound of Kreed's soft snores made him smile. Aaron lifted a finger, tracing the pad over Kreed's brow before sliding his finger across the forehead to brush away a strand of hair. It was funny to think, but he was beautiful—one of the most handsome men Aaron had ever laid eyes on. Even stranger, he'd been able to draw the attention of someone like Kreed.

There was no question that he loved this man—a life-altering kind of love. He'd remember this time with Kreed for the rest of his life. Aaron suspected that the pain that always slashed across his heart when he thought of having to leave Kreed would just grow more pronounced until he eventually died from his broken heart. Even if he could stay, Kreed's career—his entire life, everything the man had worked for—would be on the line if word ever got out that the deputy marshal was shacked up with a fugitive. Kreed would lose his credibility, and so would Mitch. He had more to consider than just Kreed. Ruining someone's life might be a little too much to overcome.

On that depressing thought, Aaron started to roll from bed, but he couldn't force himself to leave the comfort of the arms holding him. Instead he put his cheek on Kreed's chest, memorizing how his warm skin felt against his face. He gently moved up and ran his jaw along Kreed's. The stubble had grown in, and, God, did he like the feel of that. The cadence of Kreed's even breaths lulled him, somehow making him feel so safe and secure. After a few more minutes of just staring, he whispered so softly he could barely hear his own words, "I love you, but I'm not who you think I am. I've got too many skeletons to make this work. I'm so sorry."

His heart almost stopped in his chest when Kreed's eyes opened, and he was suddenly staring into those dark chestnut pools that saw too much. "I already know that. I could tell you're hiding something. You just don't understand, Aaron. Your secrets don't matter to me. I know what's in here." Kreed lifted a hand to Aaron's chest, covering his heart. "At some point, you're gonna realize you can trust me. I'm willing to give you that time."

Aaron was absolutely certain his face must have morphed into a million different expressions before he pulled his mask in place. He'd thought Kreed was sleeping. No, he *knew* Kreed was sleeping, but he'd been wrong. He should have known years in Special Forces would allow him to pick up a few survival skills. Aaron started to move away, but Kreed's arm became a vise, holding him in place.

"Don't leave."

"I can't sleep. I was gonna see if I could get some work done so we could spend the day together."

Kreed kept the intensity in his gaze, staring at him long and hard before he removed his arm, but lifted his hand to Aaron's head, drawing him closer until Aaron moved the rest of the way on his own to kiss Kreed's lips. "I meant what I said. It doesn't matter. When you're ready to tell me, we'll figure it out."

"Okay, thank you," Aaron responded and moved off the bed, covering Kreed up behind him.

"Leave the door open. I'm getting protective where you're concerned. I need to be able to hear," Kreed said, turning again to his back and draping an arm over his eyes.

Who even knew what that protective comment meant, but he left the bedroom door open and also the door to the spare room where he'd set up his equipment. Aaron took a seat at the desk and logged on to see several hundred unanswered messages. Without question, he knew he wasn't pulling his weight. It had to be freaking his crew out. He was always the one to push and barrel through every job, keeping everybody on track each step of the way.

Aaron scanned through all the messages, didn't deem anything that important, and by-passed them all. Instead, he decided to look a little closer at Derek Sinacola's death. Kreed had brought his brother up a couple of times, and Mitch had once said they were having a hard time getting information on what had really happened in the friendly fire explanation the military had released. Those answers were something he could give Kreed when the time came to call this quits. At least he could give Kreed a little something back, because the guy had given him so much.

Finding the openings was what he did best. He'd broken into the Marines' network too many times to count, and they never fixed their shit, so it didn't take long at all for Aaron to get back inside. It took the longest for him to dig through the files to find Derek's case. Aaron yawned. He was tired, but he needed to do this for Kreed. He pulled the file, made a quick copy, and got out of there before the system detected the intrusion.

Aaron propped his feet on the desk, leaned back in his chair with his keyboard on his lap as he started to sift through the hundreds of pages of information. It was the regular, standard military bullshit. Lots of words, all very official, that meant nothing at all. Legal bullshit that taxed the brain and gave someone a job, but the answers were hidden in all the mumbo-jumbo, so he had to keep going.

Hours passed and Aaron slowly began to lose steam on this idea. This massive file, with a huge amount of information, was turning out to be miles of rhetoric and babble that just made no sense at all. What Aaron couldn't figure out was why all that paperwork was necessary. Derek Sinacola was just your average enlisted Marine, nothing at all like his brother's file. So why did they document him so closely? Could they have worried about a pending lawsuit from the family? Nah, it was the military and he was active duty at the time of death. They couldn't sue, even if they had evidence of wrongdoing.

Scrubbing a hand over his face, he placed the keyboard back on the desk and stood. He stretched his tired body and yawned deeply, taking several steps around the room to help wake himself. That gnawing, tickling across Aaron's spine started. That was never a good sign, but something wasn't right in that information; it didn't make sense. Too documented, even for a government agency, and that meant something.

Most definitely the military was hiding information, but what? The time stamps on the files were legit, but that didn't mean they hadn't done that on purpose. The data seemed thorough. Aaron stared at the screen from across the room, forcing himself to think outside of the box.

Okay, so Kreed was a military badass, so it made sense that they'd recruit his brother if they'd ever realized the connection. The military could be ruthless. The price of freedom wasn't free and ethics be damned. Knowing Kreed's skills, Aaron could see the military wouldn't have used him for his brawn, though that was impressive, but for his brain, and Kreed had spent most of his time overseas.

To gather intelligence from foreign enemies required the intuitive stealth of someone like Kreed Sinacola. Aaron's eyes jumped to his computer as he moved forward. Could it be? If so, in today's world, there would be no way to hide that information. With a speculative smile, Aaron sat down and woke his computer again. If it was there, he could find it. He even knew exactly where to go. Covering his tracks, he went to work.

~~~

Kreed woke to the sounds of…a printer? He didn't even know Aaron had a printer in all that shit he'd carried around with him everywhere. Kreed opened his eyes to find the sun peeking in through the bottom of the dark shade covering the windows. Not surprising really. He'd gone to sleep in the early hours of the morning. As he rolled from bed, he looked over at the alarm clock. The bright red digital display read twelve thirty. He'd slept a long time. Must be the great company, good sex, and all these contented feelings of love he'd never experienced before that had him sleeping this long.

Whatever the reason, he was thankful, actually appreciative of a lot of things. But the biggest one was in there printing what sounded like a book from the way the machine droned on and on. He padded toward the bathroom, thinking over their evening. He hoped they'd broken ground last night with Aaron's confession that he had secrets. Yes, he'd been sleeping and Aaron hadn't meant for him to hear his disclosure, but that didn't matter. An admission of secrets meant that his guy was opening up, coming around to agreeing there could be a future between them. Those hidden secrets would come in time. It would all be baby steps, but that was okay too.

Kreed brushed his teeth and splashed water on his face, then reached for a towel. After drying his face, he haphazardly hung the towel back on the ring and went in search of his jeans. He dug through the pile of their clothing, found his, and tugged those on, not bothering with any underwear, being careful as he zipped. He walked out in the hall then stuck his head in the guest bedroom. His guy was busy working and wore those damn headphones, probably not hearing him at all. There wasn't any food or empty plates around, which meant Aaron had to be starving by now.

Resisting the urge to bother his workaholic lover, Kreed padded toward the kitchen. He began frying up some bacon and eggs before starting the coffee.

As expected, Aaron came around the corner, maybe taking the kid a little longer than he would have thought since he was almost done with cooking. Grabbing a piece of bacon, he dropped it in his mouth, chewing as he glanced at Aaron over his shoulder. He smiled at Aaron, who stood in the middle of the kitchen, not moving, his face a mask of anger and pain, and in his hands were several printed pages.

"What's wrong?" Kreed asked, turning fully toward Aaron.

"I wanted to do something for you. Give you something back, but those motherfuckers... Kreed...I'm so sorry." Aaron was shaking his head. "Those self-righteous assholes..." Tears formed in Aaron's eyes, and it confused him. Dread coiled in his gut and trepidation sent fear racing down his spine. He moved forward as Aaron handed him the pages he held. All Kreed saw was his brother's name listed on top before he lifted his eyes to Aaron's.

"What's this?" Aaron moved in closer, placing both hands around his upper arms.

"I wanted to give you closure on your brother's death. I wanted you to know what happened so there wouldn't be any more questions for you. You could begin the process of healing, but... Honestly, I never thought I'd find something like this."

Kreed lowered his gaze to the pages. "How did you get these?"

"I hacked the system."

"Do they know you did this? Can they find you?" He knew the information in his hands was life-altering, and he didn't want the man he loved at risk for gathering this for him.

"Not likely. I covered my tracks."

Kreed nodded, his eyes going back to black words on the pages. His heart sank. He'd told himself he didn't need to know what happened. It didn't truly matter because nothing would bring Derek back, but now that he had the information in his hands, his heart hammered in his chest, and he had to fight to draw air into his lungs. With eyes fixed on the documents, he moved past Aaron and headed for the kitchen table where he took a seat. Sucking in a deep breath, Kreed steeled his spine as he turned the first page and began to read. Aaron walked over to the chair across from him, put his hands on the table and waited.

Reading through the last line, Kreed continued staring at the last page as his heart filled with a sorrow he hadn't known could exist. Images of that cute kid following him around the house filled his head and his heart. He had always pretended to be so annoyed. Even when he'd come home on leave, Derek had those big brown eyes focused on him, always staying close by. He could see his brother idolized him so much that he'd followed in Kreed's footsteps and joined the military.

What Kreed hadn't known—what no one in his family apparently knew—was that his brother had followed completely in his footsteps. He'd had the same keen intuition that Kreed had and the military used that to their advantage. Where Kreed's espionage had been hidden, ultra-secret missions, where if he had been caught, the military would disavow all knowledge, Derek's had been part of a new initiative—a clandestine intelligence program performed by the United States military.

They were both assigned to the Middle East. It made sense based on their looks. Only, his brother had been found out. An internal breach. Someone from the inside fed information to al-Qaida. Derek had died a brutal death when ransom amounts had been given and the military hadn't paid. Damn it to hell, his brother had to have been scared shitless. Kreed sucked in a breath as his heart ripped wide open at the thought.

Had he known, he'd have gone to Derek. He could have tried something…anything. A tear slid down his cheek as he grabbed the papers off the table and marched to the back door. He ripped it open and went through, leaving it open as he stood on the back deck, letting the cool, salty air fill his lungs. The waves crashed against the shore like his thoughts, colliding with the disbelief and anger in his heart.

All the aggression he'd felt at the table began to fade, with desolation and self-doubt now taking hold. Why hadn't he warned his brother of everything the military had put him through? Better question, why had neither of them ever talked about this weird instinctual thing they had going on inside them?

Kreed went down a couple of the porch steps and dropped to the wood, his shoulders slumped. The United States military had so much going against it. Forever, they'd had spies infiltrating their ranks, but in today's world, our own people sold the secrets. Kreed had seen those signs all those years ago. That was one of the reasons he'd left when he had. Working undercover in a hostile country was tricky enough before you ever factored in your fellow Americans turning your name over to the wrong hands. Kreed placed his elbows on his knees and hung his head. He should have been there for his brother.

~~~

Aaron stood at the window, watching Kreed with his head bowed, those thick shoulders lowered in defeat. His heart broke a little further. He hated what he'd found; hated he had no choice but to share it with Kreed. More than anything, he hated that the man he'd grown to love had been so hurt by a bunch of hypocritical assholes who'd decided as a part of daily business who lived and who died.

He took a deep breath and stepped back from the window before turning and heading for his room. They'd pay for this. Aaron would make sure of that. Protector would make sure of that. As much as he wanted to be there for Kreed right now, he shut the door behind him. It would take a little time, but they were going to regret their lies.

Chapter 32

At sunset, Kreed finally acknowledged the rumbling in his stomach. As sick and nauseous as the day's discovery had made him, he needed nourishment and probably a cold beer or twelve. He rose from his perch on the back deck and headed for the house, deeply missing the brother he'd never really known. They'd shared so much in this life. He'd entered the military through the navy. Derek had entered through the Marines, but they'd ended up in the exact same place—stuck in the bowels of the worst terrorist organizations in the world.

Maybe if he'd talked to his little brother more, he could have helped keep him alive. He most certainly would have never allowed Derek to get involved in espionage. The problem with that line of work—it forced the spy to eat, drink, and breathe that way of life. Kreed wasn't proud of the things he'd done or seen and ignored while working his way up the terrorist cell he'd been assigned to, but he'd had to do them. Those were his orders. And a military man followed orders at all cost.

Kreed jerked open the refrigerator door. He grabbed a beer from the shelf on the door before he saw an aluminum-foil-wrapped plate of food. A slight smile formed at the corner of his lips as he noticed a note taped on the outside of the plate of food.

I didn't want to bother you. You need to eat. Please try. I'll be working for the next few hours. Don't leave and don't swim if you start drinking. I'll be out soon.

The note wasn't signed.

The thought of Aaron taking time to fix him food and the sweetness of the written words flooded that special place in his heart that Aaron had occupied, the one that only belonged to him. He liked how Aaron wanted to take care of him. It just didn't take away the indignation, pain, and betrayal coursing through him, all directed at the military. Aaron had been smart to keep his distance this afternoon, to allow Kreed time to work through all this new information. Kreed glanced up at the clock on the microwave and realized it wasn't afternoon after all. It was already evening.

He pulled the plate out, placed it and the beer on the counter, and looked underneath the foil. It was a hoagie; one of Aaron's specialties. A bag of chips and some beans were also on the plate, along with the spoon. He popped the top on the beer can and grabbed the food. He went down the hall, past the closed bedroom door. He could hear Aaron talking. It wasn't the first time he'd talked while working, but Aaron shutting the door was new.

Deciding not to bother him, Kreed took the food and went out on the patio. He placed everything on the table and lit the tiki torches close by. The magnitude of grief still overwhelmed him, and it seemed one concern led into another today. The pain over the truth of his brother's death, his fears that Aaron's early morning confession would drive the man away from him rather than closer, and then his future with the marshal service—his uncertain future now that Mitch would no longer be his partner—all of it weighed heavy on his heart this evening.

After lighting the last torch, Kreed made his way back to the table and picked up his beer. He downed that one pretty quick before heading back inside for another. He grabbed two that time and the roll of paper towels before going back outside.

Kreed took his seat and stared down at the food, unseeing, lost in images of the slop he'd eaten in the underground caves in Afghanistan. Just like always, the visions of burned bodies and the charred remains of tiny villages overloaded his brain. He would never be able to un-see that shit.

The horror and atrocity he'd endured in order to feed information to his government and… He shook his head to clear the memories. And now he knew his brother had lived that life too, except his brother had been caught. God, the death he must have endured. His stomach roiled and both hands went to his forehead, holding his head as he closed his eyes. He should have been more open and honest with Derek, been there to protect him. He'd just been too fucked up in the head. He was still working on coming to terms with that shit himself.

Kreed had no idea how long he'd sat there, playing over the images that had haunted him for years, before Mitch's shrill ringtone startled him, snapping him back to the present. The pain in the ass sound grated on his nerves. Mitch had obviously changed the ringtone at Colt's place. Asshole did that shit all the time. Kreed had just never taken the time to change it back.

Kreed rubbed his eyes and took a deep breath. "What?" he growled on the third annoying cackle.

"What's wrong?" Mitch asked, not even bothering with a greeting.

"Why aren't you sleeping?" he countered. Kreed wasn't certain of the time difference but it was already late on the island, which made it even later on the mainland.

"You haven't seen the news?" Mitch asked.

"Would you be watching the news if you were here?"

"Point. Everyone's in a tizzy. Protector took over all the military and defense sites. Had to be something big to set them off. They've broken the usual patterns, so it seems more personal. But off the record, it's funny as shit. The fire-breathing dragon, their calling card, made into a cartoon starring the director of the Defense Intelligence Agency. It shows him bouncing all over the page, trying to protect his ass from the dragon's flames. With the message, Deception Will Bite You in Your Ass."

"Seriously?" Kreed asked. Mitch captured his complete attention with that description. He sat up and pushed his plate away, having never taken a single bite.

"Yeah. Protector wasn't as clean this time. They must have been really pissed off and wanted to cause a lot of grief for those guys.

They acted fast and weren't as thorough covering their trail. Tracked it to some IP address in Nebraska."

"Like they shut down all the military branches?"

"Yeah," Mitch chuckled. "Every branch, the entire DOJ, everything is being rerouted to Protector's main page. They locked that shit down. The FBI guys are chomping at the bit to apprehend whoever's involved. Getting things back up and running's not gonna be an easy fix. It's been a couple of hours and their best guys are still locked out. Every time they get close, the dragon pops up on the monitor, cackles, and everything on screen goes up in flames."

Kreed sat there quietly, listening and thinking, unease taking root in the back of his brain. His head was too fucked up. Something kept needling at him and he couldn't shake it off.

"You there?" Mitch asked.

"Yeah. Nebraska, huh?"

"Per Masters. They're not letting too much out about the whole Protector thing. Said they would know more when they meet with me again."

"Why? Meet with you about what?"

"My future, which I don't want to discuss right now. You might want to have Aaron call Masters and see if he can help. He knows all that computer shit. Guy's brilliant. They could use him." That comment alarmed Kreed for some reason, but he pushed down that little niggling thought.

The unease coiling in his gut, tightened, then unraveled all at once. Everything stilled inside him.

The Protector hack...

Nebraska...

The dragon tattoo on Aaron's chest...

The earth shifted, knocking Kreed off balance in an almost violent reaction. The pounding of his frantic heart blasted in his ears. The air suddenly vanished as fear gripped his insides.

No!

His body lurched forward; his world tilted on its axis. Kreed dropped the phone as he shot to his feet, all his focus centered in stopping Aaron. Kreed took off running, his only focus was getting to Aaron before anyone could find him and hurt him. That realistic sobering thought drove him faster.

The possibility of losing Aaron had him sprinting across the deck and through the back door without regard to the rattling of the glass behind him. Kreed burst through the closed bedroom door, causing it to slam loudly against the drywall. Aaron jumped, startled at his unannounced entrance. The kid was working at the desk, Kreed could see the light reflecting off the monitors Aaron sat behind. Kreed slowed, his focus trained on Aaron as he cleared his mind and worked on getting a read on Aaron's mood.

Dammit, no question about it, he was right about Aaron. Kreed could feel the anxiety growing in the air around him as he stalked forward.

"What's happened?" Aaron asked. He sat back in his chair, his bare feet crossed at the desk and the keyboard in his lap. Going against every emotion in his body, Kreed forced himself to calm. He removed the earphones from Aaron's ears, then took the keyboard from his lap. Instead of smashing them all with his bare hands, like he wanted to do, he tossed them on the desk. He scanned the two screens, searching for something, anything to prove Aaron wasn't the one responsible for the hack. Hope began to fade the more he digested what he saw.

Displayed was a massive amount of gibberish with a small chat box in the corner.

"Can they hear us?"

"No, I muted them. What's wrong?" Aaron asked, looking a little spooked. No doubt, the kid had been monitoring the fed's response to all this. He could do that easily with his security clearance.

Shit, it was all starting to come together and the picture being painted so clearly in his head looked grimmer and grimmer by the second. How had he not figured this out before now?

"You've got to stop."

He watched long and hard as Aaron mentally placed barriers between them. No way was that going to work. Kreed reached down and gripped the sides of Aaron's face between his palms, keeping him from turning away.

"You have to stop this. I get what you're doing, I swear to God I do, but they'll find you and they'll either kill you or make you wish they had. This is not something that they'll forgive. They don't like being made to look like fools. If they arrest you, it's only because they fucked it up and didn't eradicate you."

Seconds passed as he watched Aaron's Adam's apple slowly dip as he swallowed. Those intense steel blue eyes searched his for seconds before Aaron's mask slid back in place.

"I don't know what you're talking about," Aaron stated, the conviction not really matching the words. His heart shattered at how easily Aaron lied to him.

Kreed understood the reason, but it didn't change the situation. He wasn't getting through to Aaron. He wasn't making himself clear. Panic dropped him to his knees. Kreed knew the things his government was capable of, had witnessed them firsthand. Hell, he'd even administered some of the blows. He had to do something, make Aaron see reason.

"The holes in my record..." Kreed sighed deeply and lowered his hands to Aaron's, gripping them tighter than ever before. "I've never said this out loud before."

Kreed bent his head, his forehead touching the back of Aaron's hands. He let Aaron wiggle one of his hands free and felt the tangle of his guy's long fingers threading through his hair.

"You can trust me," Aaron whispered. Kreed lifted his head, his eyes focused on Aaron's. The complexity of the emotion he saw in their blue-gray depths gave him more courage than he'd known in a very long time.

"I was part of a covert operation. This gut thing I've got made me attractive to the government. They recruited me into the program when I was young. I was sent to the Middle East where I identified and infiltrated al-Qaida."

"Is that how you got the scar on your hip?" Aaron asked.

"Yes. I spent years there. I was one of them, filtering information back." Kreed closed his eyes again, the images that had plagued him for most of his adult life flashed through his mind. He'd lived and breathed that terror cell every single day. He'd participated in horrific crimes against humanity to prove value and moved up the ranks quickly. He'd suffocated in that evil every day and risked his life over and over to funnel intel back to the United States government.

"I know firsthand the lengths our government will go to secure their agenda. And they will come after you. They're looking right now. We're on high alert looking for you, Aaron."

The pain of the thought had emotion driving him as he implored Aaron.

"Baby, I won't be able to keep you safe. No one will be able to keep you safe. If they don't find you now, at some point they will, because I'd stake my life on the fact that they have a team of guys just like you out there searching for…you. The bounty's too high and just increased ten-fold with this stunt on the military. They don't play. You'll disappear. Look at what happened to my brother and how they washed their hands clean. Derek followed in my footsteps, Aaron, and now he's dead."

Aaron sat there silently, watching him, his hand gripping Kreed's, holding tightly as if he'd been thrown a lifeline. What he said next gave Kreed hope, even though the words weren't quite right.

"It's not so easy to just leave."

"Whatever it takes, I'll be here beside you. I love you. I do. I should have said it sooner. I can't lose you, too. Please stop this. I get it now. I get why you kept distance between us, but you have to stop this, Aaron. Pass this torch on. Please. I love you."

"I love you," Aaron whispered. "I couldn't let what happened to Derek just pass by. I don't like you hurt."

"Then let that be enough." Kreed kissed both of Aaron's knuckles. "Please stop this. Come start a life with me. Leave all that behind."

"It's not that easy…"

"But it is, Aaron. It's exactly that easy. They're on your trail, so you just disappear, then the trail grows cold."

"There's so much more you don't know." Aaron pulled away from him, breaking the contact. His eyes were so serious, as if begging Kreed to understand. Aaron turned off the monitors, rose from the chair, and left the room, leaving Kreed on his knees in the middle of the floor.

Chapter 33

The cool water lapped over Aaron's feet at the water's edge. He held his arms crossed over his chest as he stared out into the ocean. Never in a hundred million years did he think he'd be where he was today. Protector had been his baby since high school. Every day since he and his online gaming buddy had concocted the idea, he'd focused on the notions of this being for the greater good. Never did he ever think it would become this big of a deal—a cult phenomenon that millions of people across the world followed and helped make happen for the sole purpose of being a watchdog to help control the hate and corruption in the world.

Back then, everything had seemed clearer. They'd had a plan and executed the steps to precision. He'd been strategic in hacking into the government site as a teenager. He'd planned the whole deal. Nothing too much, just a little breach...with a very loud and clear trail straight to his door. He'd needed that arrest to land him the job with the government. Just as he'd expected, within a matter of months, the agency had hired him to find holes in their systems. That was all it took. That one move allowed him to keep an eye on what the alphabet boys found when they were looking for Protector.

Aaron sighed and kicked at the incoming surf.

Mitch had complicated things. He'd found Mitch while looking for someone to friend who'd give him credibility. Aaron just never expected to like the guy so much. Guilt had been a foreign concept until he'd met Knox. That was the main reason he'd jumped in and helped him so much when Knox had finally asked for something—a way to help alleviate the guilt he had for riding on the guy's honor and integrity-filled coattails. Now, Aaron knew, that was the beginning of the end.

Patrick, his high school gaming buddy that he'd never seen in real life had changed over the last couple of years. He'd turned into a conspiracy theorist, making obvious problems into a mass of finger-pointing, digging deeper, and making broad assumptions without acquiring a shred of physical proof. They'd lost their joint vision for Protector and seemed to fight as much as they agreed these days.

Since Aaron had the fact that no one had ever made a firm or valid identification of his association with Protector, he could technically bow out. Actually, Aaron figured his partner would prefer him out. They'd fought several times over the last few months. Patrick kept hinting that Aaron was holding them back from global domination—whatever the hell that meant.

How had Kreed Sinacola figured out what no one else on the planet ever had? He couldn't even pretend to not know the answer to that question. Besides Kreed being one of the most intuitive people he'd ever known, they were connected. He connected with Kreed on a higher level than any other person on this planet. That said a lot, because Aaron had never fully connected to anyone. And it felt fucking amazing. The feelings of love soothed him, warmed him, even as the breeze blowing off the ocean became stronger and cooler.

That was another problem. He wanted what he had with Kreed to continue. Did it matter that he wasn't who he'd portrayed himself to be? Would Kreed care? Or were those just the incidentals…those little things that didn't really matter? But would they to Kreed? His name wasn't even Aaron Stuart. His given name was Aaron Drake. He'd graduated from MIT with a solid 5.0 grade-point average. And he was someone who'd used his love's best friend to further his illegal activity. That was probably a lot for a deputy US marshal to get over.

"Here," Kreed said from behind as he draped a running jacket over his shoulders. In the back of his mind, he'd registered the cooler weather, but hadn't really noticed until Kreed brought it to his attention. "You've been out here awhile. I didn't want you to get cold."

This man deserved every happiness this world had to offer. Aaron reached out and placed his hand on Kreed's forearm, stopping his retreat as he stepped away. When he turned to fully face Kreed, it wasn't the wind that chilled him to the core, it was the uncertainty in Kreed's eyes. Aaron hated knowing he'd caused that look. He hated that more than anything. Guilt and trepidation made making eye contact impossible, so he looked down at the sand.

"Rain's on its way," Kreed said quietly. Aaron wasn't sure how to reply. It wasn't like Kreed to bring up the weather or try for small talk. Kreed had always been straightforward. Aaron sucked in a deep breath and forced himself to lift his head and meet Kreed's stare. He couldn't see any contempt or regret, but the concern he found speared his heart. He never wanted to see that or the disappointment swimming in those depths.

"I love you, Kreed. I'm sorry I never…"

"I know. I love you, too," Kreed replied. His words were encouraging, but he still wasn't sure what it meant for them. The guy should hate him for lying, manipulating his friend, and jeopardizing both their careers. Aaron gathered his strength and stepped closer. Kreed wrapped one arm, then the other, around him.

"I never planned on any of this happening. As much as you've figured out, there's a lot you don't know." Aaron furrowed his brow and worried his lip. He was scared and still unsure, but relieved and touched Kreed had said he loved him. The deputy marshal was willing to forgive him and turn a blind eye. More so, he'd figured this moment would have ended in his own arrest. Since that didn't seem to be the case, he owed Kreed all of the truth.

"As long as it doesn't jeopardize your safety, I don't really care."

"You say that now…" he started.

"Aaron, you have to know things aren't just cut and dry to me."

"Yeah, you didn't arrest me in there, but you still can."

"It's always gonna be you. I'm never gonna let that happen. I'm very protective of you."

"You really see a future for us after all of this?" Aaron asked.

"Yes, and I have for a while." Kreed held him closer, rubbing his hands up and down Aaron's arms, the friction warming his skin.

"Kreed, I'm the fugitive they want so badly. I'm one of the men behind the mask. Even if I walk away, that's never gonna change."

"I've never felt this way about anyone before. I'm not letting you go for any reason. I can't stress that enough."

Silence fell between them. Aaron slid his arms around Kreed and just held him tightly. Simple acceptance was something he'd never experienced, and if Kreed believed they could have a relationship, then he had to try. There was still so much he needed to tell Kreed, but he'd hold it till Kreed was ready to hear it.

"I need you to give it up though, Aaron. What you're doing... I get it. You've brought awareness. You've started a movement. You educate the world, but that needs to be enough. Let the next generation guide the crusade."

"You're right. The group needs to grow, but without me. It was becoming a problem. My partner and I weren't seeing eye to eye on our viewpoints."

"And this person or persons knows who you are? They've already tracked y'all to Nebraska with this hack."

"They're not as smart as they think they are. They haven't figured out that when they chase Protector, they'll always end up in Nebraska. For the most part, we've kept our identity from each other. It wouldn't take much for my partner to figure out who I am—we're both pretty savvy—but we haven't broken that code of ethics since we started."

Kreed nodded and took Aaron's face softly between big palms, the touch so tender and warm against his skin that it eased his heart and comforted his soul.

"I promise if you do this for me—you give this up—I'll do everything in my power to make your life better. I'll love you, take care of you, and provide for you. If you can find a way to move in with me, I'll do everything in my power to make sure you're happy. I'll even share my Lush with you. I've seen you eyeing them. I know you want it."

Aaron smiled at the twinkle of mischief in Kreed's eyes. He needed that light-hearted moment. Everything had been way too serious today.

"As long as you're willing to share that Lush." Aaron chuckled. Kreed leaned in and kissed him briefly. "I'm nervous, Sin. This is all so fast."

"It's not fast when you know what's in here," Kreed said, lifting Aaron's palm to his heart. Aaron brought his other hand up to cup the back of Kreed's neck and held him there to deepen their kiss, making it hard and sweet. Aaron could feel the emotion behind Kreed's kiss. The sky crackled with lightning and drops of rain made themselves known on their skin. Aaron pulled back, took Kreed's hand, and led him into the house just as the storm started to gather momentum.

They had lost their clothes, shedding them as they'd come into the house. Aaron turned to face Kreed's open and honest expression. This man loved him and was willing to turn his head, look the other direction, to give him a chance to prove himself. His out. He wouldn't ever have to hide himself from Kreed again. Kreed had the ability to rip him to shreds, to destroy him in so many ways.

The wind picked up outside, and he heard the distinct tapping of rain on the windows as he pulled Kreed down the hallway. Sin slammed his mouth against Aaron's the moment they stepped into the bedroom. He pushed an insistent tongue between Aaron's lips, and he opened eagerly, sliding his tongue firmly against Kreed's, tasting him, kissing him, falling deeper in love with this magnificent man with every urgent brush of their mouths.

Kreed's tongue raked over his teeth, pushing to the back of his mouth, probing, exploring the far reaches. Aaron moaned into the kiss, giving his all, their tongues twisting and tangling, mouths working frantically to devour the other as his hands skimmed over Kreed's skin.

The wind blew against the house, making it creak. He broke from the kiss then dragged his lips across Kreed's stubbled jaw to his ear and nipped the fleshy lobe.

"Please make love to me." The need to be close to this man drove him. Kreed groaned at his words, his fingers brushing across his nipple rings, sending a surge of fire straight to his balls. Squeezing his eyes shut, Aaron threw his head back to enjoy the shock of pleasure. When he opened his eyes, Kreed's dark eyes reflected pure carnal sin.

"On the bed, now." The deputy's voice held authority, and damn, if that didn't make his cock jerk to attention.

Doing as he'd been told, Aaron pushed himself to the middle of the mattress and watched as Kreed grabbed the supplies from the drawer and joined him on the bed by slowly kissing his way up his legs. Aaron spread his thighs as Sin stretched out on top of him, cocks trapped and leaking between their bodies. He inhaled the rich, spicy scent of his lover's skin.

"You feel so good against me," Kreed said as they rubbed against each other. The friction wasn't enough to get either one of them off, but the feeling was just sweet enough to have two grown men rutting against each other like horny teenagers. With their mouths fused together and hands exploring, he swore he'd died and gone to heaven.

He felt Kreed reach across the bed and heard the cap open on the bottle of lube. Sin pulled back from the kiss and sat back on his heels. The storm outside, wind howling and rain pelting against the bedroom window, was no match for the one brewing in Sin's eyes.

"Give me your hand."

Aaron lifted his hand as instructed, and Kreed squirted the liquid on both his fingers before lowering himself to his original position.

"I want your fingers in me." Sin winked then flicked Aaron's nipple ring with his tongue before sucking his nipple into his mouth. Kreed placed wet kisses on his chest and up his neck. The spicy scent of Kreed filled his nostrils; he inhaled deeply, breathing in the powerful aroma of sex and arousal.

He gripped Sin's ass and spread his cheeks, drawing his fingers back and forth over the tight pucker before pushing in. Kreed's cock jerked against his. It didn't take long before he worked a second then third finger into his lover. Sexy sounds fell from his deputy's lips as Kreed pushed his ass against his hand.

"Need you in me." Kreed sat up, not wasting any time before he rolled the condom on Aaron then positioned himself. Lust clouded his vision as he watched Kreed reach behind him, rough fingers closed around his dick as Kreed held him in place.

A strangled sound escaped his lips when Kreed sank down oh so slowly, inch by fucking inch, on his dick until he sat fully on top of him. Heat swamped him and stole his breath. Aaron was as deep in his lover as he could be. The knowledge fueled him, urged him to lift his hips and press up into all that tight constricting warmth and try for a little deeper. It took everything in him not to move, to remain still and let Kreed set their pace.

The deputy marshal's hands splayed on his chest as he began to move up and down on his cock. Aaron slid his hands up Kreed's sides, lightly tracing the scar above his hip bone before caressing the beautiful art inked on his ribs.

"Beautiful. Ah…fuck." Aaron groaned. His deputy's hot chute tightened and fluttered as Kreed fucked himself on Aaron. The sensual movement of his body caused Aaron's breath to catch in his throat. He reached for Sin's hips, something to keep him grounded. Firm flesh pressed back against his fingers as Aaron gripped onto Kreed's hips so tightly there would probably be marks in the morning.

"So good, Sin, so tight. You feel like fucking heaven." Kreed's hips sped up, circling and grinding as he pushed those powerful thighs up and down. Aaron arched his back, driving up into Kreed, wanting to turn the man inside out, needing to be deeper, closer. He held Kreed's gaze as their bodies rocked together as one.

God, he savored the look in Kreed's eyes, the one that let him know exactly how much Kreed loved him. After being alone for so long, he'd never dreamed he would be able to build something so special. And never would he have imagined himself with a deputy US marshal. How had he fallen so deeply so quickly?

"You are it for me. Mine," Aaron whispered, his heart overflowing with the truth of every word. Kreed leaned forward, their mouths meeting in a hungry kiss. Nips and long, slow, sexy licks invaded his senses, their tongues dancing as Kreed rode him hard. The sound of flesh slapping against flesh combined with the intoxicating smell of arousal caressed his balls. He tore his mouth away from the kiss and nuzzled his face in Kreed's neck, inhaling the rich, spicy scent of his lover's heated skin.

"You own me. All of me." Kreed sat up, his gaze fixed on Aaron's, the sincerity in those words touching his soul.

Every downward snap of his lover's hips drove him deeper into Kreed. He dug his heels into the mattress and thrust up, changing his angle, intent on making Kreed come. The passion showing in Kreed's eyes seized him, wrapped around him. His orgasm flirted with the telltale tingle in his spine. He was so close. He clasped Kreed's erection in his fist and started to stroke him from root to tip. Fast then slow, his rhythm shattered.

"Always you…Aaron." Kreed threw his body back, grinding his ass onto Aaron's cock as he shouted his release. Their eyes locked as ribbons of thick, hot cream painted his chest and stomach. The look on Sin's face and the hard contractions around his dick fed Aaron's release. The air sizzled around them, and the feeling of their connection in the room sucked the air from his lungs and blanketed his entire being, the pleasure too overwhelming to fight.

"Yesss…forever, Sin." Aaron's heavy balls erupted as Kreed's contracting ass milked the weight from them. He shuddered under the pleasure coursing through him; his dick jerked, filling the condom with his seed. Kreed sagged against him, his ragged breath hot against Aaron's neck as Kreed curled his fingers in his hair. No words were spoken, because none were needed in this moment. They were right where they needed to be, in each other's arms. Their breathing finally calmed as their bodies cooled.

Aaron lightly drew the pads of his fingertips up and down Sin's back, basking in the feel of his lover's body molding against him. The way Kreed made love to him, giving himself over, had removed any remaining doubt, any uncertainty, and all barriers between them disintegrated.

"I love you," Kreed said and pressed a kiss against his sweat-slicked skin. Trust and hope stirred in the air around them. A calm knowing settled deep in Aaron's soul. Kreed had branded him, claimed his heart.

"I love you too." He meant those words. The emotion had snuck up on him, unwanted and dangerous, but he wouldn't deny the truth…not to himself and, with his actions, he would show Kreed exactly how true they were.

Kreed rolled them to their sides. His flaccid cock slipped from Sin's hot body. He didn't bother to grab the condom; they were already covered in his lover's drying come. Besides, he was so blissed out at the moment that he didn't want to move. All he wanted to do was listen to the soothing sounds of the tropical rain against the window, the comforting cadence of Kreed's breathing, and fall asleep wrapped lovingly in Sin's arms.

~~~

Kreed lay sprawled across the guest bed in the spare room, zoning out a little as Aaron went through the motions of backing out of the organization he'd helped found. Every once in a while Aaron would say something, catch him up on how the group took the news.

The best Kreed could tell, Aaron had nailed it spot-on. There seemed to be almost a relief from the other side of the computer screen, and they both acknowledged not seeing eye to eye on many issues over the last year. To move the organization along, one side was going to have to give. His partner even had someone in mind to take Aaron's spot, which was a big relief to Kreed.

What he hadn't said out loud—and what churned inside his gut—was the possibility of Protector outing Aaron in retaliation for leaving. He'd been involved in several arrests like that—very stab-you-in-the-back kinds of deals. Those groups never understood that once that started, the whole group eventually imploded. Yet, somehow Aaron's organization seemed different. Now he and Aaron just needed time and distance on their side. Kreed had enough connections and was owed enough favors that, if they could make it a few years away from Protector, he could shield Aaron from a criminal case.

The shit he knew about the government as well as key people in power... No one wanted that information out. They'd keep Aaron safe.

"He had to be planning to oust me. He was too prepared and accepting," Aaron said, looking over his shoulder toward Kreed. He took his earbuds out and dropped them on the desk. Aaron's feet were still stretched out in front of him, anchored on the desk as he leaned back as far as his chair would let him.

"You've been offline a lot lately," Kreed tried to reason, lifting up on his elbows.

"Yeah, I guess. We could tell things weren't right between us anymore."

"Are you okay with this?"

"Yeah, you know, I met Dylan Reeves and Tristan Wilder at the Rooster Teeth Expo. They had a booth there for their Secret app. I'd met Tristan before, but this time he tried to recruit me, and I didn't just shoot it down like I normally would. The writing was on the wall for me too. It feels a little…" Aaron turned away, staring off into space. Kreed watched a range of emotions cross his face. "I guess it feels like my child grew up. We never thought we'd get as big as we did. It was better when it was smaller, easier to manage. We wanted to make the world a better place. I know it all sounds dumb."

"Not dumb at all. I was like that too." Kreed sat up and scooted to the side of the bed, close to where Aaron lounged in his chair. "I did some pretty bad shit to prove myself. Once I left, it took me a long time to get over everything I'd done." He got lost in thought and shook his head. If he let himself go down that path today, it'd take hours to get his brain working right again. It was too much emotional overload. Kreed stood, grabbed Aaron's hand, and pulled the kid's chair forward until he couldn't do anything but get up. "Let's go cook dinner. We have all that shrimp that needs to be eaten."

"It's late."

"And? We're on vacation. A little midnight shrimp boil, some beer, a little more ass. I can't see that as a bad thing. Besides, I need you to show me how you do that little trick with your tongue. I like that," Kreed said, entwining his fingers with Aaron's and tugging him along.

"I'll teach you the tongue thing if you stop squeezing the shit out of the base of my dick. That's just unfair," Aaron grumbled, a little indignant. Kreed was pulling him down the hall now.

"I'm holding you off, making you last longer," Kreed shrugged smugly. "You should be thanking me."

"Really? I think you're just evil and get some kind of sadistic pleasure out of torturing me. Besides, I'm not an old man. I can still have multiple orgasms," Aaron countered, stopping Kreed in his tracks. Aaron just chuckled as he took the lead down the hall, pulling Kreed toward the kitchen.

"I'll show you old man," Kreed grumbled.

"Show me after dinner. I'm hungry." Aaron snorted. Kreed jerked at his arm, causing Aaron to stumble back against him. He quickly encircled a laughing Aaron in his arms.

He leaned in, nipping at Aaron's ear. "You've made me happy. Sure, there's shit left to deal with, but it's been a long time since I've been truly happy."

Aaron's fingers tangled into Kreed's hair, keeping him there. "Keep talking like that and I'll let you help me dye my hair before you get me drunk and do me on the beach again."

"Promises, promises." Kreed reluctantly moved out from Aaron's hold, opening the cabinets and looking for the boiling pot and spices. The sooner he fed Aaron, the sooner he could test that theory.

Chapter 34

This was the last full day of their vacation paradise, ending two of the best weeks of his life, and Kreed wasn't in a mindset to do much more than what they were doing. Kreed had his lounger buried in the sand. He'd finally opted for the Speedo, letting the warm sun bathe his skin. Aaron was beside him, keeping time, turning over every so often. Kreed had missed the last couple of turns, braving the tan line Aaron was convinced he'd get because of the sunglasses he wore.

"It's time," Aaron mumbled, turning over.

"Yeah." Kreed stayed just like he was. They'd been on an emotional rollercoaster since they'd met. Now that things were somewhat settled, the adrenaline was finally wearing off and fatigue was coming on strong. He would enjoy their remaining downtime and had no plans to do more than relax until they boarded their flight tomorrow night.

"You live in Louisiana?" Aaron asked.

"Yeah, I guess. My shit's there, at least," Kreed replied.

"That's quite a ways from me," Aaron mumbled. Kreed lifted one eyelid, glancing over to Aaron.

"All you have to do is say you want to move in. Camp Beauregard's a vacay destination. Always full, but I can manage room for you."

"Ha!" Aaron barked out a laugh. "When we get to that point, we need to move to someplace a little more happening. I bet Camp Beauregard isn't much past dial-up."

"Is that a Louisiana-might-not-be-progressive-enough joke? Don't worry. I'll keep you busy. You won't have time to miss the new millennium that much."

"You're funny. You should turn over."

Mitch's shrill ringtone interrupted the moment. It took a couple of pats under his lounger, but Kreed finally found his phone in the sand, lifted it, and swiped his thumb across the screen by the fourth ring.

"Yo, princess, how's it hanging?"

"You busy?" Mitch asked.

"Yep," Kreed replied and winked at Aaron.

"Good. Makes it better that I interrupted you. Listen, I just left Masters's office. They regretted to inform me that I was now on desk duty. Some field office in Utah had an opening, and they were moving me into administration, so I quit. I wanted you to know before anyone else."

"What?" Kreed sat up in shock. He'd figured Mitch had called about the case and hadn't really been listening closely, but Mitch captured his full attention with those words. "Start over."

"I quit. I wanted you to hear it from me. I've got about a million vacation hours, so I'm on leave right now. Once they're used, I won't be employed by the Marshals Service any longer."

"And you're good with that?" Kreed's brow narrowed as he asked the question. As long as he'd known Mitch, being a deputy marshal was all he'd ever wanted to do.

"Nah, I guess not. But I don't wanna be tied to a desk, and Utah's not good for Cody. He'd have to leave his family, his job, and his dream of becoming a ranger, or he'd stay behind for all that and I wouldn't be living with him. So, yeah."

"What's your plan?" Kreed asked.

"I haven't gotten that far," Mitch replied.

For the first time in this call, that cocky tone Knox always used faltered. His partner's voice cracked. Clearly Mitch wasn't good with any of this. Oh, man.

Kreed stayed silent for several long seconds before he spoke again. "I got an idea."

"Let's hear it."

"Stay in Dallas. We'll head back now." Kreed moved off his lounger and stood.

"I don't want you to…"

"Shut up. I'll text you the details. Find a place we can talk privately and pick us up at the airport," he instructed Mitch, not giving him any room to argue.

"All right, I guess."

"Bring Turner," Kreed said and hung up the phone.

"What's going on?" Aaron asked, turning over fully to focus on Kreed.

Damn, he hadn't considered this would end their vacation. His sexy boyfriend spread out on the lounger, looking up at him like he'd lost his mind. Well, hell, maybe he should have given the plan more thought. He moved closer to Aaron, sat on the side of his lounger, then leaned down to kiss Aaron's lips.

"We have to go back today. Knox quit." Those last two words sat heavily in Kreed's heart.

"What?" Surprise registered on Aaron's face as he jerked up into a sitting position.

"I know. They wanted to move him to a desk in Utah."

"Really?" Aaron shook his head.

"But I've been playing with an idea for a while now. I need to go back so we can talk. Maybe we can come back here in a few months. I can make this up to you," Kreed offered, wiping some sand off Aaron's leg.

"Not necessary. Mitch needs you. I get it." Aaron started to rise, but Kreed stopped him.

"You're a good boyfriend." Kreed leaned in for a kiss, and Aaron gave him a quick peck, making the move almost non-existent. Kreed lifted his hands and held Aaron's head in place as he kissed that smartass mouth. But Aaron broke off before he got too far along.

"I am. Don't forget it. Let's get going. I need to pack my equipment. I can just send it back to my house now." Aaron was off the lounger, picking up their towels and sunscreen from the sand.

"Now it makes sense why you bring that everywhere," Kreed said, trailing behind the kid as he took off for the house. He watched that perfect little ass bounce with each step he took.

"And you're supposed to have all that gut instinct. Thought you would have put that together way before now." Aaron shot him a sexy little grin over his shoulder. Kreed jogged those few steps separating them then reached out to circle Aaron in his arms and draw him back against his chest.

"I really enjoy watching you walk."

"No. One thing will lead to another, and we'll be in the bedroom—not on the plane." Aaron pushed away, but Kreed reached out and grabbed his hand. Since Aaron was being open about things, Kreed ventured into another topic he'd wondered about.

"You didn't meet Mitch by accident, did you?" he asked, tugging open the sliding back door.

"No," Aaron tried to move forward, but Kreed stopped again.

"That's why you helped him in this case. You used him, but found out he's a good guy." Kreed could tell by the look on Aaron's face that he'd hit the nail on the head.

"It's not one of my prouder moments. I liked him more than I realized I would. I was young. I didn't know there were really good-hearted people in the world. It wasn't how I was raised. I owed Mitch." Aaron stayed right there in the doorway, all his focus on Kreed. Every time he ventured into the unknown with Aaron, there was worry reflected back from that handsome face.

"He gave you credibility with the bureau," Kreed half asked, half stated, the whole picture becoming crystal clear.

Aaron was silent again, staring at him, and all he could do was stare back as the rest of the pieces fell into place like a giant jigsaw puzzle revealing a picture.

"Really?" He had to admit the kid was fucking brilliant.

"Yep. Can we go?" Aaron fidgeted with the towel in his hand.

The whole impressive plan amazed him as he figured out all the nuances. Aaron's brain was a marvel.

"You seriously got arrested on purpose?"

"Yep. I needed in the NSA. There were thousands of applicants. I had to get noticed." Aaron started to move away, but Kreed stopped him, and Aaron groaned at being detained again.

"Stuart, that's incredible. I mean, wow. You were really together to be so young. I was a stupid kid at twenty," Kreed said, trying to remove the worry he could see in the tense lines of his lover's body. He'd been very clear on this point. He'd stay by Aaron for as long as smart boy wanted him there.

"Not really. At any time that could have backfired. I could be sitting in prison right now for hacking a government website, especially back then. The Internet was only full of bad people."

"I'm impressed," Kreed said, finally letting go of Aaron. "I'll go put the loungers up. You go pack your shit."

"Don't tell Knox. I like him a lot now. I didn't really play too many video games until I met him. He got me involved. I go to the Rooster Teeth expo every year. I'm into The Creatures now and all their gaming podcasts. He opened the world to me. Please don't tell him," Aaron pleaded, following Kreed off the porch and back to the sand.

"I won't—or at least I probably won't. He can be a real pain in the ass sometimes. I might have to drop it then," Kreed teased as he reached the lounge chairs. He quickly folded the first one before grabbing the other. He finally looked up to see how Aaron had taken that joke. The evil eye he got back said it all, and he laughed. "Okay, I won't. Come on. We have a plane to catch. We need to shut this place down."

Chapter 35

"Hey, buddy," Kreed said, coming through the airport baggage claim to see Cody standing just inside the door.

"Hey," Cody replied, reaching for some of the heavy bags Kreed carried. Aaron had made a pit stop at the bathroom, but Kreed was too antsy to wait for him like he should have. The messages he and Knox had exchanged since they'd initially spoken about the resignation were becoming one-word clipped answers, and that, more than anything, told Kreed loud and clear that his partner wasn't doing well with this turn of events. "Mitch is out by the car. We're in a no-parking zone."

"How's he doing?" Kreed asked. He shook his head when Cody tried to take any of the baggage, knowing Knox would kick his ass if he let Cody carry more than his doctor-approved lifting limit. Instead, he moved around Cody toward the inside window of baggage claim. Kreed caught sight of Mitch standing on the curb right outside the airport. He was leaning against the hood of the SUV, arms crossed over his chest, his shoulders slumped as he studied the concrete at his feet. Kreed couldn't miss the pain in his partner's stance.

"Not too good. I haven't seen him like this before," Cody said, standing next to Kreed, looking out the window at Mitch.

"He doesn't do this too often. Listen, Aaron's in the bathroom. I'm going out. Can you wait on him for me?"

"Sure."

Kreed didn't wait for that answer before heading straight out to Knox, who never looked up on his approach. When he put his boots in Mitch's line of sight and dropped the suitcases, his partner finally lifted his head. Kreed reached out and pulled the bridge of Mitch's sunglasses down his nose to get a better look at his eyes. As suspected, they were full of sadness, red-rimmed, and totally sleep-deprived.

"It's gonna be all right. I promise," Kreed whispered loudly, going in for a solid I'm-here-for-you hug. Mitch loved his job more than any person Kreed knew, and his thanks for a job well done was to be sentenced to life behind a desk and have his dream yanked away from him. Skinner had to know the man wouldn't stand for that. Mitch stayed quiet in the embrace then whacked Kreed's back to get him to let loose. As he pulled away, he sniffled once and moved his thumb and forefinger over his eyes, underneath the glasses he'd put back in place.

"There some place we can talk?" Kreed asked, deciding they just needed to get this over with. He could feel Aaron and Cody coming up behind him.

Cody attempted a sneak attack, reaching down to snatch a suitcase on his way to the trunk, but Mitch moved quickly, grabbing the luggage from Cody and grumbling, "You've still got a weight restriction."

"It's not that heavy," Cody started, but let Mitch have the case with a sigh. Cody's worried gaze lingered on Mitch then darted toward Kreed. The whole scene became a little more heartbreaking when he registered the deep pain in Cody's gaze as he worried about his man.

No one spoke. Kreed opened the back door and ushered an unsure Aaron into the car as Mitch opened the back and deposited the luggage inside. Kreed tossed his duffle in the back and crawled in next to Aaron.

Once everyone was in the SUV, Mitch stared at Kreed in the rearview mirror a moment before saying, "Michaels invited y'all to stay there. Montgomery's gym is still closed. It has a big meeting room if you wanna talk there, or we can go to their house."

"Which is closer?" Kreed asked.

"It's Dallas. Who the hell knows? Traffic sucks all the time," Mitch replied.

"Whichever you're more comfortable with." Kreed shifted in the backseat. His legs didn't quite fit, even though it was a large SUV. They rode almost the whole way in silence. Of course he asked a question here and there, but all he got in reply were one-word answers, so he finally just stopped trying to make small talk. He guessed Mitch had chosen Jace's gym, when they pulled to the front of a large building with Cheer Dynasty in big, bold letters lighting the front. The place was as impressive as Colt had made it sound.

"We should have gotten into cheerleading," Kreed mumbled, getting out of the car. Cody got out of the passenger side and gave a chuckle as he slammed the door.

"Mitch says that every single time we come by here," Cody said. Mitch was already several steps ahead of them, so they followed him up the walkway to the front doors. Mitch opened the unlocked door then led them along the back wall while he lifted a hand toward a glass wall where Jace and his staff sat talking.

"He said the first door on the left down this hall would be quiet and unused." Mitch shot back over his shoulder, never slowing the pace.

"He's kind of freaking me out," Aaron whispered to Kreed as they walked side by side down the trophy-lined corridor.

"Yeah, he's not good," Kreed confirmed as they neared the room.

"I hope you have some sort of magic plan." Aaron nudged him playfully with his shoulder.

"It felt like a good idea. Now I'm not so sure. Maybe I should've just called Skinner."

Mitch flipped on the light and took a seat at the opposite side of the table. Cody followed. This quiet thing his partner did was just too weird. Kreed might not have ever seen Mitch this deep in a funk before. As the last one into the room, Kreed shut the door behind him before taking his seat. He figured the best way to handle the situation at this point would be to just dive right in.

"How'd they take the news you were quittin'?"

"I don't know. Maybe a little surprised, but they're hard to read. You know how they are. Skinner called me last night then again this morning, but it was just to talk me into their shitty plan," Mitch said, shaking his head. "I'm not interested in that."

"What are your thoughts on what to do next?" Kreed asked, watching Mitch's facial expressions for any tells. Mitch's sunglasses still covered his eyes, making it nearly impossible to get a full read.

"I don't have a backup plan. I never thought I'd need one," Mitch answered, shrugging.

If possible, his partner got smaller in that moment, looked a little more lost. Man, it sucked. Just two weeks ago, they were hugging each other in a show of solidarity and a job well done. Now the government beat the shit out of the very man who saved so many lives. Kreed would never have seen Skinner pulling this kind of move.

"Well, I figured they'd wanna move you when Cody took that bullet. I knew it was a certainty when they wouldn't let you back on the case, and I'm trying real hard to put a spin on it that they want you safe and away from ground zero, which, to them, is Texas. But listen, man, I've been thinking about something for a little while now. I don't know the logistics. It can be talked out, but I think the idea has merit and we should give it a try."

"All right, I'm listening," Mitch said, sliding out of his coat and letting it hang over the back of the chair. He could hear in Knox's voice that he'd sparked his friend's interest.

Mitch's black, cotton shirt grabbed Kreed's attention and distracted him from the conversation for a moment. He just shook his head and laughed at the picture of a strong, masculine fist filling the expanse of Mitch's broad chest, under which the words "Nothing Says 'I Love You' Quite Like Fisting" were emblazoned in bold purple and silver lettering.

"Nice shirt." Kreed nodded toward the object in question, and Mitch just grinned and slid the glasses off his face, set them on the table, then scooted up a little in his seat.

"Cody thought so too," Mitch replied, giving Cody a wink. Cody's eyes narrowed, even though his gaze stayed trained on Mitch, but his face brightened. Knox turned back to Kreed with his dark brows lifted. "So what's your big plan, Sinacola?" The guy looked almost willing to take any carrot Kreed might dangle.

"I think we should get into private corporate security." He just laid it out there as plainly as he could.

"What do you mean…we?" Mitch asked, his brow furrowed, confusion twisting his face.

"You and I have connections. I think we could make a partnership work in the private sector. Our backgrounds are solid, so the corporate world might trust us. If we can land some contracts, we know more than enough guys who are always looking for part-time work. They're trained, so whatever we couldn't handle, we'd have backup. We could have an office in Austin, keep you close to Turner, keep me closer to my parents. They need me around more."

"Are you saying you'd leave the Marshals Service to start this business with me?" Mitch studied him, and Kreed could tell he'd gotten stuck on those few first words and hadn't necessarily processed anything else he might have heard yet.

"Yeah. I can put my notice in today. I got nothin' keeping me there, especially now." Kreed didn't hesitate, not even needing to think twice before he'd spoken. No way would he ever give Aaron up or haul him in. Kreed lived by a code of conduct. He was loyal and tried for honorable to the best of his ability. Every day he continued to work for the justice department, knowing what he was hiding in his relationship, would be a day he lived a lie and that just wasn't who he was as a man.

"Why would you do that?" Mitch countered.

"I have no ties to them at all. I've been sticking around because of you. Besides, I really do need to be closer to my parents, and if this works out with me and Stuart, I have a better chance of talking him into moving to Austin than I do to Camp Beauregard."

Mitch just stared at him, and Kreed held back the smile that threatened. He'd left his friend speechless. Good, he wanted Mitch to digest everything he'd said.

"I have a decent savings. You have one too. There's a lot of shit we need to figure out in starting a business. I've never done anything like that before, but I'll invest everything I've got into making this work. You and I work well together. It seems like a no-brainer." Kreed shifted in his chair, placing both elbows on the table and leaning toward Mitch. His buddy mirrored his pose, and that caused Kreed's heart to lighten. No matter what was said from that point forward, he could tell Mitch was in.

"But is it enough to sustain a startup?" Mitch's brow lifted, clearly thinking through the possibilities.

Kreed wanted to drop a line like, "Don't think too hard, it might hurt," but decided to hold off until he got the verbal confirmation he needed.

"I haven't put pen to paper, but we can start small, invest back into ourselves for a while. However that process works. Neither of us needs a lot to live on," Kreed suggested.

"I want in," Aaron spoke up. Up until then, Aaron and Cody hadn't uttered a single word; they'd both sat there listening intently, but stayed out of the conversation. Everyone's attention shifted to Aaron.

"What?" Kreed asked, totally taken aback by Aaron's comment.

"You want in how?" Mitch asked before Kreed had the chance. Everyone in the room sat up a little straighter, waiting on the answer.

"I know you haven't ironed anything out, but there's no bigger risk to corporate security than what I do and I promise I've never met anyone better than me at finding holes in systems," Aaron said. Kreed schooled his features, hid the smirk, and turned back to Mitch. Okay, that had been unexpected.

"I don't know that we'd have a salary for you—" Mitch started.

Aaron cut him off with a wave of his hand. "Money's not a problem. I could keep us floating for a long time."

Kreed swiveled his head back toward Aaron. He'd pretty much equated Stuart to a cyber Robin Hood, but nowhere in that thought had he ever believed Aaron had taken a financial gain while working with Protector, yet Aaron sounded confident and sincere in his offer. The gesture caused his heart to do a little flip at the generosity. The kid was such a sweetheart to offer, but he doubted Aaron had saved up a whole lot with the peanuts the government paid.

Then again, the thousand dollars on earbuds came to mind. Yeah, the kid didn't save well at all. There was silence as all eyes rested on Aaron. Kreed was the first to bite, just to get the question out of the way. "How could you do that?"

Aaron's blue gaze landed on Kreed, and there was a little bit of panic in them. "Don't be mad."

Okay, with his guy, that could mean anything. He took a deep breath, re-centered himself, and focused on Aaron. That wasn't the best possible way to start an explanation, so Kreed asked the first thought that came to mind. "Should I hear this in private?"

"We can leave," Cody started to say and immediately pushed away from the table to stand. Mitch didn't follow. For the first time that day, he looked eager and completely engaged in the conversation. The Mitch he knew and loved was back, ready to hear this bombshell and no doubt unwilling to leave the room until he did. His buddy kicked back in his chair and anchored his boots on the table.

"Nah, babe, we're good. What Aaron has to say to Kreed, he can say in front of me," Mitch stated matter-of-factly.

"I think that only works if I'm the one saying that." Kreed scowled at his long-time partner who appeared to be back to his old self for the most part. Kreed cocked his head toward the door, staring at Mitch. "Go."

"No, really, I'm good. Keep going."

"Come on," Cody urged, knocking Mitch's feet off the table and tugging him by his T-shirt. Mitch finally got up and followed, but left the door cracked. How his partner could shift moods so quickly always amazed him. Kreed sighed, stood to close the door, but the door slammed shut a little harder than necessary before he moved from the table. Cody must have beat him to it.

Aaron turned completely in his chair, scooting closer to Kreed as he took his seat again. He watched the look on Aaron's face as he lifted his head and their eyes met. Kreed didn't make any sudden movements and didn't say a word. He could tell this one secret was a doozy and wondered how many more times in their lives he'd have this same moment. The breath he hadn't known he held slipped free. He'd been warned there was more to come with smart boy, but didn't anticipate that to happen right in the middle of his and Mitch's life-changing discussion. This felt like having the rug pulled out from under him twice in a matter of seventy-two hours. He braced himself as Aaron started to speak.

"My real name's not Aaron Stuart, even though it's been that for the last ten or so years," Aaron started.

"Okay, what's your name?" Kreed interrupted his story but tried to hide the anxiety of that question and swiped at the small amount of dust on the table. He wasn't sure he could look Aaron in his eyes at the moment. There were so many emotions swimming around in his head.

"Don't judge me, all right?" Aaron took a deep breath before he spoke.

"Just tell me, please," Kreed shot back.

"My name's Aaron Drake."

Kreed's head lifted toward Aaron, who looked almost apologetic at the confession. That admission sat there between them as though the name was supposed to mean something to Kreed, but he had no clue why that name might matter. When seconds passed with him evidently not responding appropriately, Aaron squinted his eyes and stared at him even harder as if trying to relay some sort of a hidden meaning with his gaze.

Oh shit.

Everything clicked in place and almost knocked the breath out of him. No fucking way! It couldn't be, could it? "Drake. Like the Drakes who own the whole fucking world? Those Drakes?"

Aaron nodded slowly. The longer Kreed stayed quiet, the more worried Aaron's expression became. The kid fidgeted nervously with his hands, picking at his nails, and honestly, Aaron should have some anxiety over that revelation. One of the wealthiest families in the world, the same ones who'd had their hands in real estate, finance, refineries, pipelines, chemical plants, and retail, who'd shaped politics and owned pretty much the entire world for centuries… Kreed exhaled deeply, yet another breath he hadn't realized he was holding. This was a game-changer.

"What else should I know?" Kreed asked, instead of stating the obvious. What would a guy like Aaron ever see in a lower-middle-class public servant like him? "Let's get it all out on the table now and be done with it."

Aaron took a deep breath, blew it out through his mouth, and said, "I graduated from MIT when I was seventeen. My family drives me bat-shit crazy. I don't live around them, only spend time with them about every other Christmas when I forget how bad they suck. I opted out of the family business, but my grandfather left the bulk of his rather large estate to me, which pissed my family off, something I still get reminded of when I'm around them. So yeah, that makes me obscenely loaded." Aaron bit his lip, worrying the plump flesh with his teeth.

"Okay—" Kreed started, but Aaron cut him off.

"And I don't live in Florida. I live in Austin. That's why this new plan would work so easy for us, if you can get past everything. You wondered how I accessed the Austin street cameras so easily when Cody got hurt. The reason I did it so quickly is I do it all the time for fun," Aaron admitted in one breath, the words coming out of his mouth so fast Kreed had to play them over in his head in order to make sure he understood.

"Fun?" He lifted his brow and the cocky smirk Aaron had added at that last sentence faded.

"Well, yeah. But I guess you have to be there to understand."

"Okay."

Aaron had stunned him speechless. Several minutes passed as he sat there and watched Aaron. Of course, it all made sense. Aaron carried himself in a privileged way. Not arrogantly—he definitely didn't flaunt it, but money was still there. Even in the way Aaron placed his napkin in his lap. Kreed had loved that move, but now those perfect manners made even more sense.

"Say something," Aaron said, back to worrying his lip, gaze searching his.

"I don't know what to say." The silence continued as Kreed tried to digest everything that his church boy just threw at him. Yeah, he should say something, but what the hell did you say when you just found out your boyfriend was wealthy beyond your wildest imagination?

Fuck! Would Aaron start to think he was only with him for the money now that he knew? Slowly Aaron's masks started to descend, making him unreadable. Kreed could sense him pulling away, and he didn't want that. Somehow it had been easier to absorb that the guy he loved was a most-wanted fugitive and a genius prodigy than from one of the wealthiest families in the world.

Sucking in a steadying deep breath, Kreed pulled his thoughts together. For the first time in a long time, he was slightly intimidated. With tremendous effort, he pushed his nerves aside and reached out, taking Aaron's hand.

"Anything else I should know?" He smiled at Aaron, hoping to ease both of their nerves.

"I don't think so," Aaron said cautiously.

"And if there is, you'll tell me right away?"

"Absolutely." Aaron smiled back at him. It was a genuine smile, the kind that made his eyes light up. The one he loved so much. His heart warmed.

"And just to make sure… Being with me isn't some kind of ploy to get your family pissed off?"

"What? Absolutely not. No, I'm already the black sheep of my dysfunctional family and I'm completely good with that."

Kreed nodded and just decided to get all the insecurity out now. "I live off what I make. It's a good life, but probably not what you're used to."

"I think those are relationship issues we can work out as we go. Besides, you're changing your job description, so don't be freaked out over something that can offer the people that matter most in your life a chance to build a better future."

"You've tossed a lot my way." Kreed couldn't think of anything else to say. Aaron had a point.

"I know, and I'd planned to tell you differently, but I want in on this business. I've been thinking about this too. Together we can offer up the whole package. I've worked with Knox pretty well over the last year, and the two of us did okay together on this last assignment, I think," Aaron said.

"We did great," Kreed agreed, and Aaron's fingers tightened around his.

"I've got a paid team of financial advisors taking care of my assets. They could easily put us on the right track to get us started. So let's do this. And you moving to Austin would be ideal for us. That takes away the long-distance issue."

"It would." Kreed nodded

"Yes, it would! I'm not rushing us, but I have a place downtown you can stay at to see how things work out," Aaron added, excitement in his voice and the look of hope in his eyes.

"I'd like that a lot."

"Good. Can you kiss me, Sin? You're making me nervous."

He laughed at Aaron. A kiss was exactly what he had in mind. He leaned in, slid a free hand around the nape of Aaron's neck and drew him closer, but not quite to his lips. He looked Aaron in the eyes. God, those gunmetal blue eyes undid him every time. Aaron had stopped wearing the colored contacts all the time just for him. "If there's anything even questionable that I should know, tell me. No more secrets. Promise?"

"Promise." Aaron's forehead pressed against his. He loved that tender move. Kreed couldn't imagine his life without Aaron. His intuition had been completely spot-on. Aaron was it for him. He had no doubt the kid would be a handful, but he was up for the challenge. On firmer emotional ground, Kreed decided then that they would make it through, no matter what.

"I love you," he whispered seconds before he took Aaron's lips. Aaron's reply got lost somewhere in the kiss.

Epilogue

Six Months Later—June

The steady rock of Kreed's oversized leather chair never faltered as he listened intently to Mitch and Skinner rehash the final changes to the investigative contract they'd managed to secure with the US Marshals Service. Mitch sat quietly, making notes, reading over each bullet-point change that would be needed to make Skinner and his higher-ups happy. They were minuscule changes. The kind of changes that just beat a man down, but all part of the tedious bureaucracy called the US government.

"We'll get these changes made—" Kreed started, but Director Skinner cut him off mid-sentence, his loud voice booming through the speakerphone. Kreed instantly reached up to mute the phone, talking quietly to Mitch.

"He forgets we don't work for him anymore."

"Whatever. He just gave us a million-dollar fucking contract. He ordered me around for far less than that before," Mitch teased, lifting a fist for a quick knuckle bump. This was turning out to be a great day for their little private security firm. They were finalizing this contract, and Aaron had Tristan Wilder in the office next door, going over the final stages of contract negotiations with Wilder, Inc. Everything was seriously coming together.

"Did either of you hear what I had to say?" Skinner barked, and Kreed quickly reached over, unmuting the phone.

"Say it again, Sir," Kreed said, grabbing his pen, hiding the laugh bubbling inside. Skinner proved he was a straight-up good man to put up with either of them after they'd left the Marshals Service.

"I'm not your boss anymore. I'm your customer. You can't ignore me like you did when you worked for me. Now, get that new shiny assistant you have to make an amendment to the contract. Don't try and change the actual contract. I have authority to sign an amendment and get it back to you by end of day."

"Will do. Thank you, sir," Kreed answered, jotting down a few notes of his own.

"Yep. Thanks, Skinner," Mitch piped in from the other side of the desk.

"Drop the sir. It scares me. Other than that, how's it going?" Skinner asked, changing the subject.

"Really well. Stuart's getting signatures on Wilder," Kreed answered. Skinner had been their number one supporter in starting this business since the day Kreed had placed his resignation on his boss's desk. He'd taken on a role as advisor, mentor, and now, top client.

"Good. They must need it. I just got a breaking news flash that Huckabee, the presidential candidate, had a breach in his website. Looks like they need you guys, too. You should get Aaron to give them a call," Skinner said, and Kreed's heart plummeted in his chest. His gaze connected straight with Mitch's. Mitch still had no idea Aaron wasn't Aaron Stuart, gaming buddy and ex-government employee.

"I gotta go," Kreed said, rising immediately. "Knox'll finish this off with you."

Kreed got as far as the door before he remembered to yell a quick thank-you toward Skinner. His heart pounded in his chest at the possibility of Aaron being behind this hack. Years fell off his life with every step he took down that hallway.

Setting up house with Aaron had been better than he'd ever imagined once Kreed had managed to learn to always stay flexible.

The kid was a pistol, and Kreed regularly had no clue what he'd be walking into. The constant hair, eye color, and clothing-style changes didn't take too long to get used to. In fact, he loved being surprised. He enjoyed teasing Aaron about how Kreed got to be with a different guy almost every day. The random tattoos and piercings taking place in their living room—not just with Aaron, but also with his small circle of friends—had become its own kind of normal. Kreed had even added a few more tattoos to his already-extensive collection and gotten two piercings that his guy loved. The generational gap of music, television, and entertainment took a little longer to become accustom to, but he'd adapted because Aaron went out of his way to always make sure he was comfortable when venturing into those parts of his boyfriend's life.

More than anything else, the extreme, progressive attitude and the lengths Aaron would go to in order to help people were ironically the hardest things for Kreed to wrap his mind around. Aaron took empathy to a whole new level. Kreed had learned quickly to channel Aaron's social-conscience into physically helping the needy instead of making a corrupt company wave the white flag. Anytime an injustice was discovered, Kreed could see the gleam in smart boy's eyes as he instantly planned a cyber-attack, and Kreed would step in and refocus his energies elsewhere.

Once Kreed managed to show Aaron there was a different way to help—a hands-on way to give assistance—he found it was nothing for Aaron to take off to the airport and lend his help to whatever natural disaster played out across the television screen. When social media came together to express their dismay over how someone was treated, his guy was already aware and forming rallies and protests around the world to help show support.

They'd switched to attending political rallies instead of Aaron hacking into the opposing side's political website in order to make a big ass out of them. Kreed was busier than he'd ever been in his life, helping his guy channel all that energy away from his previous activities. He and Aaron worked really well together, and since he wanted Aaron and his high-strung honey wanted to help the world, Kreed regularly joined in on those tasks.

But now, with the news Huckabee had a breach, Kreed instinctively knew just where that had come from. Huckabee had been on a short list of people Aaron couldn't stand. His guy had no tolerance for Huckabee's politics or attitude toward the future of this country. He could so see his mister breaking down, falling off the wagon and back into the old mode while he should be finalizing the contract with Wilder, not playing around with hacking anyone.

Anger got the best of him as he busted open Aaron's office door. Kreed held his frustrated tongue, trying to quickly come to some sort of mental plan to help save this account and pull Aaron out of his huge lapse of judgement. What he saw stopped him in his tracks. Tristan Wilder sat right next to Aaron. Both had their hands working at keyboards, their gazes fixed on the screen. Aaron looked back over his shoulder for a brief second.

"Hang on, Sin. We're almost done," Aaron said. He typed a few more strokes at the keyboard before Tristan laughed out loud, lifting a hand for a high five.

"You did it. He's gonna shit. He'll associate that with you. I know he'll remember your screen name."

"How long will it take?" Aaron asked, and Tristan looked down at his watch.

"He's all over his shit. They're very fluid at Secret. It upsets the balance of the rest of my company because they all work so well together over there. I'll say less than a minute."

"Really? Even at best, I'd have said thirty," Aaron answered, clearly impressed by Tristan's statement. Kreed watched as they both looked over at Tristan's wristwatch.

"Five, four, three..." Tristan's phone began to vibrate. "It's him." He swiped the screen and put it to his ear without checking the ID. "Hey, babe," Tristan said. His smile turned huge, again lifting a hand for a second high five, before turning to give Kreed a thumbs up. "Hang on. I'm putting you on speaker."

"Why is *En!gm4* in my house, Tristan?" Dylan Reeves asked, his voice carried loudly throughout the office space.

Kreed had met him a couple of times when they'd driven up to Dallas to present to the company, then again when they ironed out the details of the contract. Irritation was clear in the guy's voice.

"I knew you'd know that he'd been in your network, but you were quicker than I even thought. Impressive," Tristan answered as Aaron started chuckling. "We were just testing Aaron's speed and ability."

"Why are you hacking me? I told you to hire him already. *I'm* the one who found him and said we needed him." Dylan's aggravation seemed to grow with each word he uttered. Mitch came in behind Kreed, where he stood, trying to understand the dynamic here and manage his own irritation at Aaron.

"And clearly you were right, babe," Tristan replied.

"Aaron, clean up the mess you just made. And Tristan, find a hotel to stay in tonight," Dylan said flatly. Aaron slapped a hand over his mouth to quiet his laughter, apparently so tickled that he couldn't stop.

"Now, honey, don't be like that. You know I always stay with you," Tristan started, but his grin was so big that it was contagious and eased Kreed's own upset.

"Not this time," Dylan shot back. When the phone went dead, both Tristan and Aaron burst out in uncontrollable fits of laughter. Aaron held his side, obviously in pain from laughing so hard.

"I have some making up to do. Where's the contract?" Tristan laughed as Aaron reached over and slid papers across his crowded desk. His guy was still chuckling, very pleased with himself, as Tristan reached for the pen in his front pocket. He quickly scribbled his name across the bottom of the last page and rose from his seat. "Make me a copy."

Aaron's eyes lifted to Kreed's, his smile brighter than a few seconds ago. This contract had the potential to be even bigger than the one they'd negotiated with Skinner. They had their work cut out for them—that was for sure—but these contracts were the foundation for their new company and exactly what they needed.

"It was a pleasure meeting you guys. We'll have you out to California for a meet and greet. I'll make sure Dylan's in town. He'll enjoy this dynamic," Tristan said, extending a hand to Kreed then Mitch.

"Thank you for the business,"

"No, thank you guys. It's been a great afternoon. Aaron, I'll be in touch." Tristan slid out the door.

Mitch followed behind him, Kreed supposed to walk him out. He reached out and shut the door behind them. Thank God he'd gotten it wrong.

"You promised no more hacking."

"I did, but we got to talking and it was a funny idea. Safe. I didn't think you'd mind," Aaron said absently, moving the computer equipment around so he could get to all the pages of the contract. Kreed dropped down in the chair across from the desk, his relief strong. Aaron had no idea what had even driven him in here to interrupt them in the first place.

"I need to apologize. Skinner said Huckabee was hacked, and I know how much you dislike the guy. I thought it was you," Kreed admitted. There was no way to know how Aaron would take his admission, or how much making up he'd need to do, but Kreed knew he needed to trust Aaron more than immediately jumping to those kinds of conclusions.

"Oh shit. I forgot about that." Aaron turned quickly to his computer and began typing. Well, hell, he'd been spot-on after all.

"You promised me," Kreed started, his brow furrowed.

"I know, but he's friends with my dad, and my dad just gave him a couple of million to keep going in the race. And I really hate him, so he can spend that money fixing what I just fucked up," Aaron answered, never looking back at him.

Kreed rolled his eyes. Those kinds of justifications were common with Aaron. A promise always came with a certain amount of leeway. Kreed scrubbed his hands over his face as he thought about the fight they were going to have, but Kreed had to go there. One slip too many would lead the Department of Justice straight to their door.

"Babe, this doesn't fall in a gray area. Hacking Huckabee is illegal activity…" Kreed started, but Mitch busted back inside the office, cutting off his words.

"Great job, Stuart. Wilder's impressed." Mitch clapped his palms, rubbing his hands together. "Two contracts in one day. I want more of these kinds of days!"

"Yeah, me too. We need to work out the logistics, make sure we have enough help on stand-by," Aaron said, leaving the keyboard, turning toward them. Kreed immediately moved his finger in a circle toward Aaron.

"Don't stop. Fix what you did," Kreed prompted.

"Dude! Seriously, you need to lighten up," Aaron shot back.

"That might be the case, but you promised," Kreed said.

"Just for the record, you two do this shit all the time. I have no idea what we're talking about, and it's getting old," Mitch said, glancing between the both of them. "Get over whatever this is going on right now. We need to celebrate. The dynamic duo is about an hour out. Cody's off work."

Mitch left them sitting there. Kreed tended to agree; they needed to celebrate. He rose and started heading out too. Colt and Jace were the duo, and they all had reservations for dinner. "Fix that shit, babe. You promised," Kreed said at the door.

"It's only because you're so hot. You make me do crazy things, Sin," Aaron said after a brief pause. Kreed didn't move, he just stood in the doorway and smiled. He loved those words. They were still in the honeymoon phase of their relationship so little things made him all gushy on the inside. And the fact that they fucked like bunnies all the damn time had him giving in to Aaron's whims more often than not.

"I promise. A little later, I'll show how much I liked those words. But get out of Huckabee's shit first. We got dinner and dancing tonight, and I don't want to worry about men in black interrupting my grind time with you." Kreed left the office on that note and said a small little prayer that Aaron would do as he'd asked.

"Damn it! That's supposed to work in giving me more time. Would a lap dance sweeten the deal?" Aaron yelled and Kreed snickered. Yeah, they were settling into each other very well.

~~~

Thanksgiving

Kreed took the corner leading into the familiar San Antonio neighborhood. He'd grown up in this tight-knit community, and throughout his life he'd traveled this street more times than he could count. Yet somehow, this time everything seemed different. His entire life had changed for the better and it was all due to the amazing guy riding beside him.

"Any regrets?"

"Not a one. You?" Aaron asked from the passenger side.

Kreed never glanced over but he could feel the kid's gaze on him.

"I don't do regrets. I'm in. I told you that." Kreed slowed as he turned onto the street his parents lived on. Like normal for the day, the road was packed, forcing him to slow down and navigate the drive, moving in and out of parked cars and oncoming traffic. "It was cool how you got the guy to come in and ink us today."

"He owed me," Aaron replied, somewhat distracted. "This neighborhood looks like one of the fake places you see on the Hallmark Channel's Thanksgiving TV shows."

"Yeah, I know, but it's real. I keep telling you that families really do get together on Thanksgiving and spend the day eating and making each other totally miserable in the best possible way."

"I just think it's cool as shit," Aaron added. From the corner of his eye, he watched Aaron's eyes grow wide with excitement as he stared out the front windshield of the car.

As a kid, Kreed believed these same neighbors were always intruding in his life, telling his parents all the bad shit he'd done. Over the years, he'd grown up and come to realize they were only watching out for him. Now that he was older, he was thankful they had always stayed in his business. His life might have taken a much different path had they not stuck their noses in where he'd thought they didn't belong.

A smile broke out across his lips as he followed Aaron's gaze, curious as to what could possibly cause that much awe to appear on his sexy guy's face. They had spent just about every Sunday afternoon at his parents' house since he'd moved back to the area, but today, the neighborhood bustled with families enjoying the holiday. Even with all the years away, nothing had changed. Some were playing football in the front yard, some gathered by their cars talking, others struggling with armloads of food.

"Should we have brought something? Everyone's carrying in covered dishes."

"Nah, we're good. I promise."

"Are you sure? This is so different than Thanksgiving with my family. I'm glad we came." Aaron's attention remained focused outside the car.

Happiness filled Kreed's heart. He loved sharing these special moments with Aaron. His guy had been overly excited about this family gathering. This year the entire clan would be celebrating Thanksgiving dinner at his parents' place. All his aunts, uncles, and cousins planned to come. Aaron was so into the idea of celebrating this holiday that it was all he'd been able to talk about for the last couple of days.

When Aaron had arranged for matching tattoos to be inked this morning, it had come as a surprise—a very sweet surprise. Paying extra to have the tattoo artist come to the house added an extra layer of thoughtfulness to his guy's special gesture. Kreed hadn't missed the significance of what these tattoos really meant to Aaron. Being totally vested in this relationship himself, he was more than happy to commit to those ideas. This day was very special to his church boy and now it was permanently illustrated on both of them.

"My aunts and mom will cook more food than we can ever eat," Kreed said, pulling into the driveway and putting the car in park.

"I don't know about that. You might not have noticed, but I like to eat," Aaron teased as he got out of the truck then shut the door without waiting on a response. "We can bring something at Christmas, right?" he quickly added, looking at Kreed over the hood.

Kreed couldn't help but smile at the eagerness in Aaron's words and the excitement written all over his face. Kreed made his way around the front of the car, the slight chill in the November air skating across his skin as he walked. "You're gonna see that there's enough food in there for us to have leftovers until Christmas day."

"I hope so. I was trying to remember something my grandmother always made us on holidays. It was like a homemade creamed corn. It was the best ever. Everyone loved that corn. She always made me extra and would hide it so I could take it home. When she passed, my mom never made it for us; she doesn't cook. They have everything catered and it's just not the same. I bet I could find that recipe. You're pretty good in the kitchen. I think we could pull it off and make it for Christmas," Aaron suggested, falling in step beside him as they headed up the walkway.

"We could." Kreed motioned to his hip where they'd both put their tattoos as he took the porch steps up. "I was just thinking about getting your name added to this."

"Really? I left that spot open on the design, just in case. I know I kinda threw all that at you with no warning. I didn't want to push too hard," Aaron confessed, reaching for the doorbell. He stopped suddenly, and he darted his eyes sheepishly toward Kreed. "Not that I'm rushing us."

Kreed had one hand on the doorknob. He didn't bother to ring the doorbell when he visited. This was his family home. But he stopped mid-motion and used his free hand to cup Aaron's neck, drawing him in for a quick kiss. He loved those little confessions from Aaron; they caressed his heart and filled him with happiness.

Kreed's words had caught in his throat when Aaron had shown him the design he'd chosen for them— a mystical dragon and a beautifully detailed serpent, nose to nose. The lower halves of their long, sleek bodies entwined and the upper half arched high to form a heart. The tattoo had been more than perfect in Kreed's opinion.

"Rush us, because I'm already totally there, church boy. It's been almost a year now and I can't imagine being anywhere else."

Kreed knew those had been the right words when Aaron gave him that sexy little grin—the one that always made an appearance when he liked what Kreed had to say. As soon as Aaron slid an arm around his waist and drew him closer with the promise of something a little more than the quick press of lips, the door knob was yanked out of Kreed's hand and his mother's bright, shiny face came into view. The kiss would have to wait for now, but he would be hustling Aaron off to his old bedroom the first chance he got.

"You're here!" his mom exclaimed and gave them both a hug. "We've been waiting on you two. We need our tester, honey," she gushed, pulling on Aaron's arm.

Turned out his church boy had fit right into the Sinacola family. His mom and Aaron had become best buddies. She loved to cook and Aaron loved to eat—a match made in heaven. Aaron headed inside first, where his mother wrapped her arm around Aaron's waist, cheerfully listing everything on the day's menu as she guided him toward the kitchen. Kreed had actually forgotten how much his mother depended on Aaron's taste buds. She swore he made her a better cook because he could taste even the smallest hints of spices, and since Aaron was pretty much a bottomless pit, he never got too full to sample another bite.

"I'm sorry we didn't think to bring anything, Mom," Aaron apologized, settling his arm across her shoulders as they turned the corner into the dining room where covered dishes were already lining the table. His mom pointed Kreed to the back porch.

"Honey, can you please go out there and help your dad with the turkey? He got a new deep fryer at the Home Depot and it's got more bells and whistles than his old one. It even has a remote that he can't figure out. I don't know why they have to make things so complicated nowadays. You really need to get out there so we don't end up with a crispy turkey that's raw on the inside." Kreed laughed at that, remembering the past. It certainly wouldn't be the first time. He loved those memories. He looked through the house onto the back porch where he could see several men gathered around a large, steaming pot.

"Sure," he said absently, glancing back at Aaron, who'd become so completely engrossed with the desserts, he'd stopped paying any attention to him. His mom had a giant smile on her face as she watched Aaron take a finger and swipe it over some icing as he started talking again about wanting to bring creamed corn to Christmas dinner.

God, he loved the way Aaron always surprised him—simple things like asking to make the corn for Kreed's family at Christmas or how Aaron made his mother's smile a little brighter by just hanging out in the kitchen. Sweet unexpected moments like those seemed to happen about a hundred times a day, which made him love Aaron even more. His whole world revolved completely around that one man. Thank God Aaron had given him a chance.

Kreed kept walking, heading toward the back where the men had gathered. He was more than happy to help his father fry the bird, seeing as how it was his favorite Thanksgiving tradition. Well, that and ending his meal with a big slice of sweet potato pie and whipped cream. Kreed smiled at the idea of starting new traditions with Aaron, because if things went the way he planned, their next Thanksgiving would be celebrated with family and friends, creamed corn and all, at his and Aaron's new place.

The End

About this Author

Best Selling Author Kindle Alexander is an innovative writer, and a genre-crosser who writes classic fantasy, romance, suspense, and erotica.

Send a quick email and let me know what you thought of *Full Disclosure* to kindle@kindlealexander.com. For more information on future works and links, check out my website at www.kindlealexander.com. Come friend me on all the major social networking sites.

Note to Readers

Although this is the end of the Nice Guys Novels, don't despair. We love these characters as much as you do, so be on the lookout for them to show up in other works as well.

Books by Kindle Alexander

What did you think of Full Domain? Email us at
kindle@kindlealexander.com. We would love to hear from you.

If you enjoyed Full Domain, then you won't want to miss Kindle
Alexander's bestselling novels:

Closet Confession

Secret

Full Disclosure

Always

Double Full

The Current Between Us

Texas Pride

Up in Arms

Follow us on Amazon to stay updated with future projects on the
Kindle Alexander Amazon Author Page.

Closet Confession

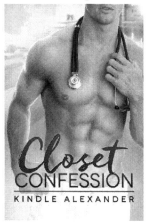

This version includes Bonus Scenes adding an additional ten thousand words to this edition. Closet Confession was previously released in the Night Shift Anthology.

Dr. Derek Babineaux is intelligent, dedicated, and one of the best ER physicians in the fast-paced world of critical care at Tulane Medical in New Orleans. Always on top of his game, he's thrown off balance when the newest medical staff member finally unleashes his hidden desires.

Justin Delacroix's job at the inner city's busiest hospital might be just what he needs to ease back into civilian life after a long stint in the military. High-performing shifts make working as a trauma nurse at TMC the perfect way to utilize his skills and quick reaction times. There's only one problem, his attraction for one sexy ER doctor is off the charts, but he has his reasons for not returning Dr. Baby's night shift advances. Or maybe he doesn't.

Learn the *Secret*

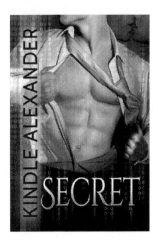

Tristan Wilder, self-made millionaire and devastatingly handsome CEO of Wilder-Nation is on the verge of a very lucrative buyout. With tough negotiations ahead, he's armed with his acquisition pitch, ready to launch the deal of a lifetime. There's just one glitch. The last thing he expects is to fall for the hot business owner he's trying to sway.

Dylan Reeves, computer science engineer and founder of the very successful social media site, Secret, is faced with a life-altering decision. A devoted family man with three kids and a wife, Dylan has been living a secret for years. Fiercely loyal to his convictions, his boundaries blur after meeting the striking owner of the corporation interested in acquiring his company. For the first time in his life, reckless desire consumes him when the gorgeous computer mogul makes an offer he can't refuse.

Meet Deputy Mitch Knox in *Full Disclosure*

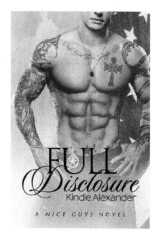

Deputy United States Marshal Mitch Knox apprehends fugitives for a living. His calm, cool, collected attitude and devastatingly handsome good looks earn him a well-deserved bad boy reputation, both in the field and out. While away on an assignment, he blows off some steam at a notorious Dallas nightclub. Solving the case that has plagued him for months takes a sudden backseat to finding out all there is to know about the gorgeous, shy blond sitting alone at the bar.

Texas State Trooper Cody Turner is moving up the ranks, well on his way to his dream of being a Texas Ranger. While on a two-week mandatory vacation, he plans to relax and help out on his family's farm. Mitch is the last distraction Cody needs, but the tatted up temptation that walks into the bar and steals his baseball cap is too hard to ignore.

As Mitch's case gains nationwide attention, how will he convince the sexy state trooper that giving him a chance won't jeopardize his life's plan...especially when the evil he's tracking brings the hate directly to his doorstep, threatening more than just their careers.

> "In the end… OMG the end… let's just say Mitch and Cody have their happy, one that touched my heart." ~Denise, Shh Mom's Reading

> "I give this story five+ perfectly delivered stars." ~Toni FGMAMTC

> "Mitch and Cody are perfect and so bloody hot, it made my IPAD melt."
> ~Jules Swoon Worthy

Experience the life and love of Avery & Kane in
Always

Born to a prestigious political family, Avery Adams plays as hard as he works. The gorgeous, charismatic attorney is used to getting what he wants, even the frequent one-night stands that earn him his well-deserved playboy reputation. When some of the most prominent men in politics suggest he run for senate, Avery decides the time has come to follow in his grandfather's footsteps. With a strategy in place and the campaign wheels rolling, Avery is ready to jump on the legislative fast track, full steam ahead. But no amount of planning prepares him for the handsome, uptight restaurateur who might derail his political future.

Easy isn't even in the top thousand words to describe Kane Dalton's life after his father, a devout Southern Baptist minister, kicks him out of the family home for questioning his sexual orientation. Despite all the rotten tomatoes life throws his way, Kane makes something of himself. Between owning a thriving upscale Italian restaurant in the heart of downtown Minneapolis and managing his long-term boyfriend, his plate is full. He struggles to get past the teachings of his childhood to fully accept his sexuality and rid himself of the doubts brought on by his religious upbringing. The last thing he needs is the yummy, sophisticated, blond-haired distraction sitting at table thirty-four.

Book of the Year 2014 Member Choice Awards ~Goodreads MM
Romance
Book of the Year 2014 ~Sinfully Sexy Book
LGBT Book of the Year 2014 eLit Awards

The word is out on *Double Full*

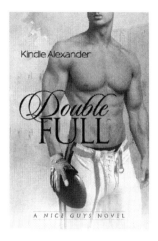

Up and coming football hero, Colt Michaels, makes a Hail Mary pass one night in the college locker room that results in the hottest, sexiest five days of his young life. However, interference after the play has him hiding his past and burying his future in the bottom of a bottle. While Colt seems to have it all, looks can be deceiving especially when you're trapped so far in a closet that you can't see your way out. When ten years of living his expected fast-lane lifestyle lands him engaged to his manipulative Russian supermodel girlfriend, he decides it's time to call a new play.

Jace Montgomery single-handily built the largest all-star cheerleading gym in the world, driven by a need to forget a life-altering encounter with a handsome quarterback a decade ago. His reputation as an excellent coach, hard-nosed business man, and savvy entrepreneur earned him respect in the sometimes catty world of competitive cheerleading. When Jace learns of his ex-lover's plans to marry, his heart executes a barrel roll and his carefully placed resolve tumbles down without a mat to absorb the shock. Can his island escape help him to finally let go of the past and move his life forward?

Everyone's talking about *The Current Between Us*

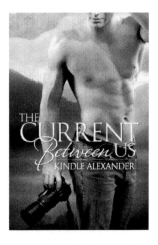

Gage Synclair, international, hard-hitting investigative photojournalist, is preparing for the final special report of his career. A story of deception and murder six long years in the making. After spending ten years in some of the worst parts of the world, he's ready to settle life down and open an art gallery in his hometown of Chicago.

Trent Cooper, electrical contractor, is surprised by the last minute request for a fast-paced electrical remodel, little did he know he'd be immediately propositioned by the gallery's owner. Being gay in the construction industry isn't easy, nor is being father to his two young adopted children. Trent keeps his life in separate zones to avoid a short circuit. Will their high-voltage passion break the currents between them forever?

"Ms. Alexander has become one of my favorite Her characters are mature, well rounded and seem to find a place in my heart."
—Denise, Shh Mom's Reading

"I loved this book! Everything about it was just perfection...great characters, surprises, and the story...seriously, it was so sweet and romantic and just really good reading." —Christi Snow, Author

"This book is an excellent love story, where even the most hardened heart and disillusioned soul can find the romantic streak hidden deep within... just go read it!!!" —Monique, Sinfully Sexy Book Reviews

Rave Reviews for *Texas Pride*

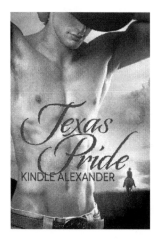

When mega movie star and two time Academy Award winner, Austin Grainger voluntarily gave up his dazzling film career, his adoring fan base thought he'd lost his mind. For Austin, the seclusion of fifteen hundred acres in the middle of Texas sounds like paradise. No more cameras, paparazzi, or overzealous media to hound him every day and night. Little did the sexiest man alive know when one door closes, another usually opens. And Austin's opened by way of a sexy, hot ranch owner right next door.

Kitt Kelly wasn't your average rancher. He's young, well educated and has hidden his sexuality for most of his life. When his long time wet dream materializes as his a new neighbor it threatens everything he holds dear. No way the ranching community would ever accept him if he came out. With every part of his life riding on the edge, can Kitt risk it all for a chance at love or will responsibility to his family heritage cost him his one chance at happiness?

Have you discovered these authors?

The wonderful world of Sara York

The Men of Halfway House series by Jaime Reese

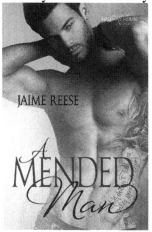

76795930R00221

Made in the USA
Middletown, DE
15 June 2018